W9-BBV-741

JUL / 2021

# PRAISE FOR TESSA AFSHAR

—— ⧜ ——

## *DAUGHTER OF ROME*

"With meticulous research and a vividly detailed narrative style, *Daughter of Rome* . . . is both an emotive biblical love story and an inherently fascinating journey through the world of first-century Rome and the city of Corinth."

MIDWEST BOOK REVIEW

"This is a lovely slow-burning, faith-filled exploration about overcoming trials and accepting past mistakes."

*HISTORICAL NOVELS REVIEW*

"Afshar brings in a thoughtful consideration of whether or not there are behaviors that cannot ever be forgiven, and her intricate biblical setting will engross readers. This is [her] strongest, most complex scripture-based story yet."

*PUBLISHERS WEEKLY*

"Tessa Afshar inhabits the world of early Christians with refreshing clarity. From life under the threat of persecution to domestic details and her characters' innermost thoughts, she makes early Christianity spark."

FOREWORD REVIEWS

"Tessa Afshar has the rare gift of seamlessly blending impeccable historical research and theological depth with lyrical prose and engaging characters."

**SHARON GARLOUGH BROWN,** author of the Sensible Shoes series

"Tessa Afshar's ability to transport readers into the culture and characters of the biblical novels is extraordinary. . . . *Daughter of Rome* is a feast for your imagination as well as balm for your soul."

ROBIN JONES GUNN, bestselling author of *Becoming Us*

———✦———

### THIEF OF CORINTH

"Afshar again shows her amazing talent for packing action and intrigue into the biblical setting for modern readers."

*PUBLISHERS WEEKLY*, starred review

"Lyrical . . . [with] superb momentum, exhilarating scenes, and moving themes of love and determination. . . . Afshar brings to life the gripping tale of one woman's struggle to choose between rebellion and love."

*BOOKLIST*

"Afshar's well-drawn characters and lushly detailed setting vividly bring to life the ancient world of the Bible. A solid choice for fans of Francine Rivers and Bodie and Brock Thoene."

*LIBRARY JOURNAL*

———✦———

### BREAD OF ANGELS

"Afshar continues to demonstrate an exquisite ability to bring the women of the Bible to life, this time shining a light on Lydia, the seller of purple, and skillfully balancing fact with imagination."

*ROMANTIC TIMES*

"Afshar has created an unforgettable story of dedication, betrayal, and redemption that culminates in a rich testament to God's mercies and miracles."

PUBLISHERS WEEKLY

"With sublime writing and solid research, [Afshar] captures the distinctive experience of living at a time when Christianity was in its fledgling stages."

LIBRARY JOURNAL

"Readers who enjoy Francine Rivers's Lineage of Grace series will love this stand-alone book."

CHRISTIAN MARKET

"With its resourceful, resilient heroine and vibrant narrative, *Bread of Angels* offers an engrossing new look at a mysterious woman of faith."

FOREWORD MAGAZINE

———— ☙ ————

## LAND OF SILENCE

"Readers will be moved by Elianna's faith, and Afshar's elegant evocation of biblical life will keep them spellbound. An excellent choice for fans of Francine Rivers's historical fiction and those who read for character."

LIBRARY JOURNAL

"Fans of biblical fiction will enjoy an absorbing and well-researched chariot ride."

PUBLISHERS WEEKLY

"In perhaps her best novel to date, Afshar . . . grants a familiar [biblical] character not only a name, but also a poignant history to which many modern readers can relate. The wit, the romance, and the humanity make Elianna's journey uplifting as well as soul touching."

*ROMANTIC TIMES*, TOP PICK REVIEW

"Heartache and healing blend beautifully in this gem among Christian fiction."

*CBA RETAILERS + RESOURCES*

"An impressively crafted, inherently appealing, consistently engaging, and compelling read from first page to last, *Land of Silence* is enthusiastically recommended for community library historical fiction collections."

MIDWEST BOOK REVIEWS

"This captivating story of love, loss, faith, and hope gives a realistic glimpse of what life might have been like in ancient Palestine."

*WORLD* MAGAZINE

*Jewel of the Nile*

TESSA AFSHAR

# JEWEL
## of the
# NILE

Tyndale House Publishers
Carol Stream, Illinois

Visit Tyndale online at tyndale.com.

Visit Tessa Afshar at tessaafshar.com.

*TYNDALE* and Tyndale's quill logo are registered trademarks of Tyndale House Ministries.

*Jewel of the Nile*

Designed by Mark Anthony Lane II and Libby Dykstra

Edited by Kathryn S. Olson

Published in association with the literary agency of Books & Such Literary Management, 52 Mission Circle, Suite 122, PMB 170, Santa Rosa, CA 95409.

*Jewel of the Nile* is a work of fiction. Where real people, events, establishments, organizations, or locales appear, they are used fictitiously. All other elements of the novel are drawn from the author's imagination.

For information about special discounts for bulk purchases, please contact Tyndale House Publishers at csresponse@tyndale.com, or call 1-855-277-9400.

**Library of Congress Cataloging-in-Publication Data**
Names: Afshar, Tessa, author.
Title: Jewel of the nile / Tessa Afshar.
Description: Carol Stream, Illinois : Tyndale House Publishers, [2021]
Identifiers: LCCN 2021006524 (print) | LCCN 2021006525 (ebook) | ISBN
    9781496428752 (hardcover) | ISBN 9781496428769 (trade paperback) |
    ISBN 9781496428776 (kindle edition) | ISBN 9781496428783 (epub) | ISBN
    9781496428790 (epub)
Subjects: GSAFD: Historical fiction.
Classification: LCC PS3601.F47 J49 2021  (print) | LCC PS3601.F47  (ebook) | DDC
    813/.6—dc23
LC record available at https://lccn.loc.gov/2021006524
LC ebook record available at https://lccn.loc.gov/2021006525

Printed in the United States of America

| 27 | 26 | 25 | 24 | 23 | 22 | 21 |
|----|----|----|----|----|----|----|
| 7  | 6  | 5  | 4  | 3  | 2  | 1  |

*For Ariana:*
*Bright, funny, gorgeous, persevering.*
*My precious niece,*
*you will always be a jewel in my heart.*

*I will instruct you and teach you in the way you should go;*

*I will counsel you with my eye upon you.*

*Be not like a horse or a mule, without understanding,*

*Which must be curbed with bit and bridle.*

PSALM 32:8,9

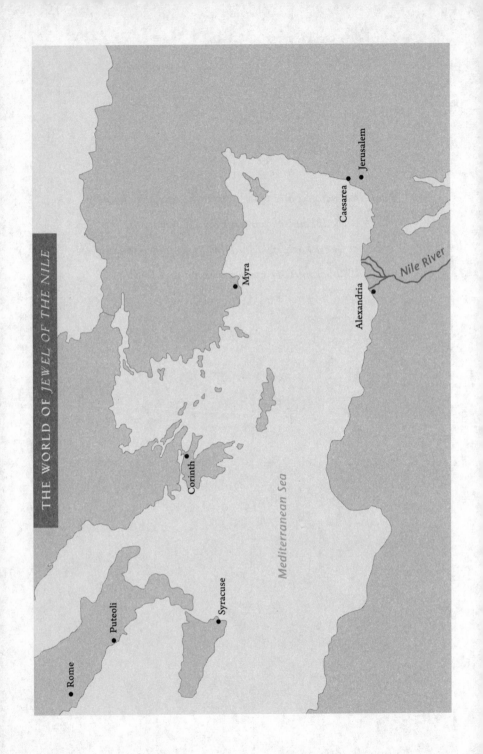

THE WORLD OF *JEWEL OF THE NILE*

Rome

Puteoli

Syracuse

Corinth

Myra

Caesarea

Jerusalem

Alexandria

*Nile River*

*Mediterranean Sea*

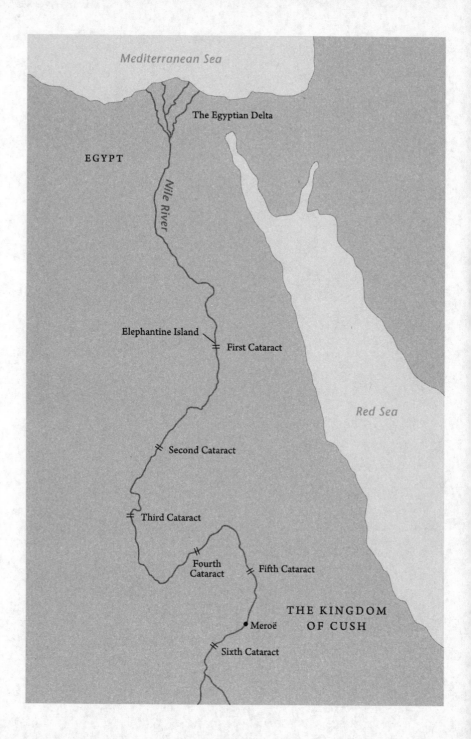

# PROLOGUE

— ❧ —

*Cush shall hasten to stretch out her hands to God.*

PSALM 68:31

AD 31

He took one last aching look outside the crumbling window; the Nile was molten gold in the light of the rising sun, a sparkling coil winding its way into the horizon. Forcing himself to turn away, he came to kneel by the pallet where his bride lay sleeping. To have this woman, he would have to give up the lush beauty of his land, give up his family and heritage. He smiled. She was worth all the loss. For his sake, she had given up as much and more.

"Time to wake up, love."

She groaned something incoherent, more asleep than awake.

"Come now, lazy. Open those enchanting sea-green eyes. We can't linger here. They will have discovered our absence by now."

He spoke in a light tone, making sure none of his mounting anxiety leaked into his voice. Still, the reminder of their vulnerability was enough to banish the last vestiges of her sleep. She snapped her eyes open and sat up in one smooth motion, holding the sheet to her throat. "How long have we been here?"

"Too long." He motioned to the window. "The sun is rising."

She turned to place a hand on his cheek. "I love you, Husband."

For an infinitesimal moment, time stood still, fears banished, their pursuers vanished, and it was just the two of them in the whole expanse of this world. Her complexion so impossibly fair resting against his dark skin, a weaving of two beautiful threads into one exotic tapestry. His chest welled up with joy and he leaned to kiss her softly. It seemed astonishing that she was his, truly and irrevocably his.

"I love you, Gemina." He said the words in Latin, the language of her birth, the language of her heart. And then broke the spell by pulling away to grab his cloak. They could not afford to remain at the dilapidated inn for another moment.

"I will settle our account with the innkeeper while you dress," he said, already pulling open the door.

He paid the surly landlord an extra coin, a fat silver one that made the bloodshot eyes widen. "For your discretion," he said.

Unsmiling, the man pocketed the coins in a dirty purse and went to fetch their camels.

He turned to look into the horizon. His chest tightened at the sight of a band of riders, approaching fast from the south.

Shading his eyes against the piercing sun, he squinted for a better view. Seven, he counted. No, eight. The camels were moving in long, smooth strides, their hooves spraying dust as they pounded the track.

His throat turned dry. They could be traders, he told himself. Merchants. Travelers making their way to Egypt. A dozen different possibilities, none of them menacing. Then he saw the flash of metal strapped to the riders' sides. Swords. He raced up the stairs that led to their room. Gemina was already exiting the chamber. Without a word, he grabbed her hand and pulled her behind him down the stairs.

"What?" she asked, breathless.

"Riders."

"How far?"

"At the rate they are traveling, not far enough. They'll be here soon."

They came to a stop at the edge of the inn's back wall where they could not be spotted from the road. The innkeeper had brought out the camels from their pen but had not bothered to saddle them in spite of his instructions.

He should have fetched the camels sooner, he thought, berating himself for a fool as he started to saddle the first beast.

Their landlord made no move to help. Instead, striding to the middle of the dirt road, he gazed into the distance. Spotting the approaching riders, he shook his head and spat into the dirt. "I knew when I clapped my eyes on you that you would bring trouble to my door."

Ignoring the innkeeper, he cinched the first saddle. He plucked a rough woolen cape out of a saddlebag and threw it to Gemina, hurriedly donning a similar garment himself.

"Pull it up over your hair," he instructed. Garbed in the fraying cotton, from the back at least, they should look like two old nomads.

His heart sank as he saddled the second camel, noting the dirt that still clung to its haunches. Clearly, the innkeeper had not bothered to rub down the beast. He threw the man a narrowed look and received a sneer in return. There was no time for an altercation. He shoved away his irritation and completed the task before him with agile fingers. He could only hope that the innkeeper had fed and watered the animals. Riding dirty camels was one thing. But riding hungry, thirsting beasts when pursued by fast, armed men . . . Sweat drenched his back in the cool morning air.

He should have seen to the camels himself. Instead, drunk on love, he had retired inside with his bride, leaving the work to a sullen stranger.

He pulled on the camel's neck to make it kneel. "Come," he said to Gemina. She approached timidly, unused to the dromedary. Encircling her waist with his hands, he lifted her into the saddle.

"We'll be traveling fast. Hold tight."

She nodded, looking pale. He gave her a reassuring smile before climbing his own beast. Using his stick, he prodded the camels into a trot, before urging them to gallop. The beasts lengthened their strides, their hard humps making for an uncomfortable trek. A fast camel ride felt nothing like the thrill of a horse race. It made your teeth rattle and your brain jar.

He cut across the rough track and made for the pale green river. The queen's men who shadowed them would not anticipate them crossing the Nile. Their pursuers would expect him to push north for the safety of Egypt. Or east for the traders who could help them navigate the desert in order to reach the lands beyond the Red Sea. He hoped that the nomads' cloaks they had donned along with their unexpected heading might fool the guards into giving up the chase. Might convince them that they were not the two lovesick runaways who had braved a queen's wrath to be together. He pushed the camels harder toward the river. The riders were gaining behind them.

As they drew close to the banks of the river, three of the riders peeled away from the rest and veered behind them. Three was better than eight. Three, he might be able to deal with, even though they were the Kandake's own guards. At least she hadn't sent Roman centurions after them.

He urged the camels on, noticing that they were already waning in speed. No matter. They did not have far to go. He led them to a deserted spot in the river's verdant shore and brought the camels to a stop. Hastily, he helped Gemina down and grabbed one of the saddlebags, leaving the other on the camel. He spared a look over his shoulder.

His breath hitched when, in the distance, he saw the other five riders swerve from the inn and follow in their wake. They must have spoken to the landlord. His silver had failed to buy the man's silence.

All his hopes for a stealthy getaway shattered in one crashing heap.

"To the boat!" he cried.

"But my clothes are in the other bag."

"No time, Gemina. Run!"

He grabbed her hand, helping her over the rushes and down the embankment. Water squished into his leather sandals and over his ankles. He wasted precious moments uncovering the skiff, which he had hidden under large palm fronds. Helping Gemina inside, he shoved the boat into deeper water and leapt in behind her.

"Stop!" a voice roared too close. "Stop or die!"

He grabbed the oars from the bottom of the boat and began pulling with all his strength. A hissing sound whistled by his ear, then another.

"Gods! They are shooting arrows at us!" Gemina gasped.

He shoved her head with one hand until she lay facedown on the papyrus reeds, his other still pulling frantically at the oar. The skiff was too modest to have a cabin where he could hide her. Cush was famed for its swift acacia-wood barges, but for this trip he had needed secrecy, not luxury, and had settled on a simple Egyptian fishing skiff.

"Keep down," he said as another iron-tipped arrow flew by his head. He was fairly certain the Kandake's soldiers were not aiming to kill them. Certainly not Gemina, anyway. He pulled harder on the oars, propelling the little boat against the drag of the wind that wanted to drive them south.

He might have lost the advantage of secrecy. But he still had a few winning tricks up his sleeve. It would take time for the guards to secure a boat with which to pursue them. He had purposely hidden his skiff far from any fishing villages where boats could be acquired with ease. And on the other side of the river, he had arranged for his own Libyan guide, a half nomad who knew all the hidden alleyways that would bring them into Egypt undetected.

The Nile spread wide here, and it cost him a long fight against the currents to get to the middle of the river. But it was far enough to keep them out of range of the arrows. A quick glance over his shoulder showed eight men standing on the shores of the east bank, staring after him, bows and arrows hanging uselessly from their limp arms. His chest expanded with the joy of victory.

"They have given up," he told Gemina, grinning. "We are safe."

But the relief proved short-lived.

He glanced back again, brows furrowing. Why were the guards so still? They should be scrambling to find a boat. They should be in desperate pursuit. The Kandake did not put up with failure. Why tarry passively by the river? Were they hoping he would simply drown? A fist twisted inside his stomach. Something smelled fishier than the Nile. Frantically, his eyes skimmed over the papyrus reeds of the little skiff. Had they found his boat beforehand and damaged it? It seemed sound enough. Surely, if they had punctured a hole somewhere, the water would have bubbled up by now?

He examined the western shoreline, thick with date palms and vegetation, and blew out a relieved sigh when he spotted a familiar thin figure.

"He is here," he told Gemina and she turned.

The nomad waved at them, his arm an enthusiastic banner pumping in the sky.

Gemina smiled. "He seems friendly."

"His mother was a nomad. They like Cushites."

He pushed away the knot of worry that twisted and turned in his gut. They were almost free. Before the skiff hit the bank, he jumped out, water dancing at his thighs, black mud sucking at his feet. The nomad came to his aid, and together, they pulled the boat onto the shore.

"I see you made it," the thin man said, his smile revealing two rows of dazzling white teeth.

"Barely," he said, pointing to the row of guards, still standing immobile on the opposite shore.

"What are they doing? Making sure you don't return?"

"I suppose." He helped Gemina out and shouldered the heavy saddlebag containing all their worldly goods.

"Pretty skiff," the nomad said, pointing.

"She's yours. We won't be able to lug her on our backs as we travel into Egypt."

"That's what I was hoping you would say." Their guide flashed another happy smile and bent to cover the boat with reeds. An odd, strangled sound escaped his lips. Without warning, the thin body pitched over and sprawled facedown into the shallows of the Nile. A long iron-tipped spear protruded from his back.

Gemina screamed.

He swerved, hand reaching for his sword. Twelve armed guards stepped forward from the shadows of the palm trees in a precise, symmetrical line. The sun glanced off their bare arms, turning flesh into ebony statuary.

A tall woman slithered through the unmoving rank, her muscular body covered in an ankle-length white gown, decorated with a pleated sash that draped across her right shoulder. Henna stained her long fingernails and hair, flashing red under the sun. On her head, she wore a metal skullcap, which supported a royal diadem.

"You did not really think you could outsmart me?" she drawled.

The manners of a lifetime transcended his shock, and he fell to his knee, arm at his breast. "Kandake."

She took a long spear from one of the guards and shoved the sharp iron point under his chin, making him wince. Blood dripped onto his tunic.

"Don't!" Gemina shouted, scampering toward him. One of the guards moved, his toned body a blur of motion, and captured her before she could reach him. Or the queen.

"Be silent, girl," the Kandake growled.

Gemina struggled harder, and the guard clenched her arms, his fingers turning vicious.

He forgot about the point of the spear at his throat when he saw her skin turning red, bruising under the guard's rough handling. With a twist of his torso, he freed himself from the queen's weapon and leapt to Gemina's defense.

"Leave my wife alone!" His voice sounded strange in his own ears, a lion's roar rather than his usually soft intonation.

He managed one step, evaded two guards to take a second, almost reaching Gemina. But a wall of hard-muscled bodies met his next stride. Fists pummeled him to the ground, knees bruising his ribs until his breath became trapped in his chest and he turned dizzy. In the background, he could hear Gemina weeping hysterically.

The Kandake's face filled the sky as she stared down at him. "*Wife*, is it?"

"We are married," he said through swelling lips. "Nothing you can do about it now."

"Is that so?" She gave him a narrow-eyed stare. "I can make her a widow."

"You wouldn't!"

She had been like an aunt to him all his life. His mother had been her closest friend. A trusted confidante in a world filled with enemies. Would she kill him because he had married without her permission? Married the daughter of a Roman official?

"You embarrassed me. I have killed men for less," she said, as though reading his thoughts.

"Forgive me, my queen."

She nodded to one of her men, and before he had time to take another breath, the royal guard had uncovered two barges from their hiding place in the reeds. They trussed him up like a captive slave, his ankles and elbows in iron chains, bound together behind his back so that his whole body folded painfully into itself, his calves pressed into his thighs, his feet touching his elbows. His muscles screamed in protest as two guards picked him up like a sack of grain and threw him into the barge. A greater agony seared his heart as he watched them drag Gemina into the second royal ship.

At the last moment, the queen stepped into the barge that carried him and signaled their departure. She would not want to be discovered on this side of the Nile. The Libyans had gained a strong foothold on the west shores of the river and had no love for her. If they caught her surrounded by so few men, they would treat her with no more compassion than she was treating him.

"Please, Kandake," he begged.

Dark eyes fixed on him. She was his senior by sixteen years, only. But the mantle of authority had added to her what years could not. She seemed at once ancient and ageless as she considered him, her lips a ruthless line.

She held up a finger. "First, she is a Roman." Another finger rose in the air. "Second, she is betrothed to some highborn Roman idiot who sits seething in my throne room at this very moment." Another finger. "Third, her father is the emperor's own official, now frothing at the mouth, flinging threats at me." Another finger. "Fourth, you sneaking little snake, you went behind my back." Another finger. "Fifth, you set a bad example for all the young men in my palace. In my kingdom." She kicked him in his exposed side, the hard point of her leather shoe making him grunt in pain. "I am running out of fingers, you fool. And I still have to deal with that blockhead father of hers."

He took a deep breath. She hadn't killed him yet. That seemed hopeful. "We should have asked your permission."

"You think so?"

"We should have asked for your help."

She gave a bitter laugh. "No, you should not. If you had dared breathe a word to me, I would have slapped you so hard, your brains would have fallen out of your skull."

"Help us now, Kandake!"

"Help you? I'd as soon squeeze the life out of you. Don't you understand? Rome is sitting at our door like a hungry lion. We barely hang by a thread, holding on to some measure of autonomy, staving them off with our rich taxes. All they need is an excuse to swallow us whole. What you did could hand them that excuse."

He squeezed his eyes shut. Once, Cush had been a

powerful nation. Seven hundred years earlier, its kings had ruled over Egypt. For a whole century, the two kingdoms had been united under the banner of Cushite monarchs. Those days were long gone now. Cush's mines and jewels as well as its wily queen had managed to hold off the sticky, acquisitive fingers of Rome from snatching them up entirely. They still had their independence, of sorts. Their riches bought them, if not the power of old, then certainly enough influence to count.

"The girl is her father's affair," the Kandake said. "But you. You are mine to deal with. And trust me when I tell you this: I will mete out a punishment you will never forget. You will learn to put your nation before your heart."

"I love this land. But I also love Gemina. I am *married* to her," he insisted.

"And how will one pathetic, hastily performed rite stand against the might of your queen and the grievance of Rome?" Again, she held him in her implacable stare. He had seen that look on her face before. The look she gave when she had made up her mind. The look that meant no power on earth would move her. The look that came before blood spilled.

Whatever kernel of hope he had held onto withered.

He turned his head painfully until he could see the other barge sailing just behind them. At least they did not seem to be mistreating Gemina. She sat with her arms wrapped around her knees, her back ramrod straight.

She would not know, yet, that she had parted from him forever.

*I love you,* he whispered soundlessly, knowing he would never say the words to her again. Knowing the Nile carried away his heart, and he could do nothing to stop it.

# CHAPTER 1

---cᴜↄ---

*Behold, if the river is turbulent he is not frightened.*

JOB 40:23

25 YEARS LATER

The boat glided past the famed statues of Pharaoh Amenhotep, two stone giants that had guarded the western shores of the Nile for over a thousand years. The first had been badly damaged by an earthquake, its face unrecognizable. But the second seemed to gaze upon Chariline with regal eyes, as if weighing her mettle. She gave the old pharaoh a lopsided smile. After years of Grandfather's baleful glares, Amenhotep could not intimidate her.

The vast breadth of the Nile spread before Chariline, its smoky blue waters as mysterious as the guardian statues of Memnon. She felt the rhythm of her pulse change, growing faster, harder, and a rush of heat that had nothing to do with the weather seeped beneath her skin. No matter how many times she made this journey, traveling on the Nile never ceased to exhilarate her.

The river itself was a battlefield, its currents moving north while the wind blew south, and their vessel became the object of a tug of war between them. Chariline watched the white sail as it caught the breeze and bellowed tight, the winds proving stronger than the waves, carrying them determinedly away from Egypt.

Just as the sun was sinking, a golden orb turning the sky into flames of crimson, they came upon the island of Elephantine, a huge landmass that had once marked Egypt's most southerly border. They would dock in its modest pier and spend the night in the anchored boat.

Her aunt's pale face appeared at the door of the cabin built into the aft of the barge. "Are we stopping for the night?"

"Yes, Aunt Blandina."

Chariline helped her aunt off the boat, guiding her up the stone staircase that had been carved directly into the river as a means of measuring the water's levels. Some enterprising merchant had built Roman-style latrines in the marina. For a modest fee, Chariline and her aunt availed themselves of the facilities before returning to the narrow cabin to retire for the night. Chariline would have preferred to sleep on the deck under the bejeweled stars like most of the local passengers. But her aunt, who would have to make a full report of their journey to Grandfather, forbade what the old man would consider an indignity.

Chariline sighed and slipped into her pallet. Every year since she had turned ten, as soon as traveling by water became relatively safe after the ides of March, Chariline had traveled from Caesarea to Cush to visit her grandparents for exactly two weeks. Fourteen days and not an hour longer. Grandfather had established those rules the first time he had sent for her. He had never wavered from them in the ensuing years.

Chariline had not wanted to change those rules either. Although she loved Cush and its capital city of Meroë, the company of her grandparents strained her nerves after the second hour. By the end of the second week, she felt as ready to take her leave as they were to be rid of her.

Her grandfather, a midranking civil official acting as an agent of Rome, had been assigned to Cush over twenty-five years ago. He had expected to rise in his career. Expected Cush to be a stepping stone to greater things. Instead, his career had stalled, and rather than a modest beginning, Cush had proven a dead end. He had become the one permanent fixture of Rome in a small kingdom. Men with greater potential and influence were sent to better posts in Egypt.

Whether his disappointment had caused Grandfather to become a sour man or his disposition had been the reason he had never risen high, she could not tell. She had tried to understand the man from the day she met him—and never succeeded.

Taking one last longing look at the indigo sky through the narrow window, Chariline closed her eyes with a sigh and fell asleep to the enthusiastic music of frogs.

The gentle sway of the boat as it raised anchor just before sunrise woke her. Careful not to disturb Aunt Blandina, she slid silently out of bed and made her way onto the deck. Even this early in the day, the wide, swirling waters of the Nile were host to a plethora of tiny and large vessels. Their captains, familiar with the deceptive eddies and sandbanks hiding under the river's seemingly hospitable waters, guided their vessels with watchful expertise.

An hour later they came upon the First Cataract in the river. The cataracts, unnavigable sections of the Nile where boulders littered the surface of the river's bed, could not be crossed except during summer's flood season. The passengers had to disembark and walk on foot, while men carried the barge on the soggy banks with the help of two bony oxen.

After the boat resumed its journey south, a boy with jet skin and a beaming white smile approached Chariline. She recognized him as one of the hired hands on the boat. He had helped carry their baggage onboard and ran errands for the passengers. Thin, naked torso glistening in the sun, he crouched down, dropping twelve smooth stones between them. With a hand, he gestured an invitation. Chariline grinned back and, glancing over to ensure her aunt remained safely ensconced in the cabin, squatted to face the boy.

She had seen him play the stones with a handful of other passengers, his fingers nimble and lightning fast. He would beat her, she knew. And although, in general, she had an aversion to losing, she would not mind it this time. Losing meant she could give the boy a coin without violating his pride. A coin that would help feed him for a day or two.

"Your name?" she asked in Meroitic.

The boy's grin widened. "Arkamani," he said, pushing out his chest.

"I am Chariline."

They drew lots to determine who should begin the game. Arkamani won and started, throwing a single stone in the air with a smooth motion. The object of the game was simple. Throw a stone in the air, pick up one from the ground, and catch the flying stone before it dropped. The next round, pick up two stones from the ground, then three, and so forth, until you held six in your palm. The second round, you threw two stones in the air and began again.

The game didn't change hands until the one playing fumbled. Arkamani did not drop a stone until the third round. Chariline held her own for a few throws, but she lacked the boy's agility and practice. With astonishing dexterity, he won the game in the next round. From her bag, Chariline extracted a small coin and one of Aunt Blandina's special cakes. "Honey," she said, indicating the pastry.

Arkamani's eyes rounded. He shoved the honey cake into his mouth, turning his cheeks into two round lumps. Chariline laughed.

"You need something in Meroë, you call me," the boy said, swallowing. "Call Arkamani." He slapped his narrow chest noisily. "I am your man, honey lady."

Chariline hid her smile. "You're a little too young to be my man."

"I'll grow," he assured her.

The captain yelled the boy's name. "Better go before you get into trouble, Arkamani." Chariline pointed her chin toward the captain.

The boy shrugged. "He is my uncle. No trouble, honey lady." Gathering his stones with care, he gave her another smile before running to do his uncle's bidding.

The next afternoon, her aunt emerged from the cabin to partake of a brief respite on the deck. The heat had turned her delicate skin the color of a mature beet, and she waved her ostrich fan in front of her face with an air of desperation. "It feels too hot to breathe."

"It's cooler outside than in that stuffy cabin," Chariline said. "Stay with me and enjoy the breeze from the river." Chariline saw a sleek silhouette slither past, a good distance from where they stood leaning against the side of the boat. She drew a sharp breath. "Look, Aunt!" she pointed.

"Gods! Is that . . . ?"

"A crocodile. Yes! Isn't it wonderful?"

Blandina shuddered. "Monstrous. I can't wait to get off this contraption." She frowned as she turned to study her niece. "You will roast your skin in that sun. Hold your parasol higher."

By which she meant that Chariline's already dark skin would grow even darker. An unforgivable offense, as far as her grandparents were concerned. With a sigh, Chariline adjusted her parasol. It wasn't as if the little bit of papyrus and wood could magically transform her complexion to the same pale shade as her aunt's.

From the first time Chariline had looked in a mirror, she had known that she would never fit in with her family. Her skin looked like cinnamon with a hint of cream. Her tight brown curls with their sprinkling of dark gold refused to be tamed into a silky fall. Her full lips, long, toned limbs, and high cheekbones all set her apart from her chalk-white, fair-haired family. Perhaps that was why her grandfather never looked her in the eyes.

Even a short stroll through the narrow lanes of Meroë was enough to show that although her mother had been a Roman through and through, half of Chariline belonged to Cush. Her mother must have met her father there.

All her life, Chariline had been told two things about her father: that he was dead, and that she was never to mention him. More than once, her curiosity had prompted her to ask the forbidden questions her heart could not set aside. Who was he? Had he known of her existence? How had he met her mother? Did he still have family living in Meroë? How did he die? An endless litany of questions that had never found an answer. In her grandfather, they had met with stony, disapproving silence. In her grandmother, a fearful and equally silent grief. Only her aunt had responded to her badgering.

"I never knew him, Chariline. I only know that your mother loved him dearly. And ran away to marry him without permission."

That was the sum total of her knowledge of the man who had fathered her: That like her mother, he was dead. That he was a Cushite. And that her mother had loved him.

And now, she would likely not discover anything else about him. After over twenty-five years of unremarkable service to the empire, her grandfather had received his marching orders. He was to retire later that spring. Leave his house in Cush and begin a quiet life in the countryside of Italia somewhere. With his imminent departure, Chariline had to discard whatever hopes she had nurtured over the years of one day discovering her father's identity. Grandfather would never crack the wall of secrecy he had erected around her parents' marriage. And with Meroë far behind them, she would lose all access to any Cushite resources. Not that it really mattered. The man was dead, whether she knew his name or not.

Arkamani interrupted the dark train of her thoughts by sidling up, armed with his stones. "Come to thrash me again?" she said, cracking a small smile at the urchin's eager expression.

"If you insist, honey lady."

This time, Arkamani won even faster than before.

She studied his grinning face for a moment. "No one will play with you twice if you beat them too quickly," she warned.

"Apologies, honey lady. Uncle needs my help soon."

"Hold one moment." She withdrew another honey cake from her bag, which found its way into Arkamani's mouth as quickly as before.

Two days, four honey cakes, and several coins later, they arrived at the Fifth Cataract. The river, which flowed narrower this far south, had turned a pale willow green, heralding their proximity to the city of Meroë. The capital of Cush occupied a gentle bend on the banks of the Nile between the Fifth and Sixth Cataracts.

After they navigated the rocks and piled back into the boat, Aunt Blandina lingered for a rare moment with Chariline. "Not far now," she said, wrapping the edges of her stola closer about her. Never talkative, she became quieter still in Cush.

"Grandmother will be happy to see you."

Aunt Blandina made a noncommittal sound.

"I love Meroë. I don't understand why Grandfather loathes it here. If he were a little less demanding, he might find himself enjoying the place."

Aunt Blandina bit her lip. "Don't let him hear you say that." She allowed herself a tiny smile. "You sound like your mother. She, too, loved Cush."

"Did she?" Chariline pressed eagerly, hoping to hear more about the mother of whom she knew so little.

A curtain drew over her aunt's face, wiping away every trace of warmth. "Hold up your parasol," she admonished before turning her back and heading for the cabin.

Fishing her roll of papyrus out of her bag, and grabbing her inkpot and stylus, Chariline settled down to work on the palace she had been designing for her friend Natemahar.

It had become a tradition between them. Every year when she came to Cush, she designed an opulent building for him. He loved her designs and told her she had rare talent. He was one of the few who did. Most believed a woman had no business wanting to be an architect. Wanting to learn engineering and construction. But Natemahar encouraged her to pursue her training. Over the years, he had sent her seven of Vitruvius's ten famed books on architecture. They had become the foundation of her growing knowledge.

The reminder of Natemahar's extraordinary support made her heart lift. She might not have been blessed with the love of a proper family, but when it came to friendships, God had more than favored her.

A few hours later, as the boat navigated a sharp bend, Chariline's attention was captured by movement on the bank. A black-and-white ibis pecked at the dark mud with its long beak. In the distance, something red caught Chariline's eye on the eastern shore. Setting her drawing aside, she leaned forward to catch a better glimpse. There it was, the first pyramid of Meroë, coming into view, followed by dozens more in bright reds, yellows, and ochres. They were nothing more than a cemetery. A burial ground for the aristocracy and royalty of the kingdom. But the pyramids of Meroë held a fascination for her that went far beyond their prosaic function. Their curious construction and enduring mystery never ceased to captivate her. Not long after, the sailors began to lower the sails and prepare to drop anchor.

Chariline headed for the cabin. "Aunt Blandina, we have arrived at the port."

Blandina came to her feet carefully, frowning at the sharp rocking motion of the boat. Signaling the captain, she arranged for their luggage to be carried to the city gate and led the way gingerly to the narrow wooden pier.

Stout walls constructed of dressed stone encircled the whole city of Meroë. At the main gate, two angular stone towers jutted out like stubborn jaws, flanking the entrance into the city, giving the guards a better vantage point as they monitored the river that brought life and goods past their city.

Chariline and her aunt entered the massive wood-and-iron gates after the soldiers gave their papers a cursory examination. Past the tower, they sat by the wall, leaning against their piled baggage, and prepared for a long wait.

Chariline stretched her neck, surveying the crowd. She knew better than to look for her grandfather. He would not meet them for another hour. He never left work until the afternoon regardless of the time of their arrival. Since their boat often anchored at Meroë earlier, they were expected to tarry at the gate and wait for him patiently.

Chariline searched through the busy throng, trying to spot her friend Natemahar. She swallowed a smile when she caught sight of him striding toward them. Not once, in all the years of her visits to Cush, had he missed her arrival. He stepped in front of Aunt Blandina and gave her a formal nod of acknowledgment. His rich clothing, as well as the young servant who stood deferentially at his side, carrying a carved alabaster box, declared him an important official.

Aunt Blandina's eyes widened a little. Natemahar smiled reassuringly. Every year, he arranged for this charade, and every year Blandina forgot.

"A small gift for the daughter and granddaughter of our honored Roman official, Quintus Blandinus Geminus," Natemahar said in perfect Latin, his words made more exotic by his soft, musical accent. "Compliments of the great Kandake of Cush." He managed to say the words with a straight face, though his ebony eyes sparkled.

Chariline bit her lip. The Kandake, or Candace as the Greeks and Romans referred to her, was the title of the queen mother who exerted more power in Cush than her own son. And if the Kandake had ever sent a present to her grandfather, Chariline was willing to eat her leather sandals. The queen had never shown the Roman official any special favors. But as her chief treasurer, Natemahar had the authority to impart gifts in her name.

"Thank you." Blandina reached for the box. She flipped the lid open and gave a faint smile. "Oh. How nice." Dried fruits and nuts had been packed in a precise pattern of arcs and triangles. Dates, figs, raisins, peaches, and almonds had been turned into an edible painting.

"That's beautiful!" Chariline exclaimed and reached for a plump date. "And delicious. Our thanks to your most thoughtful and gracious Kandake."

Natemahar bowed to her, enveloping her in the warmth

of his smile. "I am honored you are pleased, mistress." Was there more gray at his temples? Deeper lines radiating from the corners of his eyes? Had he been unwell? None of his letters had mentioned an illness. But she knew that Natemahar often struggled with his health, a lingering side effect of the procedure that had rendered him a eunuch so long ago, when he was a boy.

Chariline could not help worrying for him. Hiding her anxiety behind a smile, she said, "I couldn't imagine a better welcome to your delightful land, my lord."

"And I couldn't imagine a lovelier addition to our ancient kingdom."

This hidden dance of words had become one of Chariline's favorite games. Every time they met in public, they had to pretend not to know each other, and yet find ways to communicate. Natemahar had a genius for it, she had discovered. A byproduct of spending his life in the complexities of a scheming royal court.

"May I offer you ladies my chariot?" Natemahar suggested politely.

"Thank you. My father will be here shortly," Blandina said.

"In that case, I will take my leave of you." He bowed with the grace of a lifelong courtier and melted into the crowd. He would not be far, Chariline knew, but hide himself close enough to keep an eye on them lest someone in the packed press of people should attempt to accost them.

"Who is that man?" Aunt Blandina asked. "He seems familiar."

"I believe he is one of the Kandake's officials. He delivered a welcome gift to us last year, you may recall." And the year before. And the year before that. Fourteen years of imaginative welcomes.

"Oh yes. Now that you mention it. What a good memory you have, Chariline."

"Thank you, Aunt."

Then again, since Chariline had known Natemahar from the age of seven, and they had been communicating via secret letters for years, she was not likely to forget him.

# CHAPTER 2

——⚭——

*For everything that is hidden will eventually be brought into*
*the open, and every secret will be brought to light.*

MARK 4:22, NLT

"Let me hold that. It's heavy," Chariline told her aunt, taking
the carved alabaster box from her hands.

"That is kind of you, dear."

Chariline placed the box on her lap and opened it. She
looked at the tempting offerings inside and marveled at the
hands that had managed to use fruit as a canvas for art. Her
fingers traced the patterned cotton lining the lid, a replica of
the design inside, before replacing the cover.

The sun scorched down on her head in spite of her parasol, making Chariline's scalp itch. In her attempt to tame
Chariline's curls, Aunt Blandina had poured enough scented
oil on her hair to bury a man. She had pulled and scraped
and braided and looped and sculpted the stubborn tresses
into some semblance of order, trying to make it look Roman

rather than Cushite. But the arrangement was a miserable ache against Chariline's scalp, and she reached a finger to try and loosen a particularly tight loop.

"Leave it!" Aunt Blandina snapped with unusual vigor. "Here comes your grandfather."

"I think you mean to say here comes your father."

"Hush." Blandina stood straight, like a soldier before his general, getting ready to be inspected.

Chariline made no effort. It would only be wasted, anyhow. In truth, Grandfather did not awe her the way he did Aunt Blandina. She supposed it was because she had only spent two weeks a year under his roof, and that after the age of ten. Poor Aunt Blandina had grown up under his tyranny and still bore the brunt of it when they came to visit him. Her one act of rebellion had been to refuse to move back into her parents' home after she had been widowed. She had chosen to remain in her husband's house in Caesarea, and after Chariline was born, raised her there alone.

"Did you have a pleasant journey?" Grandfather said by way of greeting. "Of course not," he answered himself before they could. "That boat ride down the Nile is never agreeable."

Chariline, for whom the only unpleasant part of the journey had been to bake in the hot sun while waiting for him, said, "I found it most enjoyable."

"Don't be contrary," Grandfather snapped. "Your grandmother has prepared a big supper for you two. After you eat, you can help with the packing. Plenty of daylight left."

"Packing?" He meant for their move from Cush, she realized. "Grandfather, don't you have servants for that?"

"You must have baked in the heat too long. I wouldn't

allow those fools to touch my things. What they don't steal, they will break."

Chariline, who had come to know Grandfather's four servants well, and thought highly of each, frowned. "They have been packing and unpacking my baggage for years and nothing ever went missing."

"That's because you have nothing worth taking."

Chariline could not argue with that. "I will help Grandmother. Aunt Blandina needs rest tonight. It's been a long journey."

Blandina sent her a grateful look.

"In that case, Chariline, I hope you are prepared to do twice the work." As always, her grandfather winced when he spoke her name. *Chariline.* It had no family connections, no respectful nod to their ancestors. It did not even have the refinement of being Roman. Her mother, for some inexplicable reason, had chosen to give her a Greek appellation. Her grandfather, Roman to the bone, abhorred it.

Dinner, which they ate in the atrium, proved a strained affair. Grandfather felt that conversation at meals impaired his digestion, and everyone was expected to maintain a rule of strict silence. After finishing their simple meal, Chariline accompanied her aunt to her chamber and, after tucking her into bed gently, reported for duty in the tablinum.

Following her grandfather's very particular instructions, she began to wrap his extensive collection of fragile ivory carvings in rags, packing them in layers of fresh straw, while her grandmother worked silently next to her. For half an hour, Grandfather supervised their efforts like a sharp-beaked hawk, always ready with a ripe criticism.

When he finally left them to their own devices, Chariline gave her grandmother a conspiratorial smile. "I think he missed his calling. He should have been a general, ordering soldiers by the dozen."

Her grandmother placed her index finger on thin lips, as if trying to keep a smile from escaping.

Picking up a figurine, Chariline covered it with a thick layer of rags. Knowing these were her final days in Cush cast a shadow on every activity. A part of her belonged to this land. Felt a nostalgic attachment to it, an odd connection that went beyond the familiarity of annual visits. A connection that flowed from her own mysterious history.

"Grandmother, did you ever meet my father?" The words leapt from a deep place, refusing to be silenced.

Her grandmother jumped as if prodded by the sharp end of an arrow. "What?"

"My father. Did you know him? He was from Meroë, wasn't he?"

"He is dead, Chariline. You know you are forbidden to speak of him."

"Why? I am not a child. I have a right to know."

"Ask your grandfather. It's time I retired." Grandmother's fair skin looked spectral white in the lamplight as she turned on her heels and left.

Chariline's back drooped. Setting aside the packing, she made her way to her chamber. Her legs felt wobbly with exhaustion. The hours in the hot sun of the Nile had sapped her more than she had realized. Yet, in spite of a weariness that went to her bones, sleep proved elusive. She lay scratchy-eyed on the bed, tossing uselessly.

Venting a sigh of defeat, Chariline slipped out of bed, thinking to enjoy the star-filled sky of Meroë in the quiet of the atrium. Her bare feet made no sound as she passed her grandparents' chamber.

"Chariline must never know." Her grandfather's voice penetrated through the timber walls. "You understand? She must never find out."

Chariline's feet froze in place. What must she never know?

"She continues to pester me about him." She could picture Grandmother twisting her handkerchief in nervous fingers, not quite able to look at her husband.

"I don't want that . . . that degenerate anywhere near Chariline. He has no right to her. He ruined my daughter's life! Every time I see him at the palace, I want to vomit."

"After so many years, couldn't we tell her? Chariline is desperate to know her father, Quintus."

"She has no father!" Grandfather shouted.

Chariline heard the tap, tap of feet on the stone floors, approaching the door, and stole into the dark corridor before Grandfather caught her eavesdropping. Forgetting about the stars, she crept back to her room and sat slack-jawed, thinking through the conversation she had overheard.

Her grandfather's voice reverberated in her mind. *Every time I see him at the palace.* See him? But that implied . . .

Impossible! And yet those words could only mean one thing. Her father was *alive.* Alive!

He must work at one of the palaces in Meroë, within walking distance of this very house. Work in a public-enough position that forced Grandfather to see him when he attended the court.

A slow fire began to burn in her belly, radiating upward, setting a blaze in her veins. For twenty-four years she had been told that her father was dead. Twenty-four years of lies. Of subterfuge. Twenty-four years being cheated of knowing her father.

She punched a fist into the pillow beside her. Grandfather had no right! Shoving the covers aside, Chariline leapt out of bed, intending to march to her grandparents' chamber to demand the truth.

Her hand stilled as it reached for the door. Grandfather would remain as unmoved by her fury as he had been by her entreaties over the years. That man couldn't be reasoned with. He would simply bundle her on the earliest available boat out of Cush and force her to return home.

It wasn't as if she could travel back to Cush on her own. Meroë was not a popular destination. Even from a major port like Caesarea, it required two separate voyages by boat to get to Cush—and a small fortune, which she lacked. Supposing she had the funds, as an unaccompanied woman, she would not be safe traveling so far.

No. If she wanted to find her father, she had to be shrewd like a fox.

Slowly, she climbed back into bed, realizing that she could not afford to give in to rash impulses. She had to keep her wits about her and plan carefully. She only had fourteen days to unearth the identity of the man. And she would have to use every moment wisely.

Her father *lived*! That notion both thrilled and terrified her. A thousand questions churned in her mind. Did he know of her existence? If so, why had he never sought her out? And if he had never been told of her birth, how would he feel about her sudden appearance in his life? Why did Grandfather blame him for ruining her mother's life? The questions swirled in her head, a dizzying whirlpool of inexplicable mysteries.

Philip would bid her to pray. Philip, who had taught her about God and baptized her with his own hands in Caesarea's harbor one misty morning. He always began and ended everything with the Lord.

Chariline tried to tame her stormy thoughts. Tame them long enough to speak to God. But her prayer rose up like a wisp of smoke with hardly any substance. God seemed far away and inconsequential just then. Grandfather had had more influence in her life than the Lord, it seemed.

Chariline hissed a breath through clenched teeth, then bolted up as a single name rose to the forefront of her mind. *Natemahar!* Natemahar could help her! He knew everyone in the royal household. Knew long-forgotten secrets. Some old whisper of scandal in the court may lead to the identity of her father. Tomorrow, she would meet Natemahar and begin her search in earnest.

———◌◌◌———

The next morning, Chariline swallowed the accusations that burned in her throat and, schooling her features into a blank canvas, bid her grandfather a civil good morning before he departed for work. Time crawled until the women finally settled down to the noonday meal. Chariline managed to force down the yeasted Egyptian bread, swallow the vegetable stew, and drink her watered-down wine without choking.

in with their host, his greeting soft, dark eyes the kindest she had ever seen.

Chariline had promptly burst out weeping at the sight of him. He had knelt in front of her, placing an impossibly gentle hand on her head. "What's this? What's this? Tell me all about it."

Through a wave of uncharacteristic tears, Chariline had wailed, "Your skin is darker than mine. I thought I was the only one in the whole world."

Natemahar had laughed and pulled her into his arms. "You're not the only one, little one. There is a whole land filled with people like us."

"Like *me*?"

He had gazed at her, his eyes grave. "Well, more like me. You are very special; I can see that. Who is this beautiful child?" He had looked up at Philip, seeking answers.

"Her mother was called Gemina. Her grandfather is Quintus Blandinus Geminus. Come to think of it, he is a Roman official who serves in your country, Natemahar. Do you know him?"

Natemahar had stumbled back. "I know him."

That day, a special bond had formed between the two. Over the years, they had managed to meet at Philip's house whenever Natemahar traveled to Caesarea. They carved out time to be together in Cush and, in between their visits, wrote reams of letters that paved the roads and rivers that separated them.

"Why did you become my friend?" Chariline had asked once. "All those years ago, when you first met me at Philip's house. Why didn't you just forget about me?" It seemed such

If her grandmother noticed Chariline's distraction, she made no mention of it. After the interminable meal finally finished, Grandmother and Aunt Blandina retired to their chambers for their customary afternoon rest.

No sooner had they closed their doors than Chariline slipped out of the house and made her way to the spice shop. The exotic scents and vibrant colors of Cush and Egypt greeted her as she entered the colorful store.

"Good day," she said softly in Meroitic, smiling at the portly owner who stood behind his wooden counter, surveying his domain like a king.

Thick brows rose to the middle of his high forehead. "Look who has returned," he answered in passable Greek.

Having grown up in Caesarea, Chariline spoke fluent Greek as well as Latin thanks to her aunt. She switched languages with ease. "Lovely," she replied, bending to breathe in the scent of cinnamon, grated fresh in the shop.

"Like you."

Her smile widened. In Cush, as in Caesarea, she was something of an oddity, her skin too light here, the golden streaks in her brown hair a match for her amber eyes. But the people of Cush were kinder when they stared, their curiosity often mingled with admiration.

"Thank you."

"You want to send a message?"

"May I?"

"Of course. I have a new errand boy. He will get it to him in no time." He snapped a finger and the boy from the boat ran in. What was his name?

"Arkamani!" she said, remembering.

The boy's smile showed a double row of perfect teeth. "Honey lady. Told you I was your man."

"You've come up in the world." Chariline pointed at his clean linen skirt.

He shrugged. "Another uncle."

The spice seller gave Arkamani a long set of directions, spoken too rapidly in Meroitic for Chariline to catch. "Give him your note," he told her in Greek. Chariline gave the boy the tiny roll of papyrus, and tucking it into his skirt, he ran out the back door in a whirl of pumping muscles.

"How many uncles does he have?" she asked the spice seller.

"On his mother's side, fourteen. But that has always been a small family. On his father's side, our family is a lot more vigorous."

In less than half the length of an hour, Natemahar walked in. At the sight of his dear face, the iron-hard band of control that she had wrapped around her emotions broke. She ran to him, and he opened his arms to receive her as if she wasn't almost as tall as he. She felt the roiling agitation that had plagued her since the previous night break like a wave on the prow of a ship.

"Well now," he rumbled against her cheek. "What's this?"

"My father is alive!" Chariline blurted.

Natemahar took half a step back. He stared at her, his eyes wide. "How . . . how do you know this?"

"I overheard my grandfather last night."

Natemahar rubbed the back of his neck. "You better tell me all about it. Shall we have a seat?" He looked to the spice seller, who bowed deeply and whipped aside a curtain leading

to a tiny room. Two upturned wooden boxes served for stools, with a chipped concrete block in between functioning as a makeshift table.

"Thank you, friend," Natemahar said, discretely passing a short stack of coins to the spice seller. "I think you could use a little rest? Say half an hour?"

"I will lock the doors on my way out, my lord."

"Tell me all about it," Natemahar told Chariline when they were alone, his soft voice covering her like the folds of a familiar cloak.

*Tell me all about it.* Those were the same words he had said when they met for the first time seventeen years ago.

And it seemed to Chariline that the years peeled back like a ripe fig while they sat in that tiny room, the sweet perfume of the spices of Egypt and Meroë swirling around them. An image of Natemahar, younger then, and less frail, looking down at her little frame, rose up in her mind, the memory sweet and slow like dripping honey.

As with most of the best things in her life, their meeting had taken place in the home of Philip in Caesarea.

Philip had four daughters, the youngest of whom, Mariamne, had been her best friend since she could remember. Like her, Mariamne had grown up without a mother. But unlike Chariline, she had been raised with the indulgent affection of three older sisters and a doting father who didn't let the sun go down without praising his daughters. That house had become a refuge to a lonely orphan girl whose dark skin made her a stranger in her own family.

One afternoon, when she had been playing with Mariamne in the narrow atrium of Philip's house, a tall man had walked an incongruous choice for a man like Natemahar. A successful Cushite official befriending a Roman child with little to offer save a gap-toothed smile and a thousand pestering questions.

"I was a lonely man who was never going to have a child, and you were a lonely child who was never going to have a father. It seemed a good fit." Natemahar had pulled her braid. "Besides, we are alike, you and I. You are surrounded by a family who always make you feel like an outsider, while I . . . I am surrounded by men who are whole. A palace full of them. Warriors and husbands and fathers. All the things I can never be. I am an outsider in my own land. So you see, we belong together."

# CHAPTER 3

———⟨∽⟩———

*In the shadow of your wings I will take refuge,*
*till the storms of destruction pass by.*

PSALM 57:1

Theo climbed the stout mast of his ship, muscles bunching as he propelled himself higher on the smooth pole. At the top, he coiled his leg around the sturdy timber, anchoring himself in place as he looked around him. The aquamarine waters of the Mediterranean surrounded them, no land in sight.

They had been at sea for seven days, and as much as he loved his ship, he had to admit that with a dozen men on board, it could feel cramped after a week. *Parmys* was dainty: from the tip of its up-curved bow to the tail of the stern, you could lay no more than eleven tall men, head touching toe.

Theo had fallen into the habit of climbing to the top of the mast when the winds grew still, as they had this morning. He had discovered this to be one of the few spots on the ship where he could enjoy some quiet. This had become his favorite spot to be with God.

Prayer came to him easily, after years of hard practice. Four years ago, he had come to God feeling tarnished. Feeling ruined at his very core. But his friends Priscilla and Aquila and Paul had taught him to look in the mirror and see the face of the Savior instead of the nightmares of his past.

He clung to the mast and prayed for his crew, for his family, for safety on the journey ahead. His soul settled into peace.

When he finally opened his eyes, he saw his captain, Taharqa, standing patiently below.

"How goes it?" Theo asked.

Taharqa shrugged a massive shoulder. "Slooow." His lilting accent added an extra syllable to the word. "Still no sign of wind."

The charioteer in Theo had to acknowledge that the ship's speed left something to be desired at the best of times. Its deep keel, double planking to strengthen the hull, and additional ballast made the *Parmys* a reliable ship, the perfect vessel for a merchant. But it did not make her fast. Add to that fifteen hundred wide-mouthed terra-cotta jars full of the balls of soap they carried, and their pace had grown leisurely.

Even that steady, plodding pace had come to a complete stop when the winds ceased altogether several hours before. The ship's massive, square sail had dropped down, limp and useless, leaving its tiny, triangular topsail listlessly flopping to no avail.

Merchant ships rarely used oars as a regular mode of travel. It simply required too many men for practicality. On the *Parmys,* Theo had devised a system of six men at the oars when the winds grew still or ornery. That number could never replace the strength of a good wind. But it was better than standing still.

Pulling oars was hard work in a cramped space, but his crew had enough experience not to get tangled as they rowed. To a man, he trusted the rugged bunch who worked for him. They had taught him the ways of the sea, taught him to contend with its dangers and delight in its beauties.

Theo turned his face toward the sun and closed his eyes, allowing his senses to expand. He felt the breeze, subtle and warm at first. Before long, it strengthened enough to cool his flushed face. With a shift in his leg muscles, he allowed his body to slide down, speeding without a break all the way to the deck. "Wind is picking up," he told Taharqa.

The captain clapped his giant hands and rubbed them together in excitement. "Come on, men! We have a sail to hoist."

Theo helped pull the rigging, which wove its way through small wooden rings sewn into the sail, guiding a series of lines until the canvas was hauled all the way up, slowly expanding as the breeze grew, turning into a good wind.

"Now we're in business," Taharqa said.

"Up you come, boys," Theo yelled down the shallow steps to the belly of the ship where benches had been bolted to the floor. "We hoisted the sail." Men groaned with relief as they set their heavy oars aside. Theo refused to use slaves on his ship. He preferred to hire seasoned sailors, who were worth every sestertius of their wage. These men knew the rhythm of the sea as well as they knew their own heartbeat.

Within the hour, the ship had glided into a smooth tempo, sailing through the serene waters at a ladylike pace. The crew slipped into an orderly routine, the six rowers lying down for a short rest, while Theo took over one tiller and Taharqa the other. The captain maintained an eagle eye on several men who were busy making minute adjustments to the rigging.

The old Athenian sailor they called Sophocles, on account of the tall tales he liked to tell with a poet's relish, served the noonday meal on chipped plates. Stale bread softened in wine, cured olives, and fresh fish he had caught that morning with his tackle.

By the time the crew sat down to eat, the wind had increased considerably, and Taharqa loosened the lines, reducing the size of the main sail and adjusting the small, triangular sail at the bow.

When the rest had finished eating, Sophocles brought Theo's plate to him at the helm—the same rations as everyone else. Theo had no use for special privileges.

"Saved you the best, Master," Sophocles said, lisping through his missing teeth.

"Brought me the bones again, did you, Sophocles?"

The old man laughed, revealing a bank of naked gums and eight or nine rotting teeth. "Kept those for broth. You get the fish eyes."

Theo thanked the man politely and took his plate. He knew Sophocles was having fun with him. Of course, on their first journey, the fish guts and eyes hadn't been a simple threat. The men had wanted to know if their new master was made of stern-enough stuff to suit them, or if he was a linen-wearing daisy who would run screaming at the first sign of hardship. Theo had learned to eat fish guts without complaint.

"That wind is mighty strong now," Sophocles said with a frown.

Theo sopped some wine with his bread using one hand,

his other firmly on the tiller. "Been picking up steadily from the south."

Sophocles stared into the horizon. "Don't like the look of them clouds."

Theo handed his plate to the old mariner and grabbed the tiller harder when the wind almost knocked it out of his hold. His brows lowered as he studied the clouds Sophocles had pointed out. Like deer chased by a mountain lion, they were moving rapidly, barreling down toward them.

"Taharqa!" he called. His Cushite captain had stepped away from the second tiller to oversee repairs to a broken line.

"I see them." Taharqa came to stand next to him. Abruptly he turned, his movements agile for such a huge man. "Lower that sail!" he screamed. "Lower it down!"

A moment later, Theo understood the urgency in Taharqa's voice. With incomprehensible speed, the wind had turned violent, a tempest that beat at them from every side. Before the men could lower the sail, it had torn in half, flinging the ship with it dangerously into the lee of the storm.

The waves started to surge in giant, mountainous crests, tossing the ship high one moment and casting it down violently into the trough the next, causing the sailors to slip over the deck, growing ineffectual in their attempts to subdue the ship's wild flight.

A brutal burst of water loosed from the darkening sky, the downpour nearly turning them blind with its intensity.

Theo breathed a prayer as he tried to tame the tiller. He needed all his strength merely to hold on to it. Another monstrous wave broke against the bow and plunged over them, drenching them in cold water. The ship was filling too fast for

If her grandmother noticed Chariline's distraction, she made no mention of it. After the interminable meal finally finished, Grandmother and Aunt Blandina retired to their chambers for their customary afternoon rest.

No sooner had they closed their doors than Chariline slipped out of the house and made her way to the spice shop. The exotic scents and vibrant colors of Cush and Egypt greeted her as she entered the colorful store.

"Good day," she said softly in Meroitic, smiling at the portly owner who stood behind his wooden counter, surveying his domain like a king.

Thick brows rose to the middle of his high forehead. "Look who has returned," he answered in passable Greek.

Having grown up in Caesarea, Chariline spoke fluent Greek as well as Latin thanks to her aunt. She switched languages with ease. "Lovely," she replied, bending to breathe in the scent of cinnamon, grated fresh in the shop.

"Like you."

Her smile widened. In Cush, as in Caesarea, she was something of an oddity, her skin too light here, the golden streaks in her brown hair a match for her amber eyes. But the people of Cush were kinder when they stared, their curiosity often mingled with admiration.

"Thank you."

"You want to send a message?"

"May I?"

"Of course. I have a new errand boy. He will get it to him in no time." He snapped a finger and the boy from the boat ran in. What was his name?

"Arkamani!" she said, remembering.

The boy's smile showed a double row of perfect teeth. "Honey lady. Told you I was your man."

"You've come up in the world." Chariline pointed at his clean linen skirt.

He shrugged. "Another uncle."

The spice seller gave Arkamani a long set of directions, spoken too rapidly in Meroitic for Chariline to catch. "Give him your note," he told her in Greek. Chariline gave the boy the tiny roll of papyrus, and tucking it into his skirt, he ran out the back door in a whirl of pumping muscles.

"How many uncles does he have?" she asked the spice seller.

"On his mother's side, fourteen. But that has always been a small family. On his father's side, our family is a lot more vigorous."

In less than half the length of an hour, Natemahar walked in. At the sight of his dear face, the iron-hard band of control that she had wrapped around her emotions broke. She ran to him, and he opened his arms to receive her as if she wasn't almost as tall as he. She felt the roiling agitation that had plagued her since the previous night break like a wave on the prow of a ship.

"Well now," he rumbled against her cheek. "What's this?"

"My father is alive!" Chariline blurted.

Natemahar took half a step back. He stared at her, his eyes wide. "How . . . how do you know this?"

"I overheard my grandfather last night."

Natemahar rubbed the back of his neck. "You better tell me all about it. Shall we have a seat?" He looked to the spice seller, who bowed deeply and whipped aside a curtain leading to a tiny room. Two upturned wooden boxes served for stools, with a chipped concrete block in between functioning as a makeshift table.

"Thank you, friend," Natemahar said, discretely passing a short stack of coins to the spice seller. "I think you could use a little rest? Say half an hour?"

"I will lock the doors on my way out, my lord."

"Tell me all about it," Natemahar told Chariline when they were alone, his soft voice covering her like the folds of a familiar cloak.

*Tell me all about it.* Those were the same words he had said when they met for the first time seventeen years ago.

And it seemed to Chariline that the years peeled back like a ripe fig while they sat in that tiny room, the sweet perfume of the spices of Egypt and Meroë swirling around them. An image of Natemahar, younger then, and less frail, looking down at her little frame, rose up in her mind, the memory sweet and slow like dripping honey.

As with most of the best things in her life, their meeting had taken place in the home of Philip in Caesarea.

Philip had four daughters, the youngest of whom, Mariamne, had been her best friend since she could remember. Like her, Mariamne had grown up without a mother. But unlike Chariline, she had been raised with the indulgent affection of three older sisters and a doting father who didn't let the sun go down without praising his daughters. That house had become a refuge to a lonely orphan girl whose dark skin made her a stranger in her own family.

One afternoon, when she had been playing with Mariamne in the narrow atrium of Philip's house, a tall man had walked in with their host, his greeting soft, dark eyes the kindest she had ever seen.

Chariline had promptly burst out weeping at the sight of him. He had knelt in front of her, placing an impossibly gentle hand on her head. "What's this? What's this? Tell me all about it."

Through a wave of uncharacteristic tears, Chariline had wailed, "Your skin is darker than mine. I thought I was the only one in the whole world."

Natemahar had laughed and pulled her into his arms. "You're not the only one, little one. There is a whole land filled with people like us."

"Like *me*?"

He had gazed at her, his eyes grave. "Well, more like me. You are very special; I can see that. Who is this beautiful child?" He had looked up at Philip, seeking answers.

"Her mother was called Gemina. Her grandfather is Quintus Blandinus Geminus. Come to think of it, he is a Roman official who serves in your country, Natemahar. Do you know him?"

Natemahar had stumbled back. "I know him."

That day, a special bond had formed between the two. Over the years, they had managed to meet at Philip's house whenever Natemahar traveled to Caesarea. They carved out time to be together in Cush and, in between their visits, wrote reams of letters that paved the roads and rivers that separated them.

"Why did you become my friend?" Chariline had asked once. "All those years ago, when you first met me at Philip's house. Why didn't you just forget about me?" It seemed such an incongruous choice for a man like Natemahar. A successful Cushite official befriending a Roman child with little to offer save a gap-toothed smile and a thousand pestering questions.

"I was a lonely man who was never going to have a child, and you were a lonely child who was never going to have a father. It seemed a good fit." Natemahar had pulled her braid. "Besides, we are alike, you and I. You are surrounded by a family who always make you feel like an outsider, while I . . . I am surrounded by men who are whole. A palace full of them. Warriors and husbands and fathers. All the things I can never be. I am an outsider in my own land. So you see, we belong together."

# CHAPTER 3

——ↄ◖ↄ——

*In the shadow of your wings I will take refuge,*
*till the storms of destruction pass by.*

PSALM 57:1

Theo climbed the stout mast of his ship, muscles bunching as
he propelled himself higher on the smooth pole. At the top,
he coiled his leg around the sturdy timber, anchoring himself
in place as he looked around him. The aquamarine waters of
the Mediterranean surrounded them, no land in sight.

They had been at sea for seven days, and as much as he
loved his ship, he had to admit that with a dozen men on
board, it could feel cramped after a week. *Parmys* was dainty:
from the tip of its up-curved bow to the tail of the stern, you
could lay no more than eleven tall men, head touching toe.

Theo had fallen into the habit of climbing to the top of
the mast when the winds grew still, as they had this morning. He had discovered this to be one of the few spots on the
ship where he could enjoy some quiet. This had become his
favorite spot to be with God.

Prayer came to him easily, after years of hard practice. Four years ago, he had come to God feeling tarnished. Feeling ruined at his very core. But his friends Priscilla and Aquila and Paul had taught him to look in the mirror and see the face of the Savior instead of the nightmares of his past.

He clung to the mast and prayed for his crew, for his family, for safety on the journey ahead. His soul settled into peace.

When he finally opened his eyes, he saw his captain, Taharqa, standing patiently below.

"How goes it?" Theo asked.

Taharqa shrugged a massive shoulder. "Slooow." His lilting accent added an extra syllable to the word. "Still no sign of wind."

The charioteer in Theo had to acknowledge that the ship's speed left something to be desired at the best of times. Its deep keel, double planking to strengthen the hull, and additional ballast made the *Parmys* a reliable ship, the perfect vessel for a merchant. But it did not make her fast. Add to that fifteen hundred wide-mouthed terra-cotta jars full of the balls of soap they carried, and their pace had grown leisurely.

Even that steady, plodding pace had come to a complete stop when the winds ceased altogether several hours before. The ship's massive, square sail had dropped down, limp and useless, leaving its tiny, triangular topsail listlessly flopping to no avail.

Merchant ships rarely used oars as a regular mode of travel. It simply required too many men for practicality. On the *Parmys,* Theo had devised a system of six men at the oars when the winds grew still or ornery. That number could never replace the strength of a good wind. But it was better than standing still.

Pulling oars was hard work in a cramped space, but his crew had enough experience not to get tangled as they rowed. To a man, he trusted the rugged bunch who worked for him. They had taught him the ways of the sea, taught him to contend with its dangers and delight in its beauties.

Theo turned his face toward the sun and closed his eyes, allowing his senses to expand. He felt the breeze, subtle and warm at first. Before long, it strengthened enough to cool his flushed face. With a shift in his leg muscles, he allowed his body to slide down, speeding without a break all the way to the deck. "Wind is picking up," he told Taharqa.

The captain clapped his giant hands and rubbed them together in excitement. "Come on, men! We have a sail to hoist."

Theo helped pull the rigging, which wove its way through small wooden rings sewn into the sail, guiding a series of lines until the canvas was hauled all the way up, slowly expanding as the breeze grew, turning into a good wind.

"Now we're in business," Taharqa said.

"Up you come, boys," Theo yelled down the shallow steps to the belly of the ship where benches had been bolted to the floor. "We hoisted the sail." Men groaned with relief as they set their heavy oars aside. Theo refused to use slaves on his ship. He preferred to hire seasoned sailors, who were worth every sestertius of their wage. These men knew the rhythm of the sea as well as they knew their own heartbeat.

Within the hour, the ship had glided into a smooth tempo, sailing through the serene waters at a ladylike pace. The crew slipped into an orderly routine, the six rowers lying down for a short rest, while Theo took over one tiller and Taharqa the other. The captain maintained an eagle eye on several men who were busy making minute adjustments to the rigging.

The old Athenian sailor they called Sophocles, on account of the tall tales he liked to tell with a poet's relish, served the noonday meal on chipped plates. Stale bread softened in wine, cured olives, and fresh fish he had caught that morning with his tackle.

By the time the crew sat down to eat, the wind had increased considerably, and Taharqa loosened the lines, reducing the size of the main sail and adjusting the small, triangular sail at the bow.

When the rest had finished eating, Sophocles brought Theo's plate to him at the helm—the same rations as everyone else. Theo had no use for special privileges.

"Saved you the best, Master," Sophocles said, lisping through his missing teeth.

"Brought me the bones again, did you, Sophocles?"

The old man laughed, revealing a bank of naked gums and eight or nine rotting teeth. "Kept those for broth. You get the fish eyes."

Theo thanked the man politely and took his plate. He knew Sophocles was having fun with him. Of course, on their first journey, the fish guts and eyes hadn't been a simple threat. The men had wanted to know if their new master was made of stern-enough stuff to suit them, or if he was a linen-wearing daisy who would run screaming at the first sign of hardship. Theo had learned to eat fish guts without complaint.

"That wind is mighty strong now," Sophocles said with a frown.

Theo sopped some wine with his bread using one hand,

his other firmly on the tiller. "Been picking up steadily from the south."

Sophocles stared into the horizon. "Don't like the look of them clouds."

Theo handed his plate to the old mariner and grabbed the tiller harder when the wind almost knocked it out of his hold. His brows lowered as he studied the clouds Sophocles had pointed out. Like deer chased by a mountain lion, they were moving rapidly, barreling down toward them.

"Taharqa!" he called. His Cushite captain had stepped away from the second tiller to oversee repairs to a broken line.

"I see them." Taharqa came to stand next to him. Abruptly he turned, his movements agile for such a huge man. "Lower that sail!" he screamed. "Lower it down!"

A moment later, Theo understood the urgency in Taharqa's voice. With incomprehensible speed, the wind had turned violent, a tempest that beat at them from every side. Before the men could lower the sail, it had torn in half, flinging the ship with it dangerously into the lee of the storm.

The waves started to surge in giant, mountainous crests, tossing the ship high one moment and casting it down violently into the trough the next, causing the sailors to slip over the deck, growing ineffectual in their attempts to subdue the ship's wild flight.

A brutal burst of water loosed from the darkening sky, the downpour nearly turning them blind with its intensity.

Theo breathed a prayer as he tried to tame the tiller. He needed all his strength merely to hold on to it. Another monstrous wave broke against the bow and plunged over them, drenching them in cold water. The ship was filling too fast for the men to keep up, the meager bucketfuls of sloshing water they tossed overboard hardly making a dent.

Taharqa took over the second tiller. At the trough of the next wave, they dove down without warning, the ship listing sharp to its right. From the corner of his eye, Theo saw Sophocles slide, hit his back against the wooden slats, and as the ship rolled, pitch in a perfect somersault overboard.

Theo shouted his name and, releasing the tiller to one of his men, leapt to grab the rope they kept secured to the mast for such emergencies. He saw Sophocles's head emerge over a wave and, aiming, threw the rope at him. But the water carried the old sailor just beyond its reach, and before Theo could try again, another wave devoured him altogether.

His white head broke through a moment later. Theo's throat turned dry. The old mariner was barely holding on. He did not have the strength to make his way back to the ship. Not through that storm.

With no hesitation, he wrapped the rope around his middle, shouted Taharqa's name, and without waiting to confirm that the captain had heard him, dove into the wild waters of the Mediterranean. The sheer force of the sea took his breath away. For a moment he hung suspended beneath the waters, barely able to tell top from bottom. He kicked hard, all his years of intense athletic training coming to his aid, helping him find his way to the surface.

Desperation drove him, and he swam against the force of the waves, looking for a glimpse of Sophocles. His heart pounded, a fierce drum that made him deaf to everything save the beating rhythm of his own blood.

Too long. Too long since the white head had surfaced.

There! The old sailor came up again, his flailing hands beating weakly. Theo dove toward him, pushing hard, ignoring a cramp that started in his toes and moved all the way up his calf. Putting one arm ahead of another, he fought the sea and made his way to the drowning man.

His man.

One more mouthful of air, one more push, and he had his arms around Sophocles. For a tiny moment, Sophocles clung to him, bloodshot eyes staring at him with wonder and disbelief. Then, promptly, he lost consciousness, lying against Theo, a dragging deadweight.

Theo looked at the ship and realized the worst still lay ahead. Calculating the distance with an expert eye, he realized they were too far. He wouldn't be able to make it back. Not with him having to swim against the force of the wind. Not while he carried an unconscious man.

Taharqa must not have heard him when he jumped into the water. The captain was still wrestling the tiller, trying to keep the *Parmys* from drowning. No help from that quarter.

The rope Theo had knotted against his torso held, but he couldn't simply pull on the tether and make their way to the ship. The old mariner's dead weight would drag them under long before they made the hull.

His only choice was to swim against the wind.

Turning Sophocles on his back, Theo looped an arm around him and began to swim with his free arm. He took his first mouthful of water as a wave swept over them, and his second and third as he tried not to lose his hold on the unconscious sailor.

With every stroke, he uttered a prayer, asking for the

strength of the Lord to be added to his. Abruptly, he felt a tug at his waist, then another, stronger this time. He looked up, water obscuring his sight, and saw Taharqa's form bent over the side. He was pulling on the rope.

Theo broke into an exhausted grin. It proved a mistake, earning him another mouthful of the briny sea.

"Have you no sense?" Taharqa cried when he fished them out of the depths.

Theo coughed up water, his throat burning, eyes stinging. "Sophocles was drowning."

"So you decided you should join him?"

Theo watched as a couple of the men helped Sophocles below. "How is the ship?"

"It's taken in about as much water as you."

Theo stared into the gray skies with worried eyes. "The storm doesn't seem to be abating."

"It's been carrying us off course. I don't know where we are."

"Could we be close to a coastline?" That would be bad. Coastlines meant rocks. Rocks and ships were not good companions in a gale.

"I took a sounding. We aren't near any shallows yet."

The wind howled violently. Behind him, the mast seemed to waver, emitting an ominous cracking sound. "Watch out!" Taharqa shouted. The top of the mast split and tumbled toward Theo, its jagged end an enormous wooden dagger pointed at his belly.

Theo rolled out of the way just in time to avoid being gored. "My beautiful mast!" He struggled to his feet. "This storm is really starting to annoy me."

"Grab the tiller from Cleitus," Taharqa shouted. "I am going to see to this mess."

Theo forced his shivering legs to obey him and relieved Cleitus. He remembered the story Paul had once told him of the Lord calming a mighty storm and saving his disciples' lives.

The words resounded in his mind: *And there was a great calm.* At the end of that day, the Lord had not merely banished the waves. He had not only told the sea to be still. After he had tamed the storm, there wasn't merely a return to the ordinary. There was something more. There was a great calm.

Theo held on to that promise. He spoke it over the storm. Spoke it over his ship. Spoke it over his heart. *Lord, give us the something more that only your presence can give. Impart to us your great calm.* He prayed even as the tempest spit and snarled at him.

How long he stood at the tiller, his knees like egg pudding, his prayers the only strong thing about him, he did not know. Finally, he sensed the force of the rain abate, droplets falling in a drizzling mist rather than a river. The ship, too, seemed sturdier under his feet and less in the power of the rushing waves.

Ahead, he saw a break in the thick clouds, enough to allow a feeble ray of light. Theo took a deep breath. The arc of the tempest had broken.

They might be left with a waterlogged ship, a cracked mast, and a half-drowned crew. They might be lost, leagues away from their destination. But they had survived.

He felt, with a sudden and boundless assurance, that these violent winds would be used by God toward a purpose. He looked at his broken mast, his bruised ship, calculating the cost, and he conceded all of it, all of it, to God. For whatever purpose he deigned to use it.

The great calm he had prayed for descended on him then, bearing more power than the squall that had almost destroyed them. Theo settled into that calm, his tense muscles loosening.

Taharqa arrived to relieve him of the tiller. "And how did you expect me to tell Galenos that you had got yourself drowned?" he asked, his face a thundercloud.

He gave Taharqa a weak smile. "The same thing you would have to tell him if you sank his ship."

Theo and Galenos, his adoptive father, had bought the *Parmys* together, with Theo's older brother adding his wealth as a silent partner. For the most part, they used the ship to peddle German balls of soap, which they scented with perfume and sold as hair pomade around the empire. It had become quite a hit. Theo had a talent for finding new buyers in various cities, leading to larger orders every year, while his adoptive father managed the production of the soap in Corinth.

Once, long before Galenos and Theo had entered into partnership, Galenos had lost a ship—and almost his whole fortune with it. He would have a hard struggle with the news of another ship drowning.

"Galenos would have recovered from the ship," Taharqa said. "Losing you, I'm not so certain. Why did you jump into the sea? You have no more sense than you had the first time I met you ten years ago."

Theo grinned. At the age of sixteen he had survived another storm, and another dunking into the sea, thanks to Taharqa. "I owe you my life, Taharqa. Again."

The captain waved a hand in the air. "This hardly counts. I didn't even have to get my tunic wet." He laid a warm hand on Theo's shoulder. "I have never met a man so big hearted as you, Theo. Or so fearless. I am honored to work for you. Which is why I want you to know, the next time you scare me like that, I will drown you myself."

Theo scratched his head, embarrassed by Taharqa's praise. "How is Sophocles?"

"He'll bounce back. The old codger is giddy as a puppy to be alive. You should avoid him for a while. He might soak your chest with unending tears of gratitude and spin long verses that sing your praises."

Theo stepped back, alarmed. "I think I prefer eating fish eyes."

The skyline was changing rapidly, thick clouds dispersing, as the sun made a weak appearance. "What's the damage?"

"We'll need to put to port, and quick. The ship needs a lot of repair. Her keel has taken a beating." Taharqa pointed to their east.

For the first time, Theo noted the outline of land. He squinted. "Where are we?"

"Caesarea, I reckon."

Theo whistled. They had been aiming to anchor at Alexandria, where he had planned to offload five hundred of his terra-cotta jars of hair pomade in exchange for an equal load of wheat. Rome was ever eager for Egyptian grain. With a million hungry mouths to feed daily, the senate gave merchants endless incentives for carrying grain to their city.

But thanks to the storm, Alexandria lay a long way off

to the southwest of their present location. The tempest had carried them leagues off course. "Will we make it to port?"

"If we baby her. And if the weather doesn't send us so much as a whisper of wind, we'll be able to limp into Caesarea's harbor. But we'll need at least two weeks to repair her right."

Theo lowered his brows in thought. "Two weeks?" He would have to forego his visit to Alexandria. Write off the additional profit he had counted on for selling wheat in Rome. Add the hefty expenses of a considerable repair.

Losing fourteen days to the storm meant he would have to head directly for Rome, where he had promised a big shipment of soap to his best customer, an official at Nero's palace.

He sensed again, with a curious certainty, that God had allowed this encroachment on Theo's plans for a purpose. They were meant to be in Caesarea.

"We will stay with Philip and his daughters," he decided. "The men can find lodging at the harbor."

"I like that plan." Taharqa patted his flat belly. "Philip may pray too long over supper, but his daughter's cooking is fit for a king."

# CHAPTER 4

*Her children rise up and call her blessed.*

PROVERBS 31:28

"Let us start at the beginning," Natemahar said, weaving his fingers together. "What makes you think your father lives?"

Chariline described the conversation she had overheard in the night. "Natemahar, my grandfather has been lying to me all these years. My father is alive! And he works in the palace."

"How extraordinary!"

"Please! You must help me find him."

"What do you want me to do, Chariline?"

"Surely you have heard whispers about my mother."

He gave a slow nod. "As I have told you before, there have always been rumors about what happened. I have heard that your mother broke her engagement to a Roman official to marry a Cushite. But his identity is tightly guarded."

"Why is it guarded? Did my grandfather demand that it be kept secret?"

"I doubt Blandinus has that kind of influence in the Cushite court. He might have demanded it. But no one would take notice."

"Who, then?"

"The only one who could seal an event so tightly is the Kandake herself." He gave the ghost of a smile. "Shall I arrange a meeting for you?"

Chariline shook her head vigorously. She had run into the Kandake once, by accident, at the harbor, when she had been boarding the riverboat for home. The woman had looked at her the way a dragon might look at a tasty morsel. "I don't see how I could induce her to divulge any secrets to me."

"Wise girl."

"I need to come to the palace. Perhaps he might see me and recognize who I am. Perhaps he might approach me himself."

"Absolutely not, Chariline. It is too dangerous."

It was the one thing that her grandfather and Natemahar had always agreed upon. She was not to approach the palace. She now understood Grandfather's vehemence against her going there. He did not want her to stumble upon her father accidentally. And Natemahar felt that her presence in the palace would goad her grandfather too far.

"He won't find out."

"Of course he will. There is nothing secret in the palace unless the queen herself seals it. If you set foot inside the court, someone will see you. And the report of it will get back to Blandinus."

The consequences did not bear thinking of. Grandfather

already resented Natemahar because, over the years, he had gone over the old man's head to higher officials in Rome several times, seeking to obtain better trade agreements for Cush. If he discovered that Natemahar and Chariline had been friends all these years without his knowledge, he would see to it that they never spoke again.

Chariline refused to even consider losing her dear friend to the old man's vindictive maneuvering. She could not endanger this long-treasured connection. And yet, what choice did she have? "It's my last hope, Natemahar. With Grandfather retiring, once I leave Cush, I will not be allowed to return. I will never discover who my father is."

His gaze softened. "Is it so important that you know his identity?"

She brought the flat of her hand onto the makeshift table. "How can you ask that? You know it means everything to me."

"But he has never tried to reach you, Chariline. Perhaps he has good reason."

"Or perhaps he does not know I even exist."

Natemahar nodded slowly. "True. Let me think on it. In the meantime, do nothing rash."

Chariline's mouth tipped up on one side. "Me? Rash?"

"Does a bee sting?"

"No. It makes honey."

Natemahar grinned, pulling softly on a tangle of curls. "You make plenty of honey, too." He rose. "I must return to the court. I will send you a message if I find anything of interest."

———— ✿ ————

Although the flooding of the Nile kept the banks of the river fertile for most of the year, the desert did its best to encroach on the verdant fields. A brisk twenty-minute walk away from the Nile, and your feet would touch the hot sands of an arid wilderness. Cush's settled lands only occupied a narrow band of land parallel to the banks of the river.

Early in the morning, before her grandmother could assign her a lengthy list of tedious tasks, Chariline took a long walk alongside the Nile, where the busy piers and crowds of travelers ensured safety for a lone woman. The smell of fish mingled with the sweet scent of yellow acacia flowers that hung in bunches on the antler-like branches of the trees. Closer to the opalescent gray water of the Nile, a subtler aroma rose from the muddy river. A hint of sweet hyacinth, which emanated from the roots of lotus plants growing in the tiny ponds that sometimes formed along the edges of the river.

This was Cush at its best, the mystery and fertility of the river that fed its people and carried them in its twisty arms to centers of commerce and economic vitality. She never felt so at home as when she was near the Nile.

Before her grandmother could raise an alarm, hysterically demanding to know the whereabouts of her missing grandchild, Chariline headed back to the confines of the capital. Meroë was a city of twenty thousand people. But during the day, the numbers swelled to half again as many, with folks from the outlying areas pouring into the capital for work, trade, worship, or pleasure.

Chariline wended her way through the alleys and slipped into the house before anyone noticed her absence. She spent the morning packing linens made of the soft cotton of Cush, her thoughts occupied with the mystery that was her father. She jumped when her grandmother dropped a grimy box on a mound of towels in front of her.

"This is for you."

Chariline frowned, drawing a finger in the dust that spread thick on the wooden box. "You want me to pack up what's inside?"

"You can do what you wish with it. This used to belong to your mother."

Chariline gasped. She had been given few things from her mother over the years. Several pieces of modest jewelry, combs, buttons, wool and linen tunics. A pair of colorful leather shoes. She had never seen this box before.

"This was my mother's?"

Grandmother nodded. "She would have wanted you to have it." She twirled a hand in the direction of the dusty box and hesitated, as though searching for words that would not come. "She was like you," she said, finally. Without waiting for a response, her grandmother turned on her heel and walked away.

Chariline gawped at the dusty casket. Hidden in its dainty confines lay something that belonged to the mother she had never known. She cradled the box to her chest. It weighed less than a toddler. The air in the chamber had grown stale and close, and she felt a sudden urge to leave behind the oppressive walls that seemed to close in on her.

Walking carefully to the deserted courtyard, she clutched the casket with both hands. She would not have carried that box with more care if it contained the empress's favorite crown.

On the way, she grabbed a dusting rag and oil and settled herself by the diminutive pool in the atrium. Dampening the rag with oil, she gently began to wipe the wood.

A few moments later, the casket emerged from its veil of grime. Acacia and ebony wood had been entwined by a master artisan to create a delicate wave pattern on the lid. Ivory and polished jet details added luster and depth to the unusual design. Though simple, it was an exquisite work of art, a weaving of dark and light colors. Chariline laid her cheek against the cool surface and inhaled deeply, feeling as though she were touching a part of her mother. She lifted the lid slowly and peered inside.

She was not sure what she expected to unearth. It certainly was not the collection of scrolls, carefully tied with a length of faded blue ribbon. She unfurled the first and found herself staring at a pristine drawing of one of Cush's pyramids. It was not a pretty rendition, meant to beautify a room. Instead, her mother had drawn a precise depiction that paid careful attention to angles and proportions.

The steep sides of the pyramid gave it a tall, slender appearance, made more dignified by the addition of a rectangular chapel, attached to its monument by a short, narrow passageway. Next to each side, her mother had written, with neat handwriting, a number. Chariline's mouth fell open as she realized that they were calculations of the dimensions of the pyramid.

Her mother had created an architectural drawing!

Chariline opened the next roll of papyrus, this time finding a library, complete with a set of construction plans. One after another, she found exquisite drawings with careful mathematical calculations, some including intricate details such as suggestions for the type of wood, render, and color used in each building.

Over the past century, the Romans had elevated the study of architecture to unprecedented heights. An architect needed to acquire knowledge from many branches of the arts and sciences, needed to understand engineering, design, geometry, dimension, and practical construction. Her mother's drawings demonstrated an unusually keen grasp of many of these skills.

*She was like you,* her grandmother had said. What she had meant was that like Chariline, her mother had loved architecture. Had studied and designed buildings. Had tried to understand the art and science and engineering behind each form.

Chariline clasped the faded ribbon in her fist and held it against her chest. Her eyes burned with the grief of losing a mother who had shared her own passion, who would have nurtured and fostered it. She grieved the hours of conversation they could have enjoyed and never had, the endless thrill of new discoveries, forever lost. Running a trembling hand over her eyes, she pressed them closed. Her mother would have understood her. Soul-deep, to the core. Her mother would have known her and loved her just as she was.

The grief shifted and, to Chariline's surprise, became mingled with an odd joy. Joy for finding this piece of her past, which somehow made Chariline feel more complete, as if she had been an uprooted rosebush until that moment, and someone had finally planted her parched roots into good soil. Joy at finally finding a place where she fit.

Why had no one ever told her of her mother's talent?

Aunt Blandina had once shared that Chariline's mother had liked to sketch. But she had never explained that her mother's drawings, like Chariline's own, had been directed by her desire to design. These were no mere doodlings of a juvenile hand. They showed a stark maturity. They soared out of a soul created for this work.

The woman who had penned these sketches would have been proud of Chariline's hunger for creating beauty with building.

When Grandfather had discovered Chariline's interest in architecture, he had forbidden her from pursuing it in any formal way. "For the love of Venus, girl! Why don't you occupy yourself with some feminine enterprise? Whoever heard of a woman wanting to study engineering?" He had promptly banned her from continuing any endeavor connected to the design and construction of buildings.

It wasn't as if Grandfather worried that her "unfeminine" interests would drive away admirers since she had none. As the patriarch of the family, the responsibility of finding a husband for Chariline lay with her grandfather. But he had never mentioned the matter, nor had he attempted to open doors of opportunity for his only granddaughter to meet eligible men. Not once had she attended a palace function with him or met the officials who sometimes visited him from Rome and Egypt.

Not that she trusted Quintus Blandinus Geminus with her future happiness. The marriages he had arranged for his own daughters had not been successful. Her mother had chosen to break her arranged engagement to elope with a man, who did not have Grandfather's approval, presumably because she had found her betrothed objectionable. And Aunt Blandina never spoke of her departed husband with particular fondness.

No. Quintus Blandinus was not the man to choose a husband for Chariline. Just as well he seemed entirely disinterested in such an enterprise. She suspected his lack of interest was due to his belief that no respectable Roman would want her, an orphan girl with skin that declared her an outsider and parentage that seemed questionable, at least on one side.

Chariline sighed. Her life had grown small and limited in Aunt Blandina's house. If not for her friendships with Philip's daughters and Natemahar, she would have become a recluse like her aunt.

Which was why she had ignored her grandfather's demands that she give up her passion for architecture. She refused to allow him to strip her of everything that mattered to her. No doubt, he had forbidden poor Aunt Blandina from whispering a word about Gemina's interests lest they encourage her daughter's fervor. And Blandina, as always, had been unable to stand up to him. No wonder her mother had never told Blandina that she planned to elope. As close as they were, Gemina had known her sister would not be able to keep such a scandalous secret from their father.

Chariline ran a gentle finger down the lid of the beautiful box and wondered why, after all these years, Grandmother had chosen to defy her husband and share these drawings with her. She suspected that Grandmother had thrown her a bone out of pity. As far as she knew, Chariline had no idea that her father lived. If she was to be cheated out of a father, at least she might have this crumb from her dead mother.

But Chariline wanted more than crumbs. With almost no chance of marriage and a family of her own, her desire to know her father grew by the hour. He would be her true family, her heart's home. Chariline smiled slowly. This box was only the beginning. She did not intend to allow Grandfather's schemes to stand in her way ever again.

# CHAPTER 5

—— ᘓᘓ ——

*For you created my inmost being;*
*you knit me together in my mother's womb.*

PSALM 139:13, NIV

Aunt Blandina walked into the courtyard, waving her giant ostrich fan. "I could melt into a puddle. How hot the sun grows in this place." She sat next to Chariline and dipped her fingers into the warm pool. "What do you have there?"

Carefully, Chariline turned the box and showed it to her aunt. The light-green eyes dilated with alarm. "Where did you find that?"

"Grandmother gave it to me."

"Truly?"

"Truly." She snapped the lid open and unfurled the drawings for her aunt.

A sigh slithered its way from Blandina's depths. "She was always brilliant." Wiping her hands on her stola, she reached for the drawing of a villa. "So brilliant." A single tear coursed down her pale cheek as she held the aged papyrus in reverent fingers.

Chariline's mother had been nine years younger than Blandina. In that dry, emotionally putrid household, the two girls had turned to each other, more than sisters, becoming friends and family and home all in one.

Blandina looked at her niece, and for a moment, Chariline saw love well up in the wilting eyes. Her aunt's lips softened and she reached a hand to Chariline's hair, fondly patting the curls, seeing Chariline as her sister's daughter, her precious Gemina's child.

For an instant, hope rose up in Chariline. Hope that, for once, the love would linger. Would win out. But, as always, the corners of Blandina's faded green eyes crinkled, her mouth tightened, and she withdrew her hand. Chariline knew the old pain was devouring every claim of affection on her aunt's heart.

Chariline's mother had brought her into the world on a wave of tears and blood, her screams of agony ringing through the whole neighborhood. Gemina's anguish had shocked her sister, who watched in mute horror as the babe's fat body ripped her beloved sister to shreds.

Moments after giving birth, the dear woman who had brought Blandina the only true happiness she had ever known held her daughter in weak, shivering arms and pronounced her beautiful, so beautiful. She named her Chariline Gemina, kissed the top of her head, bid her sister to look after her child, and with the last of her strength told the babe that she loved her more than the world, and that her father would love her too, once he saw her, love her beyond what she could imagine. And with a sigh, Gemina had left them, Chariline and Blandina both orphaned by her death, though in different ways.

Blandina had stared at the long form of her cinnamon-brown niece, wriggling with life as she cried lustily in the arms of the nurse, and whatever they were to each other, whatever love and goodness and belonging was meant to weave them to one another, cracked. She wasn't looking at Gemina's daughter. She was gazing upon the murderer of her sister.

She had kept her promise to Gemina. She had raised Chariline, provided for her, shielded her from harm. But her love had been tarnished by the babe's birth. She could never quite separate the blame of Gemina's death from the joy of having her daughter.

Chariline understood. Truly, she did. The guilt she usually managed to push down deep raised its head and sank its sharp fangs into her heart. She winced. How could she blame Aunt Blandina? She *had* been the cause of her mother's death.

With sheer force of will, she shoved the guilt back down, down, and locked it away again. It left behind, as it always did, a hollow place, an emptiness that nothing seemed to fill.

She reached a trembling hand to caress her aunt's drooping cheek. "She loved you dearly, Aunt Blandina."

Blandina's tears overflowed, fat and salty, dribbling down her short chin. "She loved you too, child. More than anything."

Chariline nodded. She believed that. For years, she had thought that the only people in the world who could love her, love her with the wholehearted attachment she had yearned for since the day she had opened her eyes to gaze upon this broken world, were lost to her.

Her grandparents had not even sought to meet her until

it had become evident that Blandina would remain a childless widow, never destined to remarry, making Chariline their only grandchild. Grandfather finally sent for her as a last resort, the desperate act of a man with a dying family line. He barely tolerated her. Not once, in all the years she had known him, had he kissed her cheek, held her hand, ruffled her hair.

But now, she knew that her father was alive, and that changed everything.

On her deathbed, her mother had promised that he would love her, and she would not lie, not as she lay dying. Not as the last words on her lips. Her mother had believed to the depths of her soul that the father of her child would love his daughter. And Chariline trusted that dying promise.

She rolled up the papyri carefully, tucked them into her box, and snapped the lid shut.

She was not an orphan. She was not unwanted. She was not abandoned. Her father would love her. She would find him and prove it.

———— ‿ ————

It took Chariline two days before she was able to get away to the spice seller's shop again. She carried her mother's box, carefully wrapped in a clean sheet, and set it on the table in the back room. When Natemahar arrived, she pulled the sheet away with a flourish.

"Lovely," he said. "Cushite. Looks old. Where did it come from?"

"It was my mother's." Chariline opened the lid and pulled out the drawings. "She copied some of these from existing buildings. But most are her original designs."

Natemahar's mouth grew slack. "Your mother's?" He pulled a papyrus roll close, studied it carefully, his fingers running over the drawing.

"They remind me of your work," he said, finally.

"Do you think so?"

He nodded. "There is something in the general style. That blending of good structural sense with beauty. You both have it. Although your work is finer, more detailed."

"I've had more years of study. She died when she was only twenty-one." Chariline twisted the ribbons at her waist. "I never knew she loved architecture as much as I."

"Where did you find these?"

"My grandmother gave them to me."

"Your grandfather won't approve."

Chariline shrugged. "Do you have any news for me?"

Natemahar rolled his eyes. "It's been two days. You have to be patient."

In her secret search for her father, Chariline had expected to contend with danger, with difficulty, with menace even. You could not go against a man like Grandfather without preparing for some manner of retaliation. She was beginning to realize that none of that compared to the sheer agony of simple patience.

She wanted to argue, push against Natemahar's plodding exploration, and demand that he hasten his search. Before she could get a word out, he drew one of her mother's drawings toward him and lowered his head to examine it more closely.

With a light touch, he ran his finger along the surface. "Your mother used an unusually thick papyrus for some of these. I wonder why. Do you think they helped the quality of her work?"

Chariline was not fooled. After so long a friendship, she recognized Natemahar's blatant attempt at distraction. On the other hand, anything to do with her mother's work seemed worthy of being a little distracted.

She bent over the drawing. For the first time, she noticed what Natemahar had so quickly surmised. The papyrus seemed exceptionally thick.

"That's strange," she murmured.

He gave her an I-told-you-so grin. Rolling the papyrus, she waved it at him. "It doesn't make up for your slow progress. Find me a thread. A clue. Anything, Natemahar."

"Be patient," he said again. He reached for her hand. "Chariline, let us ask the Lord for guidance."

Like her, Natemahar had been discipled in faith by Philip. But he had been a much better pupil. Chariline heaved a sigh and dropped to her knees.

Natemahar began with silence. A quiet that stretched. She knew his mind was finding its way to a different realm. A place of peace. A kingdom where the dealings of the earth faded and God alone remained.

In that silence, Chariline fidgeted, her thoughts running amuck. She wanted to move to the asking. Move to the part where she told God what she wanted. And better yet, she wanted to get up and do something.

Natemahar began his prayer with simple words of gratitude, like a child bringing a posy of weeds to his mother or wrapping sticky fingers of love around his father's neck.

Chariline softened, aware that Natemahar's prayer bore a more beautiful perfume before God than all the spices in that shop.

When, finally, Natemahar asked God to help her, the tenderness in his voice pierced Chariline. "Dear Lord, show your daughter the way. You know the desire of her heart. Grant her that desire according to your will and keep her safe on every side."

After Natemahar left, Chariline lingered in the spice seller's back room. The chamber had changed by Natemahar's presence, somehow. Become safe. Become a haven. Unwilling yet to return to Grandfather's cheerless house, she examined her mother's drawings with a closer eye. Why had she used such thick sheets for some? It almost seemed as though she had glued two or three pieces of papyrus together for each drawing.

Delicately, her touch as soft as the wings of a moth, she pulled on the edge of one drawing. The corner of her nail split the pulpy sheet and she gasped, terrified that she had torn the papyrus. Then, squinting, she saw that, indeed, two separate rolls of papyrus had been adhered to one another.

At first, she thought to leave things as they were. She could visit the library in Caesarea to discover the benefits of using two sheets of papyrus as her mother had done. But she noticed that the center of the drawing was slightly thicker even than the edges.

Curiosity drove Chariline on. Once again, she began to pull delicately on the edges of the papyrus, separating the two sheets from each other. She was puzzled when she realized that the glue had only been adhered around the perimeter of the sheet, no more than the length of half a finger. When she reached the inner part, the sheets of papyrus separated with ease.

Revealing a third sheet.

Chariline gasped when she realized that the unexpected sheet was in fact a letter, hidden inside her mother's drawing in the clever pouch she had created. With trembling fingers, she freed the letter and began to read.

*Vitruvia, your faithful friend, to my dear Gemina,*

*Greetings from a hot and humid Rome! How I wish you were here so we could pore over my grandfather's books together and discuss the virtues of his teaching.*

Chariline froze. Her mother's friend was named Vitruvia. The feminine version of . . . Could it be? Could her mother have been friends with the famed Vitruvius's *granddaughter*? The Vitruvius who had authored the most magnificent series of books on architecture ever written? Heart pounding, Chariline read on and soon became convinced that, indeed, the man she had idolized for over ten years had been closer to her family than she could ever have dreamed!

Much of Vitruvia's letter concerned the construction of new buildings and the importance of functionality, beauty, and stability. One passage, however, made Chariline laugh.

*I know my grandfather believed that nature's designs ought to serve as a model for proper ratio, and that the human body, above all, displays perfection in proportion. But if he had seen my woefully small chest and ample hips, he would have thought twice about believing the*

*body's proportions to be a model of perfection. Since we*
*last saw each other twelve months ago, I have grown,*
*and in all the wrong places. I can't seem to refuse those*
*stout wedges of hot quadratus bread I so love! You, no*
*doubt, remain as lovely as ever.*

As quickly as she dared, Chariline began to pry loose the
edges of the papyri whose unusual thickness indicated another
hidden missive. Plucking the glue apart gingerly so as not to
damage the drawing on the cover page, she managed to release
the letters that had been held captive in their secret pouches
for a quarter of a century.

In all, she found four written in Vitruvia's elegant Latin.
The first three were in much the same vein. Vitruvia discussed architecture, spoke of her grandfather's military career,
dreamed of the possibility that they might one day, as women,
be able to design and build worthy monuments of their own,
and expressed a desire to be reunited with her friend soon.
Chariline felt as though she were sitting in an adjoining
room, overhearing the young women's conversation. She read
the words over and over again, flushed with pleasure at this
glimpse into her mother's hidden life.

Vitruvia's fourth letter made Chariline snap to attention.
Obviously written in haste, it began with no greeting.

*I pray our friend will be able to place this in your hands*
*without delay. By all means, flee to Rome, and I will do*
*what I can to help you. You shall be a married woman*
*when next we meet!*

*I cannot blame you for following your heart. Given
all you wrote of him in your very long letter (Egypt must
now be facing a shortage of papyrus), he is a man worthy
of you. But I fear for your safety. One thing everyone
learns in Rome from infancy: never tangle with the ruler
of an empire! If by marrying you, your beloved displeases
his queen, there is no telling how she will retaliate. I do
not believe the fact that his mother is an old and dear
companion to the queen will help you in any way. Likely
the opposite. She is liable to feel more betrayed by a
friend than a mere stranger. So please, please do not get
caught.*

*Come quickly and we shall build a palace together.
Oh, have it your way. A grand library, then. I know
how much you like your books. Only come and be safe.
I write no names in case this letter should fall into the
wrong hands.*

Chariline exhaled. Not only had she discovered a precious
glimpse into her mother's life and heart, she had found another
clue to her father's identity. His mother was an old companion
to the queen. How many officials at the palace could claim
that? Surely not many. He had to be at least forty-five. Perhaps
older. Once she shared this detail with Natemahar, it would be
a matter of days—hours, even—before she found him.

# CHAPTER 6

—◡◡◡—

*My times are in your hand.*

PSALM 31:15

Natemahar raised a dark brow as he examined Vitruvia's letter. "Clever hiding place."

"I wouldn't have found the letters if it weren't for you. You were the one who noticed the unusual thickness of the papyrus." Chariline pressed her hands together. "Don't you see what this means, Natemahar? Armed with that piece of information, you'll be able to find my father."

"You don't know the court of Cush. Everyone claims friendship with the queen."

"But not everyone can say they are a *close* companion!"

Natemahar blew out a breath. "A pile of gold, and you can be anything you want."

"Natemahar!"

"Fine. I will continue to seek him for you. Only, tame your expectations. It's not as easy as you imagine. I have to tread with care."

"You are worried that I will get tangled in something dangerous. But Natemahar, how perilous can it be to find one man? Whatever scandal my parents created by their marriage, it all happened twenty-five years ago. No one will care anymore."

"Chariline, listen to Vitruvia's counsel even if you choose to refuse mine. Your father riled the Kandake by his decision to pursue your mother. And I will tell you this about our queen: She is not a woman who forgets a grudge, no matter how ancient. Don't suppose she desires a warm reunion between you and the man who sired you."

Chariline bit her lip. Whatever had driven her parents apart at the start of their marriage, sending her mother pregnant and alone to Caesarea and swallowing every trace of her father, had as much to do with the Kandake as it had with her grandfather. Natemahar was right. Grandfather did not have enough influence at the court to silence every bit of gossip relating to the old scandal. Only the queen could have arranged for so much secrecy.

Her throat turned dry. "We will simply have to avoid her."

"On that, we agree. Which is why I proceed with care. Give me time. I will search for him discreetly."

Chariline dropped her head in her hands. A new thought pierced her with the sting of a knife edge. What if by pressing Natemahar to find her father, she put him in the path of harm? What if her entreaties were placing Natemahar on a collision course with his queen?

She snapped her head up and reached for his hand. "Forgive me, dear Natemahar! Of course you must be discreet! Please take care. Go as slow as you must."

Natemahar gave her a quizzical look. "Nothing to forgive. I understand your urgency."

Chariline shook her head. "You must ignore my prodding. Sometimes I speak before I consider. Do what you think best. With all my heart, I trust you."

Above all things, she must keep her friend safe. He must not risk his own well-being for her sake. Nor did she want him to jeopardize his position as chief treasurer and one of Cush's most senior officials.

Chariline, on the other hand, did not have such constraints. The Kandake was not her queen. In spite the color of her skin, Chariline was a Roman. And no Cushite queen was going to stand in her way.

---

"Not good," Arkamani said, followed by a long volley of Meroitic. Chariline picked up the words *important officials* and *visiting*. "Can't go to the palace now," he said. "Not safe."

She had asked Arkamani to sneak her into the palace. Clearly, he knew his way into the place since he carried secret messages to and from Natemahar without trouble. But he shook his head at her again. "Not safe, honey lady. Extra guards at the palace now. Understand?"

Chariline ground her teeth until her jaw ached. "When? When will it be safe?"

The boy shrugged. "Four days. Maybe five. Officials like to talk."

Chariline's shoulders sagged. She had already been in Cush for six days. Another five put her at eleven. That would only give her three days to find her father. Would she be able to locate him in so short a time?

"Send for me as soon as you can," she said to Arkamani. "You know where to find me."

Chariline rubbed her aching temples when the boy left. With every step she hit a wall. Came up against another insurmountable hurdle.

Squeezed between the rock of her grandfather's will and the boulder of the Kandake's power, she had ground to a halt. In spite of everything she knew about her father, in spite of the fact that he was, at this very moment, working somewhere in the court, she could not approach him. It was enough to make her want to scream.

———— ☙ ————

When Arkamani's message finally arrived, Chariline was ready. She had purchased a native tunic in the market, a simple rectangular piece of tan linen with a slit for the head, decorated with sparse orange embroidery and a short fringe at the edge of the long skirt. Many women in Cush went about bare-breasted, with only a long skirt and jewelry for covering. Peasants wore even less.

Chariline had decided that her new tunic and cheap Cushite jewelry made of ostrich eggshells was enough to help her blend in when she arrived at the court. She could not imagine her first meeting with her father, or any meeting with her father, taking place while she wore nothing but a skirt.

Scraping her oiled hair back until her scalp ached, Chariline pulled the curls into a tight knot at the top of her head, doing her best to look like a native Cushite. The women of Meroë often wore their hair closely cropped, though some adorned it in a topknot similar to the one she had fashioned.

She applied kohl to her eyes, using the thin iron wand and wooden tube that she had purchased along with her tunic. Sliding her feet into blue leather sandals secured at the front by a colorful beaded toe strap, Chariline made one last adjustment to her armband before slipping out of the house.

As prearranged, she found Arkamani waiting for her at the end of the rutted lane leading to her grandfather's house. She dropped a couple of Aunt Blandina's honey cakes into the boy's palm. They found their way to his mouth before she finished greeting him.

"How will we get in?" she asked.

The flow of Meroitic proved too complicated for her, and she squinted at him.

He grinned. "Like servants, honey lady."

She nodded and followed him down a long track. Cushites saw no point in paving their roads and thought Romans out of their minds for spending so much time on the ground they walked on. Other than one short stone road with high curbs, the city of Meroë was served by tracks. By the time she arrived at the palace, her feet were a dusty mess.

Two major palaces dominated the landscape of Meroë: one occupied by the king and the other by the queen. The kings of Cush, believed by their people to be sons of the god Amun, had dominion over the complex religious life of their nation. Priests worked closely with the king to secure the protection of their many gods and ensure a good crop and health for the people of Cush. The day-to-day running of the kingdom was considered beneath the king. Instead, it was the queen mother who managed the mundane facets of rule. Politics, diplomacy, trade, and economy were all part of the Kandake's dominion.

Chariline knew her grandfather's business with Cush concerned the interests of Rome. Taxes and trade. Nothing sacred about that. He would have no business with the king. The palace to which he had alluded in his secret conversation with Grandmother no doubt belonged to the Kandake.

A perfect square of yellow sandstone that under the potent sunlight of Meroë turned a golden hue, the queen's main residence and political hub was modest in size but beautiful in its proportions. A touch of wildness in its elaborate decorations warned the visitor that the one who reigned from within its walls was not quite tame: elephant heads at the tops of columns and carvings of crocodiles and entwined snakes added a savage air to the otherwise decorous building.

Chariline swallowed past a parched throat. She must enter the lioness's den. And then what? She had waited eleven days for this moment. Eleven days merely to walk inside these forbidden walls. But once inside, she could not very well approach every man of a certain age and ask him if he might be her father. She pushed the thought aside. Hadn't Natemahar asked God to guide her? She would improvise as the need arose.

The main entrance to the Kandake's palace was from the south. Arkamani led them to the north face of the building where a small gate was guarded by two of the Kandake's personal guards. The gate assigned to the servants.

Instead of trying to avoid the soldiers, Arkamani brazenly headed for one of them. Chariline stopped breathing and kept her gaze glued to the ground as Arkamani spoke rapidly. To her amazement, after a cursory glance, the guard waved them inside.

Chariline gawped at Arkamani. "One of your uncles?"

He laughed. "No. Only a cousin." They had entered a narrow corridor. "Come. This way."

Through a series of long hallways, he drew her toward a central courtyard, which served as a light well to the interiors of the palace. They washed their feet with water from a turquoise pool that sat against one wall and redonned their sandals. In Rome, they would be expected to enter the palace in bare feet. Here, in Meroë, bare feet were a sign of poverty. Everyone in the palace was expected to wear shoes.

On a stone bench in one corner someone had left a number of shell-thin earthenware platters and bronze vessels filled with dates, almonds, dried fruit, and roasted grain.

A harried-looking young woman stopped at the bench and picked up a large metal vessel. "Why are you two dawdling? Take a tray. I'm off my feet from running around."

"Yes, mistress." Arkamani grabbed a metal vessel piled high with figs and handed it to Chariline. "Serve!"

The young woman stared at Chariline. "Haven't seen her before."

"New as a baby," Arkamani said. "Her first day."

"Move, or it will be her last day. Take that corridor there."

Chariline bowed her head and scurried behind Arkamani. "What do I do with this?"

"Offer it to anyone who looks important."

The corridor opened to long, narrow rooms. The first few chambers seemed full of people. Chariline tried to pretend that she belonged in this place and offered figs to bored-looking men who were waiting for an audience with the queen. She kept her chin tucked into her chest and her eyes lowered.

Other servants mingled in the reception rooms, carrying large trays. Chariline noticed the plain quality of their clothing and shoes, which in contrast to her own, lacked all decoration. She hoped her own garments would not stand out so much that she would be singled out or questioned.

But nothing unusual happened. No one raised the alarm, declaring her an imposter. Then again, no one embraced her like a long-lost daughter either. She waved her tray under the noses of more men in another narrow chamber, beginning to feel foolish. What had she expected to accomplish by coming to the palace?

She shoved the figs toward a stout man's chest. Instead of taking a fig, he began shrieking at her in rapid Meroitic, shaking a finger in her face. Chariline took a hasty step back. In her agitation, she could not understand a single word. Arkamani came to her rescue and, with a bow, apologized to the irate official. Chariline caught on enough to bow and back away at the same time.

"What did I do wrong?" she squeaked when they made it safely to the hallway.

"You stood too close," Arkamani whispered. "It's disrespectful to come too close. Don't you know anything, honey lady?"

Chariline wiped the sheen of sweat from her brow with the back of a hand and tried to calm her galloping heartbeat. "Any other rules I should know?"

"Don't spill anything on anyone's toes."

"I had figured that one out. Thank you." Trying to stop the shaking in her fingers, she grabbed her vessel tighter.

The next door opened to a storage area filled with elephant tusks. The one beyond that was also a storehouse, containing jars of grain and olives. They came upon another long room crowded with courtiers, and she circled the chamber, careful to keep a deferential distance this time. She studied the faces, looking for something familiar. Something that reminded her of what she saw when she looked in the mirror. But nothing unusual captured her attention.

They came to the end of the corridor, beyond which lay the columned hall that served as the Kandake's throne room. Chariline knew she had to avoid the epicenter of the queen's rule at all cost. She was not foolish enough to risk coming to the Kandake's notice. She looked at Arkamani in despair. Nothing. She had slithered her way into the palace for nothing.

She saw the shallow steps, then, leading to an upper story, and signaled Arkamani to follow her. He shook his head. "Private," he said.

Something about those stairs pulled at her. Chariline bit her lip. She couldn't leave empty-handed. Taking a deep breath, she marched ahead.

"No, honey lady!"

"You stay," she told the boy. "I will return soon."

# CHAPTER 7

———— ✂ ————

*Do not reveal another's secret.*

PROVERBS 25:9

At the top of the stairs, she found a short corridor that led to a diminutive chamber, this one more luxuriously appointed than the ones belowstairs. Cush's famous silver embellished the ornate furniture, and bright, woven tapestries hung from the walls. Thick curtains had been drawn across the window, blocking the sunlight as well as the noise of a busy palace. Multiple lamps burned on iron stands, brightening the otherwise darkened room.

Two officials seemed in deep conversation. Chariline noticed that one of them had an eye patch, thick, ropy scars marring the skin around the patch. Beneath the scar, the man's face was handsome, with striking, angular features that gave the impression of confidence.

He turned when she came in. "What are you doing here?" he said, his voice irritated.

Chariline lifted up the platter. "Figs, Master?"

"No. Now get below where you belong."

With a bow, she turned to leave.

"Wait!"

Chariline stopped. The man walked to her, his steps slow, gold armbands and necklaces twinkling in the lamplight. To her shock, he placed a hand under her chin and lifted her face. "Who are you?" he asked slowly, searching her features.

The tray wobbled in Chariline's hand. "Nobody," she said, her voice a croak.

"What is your name? Who do you belong to?"

Here it was, the question she had yearned to hear. The question that might open a door. Lead to some scrap of recognition. She lifted her head and stared into the man's eye, trying to avoid that terrible scar. "I am Chariline, the granddaughter of Quintus Blandinus Geminus."

The single eye widened. The man took a swift breath, his nostrils flaring. "I did not know Blandinus had a granddaughter."

"He does."

"What are you doing here, Blandinus's granddaughter?"

"S-s-serving. Figs?" She lifted the platter a fraction.

The man pushed it away, almost overturning the fruit. He peered down into her face. "How old are you?"

"Sesen!" the other man in the room cried in a nasal voice. "I must quit this place shortly. Leave the wench. Let us settle our business."

"In a moment," the man called Sesen replied. He returned his attention to Chariline. "Your age?"

"I am twenty-four."

Air leaked out of Sesen's chest. "It fits. The timing . . ."

Chariline took a half step forward, forgetting to keep a polite distance. "What fits?"

"Who is your father?"

A seething throb pounded in Chariline's temples. She felt dizzy, as if the room had run out of air. Mutely, she stared at the man.

"Your father," he said again, his brow drenched in sweat. "Who is he?"

"Sesen!" the other man howled. "Shall I leave you to your diversion?"

Sesen ground his teeth. "Find me this afternoon," he commanded Chariline. "Understand?"

She nodded, an abrupt jerk of her head. On wooden legs, she forced herself to move toward the door and out into the hallway. She began to creep down the stairs and knew Sesen watched as she descended. When she reached the landing, she risked a quick look above, catching a glimpse of the man's retreating back as he returned to the ornate chamber.

She handed her tray to a waiting Arkamani and scampered back up the stairs. No force on earth was going to prevent her from returning to Sesen.

The door to the chamber was now firmly shut. She slipped past it on quiet feet and entered a tiny alcove filled with linens and pillows, situated to the left of the chamber. A curtain hung limp to one side. Soundlessly, Chariline drew it closed.

Collapsing on a fringed pillow, her thoughts ran in a jumble of questions. Why had Sesen said *it fits* when she told him her age? Fit what?

*Who is your father?* he had asked, his tone unrelenting. Urgent.

Could the answer be . . . *Sesen?* Was that what he was trying to determine? Establishing her time of birth to see if she could be his daughter?

Speaking of Cushites, the Greek historian Herodotus had once described them as the tallest, most handsome of all men. In Sesen, she could see Herodotus's ancient description come to life. Uncommonly statuesque even for a Cushite, with a chest the size of a barrel, arms that could hold up a column, and an arresting face, he was not a man to be overlooked. She could see a young Roman girl falling under his spell.

She was grasping at straws. Reaching mighty conclusions based on too paltry an evidence. Then again, why had Sesen reacted so strongly upon discovering her grandfather's identity? Was he adding up the color of her skin to the time of her conception and reaching some unspoken conclusion? What did Sesen know?

She had no way of finding answers to her questions unless she asked him. As soon as he concluded his meeting, Chariline intended to seek him out. She could not wait hours until the afternoon, as he had bid her.

Faint murmurs from next door traveled through the thin wall in the alcove, interrupting her thoughts. Chariline realized that she could make out some of the words. At first, she assumed the men were speaking of business matters. Then she heard the word *kill* followed by the name of the queen.

Chariline gasped. She must have misunderstood. In the silence, the words from next door drifted into her hideaway, hushed but discernible.

"We cannot kill her now. She has postponed her trip until summer." Sesen's voice.

"That witch! She will ruin me by then."

"She will cut your throat if you . . ." Words she could not catch. Then, "Our plan is good. It will look like an accident when her royal barge goes down and she with it. We must wait four months. Until the Kandake boards that boat in July, we must bide our time."

Chariline's head throbbed. They were plotting against the Kandake. Plotting to murder the queen.

She rubbed the pulse at the base of her throat. Had she finally found her father, only to discover that he planned to assassinate a queen?

She had to tell Natemahar!

Natemahar would have to report the plot to the queen. He would have to reveal Sesen's treachery.

Chariline thought of the twisted scar that marred the handsome face. A sudden vivid recollection made her sit up. In her final letter, Vitruvia had warned that the queen would harm Gemina's husband for daring to defy her. Was that the Kandake's mark upon Sesen's face? The punishment she had bestowed because he had dared to fall in love with Chariline's mother?

What kind of retribution would such a woman mete out for outright conspiracy?

The Kandake would surely put him to a slow and agonizing death.

Her shoulders drooped. In all likelihood, Sesen was not her father. He was a complete stranger to her. Still, the thought of causing the man's death left a bad taste in her mouth.

She bit her lip and laid her head on her folded knees. With the curtain drawn, the windowless alcove had grown pitch black. Thick dust pressed into her lungs, making it hard to breathe.

Two lives were at stake, and Chariline only had the power to save one. The queen or Sesen. Which one more deserved her help?

It occurred to her that she still had four months to decide. The Kandake's life was in no immediate danger. Sesen's plan would not go into effect until summer. Anything could happen during that time. Perhaps, one day soon, she might even be able to convince Sesen to deviate from this violent course.

For now, she would hold her peace. Tell no one what she had heard. Not even Natemahar. Especially not Natemahar! He would never keep such a grave secret from his monarch.

She heard the creeping of a door and realized the men were leaving. Holding her breath, she waited until their steps had passed the alcove. Scampering to the edge of the curtain, she drew it aside enough to peek into the hallway. Sesen turned just then, a smooth revolution of his head, and Chariline pulled away hastily. Too late, she noticed the tips of her toes sticking out beneath the curtain and scooted them inside.

She felt certain he had not seen her. In that dark corridor, the tip of a sandal and the gentle twitch of a curtain were not easy to note. Though she had no intention of revealing his secret, she did not wish him to know that she possessed it. The last thing she wanted was for the man to feel threatened by her.

She needed to speak with him privately. Needed to confront him about her birth and uncover what he knew. Even if he was not her father, he certainly held some thread of information, some understanding of her birth that would help her. Making up her mind, she shoved the curtain aside and stepped into the hallway, intending to follow in Sesen's wake.

With a hard thump, she ran into a broad chest.

"Chariline!" Natemahar's gentle voice emerged, for once not so gentle.

"What are you doing here?" he lowered his voice but could not cover the tremble in it.

Chariline might be planning to hide Sesen's plot from her friend for the time being. But she could never tell him an outright lie. "I came to find my father."

Without slowing his steps, Natemahar pulled on her tunic, forcing her to walk with him. "You are leaving. You don't understand the danger you are in."

She tried to dig her heels in. "I am not finished!"

"You are. You are absolutely finished. How did you find your way in?" By now, they had descended to the ground floor, and Natemahar caught sight of Arkamani, waiting on the landing, his hand clutching the banister. "I might have known," Natemahar murmured under his breath.

Catching sight of them, Arkamani's shoulders relaxed. "I grew worried, honey lady. Where did you go?"

"Worried, were you?" Natemahar gave the boy a stern look. "Take her home. Straight home, you understand? And if you ever help her sneak into the palace again, I will pluck you like a chicken. Hear me?"

Arkamani looked crestfallen. "Yes, master. Like a chicken."

"But Natemahar . . . ," Chariline said, trying to find a way to return upstairs in search of Sesen.

"Not a word," he instructed, his lips a flat line of displeasure. "Go to the spice seller's. I will meet you there as soon as I can."

To his credit, Natemahar did not let her wait long. He arrived like a thunderstorm, surrounded by black clouds of gloom. "Forgive me, Natemahar," Chariline said. "I know I have caused you worry. But listen. I think I know who my father is. Or at least someone who knows about my birth."

Natemahar dropped onto the box they used as a chair. He dragged in a ragged breath. "Who?"

"Sesen."

"*Sesen?*"

"Do you know him?"

"Of course I know him. He is one of the queen's six treasurers."

"He works for *you?*"

"He works for the Kandake and Cush. But yes. He answers to me. Why in the world do you think that man is your father, Chariline?"

"Do you know how he lost his eye? Did the queen punish him? Was he mauled by a lion?"

Natemahar rolled his eyes. "Try and curb your imagination, will you? More likely, it is the work of an irate husband. He has been known to leave a few of those in his wake. It happened years ago, and Sesen never speaks of it. What has that to do with your father?"

Chariline leaned forward. "What if the queen blinded him as punishment for marrying my mother?"

"Now you are worrying me. I hope you have better evidence than an eye patch for thinking the man is your father."

"I have." Chariline told Natemahar everything that had taken place in the palace. Everything save the queen's assassination plot.

Natemahar considered her silently for a long moment, his face blank. "You are jumping to conclusions."

"I don't dispute that. Perhaps we are not related. But he knows something. And the only way to ascertain what he knows is to ask him. Which is what I was about to do until you interrupted me."

The inky eyes softened. "Why don't you let me pursue this? I will approach Sesen."

"No!" She did not want Natemahar involved. She did not want him connected with Sesen in any secretive way, lest the plot should come to light and Natemahar fall under suspicion. Any clandestine meeting with Sesen could be misunderstood. "I need to do this myself, Natemahar."

"You cannot return to the palace. Promise me!"

Chariline's lips tightened with exasperation. He wanted to protect her every bit as much as she wished to shield him. Deadlock. "What if I write him a letter instead?"

"Letters can fall into the wrong hands."

"What do you want from me, Natemahar?" She leaned forward, her eyes level with his. "I am not giving up. This is my only chance to find my father. You can help me or not. But you will not stop me."

Natemahar rubbed a hand over his short hair. "It goes against my better judgment, but I will avail you of what assistance I can."

"Thank you, Natemahar!" Chariline gave him a soft kiss on the cheek. "You are the best of friends."

He gave her a pained smile. "We shall see. Here is what I can tell you: the day after tomorrow, Sesen has an audience with the king. You can approach him then, on the road between the palaces. Hand him your letter. Write it now, and I will help you. Do not, I pray, spill out too much information. You are the daughter of the Roman official in Cush, and Sesen is a courtier. If he is not your father, he will try to use you as a pawn, if he can, to gain power through Rome. The interest he displayed in you would surely not be altruistic. So word your letter with care, my dear. Else you will hand him a weapon against you and your household."

Chariline frowned. "I had not thought of that."

"Think of it now."

# CHAPTER 8

—◦◦◦—

*For behold, they lie in wait for my life;*
*fierce men stir up strife against me.*

PSALM 59:3

Chariline waited in the shadow of a palm tree, her carefully penned letter clutched in one hand. She stood close enough to the queen's palace to have a clear view of those who traveled through its main gate. Rivulets of sweat trickled down her back in spite of the majestic cover of the palm fronds.

Chariline's heart picked up speed when she saw Sesen emerge alone, his gait swift. Before she could lose her nerve, she forced her feet into motion and approached him softly.

At the sight of her, Sesen froze, the planes of his angular face growing taut. His arm, midswing, dropped as though it weighed too much.

Words hitched in Chariline's throat. She had so many questions that they tangled her tongue, rendering her speechless. She was about to stretch out her hand and offer him her letter when a commotion at the gate distracted her.

Several guards had emerged in perfect formation. Behind them, nimble as a gazelle, the queen strode toward Chariline and Sesen, her white skirts fluttering in the breeze.

Sesen heard the noise at the same time and, turning his head, spied the queen. The intake of his breath, an abrupt hiss of air that snaked its way into his nostrils, sounded louder than the soldiers' footfall.

For an infinitesimal moment, the Kandake's gaze shifted from Sesen to Chariline and settled on her with unwavering curiosity. Chariline felt that probing inspection down to her toes, like a none-too-friendly sniff from a wolf seeking its next meal. She slid back into the shadows, hiding behind the shelter of a thicket of blooming shrubs.

She almost wept with frustration when the Kandake joined Sesen, her soldiers forming a hedge about them as they walked to the king's palace together.

Her last chance. Her only chance, stolen by the queen.

It was her final day in Meroë. In the morning, the river-boat would carry her and Aunt Blandina back up the Nile for the last time.

She had failed to find her father. Grandfather had won, after all.

Chariline felt choked by a piercing loneliness. For a few days, she had grasped onto hope. Hope that by finding her father, she would finally belong somewhere. Instead, she had found a pile of ashes. The very hope that had sustained and invigorated her since discovering her grandfather's secret now became a ruthless dagger, twisting in the wound of her solitude.

Chariline headed for the ancient cemetery north of Meroë. Her mother had obviously spent hours in that place, long enough to create her accurate drawing of the pyramid. It made Chariline feel close to her, somehow, sitting where she had once sat, observing what she had once looked upon with such meticulous attention.

Entering the silent burial place with heavy steps, Chariline searched for the pyramid in her mother's sketch. A plethora of pyramids surrounded her, some built on high platforms that elevated them, making them appear taller, others sleek and compact. A few towered above the rest, while several of the older ones showed signs of age, their decaying lime render revealing crumbling brick under their elegant skin.

Chariline spotted her mother's pyramid with ease, thanks to her detailed depiction. Sinking on the arid ground in front of the monument, she pulled her knees to her chest and gave vent to a strangled groan. Around her, the pyramids stretched into the air, their eerie, triangular walls an inescapable obstacle from which their occupants could not escape.

An apt metaphor for her own life.

Walled in by Grandfather. By the queen. By time. Unable to break through.

Natemahar had asked God to guide her steps. To give her the desire of her heart. Had God guided her steps to this dead end? Was this his answer? This resounding no?

Then again, she had not bothered to ask his opinion about any of her recent decisions: her visit to the palace, her letter to Sesen, her plan to spring upon him with no warning. She had simply barreled through, leaping from one idea to the next, allowing her emotions to lead her decisions. Her mind had been tangled in its own storm of plans. Plans that had crashed around her, gaining her nothing.

*Forgive me, Lord. Tell me what to do. Where to go.*

She stared at the pyramid, a shrine to the power of death, to its finality, its implacability and inevitability. This whole monument, its desperate man-created effort to reach into the heavens, to pierce them and somehow ferry its inhabitant into a higher plane, was nothing but a clump of dirt. But there was one who *had* overcome death. Pierced it as he had been pierced, conquered it as he had been conquered by a brutal cross.

And the one who wielded that power also loved her.

She expelled a sigh as she thought of all the walls that surrounded her, the disappointments and impossibilities, the fears and frustrations. Yet none were so high that *he* could not overcome them.

*Lord. Lord. Lord.* She spoke the word again and again and again as an act of surrender. Of acknowledgment. A restoration of her heart to the right order. He was Lord. She was not. And she would stop trying to be.

Out of nowhere she remembered the lines in Vitruvia's final letter. Vitruvia had intentionally refrained from mentioning specific names in that letter. Yet she had written as one who knew Gemina's betrothed. Chariline's mother had clearly written Vitruvia a great deal about the man she intended to marry. In the enthusiastic river of information, could she have revealed his name?

Might Vitruvia know his identity? Might she be able to confirm if Sesen was, indeed, her father?

Chariline felt a sudden certainty that Vitruvia held the answers she sought.

Better still, Vitruvia would be able to paint a fuller picture of her mother, one even Aunt Blandina was unfamiliar with. Vitruvia knew the story behind her mother's scandalous marriage. Knew the full scope of her mother's dreams. Knew of her talent and her vocation.

Chariline's heart swelled with hope. Vitruvia could give her a piece of her mother that her family had withheld. Had simply not understood. A piece that had been reborn in Chariline.

Not Cush, but Rome held the answers she needed. To Rome, then, she must go. To Rome and to Vitruvia. There, she would finally be able to put her past to rest and perhaps even find a new future.

No one would understand Chariline's love for architecture quite so well as Vitruvia. Perhaps her mother's friend would be able to help Chariline pursue her dreams of becoming a fully trained architect. Help her the way she had intended to help Gemina.

With a surge of wonder, Chariline realized that her recent disappointments had not led to a dead end at all. Rather, they had pointed the way to better things. For the first time in many days, she smiled.

— ∽ —

Pulling the hood of his thin cloak farther over his head, he stepped onto the crowded boat. He had shed his customary panther-skin vest and left behind his favorite long bow and iron-tipped arrows, which marked him as a warrior. Instead, he had contented himself with a long, nasty-looking knife and a deceptively trim dagger.

His employer had stressed that he was to make things look

like an accident. Not too hard, when you were chasing after a slip of a girl. He suppressed a yawn. The money was good. But really, this was beneath him. Give him a good hand-to-hand combat to the death. An oily Roman foot soldier with his short *makhaira,* looking to gut you like a scaly perch. That seemed more suited to his dignity.

He shrugged. Work was work. You couldn't always get what your talents deserved.

He adjusted his hood, making sure to keep his face hidden in its shadows. The three precise vertical lines that had been carved on his cheeks and forehead as a boy, marking him a warrior, made him stand out on a vessel full of merchants and women.

She was sitting alone, near the prow, her back pressed into the wooden side, her hands busy drawing something on a piece of papyrus. He had to admit she was a beauty. Pity to snuff out all that youth and loveliness without even having a taste of it.

He shrugged again. Work was work, he reminded himself. He felt lucky to receive the patronage of such an exalted employee.

The assignment would be a little more complicated than he had first assumed. Passengers crammed every corner of the riverboat. He would have to pick the right time. Push her over now, and a dozen people might notice. Accidents were not so simple to arrange in a crowd. He decided to wait until they had reached the Nile delta, close to the port. Everyone would be distracted, then, getting ready to disembark.

He settled himself across from the girl where he could watch her movements. A boy approached him, his hands full of round, smooth stones.

"Game?" the boy said, eyes sparkling.

"Money?" He had no qualms stripping the boy of his hard-earned coins. Teach him to approach his betters.

The boy extracted a few coins from a wrinkled leather pouch and set them on the reed deck. "Yours?"

The warrior had to admire the boy's nerve. With a smirk, he dropped a few coins between them. They drew lots and the boy won. He began throwing the stones. He was good. The warrior scowled as the boy made it to the second round with ease.

Too good.

He snarled a curse under his breath. The boy's grin widened as he threw two stones into the air, his fingers flashing like lightning.

He watched helplessly as round after round, the boy made the stones dance in the air, catching them with impossible ease. Something made the hair on his neck rise, an old soldier's instinct that had saved his life more than once, warning him that someone was watching. He lifted his head fast and caught the girl staring at them, her teeth flashing in a wide smile.

She was enjoying his defeat at the hands of the skinny boat rat. He would wipe that smile off her face soon enough. It would be a pleasure.

The boy finished a perfect game, never giving him a chance to play even one round. Collecting the coins he had won, he shoved them into his pouch and gave the warrior a deep bow.

The girl laughed. "Arkamani, you are incorrigible. Give the man his money."

"Won it fair, honey lady. Man to man."

The warrior pulled the hood further down his face and crossed his arms across his chest. It hit him wrong that she should defend him. Like he needed the help of that slip of a girl. This whole job stank. The sooner he finished it, the better he would feel.

He settled down to watch her movements. It was going to be a long few days. Perhaps an opportunity would present itself sooner than the delta, if the gods blessed him.

They didn't. Day followed night, an interminable journey on a boat whose rocking made him faintly queasy.

Finally, just before they reached the harbor, as the boat became a hive of activity, he seized his opportunity. The girl had moved a few times to check on her aunt in the cabin. But she always came back to the same spot, her pen busily sketching something. He had sneaked enough looks at her work to know she had talent. Maybe he would keep this drawing. Better yet, maybe he could sell it for a bit of extra coin.

He leaned over the edge, mindful of her perched on the deck a few steps to his left. He didn't know if she could swim. A good swimmer could easily survive a dunking in these waters. He would have to bash her head against something before sending her into the river.

"There is an ibis swimming right next to us," he said to her.

She smiled politely but said nothing.

"Good omen. Come and see," he prodded. When she didn't move, he added, "Maybe you could draw it."

She rose and stretched before moving to stand near him. "I don't see it."

He pointed and took a step closer. Gazing around furtively, he made sure no one was looking in their direction.

His hand raised, a mighty claw ready to tangle in her hair. He heard a series of small thumps at his feet and glanced down, distracted for one moment. Too late, he saw the stones rolling at his feet.

The boat moved with the water, swaying heavily, making him take a small step to steady his gait. The ball of his foot landed on a smooth stone, slipped, skidded on the deck until he was forced to move his opposite foot to purchase balance. Only to encounter another stone, another slip, this one causing his foot to come clear off the decking, flinging into the air.

With disbelief, the warrior felt his body torque and flip, hovering between earth and sky. As he landed, he had a momentary impression of the boy's face, grinning down at him. It was the last thing he saw before his head hit the edge of something hard. Stars exploded before his eyes, and he saw nothing more.

# CHAPTER 9

*You are the most handsome of the sons of men;*
*grace is poured upon your lips.*

PSALM 45:2

Mariamne squealed excitedly and pulled Chariline inside the house before she had a chance to knock on the door. "I've been waiting for you all day," she cried. "What delayed you?"

Chariline grinned and returned her friend's enthusiastic embrace. She had arrived home two hours earlier, only taking time to wash away the grime of her long travels with a quick soak in the baths. She had donned a clean tunic the color of saffron, shoved an old length of yellow ribbon on her wet hair, and dashed to Philip's house, desperate to see her friend.

Aunt Blandina had insisted that she take along their old servant, Leda, not liking the idea of her niece traipsing about the streets of Caesarea alone. The poor woman would probably go bald with worry if she discovered all of Chariline's comings and goings in Meroë.

"So?" Mariamne poked her in the side before kneeling to

wash her feet. Philip had no servants. His daughters managed everything, including the most menial of tasks. "How was your journey?"

Chariline took the towel from her friend and finished drying her feet. "It was . . ." Astonishing? Life changing? Exasperating? "Unexpected," she said. "I have heaps to tell you." So much had happened in two weeks that Chariline felt as though she had been away from her friend for months rather than a mere fourteen days.

Mariamne looked up. Abruptly, the blast of fidgety enthusiasm that often seemed to emanate from her grew still. "Important news," she said softly, her words not a question. She had a disconcerting way of seeing through things.

Chariline nodded. "Life changing."

"Oh, Chariline! I can't wait to hear about it. But we will have to wait, I fear. We have guests, and Father has sent Irais and Eutychis to Jerusalem to keep our aunt company. Without my sisters here to help, Hermione has had to shoulder the dinner preparations on her own. You came just in time to help me serve." She gave Chariline's hand a quick squeeze. "But as soon as we finish clearing up, you and I will sneak to Hermione's chamber, and you can tell me everything."

Chariline sighed. "It's all right. I am growing quite good at waiting."

"*You?* What happened in Cush? An angelic visitation? One of the ten plagues of Egypt? A talking donkey?"

"I could have used a talking donkey. But you will have to wait to find out. Who are the guests?"

"Father's friends."

"Anyone I know?" Chariline was accustomed to meeting

all manner of people in Philip's house. Having been chosen, along with six others, to serve the poor during the early years of the church, Philip had helped many in need, most of whom still held him in great affection and visited when they could.

But Philip's friendships extended far beyond the borders of Caesarea and Jerusalem. When the church had been scattered by the first wave of persecutions over twenty years earlier, the Holy Spirit had sent Philip on a wild adventure, the tales of which would fill a book. He had come upon Natemahar on the road to Gaza during that time.

Philip and his four daughters had eventually settled in Caesarea, though the friends he had made around the empire, both old and new, still called upon him frequently. You never knew who you would meet in Philip's house, as Chariline had good reason to know.

Mariamne shook her head. "You haven't met them. Their ship sustained heavy damage in a storm, and they have been staying with us for almost two weeks."

Chariline smelled the delectable aroma of Hermione's cooking long before they arrived at the tiny kitchen, situated in the back of the small courtyard, with its chipped terra-cotta pots of herbs and spices. Hermione, Philip's eldest daughter, used them in her cooking as well as in her medicinal remedies.

Of Philip's four daughters, Hermione resembled him most, a misfortune one forgot quickly. The bony nose, the thin lips, the crooked teeth all made for a dubious first impression. But after an hour in Hermione's company, one was apt to overlook every imperfection. Such was the magic of Hermione's grace that after a few days, you might even think her beautiful.

Only the previous month, she had received a marriage

proposal from a rich merchant. It was not the first she had declined. Hermione believed that the Lord had a different calling in store for her.

She ran Philip's small but busy household with the same sweet-natured efficiency that she employed in caring for the sick. It made her one of the most beloved women of the church in Caesarea.

That uniquely nurturing quality also made her the closest thing to a mother Chariline had ever known. Hermione doted on Chariline with the same fierce affection she bestowed on her sister Mariamne, whom she had raised since the death of their mother.

Along with her many other talents, Hermione had the ability to take meager ingredients and turn them into exquisite meals. Chariline's mouth watered as she entered the kitchen. The aroma of roasting leeks, cumin, and garlic filled every corner. She arrived at the speedy conclusion that having to wait an extra hour or two to share her news with Mariamne might not require a great deal of forbearance, after all.

"What can I do?" she said by way of greeting.

Engrossed in the contents of a pot, Hermione promptly dropped a long-handled bronze ladle on the diminutive counter and flew to Chariline's side, enveloping her in the kind of wholehearted, ample embrace only Hermione could give.

"Missed you, little girl," she said, tapping Chariline's cheek. It was their private joke. Chariline had been taller than Hermione since the age of nine.

"Don't let the food burn," Chariline instructed. "I am starved."

Hermione clucked her tongue. "The only things burning

around here are the cooking fire and your bridges. Warning me not to burn food, indeed. The cheek!" But she turned back to her pot. "Can you carry this to the peristyle while it's still hot?" She pointed her ladle to a copper pan filled with steaming asparagus. "Mariamne can bring the olives and salad."

Chariline could smell lovage and coriander and fried onions mixed with the earthy perfume of asparagus under her nose as she carried the hot pan. But she forgot about the enticing aromas of Hermione's cooking and the gurgling sounds her stomach had been making for the past hour the moment she stepped into the peristyle.

Her first glimpse of Philip's guest brought her feet to an abrupt halt.

"Good evening," he said, the words stretching with an extra syllable in the musical accent she recognized from long familiarity. Everything about him declared him a Cushite. She had traveled all the way from Meroë only to meet another Cushite in Philip's house.

By the way he gazed at her, his eyes unwavering and inquisitive, Chariline knew he felt equally curious about her. She greeted him in Meroitic, which sprang to her lips readily after her recent stay in his land.

His brows drew together in puzzlement. "You are a Cushite?"

Was she a Cushite? In spite of her incomplete knowledge and frustrating lack of success in locating her father, she could answer that question, at least. "I am half Cushite," she said. "My mother was Roman."

"This is Taharqa," Philip said. "He captains Theo's ship, which almost drowned in a storm two weeks ago."

TESSA AFSHAR || 103

"I am sorry for your misfortune," she said.

"I consider it no misfortune to be saved from shipwreck and certain death by the hand of God," a warm voice interjected.

She turned to Philip's second guest. And promptly forgot the Cushite.

He had the physique of a born athlete, with wide shoulders and hard muscles that didn't bulge so much as flowed. A straight nose and chiseled mouth in a longish face made him more than pleasant to look at. But it was his eyes that caught her. Gray eyes that had contended with storms far fiercer than the one that had almost sunk his ship. Old eyes, though he was young—no older than his middle twenties.

Those eyes had known suffering. Had burned with the sting of unshed tears. They looked on her now with a curious intensity, and she felt her cheeks heat under their scrutiny.

The Cushite ship's captain had stared at her, too, though his gaze had done nothing to discomfort her. But the young man's perusal made her mouth dry and her hands tremble so that she had to set the pot of asparagus on the table, the clatter of copper on wood making her wince.

"Chariline, this is Theo," Philip said. "My dear friend from Corinth, and as you probably surmised, a follower of our Lord. I met him last year when I visited the church that gathers at the house of Titius Justus."

"*Salve,* Chariline." Theo's smile offered an easy friendliness, as if he sensed her discomfort and wanted to allay it.

Chariline managed to smile back.

Philip plucked an olive from the platter Mariamne had

brought. "I wish you could remain with us a little longer, Theo. We have so enjoyed your company. It's too bad you have to depart for Rome soon."

Chariline's head snapped up. "You are going to Rome?"

Theo nodded slowly. "As soon as the repairs are complete."

Chariline's throat clogged. *Rome!* He had a ship bound for Rome.

"You carry passengers?" she asked, trying to sound casual.

He shook his head. "Only soap. And sometimes grain."

"Soap?" Her brow wrinkled in thought. "Wait. You are the one who makes that new hair pomade!"

"Have a ship full of it."

Mariamne started to hand out plates. "My father brought some for Chariline and me when he returned from Corinth. Better than any Roman oil you can buy at the baths."

Theo flashed another smile. Chariline was already starting to realize that the combination of easy charm and the old ache hidden in the guarded eyes could be lethal. She tried not to stare.

"My adoptive father, Galenos, is the genius who came up with the idea," Theo explained. "He took what was a smelly invention from Germania and turned it into a glamorous pomade. I only deliver the thing."

"Ha! You are the one who has managed to turn soap into the new Roman craze," Philip said.

Mariamne sat on the edge of the couch next to her father. "I am not surprised your pomade has found its way into the imperial palace. For weeks, Chariline and I haunted the baths just so we could use it. We looked like crones, our skins wrinkled from too much soaking. But we smelled like the angels."

Theo came to his feet. "You must allow me to replenish your stores. It would be a relief to lighten our load a bit." He grinned. "Then I can travel faster."

Disappearing into the small chamber Philip saved for guests, he returned bearing a basket. Sorting through the different colored balls, he chose a light green orb and offered it to Mariamne. "For you . . . verbena, I think."

Mariamne smelled the soap and pretended to swoon. "I love that tangy scent. How did you know?"

His long fingers sank into the basket again, sorting through the pile until they found a dusky ball that looked like an overripe peach. "This reminds me of you." He held his hand out to Chariline.

She reached for the ball. For a moment, their fingers touched, sending a tiny bolt of lightning through her. She almost dropped the soap. To cover her reaction, she bent her head, nose glued to the slippery sphere, sniffing. "Rose?" Her voice emerged husky.

"And cinnamon." The words were mundane. *Cinnamon.* Nothing deep about tree bark that smelled good. It was mere happenstance, of course, that she always thought of her skin as the color of cinnamon. Good enough for spice, she supposed. But not, she had believed, for a woman. She had thought of it as a term of censure.

Theo said it with admiration. He imbued the word with approval. As if he could think of nothing so beautiful as a woman who reminded him of cinnamon.

Mariamne cleared her throat. "Shall we eat?"

"Please," Chariline said, although she had lost all appetite. Fortunately, at Philip's house, awkward silences never lasted. Threads of amusing conversations ebbed and flowed throughout the room. Chariline barely heard them. When Hermione served her fluffy milk custard for dessert, Chariline realized that she would soon have to leave the company of these men. And she still had so much to discover.

She turned to Theo. "You mentioned you don't carry passengers. Do you ever make an exception?"

"My ship is too small to accommodate them. Just enough room for my men and the shipments we carry. Why? Do you wish to go to Rome?"

Chariline forced herself to laugh. "Doesn't everyone?" Mariamne gave her a questioning look, no doubt wondering at this sudden curiosity about passage to a city that had never drawn her attention before.

Picking up a purple grape, Chariline twirled it between her fingers as she tried to gauge the man before her. Could she change his mind? Convince him to welcome her as a passenger on his ship, without proper accompaniment or her family's permission? No man in his right mind would take on such a responsibility.

Besides, she did not have the coin to buy passage with him or anyone else.

An idea was taking shape in the back of her mind. An idea that came dangerously close to madness. Still, she could not shake it. Had it been any other man, she would have already discarded the notion with a laugh. A woman alone on a small ship full of men?

But this was not just any ship. It belonged to Theo. And whether because of his faith or his kindness or something in him that she could not even name, Chariline felt strangely safe with Theo. Taharqa, too, gave the impression of a trustworthy man. Perhaps she was fooling herself. She did not know either of them. Perhaps this sense of safety in their presence was nothing but self-deception.

Then she thought of Vitruvia, of her father and mother. Of all that was at stake.

Putting the grape in her mouth, she swallowed it, and with it, every cautionary hesitation. Casually, so as not to raise suspicion, she set about extracting as much information about Theo's ship as she could. By the time she slipped away with Mariamne, she had managed to learn its name—and the time of its departure in two days.

# CHAPTER 10

—‿◦‿—

*Call to me and I will answer you, and will tell you great*
*and hidden things that you have not known.*

JEREMIAH 33:3

"What happened in Cush?" Mariamne asked when they were finally alone in Hermione's chamber.

Hermione, as the eldest, received the privilege of enjoying a private room. But she shared it freely with her sisters, allowing them to use the chamber whenever they had need. Before Chariline could begin her tale, Hermione herself slipped her head inside the door. "May I join you, or is this a private meeting?"

Chariline beckoned her with a wave. "Come, please. I want you to hear this too." The three women huddled next to one another on Hermione's narrow bed. Chariline picked up a wool cushion, soft from years of use, and held it against her belly. "My father is alive," she said.

"*What?*" Mariamne's voice rose in shock. "Who is he?"

"That, dear Mariamne, is the crux of my problem." She told her friends everything she had discovered about her family, showing them her mother's box full of drawings and Vitruvia's secret letters.

"Then this is where you get your talent from." Hermione squinted over the drawing of a villa. "This would make a beautiful hostel for the sick."

Mariamne gave her older sister an exasperated look. "We are not speaking about the sick now, Hermione. Forget about your villa for a moment. Focus on Chariline's father."

"Pardon me, my dear." Hermione flashed her sweet, snaggletoothed smile. "I lost myself for a moment. I do celebrate your good news."

"Celebration might be premature," Chariline said. "I don't yet know who he is."

"Celebration is very much in order. You left Caesarea an orphan and returned knowing your father lives. Isn't that cause for praise?"

Chariline frowned. "I never thought of that."

Hermione caressed her young friend's hair with a gentle hand. "Sometimes, in the frustration of what we don't have, we forget to rejoice in what we do."

Chariline played with the end of the old hair ribbon dangling against her neck. "There is something else I haven't told you." She had not revealed Sesen's secret until then. Now, she disclosed the full plot she had overheard. "I don't know what to do," she exclaimed. "What if that man is my father?"

"Poor Chariline!" Mariamne's eyes widened. "What a responsibility. To bear the weight of two lives in your hands."

Chariline nodded. "I must try and save both, whoever Sesen turns out to be. Though I have no idea how, and less than four months to do it in."

"Such an outcome may not be in your power," Hermione cautioned. "Let us ask the Lord what you are to do next."

"I am to find my father, of course!"

"There is no *of course* about it, Chariline. In my experience, God starts to tell us something, and before the sentence is out of his mouth, we finish it off the way we prefer. We assume. We presume. And we jump to false conclusions.

"No. What we need is to ask Iesous. Ask him to show you the way."

She pronounced the Lord's name as the Greeks did, who, lacking the *sh* sound of the Hebrews, ended the word with a soothing inflection. Hermione's diction made the very name feel like a balm.

Iesous.

As always, she began to pray as if she was conversing with her dearest friend. As if Iesous came to sit with her every morning and spoke to her in the watches of the night. All of Philip's daughters prayed that way. Perhaps that was why God had blessed them with the uncanny gift of prophecy. Often, they were able to perceive pieces of the future, bits of God's heart, revelations of Iesous's intentions, insight that encouraged the soul more than mere words ever could.

When Hermione asked Iesous to guide Chariline's next steps and waited in silence for an answer, Chariline did not hear anything. No words. No verses from the Scriptures. No mighty blanket of peace covered her. She saw no sign of Rome and no mystical image of her father. She took a deep breath.

And just as she was about to give up, she saw a silhouette, like a shadow, reflected in a dark pool.

It was Theo.

"Well?" Mariamne pressed her fingers. "What did he tell you?"

Chariline felt too embarrassed to confess what she had seen had little to do with her father. They would probably accuse her of having formed an attachment to their father's handsome visitor.

She shrugged and kept her lips closed tight. She did not tell them about the plan brewing in the back of her mind. The plan that involved Theo's ship.

Hermione caressed her cheek. "My dear, I see danger ahead."

Mariamne nodded. "But the Lord will shelter you from harm. I will pray for you daily and ask that he keep you safe, disarming every evil intention against you."

Hermione grinned. "And God told me that he will reveal a hidden treasure." She leaned forward and whispered in Chariline's ear so that only she could hear. "There is a small space behind a cache of amphorae in the bowels of the ship, behind where the oars are. That is a good hiding place."

Chariline's eyes widened. She opened her mouth, but no sound emerged. Hermione pressed a finger to her lips and winked.

———— ⌘ ————

Aunt Blandina had three servants. Old Leda, who had once been nurse to Blandina and Gemina and had been present at Chariline's own birth. Eurynome, a plump, middle-aged woman who cooked and cleaned and took care of the laundry. And Cadmus, the only man in a household of women, who acted as gardener, repairman, and general fetcher and carrier. As soon as she arrived home that evening, Chariline went in search of him and found him in the atrium, mending a cracked paving stone by lamplight.

"Cadmus? Does your son Telemachus still own that cart of his?"

Cadmus straightened, wiping dust from his hands. "Yes, mistress."

"Could you take him a message for me? Right away. Tell him to meet me tomorrow before sunrise. Around the corner from the house, at the edge of the Roman wall."

Cadmus's gray brows rose to his hairline. "Before sunrise, mistress?"

"Yes, Cadmus. Exactly. Tell him not to be late, and I will have a whole sestertius for him."

Cadmus rubbed a palm against his whiskered cheek. "If you insist, mistress."

She bent her head close. "I won't tell Aunt Blandina if you don't. That way, neither of us will get into trouble."

Cadmus's craggy face broke into a wide grin. In truth, Aunt Blandina did not pose much of a threat. She was just as afraid of losing her servants, to whom she had grown accustomed, as they were of losing their jobs.

Chariline retired to her chamber. She thought sleep would evade her, given the whirl of excitement that lay ahead. But she fell into a deep, dreamless slumber as soon as her head touched the pillow.

—— ᏬᏝᏬ ——

A bright moon cradled the sky when she awoke. Donning her darkest cloak over an old tunic, Chariline slipped out of the house. She ran the short distance to the wall that surrounded the city of Caesarea. Turning the corner, she exhaled with relief when she spied the outline of Telemachus's cart, the boy's head nodding against his chest.

Chariline climbed into the back of the cart. "To the harbor, Telemachus," she said, startling the young man out of his doze. He coughed, a deep, wracking sound that heaved his thin chest.

"Oh, my, Telemachus! Are you sick?"

The young man signaled his donkey to move. "Just a tickle in my throat, mistress."

"Well, if you are not better by this evening, ask Mistress Hermione to give you one of her brews. You know she charges nothing."

A thin grin split the pale face. "She charges plenty, mistress. Just not money. I will have to listen to one of her sermons."

Chariline chuckled. "That you will. And it will be as good for you as her medicine. Besides, she cooked a delectable stew last night. If you arrive early, she might still have some left over."

Telemachus expertly guided his donkey around a narrow bend. "That might be worth a sermon. Nobody in this city can cook like her." His chest rose in another paroxysm of coughs.

Chariline gave him a concerned look. "Be sure to get that medicine soon. You sound terrible."

In spite of his illness, Telemachus managed to drive his cart with easy skill navigating the broad roads toward the harbor.

Caesarea, an ancient city, had been rebuilt by Herod the Great sixty years earlier. Although belonging to the province of Judea, and the seat of the Roman governor, the city was in some ways more Greek than Hebrew. Its over 125,000 inhabitants included Hellenic Jews like Philip and Aramaic-speaking Jews, as well as Romans, and Greeks like her aunt's deceased husband.

The city enjoyed wide roads, busy markets, sumptuous baths, and lavish public buildings like the hippodrome and theater that sat cheek by jowl with Herod's luxurious palace. But in a city that boasted numerous wonders, by far the grandest wonder of Caesarea was its port.

The coastline itself offered no natural harbor. Herod had managed, through a wonderous feat of engineering, to create enormous breakwaters made of lime and volcanic ash. On one such promontory, he had built his own palace, extending straight into the sea, like a stubborn finger defiantly pointing at the briny waters.

Two massive jetties created the square Sebastos Harbor, arguably the most noble port outside of Puteoli in Rome. Within the giant man-made breakwaters, ships could take shelter, receive repairs, and be restocked before departing on their way.

It was to this port that Chariline had directed Telemachus. They passed the entrance to the harbor, the statue of Augustus twinkling pale and lifelike in the twilight. Just before reaching the harbor, Chariline directed Telemachus to pull over.

"Wait for me in the cart." She leapt down to the stone-paved road.

"Want me to come along, mistress? No place for a lady alone and in the dark of the harbor."

"Thank you, Telemachus. But I won't take long."

The young man scratched his chin, looking uncomfortable. But Chariline did not want to bring Telemachus along in case he glimpsed the ship and informed on her after she left. The last thing she wanted was to cause trouble for Theo.

She walked onto the breakwater, a part of her marveling at the sheer scale and magnificence of the structure that defied the waves, sheltering ships against the sea's unfriendly reception. A few sailors were starting to stir, though the port remained mostly quiet so early in the day.

She searched for Theo's ship until she saw the name etched in blue-and-gold relief on the sternpost of a dainty vessel. The *Parmys* had only one large central mast, its great square sail hanging limp from its lines.

From Mariamne's description, she recognized the distinctive carving of a windswept charioteer that occupied the ship's prow. Mariamne had told Chariline that seven years earlier, Theo had won one of the most exciting chariot races in the history of the sport during the famed Isthmian Games. That race had instantly catapulted Theo into legendary success in Corinth. The carving had been a gift from his brother, another beloved winner of the Isthmian Games.

Hiding behind a large potted palm, Chariline stood as close to the *Parmys* as she dared and studied the ship intently. On one end stood a modest, square cabin with a flat roof, which sported a wooden railing, allowing sailors to use its added height as an observation deck.

Only one sailor seemed to be guarding the ship. He worked sleepily on a net, his fingers plying an iron hook to repair invisible tears. Chariline watched, motionless, looking for movement elsewhere on the ship and saw none.

Hermione had told her to seek the bowels of the vessel, where the oars were kept. She spied a rectangular hatch midway in the deck. She could make out a few steps leading down, melting into the dark. This must be the hatch that connected to the lower deck and the oar benches.

She lingered in her hiding spot, observing every detail of the ship and memorizing its lines until the sun started to rise. Not wanting to be seen, she made her way back to the cart and arranged for Telemachus to pick her up at exactly the same time the following morning.

———

Aunt Blandina loved poppies. Chariline took time to pick a dozen, weaving the bright blooms into a jaunty garland. At breakfast, she placed the wreath on her aunt's brow, making her laugh. Romans had a particular fondness for garlands and often used them at their feasts. This might be the last day she saw her aunt for a long time. She wanted to leave behind a handful of joyful memories. She fluffed Blandina's pillow on the couch, fetched her favorite wine, washed her feet after they walked around the garden, and listened to her complain about her corns.

She should have had more days like this with her aunt. But she knew the experience was bittersweet for both. Aunt Blandina would shut down at some point. Grow monosyllabic and withdrawn. And Chariline would ache from the rejection of it.

They had fallen into a rhythm of mutual isolation, living together and apart at the same time.

When Aunt Blandina retired for her afternoon rest, Chariline decided to visit the baths. It might be weeks before she could enjoy a proper soak again. She washed her hair with the rose-and-cinnamon ball of soap Theo had given her and, after a leisurely dip in the caldarium, decided to indulge herself thoroughly and used the soap to wash her whole body.

Inhaling the sweet scent of roses and cinnamon, she leaned against the side of the pool and let her eyelids drift closed. Was she truly going ahead with this insane plan?

She could continue to live the life she had known for twenty-four years. Forget what she had discovered in Cush. Settle back into the routine of living with her aunt, together but alone.

Or she could risk everything to find the father she ached to know.

She took a deep breath and stepped out of the pool. Her plan might be perilous. But at least it opened a door to hope. A door to a fulfilling future. A door to love. Yet before she could grasp that future, she would first have to confront the past.

In the evening, after the household went to bed, Chariline gathered a few essentials in a sheet: extra tunics; some personal necessities; enough cheese, bread, dried fruit, and nuts to last three or four days; a small wineskin of watered wine; a modest purse of coins. She carefully packed her mother's drawings and Vitruvia's letters in her mother's box, adding a thick roll of papyrus and a full inkpot for her own sketches. She tied a secure knot in the sheet and stuffed her bundle in the chest at the end of her bed.

Pulling out her stash of papyrus, she wrote two letters. The first she addressed to her aunt.

*Chariline, your faithful niece, to my honored aunt, Blandina,*

*By the time you read this letter, I will be gone. I cannot tell you where, as I do not want Grandfather to come marching after me. Please don't worry. I will be safe. And, no, I am not running away with some unsuitable fellow. Or any fellow. But I have good reason to go. I hope one day I will be able to tell you about it.*

*Your loving niece, always*

She wrote another letter for Mariamne and Hermione and, sealing them, left both on the narrow shelf over her bed where they could easily be discovered.

# CHAPTER 11

— ⚬ —

*If I rise on the wings of the dawn,*
*if I settle on the far side of the sea,*
*even there your hand will guide me,*
*your right hand will hold me fast.*

PSALM 139:9,10, NIV

He came awake with a throbbing headache and a bilious stomach that demanded to be emptied. It took a few moments for the double vision to clear. He remembered the stones rolling under his feet. Remembered hurtling into the air, followed by a spectacular fall. Touching the back of his head, he winced at the tender bulge the size of an ibis egg that ached under his exploring fingers.

It didn't take long to discover that all the passengers on the riverboat had already disembarked, including the girl. And the boy with the stones whose neck he wanted to wring had vanished as well.

Thoughts of revenge would have to wait. He had a job to do. His master would not be pleased with his failure.

The warrior managed to pick up the girl's trail after a few hours. She had boarded another vessel headed for Caesarea.

He paid passage on an Egyptian ship full of grain but had to wait until the next day before they set off for Sebastos Harbor.

By the time he arrived at the girl's house, it was the dead of night. He sat hidden by a clump of shrubs, watching from the shadows. Weariness and the pounding in his head finally wore down his reserves and he fell asleep. A slight sound roused him from his restless slumber. His senses instantly alert, he picked out the slim, tall figure, wrapped head to ankle in a dark cloak, emerging from the house.

At first, he dismissed her as a servant, leaving the house before sunrise to run the daily errands of a small household. Then something in the girl's gait caught his attention. The height was right. He crept out of his hiding place and followed the lone silhouette a few steps. A flutter of wind blew aside the cloak and bright moonlight caught the length of a calf. He smiled slowly, recognizing that distinctive skin.

The gods were smiling upon him, after all. Here she was, handed to him on a platter, utterly alone in the dusky predawn hour. What kind of accident should he arrange? He could throw her in front of a cart. But that wouldn't assure her death. He could break her neck first. He was considering the merits of this plan when she turned a corner. Following behind, his eyes bulged when she climbed into the back of a cart.

*What is she doing?*

He had assumed he would have plenty of time to fake an accident as he followed her on foot. This unexpected and clearly prearranged ride turned his plan on its head. Instead of a leisurely pursuit, he now had to run behind the cart to keep up. With every step, tentacles of pain shot through his injured head.

He couldn't wait to get rid of the girl.

As the cart gained speed, he fell behind, until he lost sight of it. Cursing under his breath, he pushed harder, trying to catch a glimpse of them.

At the next intersection, he came to a stop, panting heavily, dry throat burning. Should he turn right toward the aqueducts, or left toward the harbor? He hesitated for a moment, undecided. There were more shops near the harbor. He turned left.

In the distance, he spied the cart again, pulled over to the side of the road. It was empty.

He stopped and cast about uneasily, looking for the girl and the driver. He spotted the driver first, speaking to a couple of sailors at the entrance to one of the breakwaters.

Just behind the cart driver, he finally spied the girl standing behind a potted palm tree, barely discernible in her dark cloak. Breathing a sigh of relief, he began to run in their direction.

By now, he had drawn close enough to hear the driver, who was speaking in the loud voice of a hawker. A pale boy with thin arms and a bony chest, he yelled enthusiastically, his arms spread wide for emphasis. "Pretty girls? Anybody want a visit by pretty girls?"

Heads were turning his way. On the ships that bobbed up and down in a tidy line ahead of them, sailors hung over the sides of their vessels, grinning.

Noticing their attention, the driver bellowed even louder. For a puny lad, he had a surprisingly deep voice. "I know beautiful girls. I can arrange to have them here before your captains arrive to ruin your fun."

The sound of hooting and catcalls from multiple decks broke the predawn peace.

On a ship docked toward the end of the breakers, an athletic man advanced toward the prow of the vessel, leaning against the railing, his mouth a grim line. A dark-featured giant joined him at the helm, taking hold of the tiller. The warrior noticed he looked like a Cushite. "I *am* the captain," he called out to the driver, "And I don't like your kind of fun. Keep your pretty girls. We're casting off. Raise that anchor, boys!"

For a few moments, the driver's boisterous spectacle had distracted the warrior. He had wondered if the skinny lad meant to sell the girl. Then, with an abrupt hiss of breath, he realized that she had disappeared right under his nose. There were no pretty girls for sale. The whole thing had been a ruse to divert everyone's attention. But why?

Frantically, he viewed the jetty. Where had the girl gone?

Then he saw it. A shadow creeping down a hatch on the ship that was leaving the harbor.

It was her! He was sure of it. She had snuck onto the ship while half the sailors had been absorbed in their tasks and the other half had grown distracted by the cart driver.

That sly fox! She had stowed away on a ship bound for who knew where, with no one the wiser.

The warrior began to run, jumping over obstacles in his way. But even as he pushed himself until his vision blurred, he knew he would never make it in time. The ship was already gliding toward the open sea behind a small pilot boat. She had slipped through his fingers. Again!

He grabbed a sailor. "Where is that ship headed?"

"Don't know. Don't care." The man shook his arm loose.

He grabbed another sailor, his fingers rough. "Where is that ship bound?"

"How should I know?"

The warrior's ire became a red haze. Any moment now, that ship would hit open water, raise its sail, and vanish into the horizon, where he would never be able to find it—or the girl—again.

His fist became a hammer and he slammed it into the sailor's face with a satisfying crunch. "Do you know now?"

The sailor raised his hands in surrender. "Didn't mean to . . ."

Another punch. "Where?"

"Grrr." A rivulet of blood carrying a tooth trickled down the side of a stubbly chin. "Thimmer down! I don't know. But I'll find out." He held up both hands again.

The warrior stepped away. "Be quick about it."

A few minutes later, the sailor returned, holding a dirty towel to his lip. "That'th the *Parmyth*. It'th headed to Puteoli. Thatithfied?"

This whole job stank worse than the dead fish floating in the harbor. "Where do I find a ship bound for Puteoli—*now?*"

———— ⚭ ————

Chariline wriggled down until her shoulders were reclining against the wall, the cache of terra-cotta amphorae hiding her body from the casual observer. The ship had left before sunrise, and in the cover of darkness, she had managed to slither her way into its bowels, undetected. She hoped that even Telemachus had not seen which ship she had boarded.

If Grandfather ever managed to follow her trail to the harbor, she wanted to ensure that Theo would not catch the brunt of the blame for her disappearance.

The amphorae were stacked in the aft of the ship, shadowed by the curved cedar hull that surrounded them and the solid planking of the cabin floor above. Arranged in neat rows on the opposite corner from the oarsmen's benches, they provided the best hiding place the *Parmys* offered.

Chariline thanked God for Hermione's whispered direction. She had not asked if her friend knew this detail because she had been invited to tour Theo's ship during his stay at their house or if the Lord had revealed it to her. Either way, Hermione had clearly heard from Iesous about Chariline's intention to stow away on Theo's ship.

The advice she had given was the only reason Chariline's harebrained plot had succeeded thus far. In a diminutive ship populated by men, she had managed to find the only spot that was left alone much of the time.

Two hours into their journey, no one had yet ventured below. The wind had been strong enough to raise the sail as soon as they had left the harbor, and they were now traveling at a steady pace without the need to resort to oars.

For the first time in hours, Chariline took an easy breath. She had done it! She had stowed away on Theo's ship!

Her heart exploded into a deafening rhythm. What had she done? She had stowed away on Theo's ship!

Back and forth it went, elation followed by horror.

They had not traveled so far from Caesarea that she could not change her mind. She could march upstairs this very moment and ask Theo's pardon. Accept his scorn. Bear his frustration. Be returned home and wait for a more honest opportunity to get to Rome in order to find her father.

Except that such an opportunity would not come. Grandfather would never allow it, which meant Aunt Blandina would not allow it, which meant that she would not be able to undertake the single most important journey of her life.

Once again, she was faced with a disagreeable choice. Choose a world without her father or face Theo's loathing. The choice felt like a kick to her solar plexus. Her breath caught. The ship's walls seemed to close in on her.

The thought of the aggravation she would cause Theo made her wince. He had clearly indicated that he had no desire for passengers. She would bring him a load of trouble by her mere presence, disturbing a crew of crusty sailors unused to female company.

She pulled her cloak over her head and hunkered down, the sound of the wind beating against her ears. From the clutch of amphorae surrounding her arose a confusing array of different scents: myrtle and pomegranate, cypress and rose, honey and sweet marjoram, yellow clover and ambergris. The overwhelming effluvia of too many perfumes made her dizzy and she closed her eyes.

She must have fallen asleep. When she came to, her hiding place had grown sweltering, making her tunic cling to her in damp, unwieldy lines. Through the opening in the hatch, she glimpsed a bright sky, the sun's rays glaring hotly. Late morning, she guessed. They had been at sea for six or seven hours already.

Too late to turn back.

A man laughed and a long shadow fell across the opening

of the hatch. Theo descended the seven steps that brought him to the lower level. Chariline ducked, bending and twisting until her joints ached. Through the thin spaces between the amphorae, she saw Theo walk toward her. He came to a sudden stop, hesitating before doubling back.

One of the oars had been knocked out of place and lay crookedly on the bench, its paddle hanging precariously off the end.

Chariline squeezed her eyes shut. She must have brushed against it on her way to her hiding place. Theo frowned, straightened the oar, tapped it a couple of times thoughtfully, then turned. Toward Chariline.

He sauntered to where the amphorae sat in stacks, leaning against the wall and each other. Chariline slipped even lower. Sweat trickled down her back. Theo bent over an amphora close to the front, sorted through the balls, and grabbed one.

"Sophocles," he cried. "I found one that will make even you smell good."

Sophocles yelped. "You might as well try to lather a dolphin with your soap. I won't do it, I tell you." The sound of raucous laughter came from above.

"You're going to smell as pretty as Cleopatra, the queen of Egypt," someone yelled.

"Cleopatra, sure!" said another. "All mummified and lying in her crypt."

Theo grinned and threw the ball into the air, watched it twirl before catching it behind his back, then bounded up the stairs in two leaps.

Chariline exhaled, stretching her aching back.

She could not expect to remain hidden for the full duration of their journey to Rome, which would likely take weeks. She would run out of water long before then. But she wanted to avoid discovery for as long as possible. Once they found her, the whole crew would likely resent her for sneaking on board. Not to mention Theo's displeasure. Besides, he could always drop her off at the next harbor and leave her to make her own way home.

Chariline doubted this outcome. Though she deserved it, she suspected Theo would not act with such callous disregard for her safety. She had sensed a deep kindness in him. And Philip had said he was a man of faith. Surely, he would not simply banish her from his ship and leave her to fend for herself?

The butterflies in her belly reminded her that she did not feel as secure in Theo's response as she told herself. He would be well within his rights to abandon her at the first convenient port.

The other possibility, that of Theo turning his ship around and returning her to Caesarea, seemed more likely to Chariline. She could only hope that Theo would feel honorbound to keep his word to his important patron in Rome so that returning a stowaway to a harbor that lay far out of his way would become an untenable option.

She took a small sip of her watered wine, trying to soothe her parched throat.

Judging by the howls and shrieks coming from the deck above, the men had managed to get some soap on Sophocles. Chariline hoped it wasn't the one scented with rose and cinnamon. For some odd reason, she had formed a proprietary attachment to that particular soap. She had come to think of it as *her* special scent. The idea of sharing it with some dour sailor who, save for a swim in the sea now and again, had probably not bathed in a decade, seemed wrong. Which was ridiculous, of course. Theo would be selling bushel loads of the stuff to any interested buyer across the empire.

Tearing off a piece of bread, she took a dainty bite and chewed slowly. A shadow fell across the opening of the hatch. Instinctively, she took a sharp breath, making the morsel of bread catch in the back of her throat. She choked. Eyes watering, she shoved a hand over her mouth, trying to suppress the tide of coughing that threatened to let loose.

Theo descended the stairs again. Halfway down, he stopped and turned to face the deck. "The lot of you stink. Couldn't you have visited a bath before you boarded my ship?" he shouted.

Chariline could not hold the coughs back any longer.

By some miracle, Theo's monologue covered the noise. A tiny piece of bread flew out, and she took a deep, steadying breath. While his back was turned, she slithered farther down against the wall, silent as a feral cat, hoping the top of her head remained invisible.

Theo descended the rest of the way, still speaking to the crew. "I am a soap merchant, not a pig farmer. In your present condition, you are liable to scare away all my refined customers." He grabbed a handful of soaps from the first container before him and returned up the stairs again.

Chariline sagged, feeling exhausted. How was she supposed to live this way for days?

Above her, on the deck, extraordinary amounts of whooping and teasing and hollering went on for a good hour. Every once in a while, a man streaked across the top of her vision as he ran past the open hatch. After the shock of seeing her second set of naked legs, she learned to screw her eyes shut and keep them that way.

It dawned on her that the life of a stowaway was more complicated than she had imagined.

# CHAPTER 12

—cɯɔ—

*Would not God discover this?*
*For he knows the secrets of the heart.*

PSALM 44:21

On the fourth morning of her voyage, Chariline stared bleary eyed into the dark space before her and began seriously to consider surrender. Her watered wine would soon run out, and except for a handful of nuts, she faced a long battle with hunger.

Worse than hunger and thirst were the frequent and unforeseen interruptions. On numerous occasions, the sailors traipsed down the stairs, sometimes in the middle of the night, looking for an odd piece of tackle or rope they had stored there. This continuous and unheralded disturbance meant that Chariline could never lower her guard, never fully give in to sleep. Taking care of personal needs had turned into a nightmare.

Over against this nerve-wracking stream of disruptions was Theo's inevitable anger. Every time she felt tempted to walk on wobbly legs up those seven steps, the thought of having to face him dissuaded her. What excuse could she offer that might win, if not his acceptance, then at least his compassion?

She had spent hours forming speeches for that first meeting. None seemed sufficient. In the end, she had settled for the truth. She would tell him everything and let him come to his own conclusions.

Her throat felt dry and swollen from thirst. She took a small sip of her warm, stale water. The wine had started to go sour, and it tasted more of vinegar than grape juice.

A set of feet rattled slowly down the stairs. An old sailor she had not seen before appeared, white hair matching billowy whiskers. He approached the terra-cotta amphorae in the back. Closer to the wall, separated from the soap containers, sat five or six narrow-necked amphorae, filled with cured olives, oil, and wine. Extra rations, Chariline suspected.

With sure steps, he negotiated around the vessels and approached the back wall.

Chariline's heart stopped.

The old sailor stood so close she could smell the briny odor of fish wafting from his short tunic. Dragging a jar toward him, he shifted his body to allow the amphora to lie securely against him. His body turned to accommodate the heavy jar. His line of vision shifted, angled toward the stowaway he did not know they carried.

Chariline knew the moment he saw her.

Opalescent eyes widened. He screwed them shut, as if unable to believe what he had seen, before opening them again. His jaw grew slack.

"Oh, Captain!" he cried, his voice wobbling. "You better get down here. And bring the master."

Chariline gulped, nausea clawing up her belly. The moment she had dreaded had finally arrived.

"What you want, Sophocles?" a voice cried from the deck.

"I reckon we caught ourselves a sea nymph," the sailor said, not taking his gaze off Chariline.

She raised her fingers and waved half-heartedly at the old man, hoping to convince him that she was friendly. The wrinkled, leathery face, still sagging with astonishment, cracked into a grin, exposing more gums than teeth. He waved back.

"I think she's sociable," he called.

Taharqa's massive shoulders darkened the opening of the hatch. "What are you spouting about, Sophocles? I don't have time for one of your tall tales."

"See for yourself," the old sailor said. "A sea nymph, in the flesh."

Chariline rose, preferring to meet her fate with a sliver of dignity rather than slinking on the ground like a dried-out earthworm. Her knees shook after four days of being bent into awkward angles.

"Captain," she croaked.

Taharqa froze. A frown, ominous as the smoke emerging from the mouth of a volcano, darkened his face. "That's no sea nymph," he thundered. Pointing his chin at Chariline, he said, "You're a long way from Caesarea. Or Cush. Or wherever you belong."

"I apologize for the inconvenience."

"Theo!" the captain bellowed.

Theo rushed down the steps. "What's all the . . . " He skid-ded to a halt. "Ruckus . . ." His voice tapered off. A mask of disbelief congealed over the sun-bronzed features.

After a long silence, he said, "You!" Incredulity, uncer-tainty, and shock wove through that single word. "What are you doing on my ship?"

Every word Chariline had painstakingly rehearsed for end-less hours promptly vanished from her mind. She watched as astonishment and confusion turned into irritation on the handsome face. And was finally replaced by hot anger.

His gaze took in her rumpled appearance, wisps of flyaway hair sticking out from her untidy braid, and traveled to the sheet on the floor where she had been hiding for four days.

"I did not realize you were so fond of my soap that you wished to sleep with it," he said dryly.

"I . . . I am sorry for this dreadful intrusion, Theo. If you allow me, I can explain."

The sculpted lips grew flat. "I doubt that. I doubt that very much."

———— ⚭ ————

The first time he had seen her in Philip's house, he had thought her one of the most dazzling women he had ever set eyes on. She reminded him of an exotic bird, full lips and carved cheekbones and a smile that had melted something old and crusted in his soul. Listening to her low voice, he had felt feelings stir inside him that he had believed long dead.

Interest. Admiration. Fascination.

He had shoved all of it down, unwilling to complicate his life for a woman he would leave behind in a matter of hours.

That she had shown up on his ship—his ship!—in the middle of the sea was no less disconcerting than his first engrossed glimpse of her had been.

He gazed at her now, her tall, narrow-boned limbs folded awkwardly on the stool in front of him as if every muscle ached. They probably did, from her long hours of confinement in the bowels of the ship.

After finding her tucked among the soap amphorae, looking annoyingly composed and oddly regal in her wrinkled tunic, he had escorted her to this tiny cabin, the only place on the *Parmys* with a door on it. All the way here, he had smelled cinnamon and roses, his own soap, perfectly matched to something in her skin, wafting in a way that had disturbed him to his core.

As soon as he had stepped over the threshold of the cabin, he had slammed the door shut in a dozen inquisitive faces. By the time he reached the deck, every man on the ship had heard they had a stowaway and trailed after him like a giant cloud of hornets shadowing his steps. Shadowing her.

The cabin was stuffy and hot, one of the reasons he rarely used it.

What *was* she doing here?

"What are you doing here?" he barked, voicing his most pressing question. Truly, he did not need this mad complication. What was he to do with a woman on a ship full of rowdy men?

Her tongue darted out, trying to lick dry lips, and for the first time he noticed how chapped and painfully cracked they looked. He reached for the jug of water resting on a corner table and poured some into a goblet and held it out to her.

She gave him a grateful look before drinking down the warm water thirstily. "Thank you." Her voice emerged a whisper. He noticed her fingers twisting agitatedly around the stem of the goblet. For the first time, he realized she was afraid. And something more. Something more heated than fear.

She was ashamed.

The line of his back, which had grown as ramrod straight as a general facing an enemy army, loosened a little.

"I beg your pardon, Theo," she said, her voice trembling in spite of the way she held up her chin. "I know I am a terrible inconvenience. And I would never have presumed to impose upon you if I were not desperate."

"*Impose* upon me?" He flicked a hand in the air as if sweeping away her apology. "You would have imposed upon me if you had shown up an hour early for a dinner invitation. This . . . !" He pointed to where she was sitting, words failing him. "This . . . stowing away on my ship when I had already made it clear that I take no passengers . . . This is not a mere imposition. It is an intrusion. An invasion. This is an outright violation." He pressed his index finger down like a silent exclamation.

She bit her lip. "I beg your pardon," she said again.

"And why, may I ask, have you taken it upon yourself to sneak on board? To wriggle your way inside a merchant vessel full of rough sailors who are unaccustomed to having women on board? You wish to see the sights of Rome? Go shopping, perhaps, in its glittering stores? You are longing for an adventure?"

Another thought momentarily wiped out every other concern from his mind. "You are on your way to meet a secret lover?" He tasted gall as he spit out the words. Disconcerted by his own response, he clamped his mouth shut.

She shook her head vigorously. "I am going to find my father."

That silenced him for a beat. He felt as if someone had knocked the wind out of his sails. "Your *father*?" He frowned. "Couldn't you have sent him a letter, like normal people?"

"I could not."

"Why?"

"I don't know where he is, exactly. Or *who* he is, for that matter."

Theo's mind came to a crashing halt, like a skiff run aground on a deceptively calm shore. He sank down on the edge of the narrow cot, which took up half the space in the cabin. "You don't know who your father is?"

"I do not. My grandparents had always told me he was dead. I only recently discovered they had lied to me all my life. My father is alive. I don't know his name. Grandfather refuses to tell me. But I need to find him, don't you see?"

"And you think he resides in Rome?"

"No. He lives in Cush."

"Of course. That makes perfect sense. I can see why it's so important that you head for Rome."

"I am going to Rome because my mother's friend lives there. I believe she can reveal my father's identity."

"Why don't you ask your mother?"

"She died when I was born." She said the words without inflection. But Theo knew something about the writhing force of guilt. Knew something about the agony of blame over a mother's death. He sensed the foul presence of it under

Chariline's calm pronunciation. The poisoned dagger that never stopped pressing its point against the heart. The belief that she had caused her mother's death.

Every impulse toward sarcasm, every antagonistic barb instantly lost its allure. He leaned toward her and gentled his voice. "Couldn't you write your mother's friend?"

She shook her head. "I don't know where she resides. Once I find her, I know she will help me." She bent down and searched through the small bundle she had carried from her hiding place.

From her meager pile, she extracted a thick roll of papyrus. "Here. Let me show you."

There followed such a tale of intrigue and mystery that Theo would have doubted her veracity if not for the earnest manner with which she told it.

Theo opened one of the pouches of papyrus Gemina had created all those years ago and studied it in silence. He had to marvel at the ingenuity of the young woman who had found a way to hide precious letters from prying eyes.

"Your mother was resourceful."

"It seems so."

Shuffling through the drawings, he looked up. "This one has your name."

She offered him a wan smile. "Like my mother, I love architecture."

He thought of the way Chariline had managed to sneak aboard a cramped ship, evading discovery for four days. She had inherited more than her love for architecture from her mother. "And you think you can find this Vitruvia in Rome?"

"I do."

"What if she has moved? What if she has died? What if you can't find her?"

She tucked her hands under her arms. "Then I have lost nothing. I can go on knowing that I tried my best."

Sometime over the past hour, it had become clear to Theo that she had not stowed away on his ship because she had an irresponsible thirst for adventure. Nor was she thoughtless and selfish as he had suspected when he had first discovered her hiding amongst his jars of soap.

He had started to read her inflections better over the past hour. She reined her emotions tight and worked hard to conceal them. But in the close quarters of the cabin, with her life opened before him like rolls of papyrus containing an ancient poem, he saw beyond her reserved expression. He slithered under her guard.

And he learned something interesting.

On their march from the ship's bowels to the cabin, he had thought her uncomfortable with twelve pairs of eyes shadowing her every move. Now he realized that she must have felt petrified. Teeth-chatteringly intimidated by the unfriendly faces of his men as they followed her.

Yet she had risked this difficult journey, faced the disquiet of being the only woman on board. Risked his own power to humiliate and harm her. Not because these things mattered so little to her, but because finding her father meant so much more.

Her illicit presence on his ship spoke volumes about her desire to encounter a man she had never even met. Instantly, he knew why. She was painfully hungry for love.

A subject in which Theo happened to have some expertise.

He also knew, firsthand, the guilt she carried for her mother's death. Oddly, he could even identify with her baffling ignorance when it came to her father's name. Of course, unlike her, he had as much interest in finding the man who had sired him as he did in coming face-to-face with one of the monsters of the deep.

His jaw ached as he thought of this long chain of unlikely coincidences. He could say, with some assurance, that there was not another man sailing the seven seas so well equipped to understand, even sympathize, with this woman and her quest.

His mind dredged up a memory of the storm that had crippled his ship and landed him in Caesarea. The storm that had forced him into her path. Remembered again with perfect clarity the assurance he had felt. The assurance that God had guided his steps into that shore for a reason.

Was *she* the purpose God had intended all along? Had he been drawn into Caesarea to help Chariline?

He rubbed the back of his neck. "Did you tell your aunt that you were stowing away on the *Parmys*?"

"Of course not! I do not wish to cause you trouble, Theo. The last thing I want is for my grandfather to come traipsing after you, hurling accusations."

"That's reassuring."

"I left my aunt a letter so she would not worry overmuch. But I did not even tell her that I was headed to Rome, let alone divulge any particulars about you. Although . . ."

"Although?"

"I think Hermione knew. She has an uncanny way of seeing things without being told. But she would never violate a confidence."

Theo nodded. He had heard of the extraordinary gifts of Philip's daughters. "I must pray on this, Chariline. Ask God what I am to do."

She gave a short nod. In that tremulous movement, he sensed a vulnerability so fragile it made his insides ache. Whatever decision he made, it would have a profound impact on her future. On her heart.

All the more reason to pray. God must direct him, for he could see that something fundamental to her well-being was at stake in this decision.

Then again, hauling her to Rome and setting the woman loose upon the world hardly seemed safe. And at that moment, he was not even sure if he worried more for the world or for her.

He rose to his feet. "You must be hungry. I will ask Sophocles to bring you dinner. We eat simply on this ship."

"That will suit me perfectly. Thank you."

At the door, he turned to face her again. "Please do not try to leave this cabin." He held her gaze. "My men are not savages. They are trustworthy, in their own way. But I cannot vouch for their manners. Best you keep out of the way for now."

She rose. "Theo?" She held on to the corner of the stool, her knuckles turning white from the force of her grip. "I am grateful to you." She held up a hand. "I know you have made no decision. I am grateful, nonetheless. That you listened to my story." Her fingers twisted painfully on the edge of the stool.

Looking at those fingers, long and slender and unsure, he felt an odd hollow in his chest, as if someone had taken his heart out of its comfortable cavity and wrung it out before replacing it. He shook the odd image out of his mind. Before more fanciful thoughts could lay ahold of him, he slipped out of the cabin and pulled the door firmly shut behind him.

# CHAPTER 13

—❧—

*If any of you lacks wisdom, let him ask God, who gives generously
to all without reproach, and it will be given him.*

JAMES 1:5

Chariline collapsed on the stool as soon as the door closed
behind Theo. Her throat felt dry. She coughed and was surprised by the hacking sound that emerged from her lungs.
Reaching for the flagon of water, she poured herself a cup and
drank down a few mouthfuls.

On the whole, Theo had treated her with more compassion than she deserved. She winced as she recalled his initial
sarcasm, the open ring of accusation in his tone. His disgust
had been every bit as painful as she had feared. But somewhere
in the retelling of her story, his rigid shoulders had dropped
from around his ears, and he had started to really listen.

It was a heady elixir, being listened to by Theo, being the
sole object of those searching gray eyes that seemed to have a
language of their own.

Rising on shaky legs, she approached the closed door. The

wood was ancient and warped in places, leaving a long slit between two pine planks. Pressing her face against the crack, she eyed the world outside. On their march into the cabin, she had been too overwhelmed to notice her surroundings. Now she saw that it was a bright day, the sky the dark blue of cornflower petals. She tried to take a deep breath, filling her lungs with the fresh air that the cabin lacked. It only made her cough again until her chest ached.

The wind must have finally dropped; the sailors were busy pulling on flax ropes, lowering the linen sail. A strange silence had fallen over the usually boisterous ship. Every once in a while, one of the men cast a curious glance toward the cabin.

As soon as the sail was safely lowered, Theo began to climb the mast. Chariline's lips hung open as she watched him scale the smooth pole without the help of a ladder or ropes. Graceful as a feline, his muscles bunched and loosened, propelling him upward until he sat, anchored securely by one leg wrapped around the mast. To her bafflement, she saw him lower his head and knew by his attitude that he was praying.

She stepped away from the door, feeling as if she had intruded on something private and holy. He had found an odd roost for prayer. Then again, he was not likely to find many distractions up there.

Iesous liked to retreat to the mountainside to pray privately, she remembered. Theo had withdrawn to the closest thing to a mountainside he could find on a ship.

A sudden wave of exhaustion rolled over Chariline. It had been four days since she had been able to fully stretch out her body and sleep deeply for any length of time. Parts of her ached that she had no name for.

She stared at the narrow bed longingly. She supposed this must be where Theo slept. Having violated his ship by her uninvited presence, she found herself unwilling to add insult to injury by taking over his cot as well.

With a sigh, she grabbed her sheet and, folding it lengthwise, laid it on the only narrow bit of space on the floor long enough for a body to stretch on. Using her cloak as a pillow, she lay down, cradled tightly between the base of the bed and the wall. It was like sleeping in a cave.

The ground proved unyielding and hard. Whoever had put down these wooden slats had not meant them to serve as a bunk. She groaned, turned half a revolution, and yelped when she hit her elbow on the wall.

Her eyes closed. "Praise you, Iesous, for bringing me this far. Please carry me the rest of the way."

She had almost drifted into sleep when the door slammed open, narrowly missing her head. With a half-strangled squeak, Chariline sat up, her eyes saucers.

The old man who had discovered her a few hours earlier walked in, carrying a wooden tray, flashing her a wide, unselfconscious grin, as if bursting unannounced upon young women was something he did every day.

"Master Theo said to bring you food." He placed the tray carefully on the corner table. "You must be hungry, eh? Unless you got your hands on my olives and wheat?"

"I wish I had thought of it."

The man threw his head back and laughed, Adam's apple bobbing up and down in his skinny, sun-scorched throat.

"I'm Sophocles. You're my first stowaway." He gave it some thought. "Well. The first one we didn't throw overboard right away."

"There's still time."

He laughed again. "You've got spunk, girl. Sent the master right up his mast, you did. Praying to his god."

"He's my God, too."

"Then there's hope for you. But you better eat, in case."

"In case?"

"In case the boys decide to haul you overboard. If you've got to go, you might as well do it on a full stomach."

Chariline grinned. She was beginning to like the old sailor. "What did you bring me?"

"Fish eyes and octopus entrails."

"I was hoping you would say that."

The old sailor cackled. "Spunk. That's what you have." He offered her a chipped bowl and a round of flat bread, slightly charred on one side. Chariline examined the inside of the bowl and found, to her relief, no sign of eyes or entrails.

Taking a cautious mouthful, she discovered fresh fish, hot and fragrant with a hint of olive oil and some kind of spice she could not identify. "I can see Theo stole you from the emperor's kitchens. This is tasty, Sophocles."

"Caught it myself, just now. Practically jumped in my lap."

"Maybe you can teach me that."

"How to jump in my lap? I'm a bit old for that sort of thing. But I'll see if I can oblige."

Chariline choked. "Teach me how to fish, cheeky old man."

Sophocles shook a crooked finger in her direction. "See?

Got a bit of color in your face. You were looking as faded and dried up as last year's barley." He stared down at her. "What are you doing down there, anyway? Seems you like squirming yourself into awkward places. No need to hide anymore, girl. Everyone knows you're here now."

Chariline took a bite of the warm bread. After four days of stale rations, the steaming, flaky fish and slightly lumpy bread tasted like ambrosia. "I was trying to sleep until you burst in, unannounced."

"You got eyes in your head or what? There's a perfectly good bed over here." He sat down on the edge of it and patted the blanket as if to prove his point.

"That belongs to your master, if I'm not mistaken," she said, sloshing water to wash down a mouthful of fish. "It would be rude to take it without permission."

"You're awfully cordial for a stowaway. If you are so fastidious about asking permission, perhaps you might have given it some consideration before climbing aboard our vessel."

"I know, Sophocles. I am trying not to add to my sins."

The sailor laughed. "We're just sore cause we didn't catch you, see. Made a fool of the lot of us. We like to think we are clever."

She leaned her back against the wall and stopped chewing. "Are the men very angry with me?"

Sophocles shrugged. "A few have a mind to drown you straightaway, to ensure you cause no more trouble. Most of them don't care much one way or the other. Though, of course, they wouldn't object to a good romp, if you be willing."

Chariline choked again. No wonder Theo had warned her not to step outside the cabin.

Sophocles clicked his tongue. "No need to fret, now. The master has warned them something fierce. No one would touch a hair on your head. Unless you want your hair touched, in which case, you will have no lack of volunteers."

"I have no need for volunteers," Chariline said, her voice high. "And I would be most obliged if you let the men know it." She set her empty bowl back on the tray.

"I will. Don't get your curls all tangled with worry. The boys won't do a thing to rile the master. They would kiss the ground he walks on, if he asks." He came to his feet. "I will bring you more food this evening. Seeing how the wind has died down, we'll be anchoring at the port of Myra tonight. That means fresh milk and cheese. So, porridge for supper."

"Thank you, Sophocles. And, ah . . . perhaps you might consider knocking on the door before entering next time? In case I am indisposed. I wouldn't want you to be embarrassed."

"Graces, I wouldn't be embarrassed if I saw Venus herself in her skivvies. No need to distress yourself on my account."

Chariline rubbed her forehead. "Then perhaps we should worry for me, Sophocles. Knock! Please."

"There you go issuing orders, already." The old sailor shook his head. "I knew it wouldn't take you long."

When Sophocles left, Chariline sat staring at the closed door and worried. If they were to anchor at Myra this night, a principal port with numerous connections to Caesarea, Theo might just consider bundling her back home. Pay for her passage on a ship headed the other way, while he continued west to Rome with a clear conscience.

She swallowed past a lump. A fit of coughing robbed her of breath, and she lay back, panting, feeling weak and shivery.

It seemed Telemachus had given her something besides a ride to the harbor.

———— ∞ ————

She had already wrapped Sophocles around her finger, Theo could see. While the rest of them had plain porridge for supper, the old sailor had managed to produce wildflower honey from somewhere and drizzled it all over her bowl. On the tray next to the porridge sat a shiny red-and-yellow apple. What next? A bunch of spring blossoms tied with ribbon?

Theo's chin dropped to his chest when the old man knocked before entering the cabin. Theo had tried to teach Sophocles this basic courtesy for three solid years without a glimmer of success. Not once had the crusty mariner bothered to announce his presence before banging the door open.

Two hours earlier, they had docked at the port of Myra without incident. But his men remained on high alert, concerned that if a slip of a girl could sneak past them, worse things could get by in the moonless harbor. Usually they let their guard down once they anchored. That was their time to ease back. Rest. Now they were more vigilant than they had been at sea. He could feel the tension in their stretched muscles. Everyone was acting jumpy. Theo sighed, hoping that the weight of unaccustomed watchfulness did not lead to tempers flaring.

He had spent considerable time in prayer regarding the tangle his uninvited guest had forced upon him. He knew his answer. But it had taken him some hours to make peace with it.

Strangling another sigh, he forced his legs to move toward

the cabin. She had been waiting on him for hours. Waiting to discover her fate.

He knew the waiting must have been an agony of the soul, full of fears and uneasiness. And he suspected she had the kind of robust imagination that could dream up the worst possibilities. Yet she had honored his request that she remain in the cabin. Not once had she tried to venture outside during the long delay. Anticipating a decision that must be hanging over her head like the sword of Damocles, she had still chosen to abide by his wishes.

In spite of himself, Theo felt a spark of admiration for the woman who had violated his ship.

He knocked on the sun-bleached door and, at her calm bidding, entered. Sitting on the cabin's only stool, she was leaning over a piece of papyrus, putting final touches on a drawing. He took a step closer and saw that she had sketched the *Parmys*. She had managed to reveal something of the unique personality of the vessel, its elegant lines and curves, its air of solid reliability. She had made the ship look as dependable as an ancient rock and yet as fragile as gossamer. His eyes widened with wonder. By some inscrutable trick of her pen, she had captured what he loved most about the *Parmys,* a weaving of both strength and frailty.

"You have quite an eye."

She put the papyrus away. "I am not good with ships. Buildings, now. Those I understand."

"If that's you not being good, I would like to see your best work."

Her amber eyes, almost the exact shade of her luminous skin, rested on him, full of hope. Brimming with dread.

He found he had to gulp down a mouthful of air.

Although he understood her reason for wanting to go to Rome, understood, even, the manner in which she had done it, Theo knew in his bones that her presence on his ship meant trouble. It intruded upon the easy camaraderie of his crew. It heralded the coming of burdensome strife, weeks from now, when her grandfather started looking for someone to blame.

Then again, trouble and strife did not mean Theo was free to walk away.

"You can come with us to Rome," he said. "But there are conditions."

# CHAPTER 14

*I am making a way in the wilderness
and streams in the wasteland.*

ISAIAH 43:19, NIV

Chariline exploded to her feet, her movements awkward with irrepressible excitement so that her foot tangled in the stool, flipping it against the wall. It crashed and bounced back.

Before it could catch her in the thigh with bruising force, Theo's arm flashed out, fingers grabbing the stool in midair and setting it gently, harmlessly, back on the floor.

For just a moment, she forgot about Theo's pronouncement. Forgot about Rome and her father. For a moment, she saw only Theo, lightning fast, in control, bringing order into her chaos, and her heart banged against her chest with an entirely different kind of excitement.

Shaking her head, she forced her mind back to his words, rather than the mouth that had proclaimed them. "Anything. Anything you say."

He frowned. "Do you want to know my conditions?"

She tried to tamp down a grin and failed. "Yes, please."

"I am unwilling to bring a young woman to Rome and dump her there to fend for herself."

"That would be terrible."

"Who knows what kind of trouble you will find."

"Likely the worst."

"That's what I think. It's settled then."

She suppressed a cough and leaned forward. "What is?"

What would Theo say if he realized she was coming down with something? Would he change his mind and send her home, after all? Would he consider her simply too much trouble?

Perhaps she could pretend nothing was wrong and hope whatever ailment was trying to take hold in her would pass quickly. Theo might not even notice. After all, he likely wanted to avoid her company as much as possible.

"I will be staying with my friends Priscilla and Aquila in Rome. You will come with me. They are hospitable people who love the Lord. I know they will welcome you."

Chariline's grin widened. Her greatest concern, once she managed to arrive in Rome, had always been safe lodging until she could find Vitruvia and seek her help. "Done."

"They live in a house on the Aventine. Nothing luxurious. But you will have a safe nook to yourself."

Chariline had no idea where the Aventine was. "Couldn't be better."

Theo cleared his throat. "Once we are there, we will try and find the whereabouts of this Vitruvia."

Taking a cautious step back, Chariline thought for a moment. "*We?*"

"We."

"You do not need to play chaperone and bodyguard to me, Theo."

"That is part of the condition. As I said—I am unwilling to let you fend for yourself in Rome."

Chariline's eyes narrowed. "Look—"

Theo slashed his hand in the air, cutting her off. "This is not a discussion. These are my terms. If you want to come to Rome on my ship, you agree to them. Understand?"

Chariline crossed her arms, a barricade over her chest. "What else?"

"You don't sneak anywhere by yourself. We are in this together. When I am unavailable, you wait. Either we look for Vitruvia as a team, or you don't do it at all."

He lifted his finger and pointed at her chest. "You don't lie to me. You don't hide anything from me. You don't prevaricate."

She huffed an offended breath, then wished she hadn't, as it threatened to bring on another coughing fit. "Really! Anyone would think I was a criminal."

"Or a stowaway." Theo crossed his arms, an even bigger barricade than hers. "Do we have a deal?"

Chariline considered his terms. What choice did she have? It was a miracle he had agreed to take her to Rome at all. To find her shelter on top of free transport. She could put up with his overbearing rules for a few days until she found Vitruvia. How hard could it be?

"We have a deal."

Theo shoved a hand through his hair, making it stand in spikes. For the first time, she noticed a streak of premature silver where his forehead and hairline met. It added a different aspect to his face, a touch of age that suited whatever history he had buried behind those eyes.

Noticing the angle of her gaze, he pressed a quick hand over his disordered hair, taming it, hiding the patch of silver. She wondered if vanity for this untimely sign of aging drove him to hide it with such fervor. But she sensed something deeper attached to the movement.

Something furtive and painful.

Theo had his own secrets, it seemed. Well, he was welcome to them. All she needed from him was a voyage to Rome.

"Write a letter to your aunt and let her know that you are safe. You can write another to Philip and his daughters, if you wish. I shall find a courier at the port. That way, they won't have to wait for weeks to hear from you."

"That is thoughtful. I am grateful to you." She reached into her pile, where she had placed the drawing of the *Parmys*. "This is for you," she said. "With my thanks."

He studied the drawing. "You made this before I came to tell you my decision. Were you so confident I would let you accompany us?"

She grinned. "No. I thought you would send me packing. I drew it for me. To help me remember this time. Now that I am going to sail with you all the way to Rome, I won't need a memento."

He rolled the papyrus carefully and turned to leave. At the door, he hesitated, his hand hovering by the latch. "Sophocles tells me you refuse to use the bed."

She reddened. "I am not completely devoid of manners."

He turned to face her. "Nor am I. I won't come in here while you occupy the cabin. Use the bed. I often sleep outside, in any case. Much more pleasant in the fresh air."

On that, they could agree. But Chariline refused to complain about the stuffiness of her lodgings when the very fact that she had them came as a gift. A veritable miracle.

Theo held up her drawing. "This is exceptional. A few more like it, and you can consider your passage paid for." He strode out, not waiting to see her reaction.

He thought her drawing exceptional! Good enough to be considered a payment for her passage! The part of her soul parched for admiration clutched that accolade eagerly. Pulled it close and cradled it with a touch of greed.

Shaking her head, she sank down on the edge of the bed, her legs finally giving way. "Forgive me for my pride, Iesous," she whispered. "For my hunger to receive praise. My need to be admired by others." She lay down, flinging her arms into the air. "Thank you, dear Lord. Thank you for making a way where there was no way."

She was truly bound for Rome! In a few weeks, she would discover the identity of her father and find a way back to him. Back to Cush.

With the question of her immediate future settled and the mountainous weight of worry lifted, she realized for the first time how achingly tired she felt. Stretching out her long legs, she groaned with relief. The lumpy mattress seemed to her as luxurious as a king's silken bedding. Within moments, she was asleep.

The muted sound of water sloshing against wood filled the stillness when Chariline awoke. Like a mother's lap, the narrow bed moved gently to the rhythm of the waves. Confused, she reached a groggy hand over her chest. It felt like something was sitting there. Something heavy that was making it hard to breathe. Her fingers grasped at air, finding nothing.

Pushing against the wall, she forced herself to sit up. Everything hurt, as if she had been run over by an oxcart. The small effort left her dizzy and gasping. Her breaths emerged fast and shallow, not enough air getting inside to satisfy her lungs.

She laid a trembling hand against her pounding head. The cabin was drenched in anemic light so that she could just make out the cup of water Sophocles had brought her the night before. Reaching for it, she bent forward and immediately regretted the movement. Her eyes narrowed as a mallet of pain crashed against her skull.

Her fingers trembled against the wooden cup, causing her to spill more of the lukewarm liquid than she swallowed. It burned its way down her throat, making her cough. Blindly, she slapped the cup back on the side table.

Trying to take inventory of the pounding and throbbing in her body, she forced herself to focus.

She felt sick. Sicker than she ever remembered being.

Chariline moaned. How was she to cope with illness on a ship full of men, every one of them a stranger to her?

A wave of loneliness threatened to crush her beneath its weight. For the first time, she felt homesick for her aunt. Aunt Blandina might not offer the warm affection for which

Chariline hungered, but all her life, she had tried to keep her niece safe.

Longing for Hermione and Mariamne pierced her. She ached for their soothing touch, their reassuring words. Hermione would know how to alleviate this ailment. Chariline decided that she even missed old, cantankerous Leda, who had nursed two generations of children in her family and had sat by her bed through many a minor childhood ailment. Running through Leda's dour manners lay a gruff but genuine devotion.

She rubbed a weak hand against her forehead. Her skin felt hot and clammy. Shivering in spite of the heat, she pulled the thin blanket she had pushed to the bottom of the bed back over her shoulders.

How would Hermione treat a fever?

She would tell Chariline to rest! Lacking Hermione's herbs and brews, she could at least sleep. Chariline closed her eyes. But her aching body and shivering limbs refused to cooperate. Sleep eluded her. She lay in the semidarkness, trying not to panic as the dizziness threatened to swallow her.

Another paroxysm of coughing shook her, making her chest burn. She grabbed her handkerchief and spat out the thick sputum that had started to clog her throat and lay back again, exhausted.

The cabin seemed devoid of air. Every panting breath left her more desperate for another mouthful. The fresh outdoor air beckoned like a panacea. If she could only breathe, she would feel better.

Convulsed by another excruciating fit of coughing, she realized she was drowning. Drowning in the waters of her own body and the never-ending stream of thick yellow sputum that congested her chest.

She needed help. She needed to get out of this cabin.

Supporting herself on a trembling hand, she forced herself to sit up. For a moment, she could move no further as she battled a wave of nausea. When her stomach settled, she pushed herself to stand. It took several tries, but finally, she managed to get out of the bed, bent over at the waist, panting.

She had never known such weakness. Every stride, as she moved toward the door, became a battle.

In the diminutive cabin, only three steps separated the bedside from the door. She forced her feet to move: One step. Two. She stopped. Staggered. Her body started to topple over. Reaching for the stool, she managed to keep herself upright. "Iesous!" His name emerged, a huff of air. A desperate prayer. With the last of her strength, she pressed forward.

Three.

Laying her head against the warped wood, she rested until the shivering in her limbs grew bearable. With a shaking hand, she pulled on the latch. It did not move under the feeble pressure of her fingers. She tried again, and finally, the door opened.

Gulping a breath, she stepped outside, into the pale light of the dawn. "Iesous," she whispered again, the very name a shelter.

# CHAPTER 15

—— ⚮ ——

*Heal the sick, raise the dead,*
*cure those with leprosy, and cast out demons.*
*Give as freely as you have received!*

MATTHEW 10:8, NLT

A decent wind had finally started to rise, and Theo helped with the rigging, guiding the boltrope through the canvas. The previous afternoon, as soon as they had docked at the port of Myra, he had gone in search of new business. In the harbor's noisy tavern, he had run into an acquaintance, a crusty merchant from Athens bound for Hispania. Theo had managed to offload a sizable cargo of soap on the fellow. In its place, he had purchased five dozen amphorae of wheat from Myra's massive granary. With one million mouths to feed daily, Rome was always hungry for grain. Buying the grain at Myra's higher prices would not gain him as sizable a profit as he could have had if he had managed to purchase the wheat from its source at Alexandria. But all told, he would still make a decent income from his voyage.

Feeling pleased, he stretched and turned his face into the

wind. He planned to leave the harbor within the hour. If conditions proved favorable, they might even be able to anchor at Cnidus that evening rather than face the night on the dangerous open waters of the northern Mediterranean.

He could hardly believe his eyes when he saw her leave the cabin. After all his warnings, the woman couldn't even obey one simple rule. He let Taharqa take over the rigging and marched over to where Chariline stood, leaning against the door, her eyes closed.

"I told you not to leave the cabin," he snapped, his voice tight with frustration.

"I am sorry, Theo." Her eyes opened, narrow slits against the pale sun. For the first time, he noticed the sheen of perspiration on her skin. A series of harsh-sounding coughs shook her body and she gasped, as if short of breath.

"Sick," she choked out.

She was shivering, he realized. He reached out a hand as she staggered, grabbing her arm to steady her. Her skin felt like a brazier. "You're burning up!" he exclaimed.

"I am sorry," she said again. To his utter astonishment, her limbs folded and she began to fall. Catching up her limp form before she crashed on the deck, Theo hefted her against his chest.

"Chariline!" Her eyes fluttered but did not open.

Alarmed by the heat of her body, he shifted her in his arms, settling her more securely.

Sophocles appeared by his side. "What happened?"

"She fainted." He pointed with his chin. "Door, Sophocles."

The old sailor dragged the door open and stood aside, giving Theo a wide berth. He stepped in and, with a quick glance, took in the disordered bedding, still damp from her perspiration, as if she had tossed and turned restlessly for hours. His heart hammered in his chest. He could feel his hands shaking against her back.

"Tell Taharqa to send for a physician. Quickly, Sophocles."

For once, Sophocles said nothing. He rushed out of the door like a man chased by an inferno.

Theo laid Chariline gently on the bed, keeping one hand behind her shoulder, unwilling to let her go.

Her eyes opened. "I am so sorry."

"Why do you keep saying that?"

"I'm ill."

"I gathered. Stop apologizing. It's not your fault. We'll try to get you better."

She flashed him a weak grin. The sight of the full lips, chalk-white and smiling, turned his pulse into a throbbing drum. "Are you often subject to fevers?"

"No. Never. Healthy as a horse." She half rose as a paroxysm of coughs shook her.

"I see that," he said, relieved to know the fever was not a recurring one. Sitting behind her on the bed, he shifted her body so she could lean her back against his shoulder, taking on the weight she seemed unable to bear.

He held her until the wrenching coughs subsided. Carefully, he rose, still supporting her back, while with his free hand he arranged the pillow against the wall. Trying not to jostle her too much, he settled her against the cushion. "I've sent for a physician. He will be here soon."

"I only need a bit of rest and fresh air."

"We shall see." Theo sent up a stream of silent prayer. He

noted her short, rapid breaths, the shivering limbs, the profuse sweats. He was no physician, but even he could see that whatever ailed her was no passing malady.

She gasped suddenly and sat up straight, looking around with desperation. "Your shoes," she said, as she leaned to the side.

It took him a moment to take in her meaning. He had barely enough time to leap out of the way before she vomited. Sophocles walked in just as she sat back, closing her eyes, looking wan.

"I'll clean that up," the old sailor said, his voice matter-of-fact. It wouldn't be his first time, though usually he rendered such services for his sailor brothers following a cheerful evening featuring too much wine.

"The physician?" Theo asked, his throat dry.

"Taharqa went to fetch him. Should be here soon. Lives on a street behind the harbor."

Sophocles reached a hand to stroke the top of Chariline's head. Theo had never seen the old mariner so tender. "Chin up. You'll be hale as an ox soon," he said. "Back to telling us what to do by tomorrow, I reckon."

She tried to smile and failed.

"Can you fetch her some water, Sophocles?"

"Right away, Master. And I'll bring her some of your good wine with honey." The old mariner scooted out, leaving the door open to allow the sea air into the stuffy cabin. Theo noticed a few of his men congregating too close, ogling with curiosity. He gave them a narrow-eyed look, and they dispersed as fast as tumbleweeds in a desert wind.

"Did I get your shoes?" she rasped.

"I'm too quick for you."

"That's a relief. Already owe you for passage to Rome. Don't want to add the price of shoes to my debt."

"You don't owe me anything."

Theo laid his hand against her forehead and swallowed. Her fever burned too high. Her eyes glittered with it. "Where is Sophocles with that water?" he growled.

"Don't tell him off."

"I won't." If she had asked him for his entire cargo, he would have agreed, if only to put her mind at ease.

Sophocles returned, his hands piled high with sheets and jars. "Here is water." He handed a flagon to Theo.

Glad of something to do, Theo poured a fresh cup for Chariline while Sophocles fell to his knees to clean the floor.

"Beg your pardon, Sophocles," Chariline said.

"Aw, it's just a dainty morsel. You should see what the boys manage after a good festival celebration."

"Here," Theo said, holding the cup to her lips. "Take a sip and rinse your mouth. You can spit into this bowl."

He was alarmed to find her too weak to sit up. Theo wrapped a supporting arm about her shoulders and held her as she cleaned her mouth. He mixed a bit of the honeyed wine in water and urged her to drink. She took a small sip. But he could see she had exhausted herself and laid her back against the pillow. Her eyes closed, though he sensed from the labored rhythm of her breathing that she was not asleep.

In the heap of things Sophocles had brought, he found a clean rag and, dipping it into water, dabbed her forehead, cheeks, and neck, trying to cool her off. He felt helpless. His insides squeezed with anxiety as he stared at her flushed, listless face.

"We ought to change the sheets." Sophocles pointed at the wrinkled bedding. "I brought some clean ones."

"Right." Theo frowned. The tiny cabin left little room for maneuvering. "I'll lift her. You change them."

Slipping his hands under her body, Theo lifted her once again and cradled her close to him. If she had been less weary, she might have squawked at being forced into such unusual intimacy without regard for her modesty. But in her exhaustion, she laid her head against his shoulder. Without meaning to, he allowed his hands to tighten around her, feeling a curious surge of protectiveness that caught him off guard.

"I'm not skilled as a lady's maid," Sophocles said when he had finished changing the sheets. The linens looked as wrinkled as before. At least they were dry and clean. Gently, Theo laid Chariline on the bed.

"Thank you," she murmured with a sigh.

Taharqa appeared at the door, his barrel of a chest cutting off the sunlight. "The physician is here. Teretius of Myra."

Theo exhaled with relief. It seemed to him that Chariline's condition had deteriorated even in the short hour since he first found her.

The physician, a pale-skinned man with a thin nose and clever eyes, asked Sophocles to vacate the cabin. At Theo's nod, the old mariner scurried out. Refusing to budge, Theo stood at the door like a sentinel, keeping a wary eye on Teretius. Not every physician could be trusted. There were even those who did more harm than good.

If Teretius felt any alarm at Theo's narrow-eyed scrutiny, he hid it well. Theo supposed in his line of work, the man had grown accustomed to wary inspection by the concerned relatives of his patients. He began, in a calm voice, to ask Chariline to describe her symptoms. Only after he had exhausted every inquiry did he begin an examination. Theo felt relief wash through him when he noticed the man's silent competence.

The physician pressed his ear to Chariline's back and listened to her breathing, listened intently with a large ear pressed to her chest as she coughed, examined the color of her sputum, and felt the rhythm of her pulse. Finally, he straightened.

"The acute fever, serrated pulse, and chills could be caused by many things," he said. "But the dyspnea, the severe ache in her chest, and the color of the sputa are a sign of pleuritic affections."

Theo frowned. "What is that in plain Greek?"

"She is suffering from what Hippocrates called peripneumonia. A malady of the lungs."

"What is the cure?" Theo forced his voice to sound calm.

"According to Hippocrates, you open the vein here." He held Chariline's arm up and pointed to a pale blue line before letting go. "The bleeding will balance the humors."

Chariline's eyes widened. She coughed, her face crumpling in pain. Theo reached out and clutched her hand, squeezing it softly. Her fingers wrapped around his, clinging.

Teretius shrugged. "Four hundred years later, many physicians still hold to Hippocrates' methods. I have never found them helpful with such maladies. They only weaken the patient. She is young and strong. An old man would have little hope of recovery. But your friend here . . ." He shrugged again. "She should regain her health. With careful nursing."

"She'll regain her health. Tell us what to do," Theo asked.

"We reduce the fever using the herbs I will prepare. Eight times a day, steep a spoon in boiling water and give her a full cup. You can add honey to sweeten the brew. I will also prepare an analgesic to help with the pain. Don't give her too much, as it will slow her recovery. Enough to help her sleep. Rest is the cure for this malady."

"How long?" Chariline asked, her voice wobbly. "How long will this last?"

"The worst should pass in two weeks. One if you are exceptionally strong. But you will need to rest until the cough is gone and you feel no more pain in your chest as you breathe."

She groaned. "Impossible. I won't delay the ship that long."

Theo waved away her response. Before he could assure her that they would work out a solution, Teretius spoke. "You won't have to. Once I give you the herbs, you can be on your way. You can rest on the sea as well as at the harbor."

Theo turned to the physician. "Do you not need to examine her again?"

"I could. And charge you a bundle for my services. In truth, I can do no more for her than I have already said. I will bring you the herbs and the tincture I mentioned. Follow my instructions. Skip no doses. Do you have a slave who can look after her?"

Theo squeezed the slim, shivering hand again. "I will look after her myself." He cast a glance at Chariline, noting the downturned line of her lips. Reading her thoughts with ease, he said, "Don't apologize again."

She dropped her gaze, but not before he saw the glitter of tears. Gritting his teeth, he rolled his shoulders. "I have watched over colicky horses for many a sleepless night. Nursed sick foals for days on end. An ailing girl does not daunt me. At least she won't try to kick me when I pour your brew down her throat."

The physician smiled. "I would not be too certain of that. That remedy can grow quite vile by the third day." He wiped his hands on a linen towel. "I suppose there is not much difference between nursing a sick horse and nursing a sick woman."

Theo hid a grin when Chariline gave Teretius a poisonous look.

Unfazed, the physician went on. "As long as you remain persistent and accurate in your care, I have no objection. I will deliver the herbs to your ship once I have mixed them. Lest you forget, I will write out the instructions. Follow them without fail."

"You can trust me."

"In that case, you can sail at your convenience. The herbs will do their work equally on land or at sea."

Chariline sat quietly through Teretius's instructions. As soon as the physician left the cabin, she burst out, her words overflowing like hot lava that refused to remain trapped inside, "I *am* sorry, Theo. And thank you!"

Only then did he realize that he was still holding her hand. Holding on to it as tightly as he had held on to the rope Taharqa had used to pull him to safety in the midst of the storm.

# CHAPTER 16

—— ࠋࠋ ——

*I have told you these things, so that in me you may have peace.*
*In this world you will have trouble.*
*But take heart! I have overcome the world.*

JOHN 16:33, NIV

Chariline made a face as she drank down the tincture. Her third cup of the day. Not all the honey of Attica could conceal the smell of fenugreek, an herb she had disliked since childhood. Four days into her sickness, and the fever had not budged. Her body still shivered and quaked, and she continued to feel as if she was drowning with every labored breath.

Theo had barely left her side since the physician's visit. His chin, shadowed by the start of a thick, dark beard he had not had time to shave, matched the dark circles under his eyes. He had made up a pallet for himself on the cabin floor, in the narrow cave she had occupied earlier, though she suspected he slept little.

Sophocles seeped her herbs and prepared her tinctures. He made her fish broth and warm bread. But Theo would not allow him to step inside the cabin. It took her a day to realize he feared contagion. The physician had warned them that the disease would be deadly to an old man. She could not bear the thought of causing Sophocles harm.

She remembered sitting next to Telemachus on his cart, and the way he had hacked away the morning she had sneaked onto the *Parmys*. She hoped he had fared better than she had.

She worried most for Theo. Was her mere presence a danger to him? What if he fell ill? Yet regardless of how much she urged, he refused to leave her side, irked by her pleading.

She had learned that Theo was unshakable as granite. The man's blood pulsed with loyalty. Once he made a commitment, nothing would shake it. In his steady, quiet way, Theo *claimed* people. Took them into his heart and made a home for them there. Gave them a place where they belonged. And for some strange reason, he had claimed *her*, the stowaway on his ship, the Great Inconvenience, the thorn in his side. Claimed her alongside Sophocles and Taharqa and only Iesous knew how many others.

In the end, she admitted defeat and gave up urging him to leave. Instead, she did her best to accept his care with grace.

For all she had learned about Theo over the piling, restless hours, in many ways he still remained a mystery. She had tried asking him polite questions about his past. His parentage. His upbringing. She had never met a man so adroit at deflecting personal inquiries. After four days, she still did not know much about him. She had laid herself bare before the man. Shared the mortifying secrets of her family. Yet not once had Theo returned the favor. Whatever mystery haunted him, he guarded it jealously.

She watched him now as he sat leaning against the wall, writing on a roll of papyrus, his brows knotted in thought.

"Are you writing a love letter?" she teased and was surprised by the flush that spread over his cheeks.

Her belly spasmed. Did Theo have a sweetheart? To her shock, she found the notion more unpleasant to swallow than Teretius's disgusting tincture.

"No," Theo said. "No love letters here."

Chariline exhaled. "Surely not your accounts. That look of deadly concentration could not be for a column of numbers."

"No."

Theo's features grew inscrutable. Closed off like the iron gates of a walled city when the enemy approached. The fever may have turned her mind into a bog, but she knew it was time to back away. Gingerly.

He rolled up his secret papyrus and set it aside with a thwack. "Do you want to know one of Yeshua's favorite sayings?" he asked, changing the subject without even a pretense at subtlety.

"Yeshua?" she asked. He pronounced the Lord's name the Jewish way, having come to faith through the friendship of the famous rabbi, Paul, and his friends Priscilla and Aquila. But although he used a different version of the Master's name, he said it the way Hermione said "Iesous." With a world of emotion. With honest love. Like a son to a beloved father.

"Yeshua." He nodded.

"Tell me."

Theo had set a rhythm for the long hours they spent together. In the mornings, they prayed. In the afternoons, he would recite Scripture or tell a story about the Lord.

Sometimes they just talked about the places they had visited, few in Chariline's case, but eclectic and fascinating in Theo's. He was insatiably curious. Having never been to Cush, he asked endless questions about Meroë and seemed fascinated by the most mundane details. In the evenings, they prayed again, Theo often taking the lead, as if this was a natural part of his own routine that he shared with her.

And in between, she drank a lake of steeped herbs. Enough to drown in. Enough to float on.

To add to her misery, Theo plied her with Teretius's sticky analgesic paste to dull her pain so that she could sleep. Still the fever raged, fraying her at the edges. The endless, suppurative cough continued to afflict her, robbing her of breath.

She was careful never to complain. Not one word. She would not reward Theo's determined efforts to nurse her back to health with spurious grumbling.

"Take heart," Theo said, and in the fog of fever, it felt as if he had read her thoughts and wanted to encourage her.

"Thank you."

"I mean, that was one of Yeshua's favorite sayings. *Take heart.* He used to say it to all sorts of people. He said it to his disciples when they were overcome by fear. Said it to a paralytic man with no hope for healing. Said it to a woman who had been sick for twelve years. *Take heart.*

"Take heart when you are afraid. When you are overwhelmed by trouble. When you are ashamed. When you are hopeless. When you are despondent. *Take heart.*

"Not an empty, meaningless phrase, you understand? Because Yeshua never wasted words. When he whispered *take heart*, he was making a mighty proclamation. An impartation.

A divine assurance. His consolation and his promise present in those words. *Take heart,* he said, and his Spirit stepped into the words to inhabit them with power and comfort."

Theo leaned close, his voice growing quiet. "*Take heart,* Chariline. Yeshua is here with you, as surely as he was with the bleeding woman and the paralyzed man."

It was not until he said the words that she realized she had lost heart. Somewhere in the endless hours of feverish pain, discouragement had managed to wriggle inside and take residence. Spreading its roots.

*Take heart.*

Theo's lips had formed the words. His voice had spoken them. But Chariline felt Iesous capture them. Felt his Spirit impart strength to them. Her eyes drifted closed. Startled, she became aware of the weight of fear she had been carrying without realizing.

*Take heart.*

The words reverberated in her spirit, more powerful than Teretius's herbs. The burden of fear sloughed off slowly, measure by measure, and peace inhabited where there had once been the darkness of discouragement. The drowning pressure that had been sitting on her chest lightened. And she fell asleep.

When she awoke, the fever no longer raged but burned low, a simmering heat that lacked its initial fury.

"You look better," Theo said, in surprise.

She studied him with the fresh insight of a mending body. "You look terrible."

Theo grinned and rubbed his scratchy cheek. "I'm insulted."

"Theo, you need to leave me for a few hours. Rest. Eat. Or you will also fall ill. And take time to bathe! My nose is starting to work again."

Theo laughed. "Sophocles said you were bossy."

———cᴕᴐ———

When Theo left, closing the door softly behind him, Chariline set to work. She might have told Theo to bathe, but her own need for a good wash surpassed his. Stripping off her stained, wrinkled tunic, she dipped a cloth in the tepid basin of water Sophocles had delivered earlier in the day. On a ship overflowing with soap, she could not find a single sliver in the cabin. Too afraid to ask Theo lest he forbid her from too much activity, she settled for a simple rinse, washing away the sweat and grime of fever.

By the time she finished her ablutions, hair braided in a neat rope down her back, she felt weak with overexertion, legs quivering like jellyfish tentacles. It took all her strength to fetch a fresh linen tunic from her bundle and draw it over her head. When she was done, she lay back against her pillow, panting with exertion, but feeling oddly improved.

She ignored the slight nausea born of fatigue and allowed herself a tremulous smile of triumph. She was not dead. She was not in Caesarea. She was more or less clean, on a ship bound for Rome. And perhaps, just perhaps, in spite of the endless trouble she had caused him, Theo had started to look upon her as a friend.

Her new friend knocked on the door much too soon for her liking, a certain sign that he had not taken time to rest. He had accepted her advice to bathe, however, and now stood in a white tunic that made his bronzed skin shimmer like a polished shield, his hair combed carefully to hide its tuft of silver.

"You changed," he said, sounding surprised.

She drew a hand down the light-blue linen of her garment. "I had been wearing that tunic since Caesarea. You could have grown a flower patch in its dirt."

Theo drew the stool near the bed and sat. This close, she could smell cypress with a hint of sweet styrax on his skin. Inexplicably, she felt blood rushing to her cheeks.

For four days, the man had fed her one spoonful at a time, held her as she drank, wiped her sweat. For four days, he had sat closer than this. But she had been too sick to appreciate the intimacy of their position.

Now she was well enough to take note of it. Her insides twisted, as if they, too, were blushing.

Theo shifted. Closer. For a moment, she squeezed her eyes shut.

"I have a surprise for you," Theo said, his deep voice sounding pleased.

"We are about to arrive in Rome?" she croaked hopefully.

He chuckled. "Not even close. This time of year, a bigger ship might get us to Rome's harbor at Puteoli in two weeks. But *Parmys* will need five. Six, if the winds prove ornery."

Her mouth turned dry. She leaned away until her back hit the wall. Six weeks! That did not leave her much time to find Vitruvia, discover the identity of her father, and deal with Sesen's plot against the queen. Her hand fisted against her belly. "What surprise?"

"You are coming out on the deck today. To sit in the sun.

Teretius told me that once the fever became less acute, fresh air would do you good."

"Truly?" She grinned.

He grinned back. "Taharqa and Sophocles have made a nice chair for you. Come and see."

Chariline hung her legs over the bed. Holding on to the rough wooden edge, she pushed herself up. A deep cough rattled at the bottom of her lungs and made its way out, leaving her gasping. Without warning, her knees buckled.

Before she could collapse, Theo's hand snaked out to wrap around her waist, pulling her to him. For a moment they stood, chest to chest, Theo holding her up.

Her heart raced. He shifted his hold and, grasping her under the knees, swung her up into his arms.

She gulped a startled breath.

"Allow me to be your chariot," he said with perfect courtesy, but his voice emerged husky.

He was only being kind she reminded herself. But her galloping pulse had no interest in courtesy or kindness. Tucking her runaway feelings out of sight, she lay against his chest like an unyielding timber pole.

As they emerged onto the deck, she worried the men would ogle her with curiosity, if not outright animosity. But they remained busy at their tasks, ignoring her presence. She suspected that either Theo or Taharqa had warned them to leave her in peace.

Theo carried her to a low chair, which had been set up at the stern of the ship, and deposited her gently into the downy folds of a thick cushion. As his hands withdrew, she felt at once relieved and disconsolate, as if she had lost something precious.

From her seat, she could see Taharqa at one of the steering oars. The ship had two tillers on opposite sides of the stern, but it did not always require two pilots. Depending on the wind, it could be manned by means of only one of the rudders.

She drew a mouthful of sea air into her chest and felt life return to her veins. "What a beautiful day," she whispered.

Someone had erected a wide canopy made of canvas and rope over her chair, protecting her from the harsh rays of the sun. Theo adjusted the angle, throwing more shade over her. "We will start slow. Just a few minutes today."

"Theo." She held his gaze, something she could do now that she was out of his arms. "I can never repay your goodness."

He yawned and stretched. "Don't want repayment. Besides, I need to keep you alive. Clearly, you like my soap, and devoted customers are hard to come by."

———

The fever broke after eight days. But it wasn't until the third week of her convalescence that the painful coughs and the exhausting dyspnea finally ceased. Not until then did Theo consider Chariline well enough to be in the company of Sophocles.

After that, the old mariner fell into the habit of seeking her out every day, doing his chores while sprawled next to her so they could converse. One afternoon, as she slouched in her comfortable chair, working on a new design, Sophocles dropped by her side, a large spread of sailing canvas on his lap.

"Can you sew?" he asked hopefully, holding up the unraveling leather patches in the corners of the stiff linen.

"Not a stich. Can you draw?"

"Not a stroke." He pulled a large needle out of a leather pouch and set to repairing his canvas with dexterous fingers.

"Why is the ship called *Parmys*?" she asked, turning her attention back to her scroll, another drawing of Theo's beloved ship.

"It was named after the master's mother."

She frowned. "What kind of name is *Parmys*? It isn't Greek or Latin."

Taharqa, who stood within earshot manning the steering oar, said, "It's Persian. Theo's mother was a freed slave."

Chariline set the drawing aside. Finally, someone willing to shed light on Theo's mysterious background. "Who freed her?"

Sophocles tightened an unraveled cord of leather. "Master Justus's father, wasn't it? Before he married her?"

Taharqa made a sound of assent in his throat but did not expand any further.

Recognizing the name of Theo's brother, she asked, "*Their* father, you mean? He freed their mother?"

"They have the same mother, but different fathers," Sophocles explained.

Taharqa gave the old sailor a quelling look. Sophocles shrugged. "It's all I know, anyway. No need to beat me up with your menacing stares."

Chariline considered Sophocles's answer. Theo's mother must have been widowed, or divorced, and then remarried. She had a vague recollection of Theo mentioning an adoptive father. What was he called? Something Greek. Galenos! That was it. Was Galenos Justus's father? Perhaps after having Theo, Parmys had been widowed, and Galenos had married her and adopted Theo.

No. That could not be. Slaves were forbidden to marry. If Justus's father had been the one who freed Parmys, that meant she could not have been married before him.

She leaned forward. Theo may have been born to a slave woman. An unmarried slave woman. "Sophocles, who is older? Theo or Justus?" she asked.

"Justus."

So Parmys had been freed by Justus's father, married him, and had Justus. She must have married Theo's father after that. Obviously, Theo's father had died, and Galenos had adopted him. Adoptions were common enough in Roman society.

"How long have you known Theo?" she asked Sophocles curiously.

"Three years now." Another unraveled cord tightened under the nimble fingers. "Found me in a heap at the port of Alexandria, he did. Unwanted flotsam, that's what I was. Too old to be of proper use on a sailing vessel. My last master dumped me there and said I wasn't worth the food I consumed.

"I sat on the jetty not knowing what to do with myself. Been a sailor since before I turned twelve. Sixty years I been sailing, and of a sudden, I am not fit for the sea.

"A dozen men and women walked past me by the hour. Not one offered a hand. Master Theo, he stopped. Asked my name. Asked me where I used to work and if I had any skills. Hired me on the spot."

She smiled. "Sounds like Theo, all right."

Sophocles set to tackling another tear in the canvas. "I can't do what these louts do, anymore." He pointed his chin at two sailors adjusting the spars in the square sail. "Too old to climb up and down or pull on oars or haul rigging. But I know how to cook . . . some. And the master isn't particular. Pays me the same as he pays the other men." Sophocles grinned. "I'm wiser now and don't spend it all on cheap wine. Got me a little nest egg." He stretched his back and gazed into the sea.

"Almost didn't get to spend it, though. Nearly drowned in that storm."

"I am sorry, Sophocles! Thank God you survived."

"Thank Master Theo. He jumped into the water to pull me out. Just about drowned his own fool self, so a useless sailor wouldn't die."

"I told you, old man," Theo said, appearing on silent, bare feet, his shadow falling over them. "Saved you, because Yeshua saved me. He is the one you should thank. If not for his help, we would both have drowned that day."

Sophocles looked up. "Haven't believed in a god since I was a boy. But I like yours. If he is a made-up story, he is a sweet one."

"He's no story, Sophocles."

Sophocles nodded. Under his breath he said, so only Chariline could hear, "When I look into his eyes, I almost believe it."

# CHAPTER 17

—⌘—

*And behold, I am with you always, to the end of the age.*

MATTHEW 28:20

"Are you going to tell me what you've been writing in that scroll?" Chariline held up her own sheet of papyrus and examined the outline of the house she had been drawing. She had decided she would design a garden for Vitruvia as a gift.

"No," Theo said without looking up.

They were sitting next to each other on the deck, Chariline on her chair, where she spent several hours each day, and Theo stretched out on his side. In the sun, his gray eyes turned into a peculiar shade of silver, ringed by black. Chariline realized she was staring and looked away.

"I show *you* all my drawings," she pointed out.

"And they are very good. You still owe me several, by the way."

"I gave you three!"

"I would like a villa next."

"Would you, now?"

"Not a drawing. But a proper architectural design. With construction plans."

"And what would you do with the plans of a villa?"

"Build it."

"Where?"

"On my land."

"And where is that?"

"Aren't you full of questions."

"I can't design a villa for the shores of heaven. I need to know about the land. Is it flat? What kind of soil does it have? Does it enjoy a mild climate? Does it have access to water?"

"It's an olive grove just outside Corinth with soft, rolling hills. One day, I would like to build a villa in it. And I am commissioning you to design it."

Chariline sat up. "Do you mean it?"

"Perhaps." Theo shrugged. "I would have to check your calculations, first. Make certain you have made no grievous errors that would bring the walls down over my head the first time there is a strong wind."

She laughed. Theo had an abhorrence for sums and calculations. As soon as he had discovered her dexterity for geometry was matched by her talent for arithmetic, he had dumped reels of his accounts on her lap and asked her help for his dealings with the officials at Rome.

She had embraced the work with enthusiasm. Never mind her passage to Rome. She owed the man for the hefty physician's fees. For the big bag of curative herbs. For her food. And likely, she owed him her very life. No physician could have provided better care for her as she battled fever than Theo's quiet, capable ministrations. He had pulled her through the darkest days of her infirmity.

"Do you truly own an olive grove?" she asked.

"I do. A gift from my brother."

"If I owned my own olive grove, you couldn't convince me to leave it. Justus sounds like an exceptional man."

"I could not ask for a better brother," Theo said, his voice grave. But Chariline saw something flicker in the gray eyes, like an old specter, present, yet invisible.

She sighed. "I wish I had a brother. Or a sister. Besides Aunt Blandina and my grandparents, the closest person I have to family is Natemahar."

"The Cushite treasurer?"

She nodded. "I've known him longer than I've known my grandparents. But living on different continents means I don't see him often." She shrugged. "It can grow lonely."

Theo rolled up his papyrus and placed it in the wooden box where he kept his writing implements. "My friend Aquila once told me that the Lord made a special promise to his followers. After his resurrection, he told them, *I am with you always.*" Theo's gaze bored into her. "*Always. To the end of the age.*"

"I know," she said.

"You do here." He pointed to his temple. "But not yet here, I think." He pressed his hand over his heart. "I tell you this because I understand the difference. There was a time when I needed to hold on to that promise tightly. Needed it to pierce my heart."

She slid closer. "You were lonely?"

"I felt forsaken."

He stared into the distance. "Day after day, the world went

on around me as before. But I had come *to the end of the age* in my life. The age of dreams. The age of hopes. The age of belonging. It had all come tumbling around me. And I needed the *always* of God in the midst of those endings.

"I needed to learn that Yeshua does not abandon. He does not walk away. He does not leave and forsake. His *always* is trustworthy. Even when the people you love fail you, he does not. He does not leave you. He is with you. Always.

"This is what I learned in that dark time, Chariline. Though I had no mother and no father, though I did not have the desire of my heart, I was never alone.

"You may have no brother or sister. I don't know if you will ever find your father. But I do know this. As one who calls God *Abba, Father,* you are never alone. Your earthly father may have abandoned you. Knowingly left you, even. But your heavenly Father will not. He will remain with you always. And in his presence, there is fullness of joy. Soul-deep calm. Favor and grace."

He dropped his head, as if in thought. "Don't bank your life on finding Vitruvia. Or your father. Don't bank your life on besting your grandfather." He looked up. "Those things may come to pass, or they may not. You may find your father and feel lonely in spite of it. Feel the sting of his abandonment worse than you do now. But whatever happens, you can bet your whole life on this: God is not an abandoner. Yeshua will not leave you or forsake you."

He grabbed his wooden casket and rose to his feet. "Lecture finished." Flashing a smile, he bowed like a courtier at the Kandake's court. "Now, I must attend to my duties."

Chariline followed him with her eyes as he disappeared

into the hold. He had revealed more of himself to her in the past hour than he had in all the days she had known him. And yet, thinking over his words, his confession of pain and loneliness, she realized that she still knew as little about this enigmatic man as she had known before. He was, she decided, a true paradox, at once candid and secretive.

With a start, it dawned upon Chariline that she longed to *know* Theo. Know him to his core with no secrets between them. She sensed in this man a goodness, a depth, both of faith and emotion, that she had rarely encountered in anyone. Everything in her was drawn to him.

With creeping dread, she began to suspect that Theo's decision to withhold a part of himself from her would one day prove as painful as the worst agony she had suffered during her infirmity.

———∽∾———

In spite of the prevailing westerly winds, the currents of the northern Mediterranean allowed the *Parmys* to swallow up the leagues on the open sea at a steady pace. Encountering few obstacles, in the fifth week of their journey, they arrived at the port of Syracuse, where they dropped anchor for the night.

Tucked into the southeastern corner of Sicily, Syracuse offered all the lavish charm of a prosperous Roman city. As well as two theaters, the city boasted an amphitheater, temples, altars, and aqueducts, not to mention numerous taverns offering a bottomless fountain of wine and fermented barley. Not that Chariline got to see any of it. She had promised to remain on board until they arrived at Puteoli.

After interminable days on the sea, *Parmys's* men abandoned ship as soon as they anchored in the early afternoon, ready for some entertainment. At Theo's behest, Chariline wrote new letters for her aunt and Mariamne, which he entrusted to couriers at the harbor.

Gazing longingly at the pretty port from the confines of her chair, Chariline smiled in welcome when Sophocles returned from his jaunt early, carrying a hefty satchel. He dropped next to her, tucking his legs under him in a tight fold. From his satchel, he extracted a fresh pomegranate and delicate almond cakes, still warm from the ovens.

"A gift for you," he said.

"Sophocles! You shouldn't spend your money on me."

"Well." The old man started fiddling with the strings hanging from his satchel, looking cagey.

"Well, what?"

"I only have the money because of you."

"I don't understand."

"When you got sick, we made a bet, see? The boys and I. The boys all said the gods had cursed you for sneaking on our ship without permission. They were sure you would die. I bet them you wouldn't. I knew you were too stubborn."

Chariline smirked.

"Besides, the master was praying for you. Day and night. In between fluffing your pillows and wiping your brow, he prayed. His god had to cure you, didn't he? Or he would never hear the end of it."

Chariline cuffed Sophocles on the shoulder. "Some respect, if you please."

He laughed. "Well? Eat up. You won't get another chance. Not like I'm going to bake you almond cake."

Chariline carefully divided the cakes and, using Sophocles's short knife, cut the pomegranate into two halves.

"I've got my own," the old man said.

"It's not for you. It's for Theo. Since he did all the praying and the arduous work of keeping me alive, it seems he deserves at least half the winnings."

"Come to think of it, he does."

White flyaway hair blew into the old man's wrinkled brow. The saucy grin, always so close to the surface, flashed, revealing mostly toothless gums. Chariline's heart swelled with a burst of affection. She wished her grandfather were more like Sophocles. Warm-hearted and playful. Bringing her head close, she whispered, "Iesous sent Theo to find you when you were deserted in Alexandria, Sophocles. Sent him to save you. The Lord must love you very much."

The old mariner's face fell. "I'm not worth saving, girl. Not worth loving, either."

"But you are. Theo almost died proving it to you."

The brown, opalescent eyes filled. "Since that day, I been trying to be a better man. When someone so good as the master is willing to die for you, it gives your life a new worth."

Chariline nodded. "Someone even better than Theo did die for you, Sophocles. Died so that all your past mistakes might be redeemed and your future made secure. Died to restore to you the worth you lost. His name is Iesous, or as your master calls him, Yeshua. And he loves you dearly, Sophocles."

Sophocles hung his head. He didn't say a word, but in the reflection of the setting sun, Chariline saw a lone tear sparkle on his cheek.

———&———

Two days later, they arrived at the harbor of Puteoli, marking the end of Chariline's sea voyage. She was days away from Rome. But she could not leave the ship just yet.

Theo had left to arrange a berth for his ship and to organize the short-term storage of his goods at a nearby warehouse. He had forbidden her from leaving the *Parmys* without him, and she stood in the afternoon sun, chafing at the required delay.

Theo's men were a whirl of activity around her, transporting the heavy amphorae of soap and grain onto the dock. Impatient to disembark, Chariline leaned against the sternpost and studied the harbor. Having grown up in a port city, she had expected to be met with familiar sights and sounds. But Puteoli proved a new experience. Not as charming or beautiful as Caesarea, the ancient harbor of Puteoli was sprawling and industrial.

The sounds of dozens of exotic languages mixed with the shrill cry of seagulls. Dockers pushed barrels of wine; slaves loaded crates full of cloth and pottery; sailors off-loaded more wheat than she had ever seen in one place. The massive flat-bottomed ships that had carried the grain from Alexandria could not actually dock at the harbor. Immense as floating cities, the ships had to drop anchor in the open sea while smaller vessels carried their cargo to shore.

A line of poorly dressed women caught her attention, and Chariline turned to study them more closely. Only then did she notice the chain that bound them together at the neck. Some were half naked, exposed to the sun and the leering

188 || JEWEL OF THE NILE

gazes of men. They stumbled toward the quay, urged on by the cracking whip of the man who shadowed them. A slave trader.

"A terrible sight," Theo said grimly, startling her. She would never grow accustomed to how silently the man moved.

"Appalling," she agreed. The Roman world was built on the back of such horrors. She remembered that Theo's own mother had been a slave, which explained the bleak cast of his features as he watched the deplorable scene unfold.

He stepped away from the sternpost. "We can disembark now. Are you ready?"

Chariline picked up her small bundle and waved it at him. He took the knotted sheet from her hand and helped her down the gangplank. And finally, after six long weeks, her feet touched land.

———— ༄ ————

Like a hawk tracking its prey, the warrior watched her as she made her way to the quay. He was not going to lose her this time. He recognized the tall man walking next to her as the one he had seen briefly on the ship. He preferred not to tangle with that one. He would, if he had to. But for the moment, he wanted to wait and see if a better opportunity presented itself.

He did not have long to wait. His mouth opened in a satisfied smile. The man left the girl to speak to his Cushite captain. They were only a few steps farther up the quay. Enough for the warrior to accomplish what he must. He had looked forward to this moment for a long time.

The girl stood at the edge of the water, staring at the elegant trireme that was preparing for departure, fifty oars up on each side. The oars came down in perfect unison, as if conducted by music.

The warrior timed his movements with infallible precision.

The trireme's oars lifted out of the water and swung up.

He grabbed the girl from behind in a hard grip, his fingers digging into her tunic and skin. Pulling her back, he gained all the momentum that the solid muscles of his arms and back gave him.

She gave a strangled cry. In the cacophony of the harbor, no one heard.

He heaved her body in an arc and flung her into the path of the first oar. Right where she would be hit a mighty blow to the skull.

The oars came down just as she landed in the water, headfirst.

# CHAPTER 18

— ✦ —

*He will send from heaven and save me;*
*he will put to shame him who tramples on me.*

PSALM 57:3

Chariline felt her body fly through the air. From the corner of her eye she noticed the trireme's oars. Coming down.

Her head hit the water. She was blinded for a moment by foam, her eyes stinging from sea salt and the flotsam of the port. The momentum of her fall had placed her in the direct path of the first oar as it descended toward her.

There was nothing she could do to stop it.

Having grown up by the sea, Chariline had learned to swim like a fish. But even her skills in the water could not save her from being struck by that oar.

She felt them then. Forty-nine oars lowering as one, churning the waters around her, coming within a handsbreadth of bruising and breaking joints and bones. But the first oar, the one that was descending toward her head, stopped. For a tiny fraction, as time stood still, she saw it, jiggling just above her, as though caught, stuck on some unforeseen impediment, the rower frantically trying to loosen it.

Every instinct demanded that she swim up, toward sunlight and breath and shore. But she knew that the safest way was down, below the striking reach of the oars. Any moment now, that solid piece of thick oak, created for wrestling with oceans, would manage to lower, and if she was not out of its way, she would get herself battered and likely drowned.

Her lungs were still not working at full capacity, and they were beginning to burn already, demanding air. Chariline ignored their clamor and pushed toward the murky bottom. She swam past the giant hull, past the oars, which had pulled out and were descending again, once more directly headed her way. Feet scissoring, arms stroking rhythmically, she pushed herself lower, out of their path, until she started seeing black dots before her eyes.

Finally, she saw that the slow-moving trireme had floated just beyond her. A cylinder of safe space opened up above her in the sea. With the last of her strength, she pushed toward the light. Clinging to the edge of the pier, she gulped in the air, her vision blurred. Theo and Taharqa flew to her side, almost slipping into the water in their haste to reach her.

"What happened?" Theo cried as he fished out her dripping body safely onto shore. "Are you all right?"

Chariline could only manage a slight nod.

"Did you faint again?"

She shook her head.

"By the time I saw you, you were already pulling yourself out. It's a miracle you weren't struck by one of the oars of that trireme."

Thinking of the oar becoming stuck at the last moment, barely missing her head, she could only agree. A miracle, indeed.

Theo had stripped off his light cloak and was wrapping it around her shivering body. "Did you trip?"

She shook her head, again.

Taharqa, who had crouched on one knee next to her, squinted. "What then?"

"Someone pushed me," she managed, finally.

"You mean they ran into you, and you fell over?"

"I mean they grabbed me from behind and shoved me into the water."

Theo's face jerked back as if slapped. "Are you certain?"

"I can still feel the marks of his fingers on my back."

"Did he rob you?"

Chariline reached for the leather pouch tied to her belt. "Still here." Her bundle also sat untouched on the quay, getting damp with sea spray.

Theo shook his head. "I don't understand."

Chariline bit her lip. "Natemahar warned me that trying to find my father would be a dangerous undertaking. He seemed to think the queen would not approve."

Hauling her to her feet, Theo pulled the edge of the cloak over her sopping head. "You think the queen of Cush sent someone to assassinate you?"

"It sounds mad, I know. But someone did just try to kill me."

"How would the queen of Cush know you would be arriving at Puteoli?"

Chariline's shoulders sagged. "I don't know."

—⁂—

The warrior ground his teeth. He could not believe the girl had survived that fall. He had arranged for the perfect accident. She should be dead twice over. He had pitched her into the water at the perfect angle. He could not believe his eyes when the oar refused to lower, stuck in the air like a defective wing.

After that, she had remained underwater for so long that he grew hopeful. Perhaps she had drowned in spite of the unfortunate obstacle. But the creature would not die.

He wanted to crush her under his feet like a lizard. He wanted to squash her in his fist like a ripe melon.

He would have to wait. Yet again.

With those two goons standing on either side of her like a blockade of impenetrable muscle, he could not lay a hand on her now. Once again, he was reduced to stalking her in the shadows, looking, but not touching.

He watched as the Cushite captain hired a two-horse *rheda*, and the three piled in with their baggage and set off on the link road north toward Capua. The warrior smashed his fist into a clay amphora. It cracked, spilling some smelly spice all over the wet concrete.

"Hey, you can't do that!" a docker cried. The warrior turned one revolution to face the man. Seeing the look on his face, the docker backed up several steps.

"Where do I hire a horse?" the warrior snapped.

—⁂—

It took four days, two roads, and three inns, including the famed Tre Taverne, before they arrived in Rome. Determined to put her chilling experience at the port of Puteoli behind her, Chariline started to enjoy herself more the closer they came to the great capital of the empire.

They traveled most of the way on the famed Via Appia, its heavy stone and lime mortar foundation covered by lava blocks, which made for a relatively comfortable ride in the horse-drawn *rheda*. Passing a series of breathtaking monuments, travertine facades glowing like an oyster shell in the sun, the architect in Chariline sat breathless, studying the grandeur.

The way grew more jammed with crowds the closer they drew to the city, the monuments flanking the road giving way to shops and hawkers. The sheer noise, smell, and denseness of the population was dizzying. Municipal law forbade the use of carts and carriages within Rome in daytime hours to help with the incessant congestion. Theo arranged for their baggage to be delivered to his friends' home that evening, and they resumed their journey on foot. Clinging tight to Chariline's hand, Theo made sure that the crowd would not sweep her away.

Upon entering the city gates, Chariline spied a sprawling bathhouse immediately to their right, its slightly faded facade not detracting from its splendor.

"They carry my soap," Theo said, noting her stare.

"When can I visit?"

"There is a better one when we turn left on Via Nova."

"Do *they* carry your soap?"

"Indeed."

"Then they are worthy of my patronage."

The corner of Theo's lips tipped. "We are entering the

Aventine neighborhood. At its northern border, some residents can watch the chariot races at the Circus Maximus from their rooftops. You can even see the Caesar's palace and gardens from some of the taller villas."

"Can you see them from your friends' rooftop?"

"No. Aquila and Priscilla's house is on the south side of the Aventine in a more modest neighborhood. They are workers of leather. Their shop occupies most of the ground floor, and their private chambers are on the second story."

It dawned on Chariline that she was about to oblige two perfect strangers to welcome her into their home. "Are you sure my presence will not inconvenience them?"

"Quite sure. They are used to welcoming strangers. Set your mind at ease on that score. They will know to expect you. I sent them a note ahead of us."

Priscilla and Aquila's house, a rectangular, two-story building, had whitewashed walls that were brightened with clusters of pink flowers cascading from several oleander bushes. The main gate was flanked by two jutting chambers. Through the open shutters of large windows, she saw that one chamber housed a shop and the second a workshop where a couple of men were cutting a large piece of leather.

A fine black awning embossed with a scalloped design at the edges hung jauntily over the gate, providing shade to visitors. Theo rapped his knuckles on the open door and called out a short greeting.

A woman with dark red hair arranged in a coronet of loops and braids hurried toward them. "Theo! I am so happy to see you, my dear." She spoke an elegant Latin, more suited to a senator than a worker of leather.

Theo's eyes seemed to melt at the sound of her voice. "Priscilla. It's good to see you."

"And Captain Taharqa! How is your dear wife?"

Taharqa was married? Chariline remembered to snap her gaping mouth shut.

The big captain's handsome features softened as he smiled at Priscilla. "She is well. Thank you. And she loved the red leather cloak you sent her."

Chariline stared at the woman whose mere presence seemed to have transformed her companions from men to puddles. Close up, she saw that Priscilla was striking rather than pretty, with an angular face, delicate lips, and skin so fair it seemed to glow.

Her bright-blue eyes held more warmth than cordiality as they rested on Chariline. "You are most welcome, my dear." She managed to imbue each word with such sincerity that Chariline immediately joined the puddle.

"Thank you for allowing me to stay at your home."

"Where else would you stay?" She took a step back. "Where are my manners? Come inside, everyone. You must be exhausted from all your travels."

Walking through a passage, they approached a bright courtyard. An open door on her left gave Chariline a glimpse of the shop, which had two long stone countertops and neat shelves stacked with colorful leather samples.

The long, narrow entryway led to a courtyard so fiercely verdant, it made Chariline stand still in astonishment. The scent of flowers mingled with that of mint, thyme, basil, and tarragon. Around a small fountain in the center, someone had created a garden made up of a profusion of herbs, climbing cucumbers, peas, beans, and fat squash plants whose wide leaves spread like a viridescent cloak. On the outer edges of the courtyard, flowers bloomed in rich clumps of color, roses, lilies, violets, and irises turning the small space into a canvas of purples, pinks, and whites. Silvery and mossy greens nestled against dots of yellow and orange.

The combined explosion of color and perfume made Chariline gasp. "It's breathtaking!"

"And most of it tastes good," Priscilla said.

From one of the rooms lining the left side of the courtyard, the sound of fierce barking emerged.

"That's Ferox." Priscilla made a face. "He has taught himself how to open closed doors, I'm afraid. Any moment now, he is going to bound out here. Forgive his enthusiasm. He's entirely safe."

Before Priscilla had finished speaking, a large dog with black shaggy fur ran toward them, barking.

"Ferox!" Theo cried, and the hefty creature rose to place his paws on his chest. His big tongue darted out toward Theo's face, doing a good job as a face towel.

Theo laughed, avoiding the missile. "Sit, you monster." When Ferox obeyed, he rubbed the black floppy ears. "Still no manners, I see."

The dog stared adoringly at Theo, tongue lolling, before turning to Chariline. She gulped, thinking the beast might try to jump on her the way he had Theo. As if sensing her dread, Ferox merely stuck his black muzzle into her hand, sniffed, and giving her a friendly lick, settled down once more.

"I apologize for our beast." Priscilla rolled her eyes. "Come. Let me show you to your rooms. Chariline, we have put you in my son's room. Marcus is visiting his steward at his country estate in Ostia."

Chariline frowned in confusion. Their son owned a country estate?

"Theo and Captain Taharqa, you can share Uncle Benyamin's chambers. He insisted on accompanying Marcus, saying the boy is too young to travel alone."

"I am sorry to miss Benyamin," Theo said.

"I think he was looking for an excuse to vacate the premises. We have a large order due, and the workshop has been toiling far longer hours than usual. Which is why Aquila is not here to greet you in person. He asked me to apologize. He will join us for dinner."

Priscilla turned to Chariline. "Are you hungry, my dear? Thirsty? Would you like to visit the baths? I want you to feel at home here."

Chariline decided that if Aquila was half as winsome as his wife, she might never leave.

———— ⟐ ————

"What brings you to Rome, Chariline?" Priscilla asked, passing a dish of pear patina to Theo. The pears, stewed in sweet wine and honey before being smashed and cooked in eggs, melted on Theo's tongue. They had gathered for supper in the long room on the second story of the house. Priscilla and Lollia had prepared a delicious meal of chicken seasoned with fresh dill, leeks, and coriander alongside carrots and parsnips, with a loaf of hot *quadratus* bread still steaming from the baker's ovens. After weeks of eating fish and flat bread, every bite of Priscilla's mouthwatering feast felt like a celebration in Theo's mouth.

"I am here to look for my mother's friend Vitruvia. She is the granddaughter of Marcus Vitruvius Pollio."

"The famed architect who dedicated his books to Augustus?" Aquila's spoonful of dessert hovered in the air for a moment. "He's still a well-known figure in Rome, though he died over seventy years ago."

"Do you know where his family might live?" Chariline asked eagerly. She had visited the baths with Priscilla earlier and changed into a simple cream tunic, her curls loose over her shoulders. Theo had given her a basket full of cinnamon-and-rose soap when they disembarked from the ship, and the scent lingering on her warm skin teased him every time the breeze blew in through the open windows.

Theo's mouth turned dry and he looked away.

Something had shifted in his heart as he had cared for her during her illness. For long days, she had depended on him for everything. The unusual circumstances had woven a deep closeness between them. An attachment unlike any he had known, save perhaps for what he had once felt for his foster sister. But he had grown up with Ariadne. Known her from the day of her birth, inseparable through the worst and best years of their young lives.

How had this woman wrapped herself around his deepest core in such a short time?

Mentally shaking himself, Theo tried to refocus on the conversation.

"Priscilla, do you know where Vitruvius's granddaughter might live?" Aquila was saying.

"No, but I can ask Senator Pudens and his wife when they return from their estate in Antium. They should be back in

Rome next week. Senator Pudens has a talent for unearthing all manner of information. If anyone can help you, it is he."

"Next week?" Chariline's shoulders slumped. Ferox, sensing her dejection, padded over to her and dropped at her feet, laying his massive chin on her toes like a blanket.

Theo placed his cup on the table. "Tomorrow, I am meeting with my contact at the palace. I will ask him. Given Vitruvius's connection to Augustus, someone at the palace may be able to provide us with a lead."

"Does your mother know Vitruvia's last known address?" Priscilla asked. "We could always start there."

"My mother died at my birth."

Priscilla immediately reached out a comforting hand. "I am sorry, my dear."

"That's partly why I want to meet Vitruvia, you see. They were close friends in their youth, she and my mother."

"Of course." Aquila smiled at Chariline. "I was very young myself when my mother died. Only a boy. I can only imagine the pleasure of speaking about her to someone who knew her well."

Chariline wove her fingers together distractedly. She lifted her head. "I also hope to find my father."

Theo noted the quick rise and fall of her chest, the darkening flush on her cheeks. "You don't need to divulge anything if you don't wish, Chariline."

"Absolutely!" Priscilla leaned forward. "You are welcome here as you are. No explanations needed."

Chariline looked down. "All my life, my grandparents lied to me. They hid the truth because, from their perspective, they were doing me a service. If I have learned one thing from their example, it is this: hiding the truth gains nothing but an invitation for the powers of darkness to multiply.

"I have nothing to hide. The Lord knows it all. You are welcome to my story."

Theo sat, thunderstruck, as Chariline unfolded her life. Laid bare the skeletons that had shaped her and left her bruised. Her past was not nearly so dark as his own, certainly. But it contained enough shadows to make anyone think twice before revealing it. Her mother's decision to break an engagement in order to elope with a man of whom her father disapproved was no small offense in a Roman household. Her grandfather's controlling cruelty and deceit, her aunt's inability to forgive, even her own decision to stow away on his ship were secrets most would prefer to hide.

Secrets *he* would prefer to hide.

Theo thought of his own past. The story of his own conception and birth. His own upbringing. The idea of revealing all that to this woman turned his stomach. He could not bear the look he would find in her eyes. Horror. Disgust.

He listened to her as she opened her life and decided more than ever to keep his hidden.

# CHAPTER 19

—❦—

*Confess your sins to one another.*

JAMES 5:16

The next afternoon, Theo returned from the palace, a tiny scrap of papyrus in his hand. "We have a lead. The official I know at the palace located an old address for the Vitruvius family."

Chariline had been helping Lollia shell peas in the courtyard and almost upended the bowl when she leapt up to reach for the scrap. "Can we go now?"

"If you wish."

Chariline flew to the stairs, intending to change into her good tunic.

"Chariline."

She stopped, her foot dangling over the last step, itching to move. "Yes, Theo?"

"I don't want you to build up too much hope. They probably moved long ago."

She jerked her chin down in a nod. He was likely right. All the same, someone in the neighborhood might know where the family had moved.

"Is it far?" she asked Theo as she put on her sandals.

"The house is on Via Tiburtina to the northeast of us. A lot of hills, Priscilla tells me."

"I like hills."

"We are walking."

"I like walking." Chariline tightened the strap around her ankle.

"It will be busy this time of day. People heading home for supper."

Chariline opened her mouth but was forestalled by Theo's raised hand. "I know. You like crowds."

She grinned. "I was going to say I like supper."

"Well, if this Vitruvia of yours lives there, she might offer us some."

As they were about to leave the house, Ferox ran to their side, his tail wagging with enthusiasm. Here was a dog who knew how to beg with charm.

Priscilla emerged out of the workshop and put a steadying hand on his leather-and-bronze collar. "Come, boy. You are not invited."

Ferox, unwilling to give up, licked Chariline's fingers, making her laugh. She had never owned a pet or lived in a household with a dog. But she was thinking that if all dogs were as friendly as this one, she might one day like to have one. "May we take him with us?" she asked impulsively.

"If you are certain he will not be a nuisance?"

"You won't be a nuisance, will you, boy?" Chariline asked.

Ferox sat perfectly still, a model of good behavior, not taking his eyes off her. Lifting one paw, he offered it like a gentleman.

They laughed. "That settles it," Chariline said. "He is more well-behaved than I am." As if sensing his welcome, the dog pranced around their feet, running from Theo to Chariline.

"Yes, we are all aware that you are excited," Theo said, patting the dog. "But you must comport yourself. Understand?" Tying a long leather leash to the collar, they set off, Ferox in tow. Used to long treks accompanied by humans, the dog managed to stay out of trouble.

They walked in silence for some time. Apprehensive at the thought of meeting Vitruvia, or worse, finding a dead end as Theo feared, Chariline barely noticed the grand parade of monuments they passed. Young Nero had ruled as emperor for two years now, and as they walked by the Palatine, one of the seven hills of Rome where Nero's palace stood, she noticed that the sharp smell of garbage and human waste gave way to a faintly sweet smell.

Theo must have seen her whiffing the air like a hound. "Nero has had new pipes installed under some of the rooms in the palace. They flow with a steady stream of perfume. His favorite is rose water. Apparently, he finds the Palatine too foul-smelling for his delicate sensibilities."

Chariline laughed. "No wonder they are buying your soap by the crateload."

"Yes. The emperor's nose has been very beneficial to my business, although it is not doing much for the treasury. Rose water is not cheap, not when you have rivers of it flowing through the palace."

By the time they arrived at the house on Via Tiburtina, Chariline's chest was burning with exertion. To her annoyance, Theo merely seemed invigorated by all the hills they had had to ascend and descend.

A young slave with a polite smile answered their knock. "May I help you?"

"We are looking for the granddaughter of Marcus Vitruvius Pollio."

"He does not live here," the fair-haired slave said.

"I would be astonished if he did." Theo smiled. "He is quite dead. We are seeking his granddaughter Vitruvia."

"No one by that name lives here either."

"The Vitruvius family lived here fifty years ago. Is there an older servant in the house who might recall something?"

The slave scrunched his face in thought, turning his pleasant features into a white prune. "I can call Pomponia. She's worked here all her life."

"We would be obliged," Theo said.

After an interminable wait, Pomponia shuffled to the door, her rheumy eyes squinting. "Yes, Master?"

She had the servile manner of someone born into slavery. Across one arm three long, narrow scars twisted like the tail of a snake. Chariline flinched, recognizing the mark of a whip. "We are sorry to disturb you, Pomponia," she said gently. "We are looking for Vitruvia. Granddaughter to Marcus Vitruvius Pollio."

"Vitruvius?" The old woman hung her head. "I know that name. Wait. It will come to me." She scratched the side of her nose. "Is he a butcher?"

Chariline swallowed a groan.

"Not a butcher, no," Theo said. "An architect who lived here many years ago."

"Oh, that one!" Pomponia nodded. "My first master bought this house off his son."

"Do you know where the son might have moved?"

Ferox, who had been lying on his side, yawned hugely, drawing the old woman's notice. "He doesn't bite, does he?" she asked fearfully.

"Not at all," Chariline assured her. "He is very tame. About Vitruvius's son . . ."

"Him. He moved. A long time ago."

Theo gave Chariline an amused glance. "And do you know where he went?"

"Somewhere near the baths of Agrippa. On that crooked road off Via Lata. What's the name?" She shrugged. "Don't remember. I am sorry, master."

Theo smiled reassuringly. "You've been very helpful, Pomponia. Our thanks." He handed the old woman three small coins. She wrapped a veiny fist around them and bowed her head.

As they walked away, Chariline said, "Shall we head there now?"

Theo shook his head. "It's growing dark. Considering neither of us knows Rome, we will find it impossible to locate the house. In any case, people are closing their doors for the evening. We should go home and start our search again early in the day."

"Tomorrow?"

"I'm sorry. Not tomorrow nor the next day. I will be making the rounds at the baths, replenishing their stores of soap and trying to establish new accounts. The day after that, I promise."

Chariline bit her lip. So close to discovery, and yet another round of waiting. "Could Taharqa accompany me?"

"I need him with me."

"I could go alone," she suggested.

Theo's head whipped toward her. "Absolutely not, Chariline. We had a deal. You will not go without me."

Chariline lowered her head so that Theo would not detect the mutinous set of her jaw.

———— ❦ ————

The warrior smiled when the girl emerged from the white-washed house. She was alone, except for a large black dog. He curled his lip. He did not like dogs.

Waiting until she turned into a long, narrow street, he scanned the way ahead. There were no alleys or intersecting streets for several blocks. His eyes turned upward to the flat roofline of the houses, two or three stories high in this part of the city. Spying what he wanted, he picked up his pace and passed her on the other side of the street.

The climb was easy. A few good footholds and he pulled himself to the empty rooftop. A row of massive stone pots planted with short palm trees lined its edge. He knelt behind one, estimating his timing. Given the girth of the pot, he might be able to get the dog as well. That would be extremely satisfying. Heaving the bulky pot, he positioned it at the edge.

The girl appeared, a few steps short of his position. A slender bee, with black and yellow stripes, buzzed around his face, annoying him. He waved it off and returned his gaze to the street. The bee returned, sounding angry. The warrior swatted it away as he placed his shoulder against the pot. One more moment and his problem would be squished on the sidewalk.

He felt a burning sensation on the back of his neck and gasped. The benighted bee had stung him! Ignoring the pain, he started to shove, and then froze. That sound!

His eyes widened as dozens of bees started to swarm around him. Too late, he saw the nest at the base of the pot he had moved.

He teared up helplessly as sting piled upon sting, angry bees attacking the exposed skin of his neck and wrists. Grinding his teeth, he refused to give up. Success beckoned, so close he could smell it. Putting his whole weight behind the pot, he gave it one mighty shove.

—— ⁐ ——

Ferox began to bark furiously, his nose pointed to the roof above them. Chariline slowed her gait to look up. She had the impression of a man crouching behind a massive stone pot before it came tumbling down.

A jumble of thoughts crashed through her mind in half-formed sentences. *He pushed the pot on purpose . . . I will be crushed under its . . . Ferox might be hurt . . . There is no time to . . .*

The pot crashed with an earth-shattering sound. It landed just ahead of her, missing her and Ferox by a handsbreadth. Chariline gasped as shards of stone, dirt, and palm fronds exploded in every direction. Amazingly, save for a few shallow scratches, she was unharmed.

Ferox's barking had caused her to slow down a beat, and

the delay must have been enough to cause them to miss the heavy projectile. Or perhaps the man's timing had been off by a blink.

Above them, the man was waving his arms in an odd, frantic dance. He threw himself toward the edge, and she realized that he was climbing down.

In pursuit!

She began to run, Ferox at her side, growling like Cerberus, the three-headed hound who guarded the gates of the underworld. Chariline managed to put a good distance between them by the time the man's feet reached street level. Looking over her shoulder, she saw him gaining. For a moment, the wind blew his dark hood down, and she saw his face.

A Cushite face, marked by the scars of a warrior.

Chariline was a fast runner. But the warrior was faster. With every flying step, he gained a bit of ground. Soon, he would catch up with them. She reached a cross street. A rider atop an immense stallion was ambling toward her, slowing a long line of litters and riders behind him.

At the last moment, Chariline jumped in front of the horse, heaving Ferox's leash to keep him at her side. The horse reared, hooves flying in the air. The rider swore, pulling on the reins, arms bulging as he tried to control his spooked beast. Everything turned into a slow motion of horrors. The warrior followed close behind, while the panicked horse threatened to crush Chariline and Ferox under its wide hooves.

Chariline pressed harder, urging Ferox on. They managed to get to the other side of the road, barely missing being trampled.

A quick glance over her shoulder showed the warrior stuck on the other side of the street, unable to cross.

That delay gave Chariline enough time to turn a corner and arrive at the Palatine Hill, which was swarming with soldiers. She knew that even if the Cushite warrior managed to track her here, he would not dare to come near her with Nero's guards stationed at every corner. She ran down the street that hugged the corner of the Circus Maximus. It was the road that cut into the heart of the Aventine, leading her to the side street where Priscilla and Aquila's house was located.

Ferox panted heavily next to her. "I know just how you feel, boy," she huffed, hand hugging a stitch at her side.

———— ⟳ ————

Theo glared at her in silence, the vein in his neck pulsing rhythmically like a purple whip. If he had yelled, stomped his feet, hissed with anger, she would have felt better. Instead, he exhibited an iron control, his silent indictment worse than a tongue-lashing could ever be.

"I apologize, Theo."

He leaned forward. "You gave your word."

She grimaced. "I did. I shouldn't have gone without you."

They stood in the courtyard, where the scent of mint and roses mingled with the aroma of damp earth. The clouds had turned a nasty charcoal gray and sent a razor-cold downpour earlier, which had only ended a half hour before. Any moment, they might open up again and pelt them with more rain.

Theo pressed his thumb over the tiny muscle that pulsed in the corner of one eye. "It's a miracle you weren't killed."

"I should have waited for you," she acknowledged.

He pulled an agitated hand through his hair, for once too distracted to cover the silver patch immediately. "At least you told me the truth."

She dropped her head. Thanks to her headstrong ways, she had almost gotten Ferox killed! She could not keep that to herself. "I wish I hadn't broken my word to you, Theo."

"The trouble is, now I can't trust anything you say." He turned on his heels and left her standing in the damp courtyard.

Watching him go, striding away from her as if he could not wait to flee from her presence, Chariline fought a rush of tears. She had spent long hours, when she had first stowed away on his ship, worrying about what it would feel like to be subjected to Theo's disappointment and anger. Now she knew. And it was worse than anything she had imagined.

# CHAPTER 20

———— ༄ ————

*But for you who fear my name, the sun of righteousness*
*shall rise with healing in its wings.*
*You shall go out leaping like calves from the stall.*

MALACHI 4:2

In the evening, as was their habit every week, Priscilla and
Aquila hosted a worship gathering at their home. Everyone
congregated in the long upper room above the courtyard
where they had eaten supper the night before. Chariline sat
alone at the back of the room, not wanting to intrude upon a
company who already seemed to know each other well.

She counted thirty-seven people, some occupying couches,
others on cushions and carpets scattered on the mosaic floor.
Senator Pudens and his family were still visiting their estate in
Antium, but many of their servants and slaves who worked at
their house in Rome were in attendance, as were a baker, two
lawyers, and a retired member of the Praetorian guard.

"I want to speak of darkness, tonight," Aquila began,
"because we all have to contend with darkness in our lives."
He cleared his throat. "I want to speak of the darkness
that plagues us: The dark thoughts that torment. The dark

circumstances that wound. The dark desires that hound. The dark choices that hurt. The dark warrens of our fearful imaginations. Sometimes, under the weight of the darkness, we feel hopeless. Overcome."

Chariline held her breath. The rest of the gathering must have felt the same. The chamber had grown silent like the depth of the sea. One person moved and the rustling of his tunic could be heard in every corner of the room.

Aquila stopped as if in thought. "I want you to know, the Lord had to contend with darkness also. Unimaginable darkness.

"The darkness of physical pain when he was beaten and crucified. Then, as he hung on the cross, for three hours the world plunged into darkness. The sun was expunged from the sky as he suffered. No light to comfort him in the end. The world became a place of shadows.

"But still greater darkness awaited him. The darkness of utter loneliness. For the first time in his eternal existence, his Father forsook him. Withdrew the light of his presence. And Yeshua had to suffer through the darkness of death, alone."

Aquila looked toward Priscilla and nodded. She came to stand next to him, reaching for his hand. "We all contend with darkness in our lives," she said. "I know I have. But this truth consoles me: Our Lord, who passed through the worst darkness, endured the most grievous and fearsome evil, the deepest loneliness—he himself helps us in our darkness. Helps us to navigate the shadow places of our lives without sinning. Helps us to persevere through them without breaking.

"He endured the loss of every light so that we may always have the light of his countenance shining upon our path.

"Perhaps you feel the darkness of your own failures pressing in upon you this night. Feel oppressed by the weight of your sin. But even now, at this very moment, the sun of righteousness is waiting to rise upon you with healing in its wings. The light of God will swallow up the darkness of your guilt and shame, if you only reach for him."

Chariline drew her knees to her chest and dropped her head. Theo might never trust her again. She might have ruined their friendship. But Iesous extended his forgiveness.

She remembered that the Lord's dear friend Peter had broken his word also. His word never to deny him. Three times, Peter had broken that word, and yet Iesous had sought him out and loved him. *Forgive me, Lord, even as you forgave Peter.*

The greatest darkness had tried to swallow Iesous and failed. Now he stood victorious, able to swallow her darkness, which she had created with her own hand, her own choice.

*Take it, Iesous. And set me free, I pray.*

---

After the guests departed, Chariline helped Priscilla and Lollia clean up the leftovers of the modest meal they had served. Aquila had returned to the workshop, laboring on a tent that was due in the morning.

"You are gifted," Chariline told Priscilla shyly. "Was it not the prophet Isaiah who said:

> *"The Lord GOD has given me*
> *the tongue of those who are taught,*
> *that I may know how to sustain with a word*
> *him who is weary.*

"That describes you, Priscilla. Your words sustained me."

Priscilla smiled as she scoured a platter with a rag. "I see you know your Scripture."

"Not as well as I should."

Scrubbing a stubborn spot, Priscilla frowned. "Theo will come around, you know."

Chariline felt her cheeks warm. "I had given him my word, you see. Never to venture out without him."

Priscilla's hands stilled in the water. She stared at Chariline for an unbroken moment. "Why did you? What made you break your word?"

"I found the thought of waiting two whole days unbearable. It seemed impossible to sit home and do nothing when Vitruvia might be a few streets away. I told myself that I had no choice when I gave my word to Theo. That it did not count, because I was forced into making that promise."

"And did you? Have a choice?"

"Of course. I could have returned to Caesarea."

Priscilla nodded. "Did you ask Yeshua about it? Ask if he wanted you to go to Vitruvia this morning?"

Chariline shook her head. It had not even crossed her mind. "I asked for his help."

Priscilla passed the platter for Chariline to dry. "His help, but not his permission?" She dipped a clay cup into the water. "So, you placed your desire before the Lord's will."

"It wasn't such a bad desire, I thought. Except for breaking my word to Theo. Why should God not approve of me finding my father?"

Priscilla smiled. "It's not the nature of your longing that is at issue. It is the fact that God does not reign over it. Finding your father has become the jewel you refuse to part with. Not even if God asks it. In that part of your heart, at least, your flesh still rules.

"The problem is that when you are flesh-driven, you cannot be Spirit-led."

Priscilla's blue eyes bored into her. "You are aching because Theo is angry. But my dear, you have a greater problem with Yeshua."

Chariline dried the cup with trembling fingers. She thought of Natemahar, and the way he prayed with all his soul bare before God, waiting upon him. Thought of Hermione, who asked for Iesous's direction even in the small things. Of Mariamne, who never presumed to jump into action without God's confirmation. Of Theo, who climbed his mast to be alone with God.

It had been a long time since she had settled in the Lord and allowed her soul to be still. To surrender.

She had wrestled the reins of control out of Iesous's hands, taken charge of her life the moment she discovered her father still lived, because she had been afraid that God might not give her what she most wanted. Afraid that he would deny her the father she longed for.

At the root of this mad chase, this headlong spring into thoughtless pursuit lay this simple truth. Chariline did not trust God to say yes. He had withheld her father from her all her life. Why should he change his mind now?

She had betrayed Theo, put her own life at risk, dragged Ferox into her mess, worried her poor aunt half to death for this simple reason: She trusted herself more than she trusted God.

*When you are flesh-driven, you cannot be Spirit-led,* Priscilla had said. Well, Chariline was done being flesh-driven. "I want to be Spirit-led," she said to Priscilla.

Priscilla reached her damp hand and squeezed Chariline's trembling ones. "So you shall be."

———⁂———

Late that night, unable to sleep, Chariline crept down the stairs, longing for the peace of Priscilla's enchanted courtyard. She had just sat down on the bench by the fountain when she caught a silhouette on the bench across from her. Startled, she vaulted to her feet.

"It's only me," Theo said quietly. "I did not mean to alarm you."

"I'll leave." Chariline took a step back, not wanting to disturb Theo. She must be the last person he wanted to see.

"Stay," he said, also rising to come to her side. She noticed his mysterious scroll of papyrus clutched in his fingers.

"Still writing that love letter?"

His lips twitched. "Not a love letter." He extended a hand, inviting her to sit again, and joined her on the narrow bench.

She could feel the warmth of his body where they almost touched and drew her legs in, tucking one foot behind the other.

"Tell me about this Cushite," he said.

She snapped her head up. "The Cushite?"

"You called him a warrior. What makes you think that?"

"He had scars on his cheeks and forehead. In Cush, young boys who want to become warriors often receive these cuts to prove their courage. Many soldiers bear them."

"Was he someone you knew?"

She frowned. "He seemed familiar. But I can't place him."

Theo folded the scroll tighter. "Taharqa says that a warrior like that is not cheap to hire. Apparently, you've made yourself an enemy in high places."

"The queen would be my guess."

"But why? Does she know you are on your father's trail?"

"She saw me with Sesen on my last day in Meroë. If Sesen is my father, or knows his identity, the Kandake would have known that I was close to finding him."

"And that is enough for her to want you dead? Enough to send an assassin halfway across the world?"

"It seems so. Theo?" She swallowed. "If he knew where to find me today . . ."

Theo nodded. "He knows where you are staying. That occurred to me also. He must have followed us from Puteoli. I don't want you to worry about it. As determined as he is, he can't hurt you while you are in this house. He would have to get past too many of us to reach you."

She exhaled, allowing the relief of his assurance to wash over her. "I wouldn't want anyone to be hurt on my account."

His expression hardened. "No one is going to get hurt."

Looking into the flashing eyes, Chariline believed him. "Have you noticed an odd thing?" she asked.

"You mean apart from someone trying to kill you?"

"Exactly. Here is a trained warrior sent to Rome all the way from Cush. But he does not use swords or daggers or arrows or pikes or spikes . . ."

He bit off a smile. "I think I see your point. He tried to drown you the first time. And then he attempted to squash you under a giant stone pot. In either case, had he succeeded, no one would have suspected foul play. It would have appeared to be a mishap."

"Exactly."

He arched a brow. "I am impressed."

"By what?"

"Your powers of observation." He rubbed a finger along his chin. "This could work in our favor. If his mandate is to make your murder look like an accident, he is constrained by how he can attack you. We'll be able to protect you better." They sat in silence for a moment.

Theo sighed. "Chariline. I spoke more harshly than I intended, this afternoon."

She looked up. "I understand. If I had died, you would have felt responsible. All your life, you would have carried that weight."

The tight knot in his jaw loosened. "If you knew that, why did you do it?"

"I did not think of it until I saw your face when I confessed. Theo, I want you to know I will never break my word to you again. Whether I find my father or not. Whatever is at stake. I won't do that to you again."

Theo inhaled. Tapped the scroll into his palm for a beat, then grinned. "It seems my curse."

"What does?"

"To be forever bound to stubborn women."

Before she could ask what he meant by that cryptic comment, Theo had disappeared into the shadows. What *women*? Then a slow smile spread over her face. Theo felt *bound* to her.

———— ⟳ ————

In the morning, Chariline went to the diminutive kitchen in the corner of the courtyard to help Lollia make hot wheat pancakes. A freed slave, Lollia was more a member of the family than a servant and felt free to order everyone around, including Aquila.

"Lord, have mercy," she said, waving her wooden spoon at him as he swooped into the kitchen to pinch a couple of dates. "Look at the circles under those eyes. They are deep enough to plant a hedge of strawberries in."

"Yesterday you called me handsome," Aquila said, pilfering half a pancake with no apology.

Lollia tried to rap the back of his hand, finding him too fast. "That was before you stayed up half the night, working on some impatient fellow's tent."

"One bite of your wheat pancakes, and I am restored."

"Did I hear someone mention pancakes?" Theo said from the door.

"Mercy! We are being ambushed by barbarians," Lollia cried. "Where is Priscilla when I need her?"

"You don't think I would dare to come anywhere near the kitchen if Priscilla was in it, do you?" Theo reached for the pancake half that Aquila had left behind.

Chariline laughed. "She is the gentlest of women. Don't you dare malign her. I won't have it."

"Gentlest of women, is she?" Theo managed to grab a date and stuffed it into his mouth before Lollia could blink. "I will have you know she once slapped me so hard, I almost lost my teeth. Had a bruise on my cheek for weeks."

"Are you still going on about that little incident?" Priscilla said from behind him.

"Every chance I find." Theo grinned.

Chariline looked from one to the other. "Surely you did not . . . That is to say, Priscilla never would . . ."

"She would and she did," Theo said.

"It is true enough," Aquila added. "You should have heard the screeches that came out of these delicate lips." He bent to kiss the delicate lips. "I still blush when I think of it."

Priscilla rapped him on the shoulder. "It was all in a good cause."

Chariline raised a brow. "Can I join in?"

"The cause that leads to my abuse? I think not," Theo said, reaching for another pancake.

"I will abuse you myself if you take that," Lollia hissed, and everyone backed out of the kitchen very slowly.

Priscilla led them out to the courtyard. "In truth, Theo helped save the life of our friend Paul," she told Chariline. "He may be a stodgy old merchant now. But there was a time when he did not mind climbing up walls and sneaking through windows."

"That was the easy part. Being slapped by you was what made me realize a life of adventure held too many dangers for the likes of me," Theo said, making Priscilla chuckle.

Chariline tucked a tuft of hair behind her ear. Theo had helped save the life of one of the church's most famous leaders. Another Theo mystery to add to her long list.

An hour later, Theo and Taharqa left to tend to the sale of soap at several baths, and Lollia went off to shop for their noonday meal, while Priscilla and Aquila retreated to the workshop.

That left Chariline alone with her mountains. The ones

she could not move. God was her mountain mover. Chariline sat at his feet and gave those mountains back to him. Then she spent a day watering Priscilla's garden, clearing dead flowers, collecting herbs for Lollia's cooking, sweeping the floors, and generally making herself useful to her hosts. Hard work might not find her father or find answers to the puzzle of the Cushite assassin pursuing her. But it did quiet her soul.

# CHAPTER 21

—— ✤ ——

*Wait for the LORD;*
*be strong, and let your heart take courage;*
*wait for the LORD!*

PSALM 27:14

Although the implements of Priscilla and Aquila's work—awls, needles, blades, hole punchers, sheers, stamps, threads, and cords—required little space, the leather itself could be cumbersome to store so that after a few hours of labor, the workshop looked and felt cramped.

Noticing the height of the room, Chariline realized that with a few simple adjustments, she could help create a more orderly environment for her new friends. She drew a series of shelves overhead, stretching across every wall. They were too narrow to interrupt the light, but substantial enough to add a convenient space for storage. She also designed a wide cutting table for the center of the room that contained a chest underneath, as well as a drawer where they could keep the smaller implements of their trade.

She was drawing a long bench with a retractable stool

when she heard Ferox barking and heard Theo's and Taharqa's voices at the door. She rose to greet the men. Her smile wavered at Theo's expression.

"Did you not fare well at the baths? They are fools if they rejected your soap," she said.

"The baths were fine." Theo rubbed his neck. "In fact, Taharqa and I finished early. We were close to the neighborhood Pomponia had mentioned and decided to investigate."

A fist twisted in Chariline's chest. "You could not find the house."

"We found the house. But she does not live there. No one connected to the Vitruvius family does. The current residents have no idea where they have moved. Apparently, they did not reside there for long. None of the neighbors were able to help us, though one old man said he thought they had left Rome. I am sorry, Chariline. It was a dead end."

All at once, the warm atrium seemed cold. "Thank you for trying, Theo," she said, twisting her arms into a tight knot.

"Don't give up just yet. We still have Senator Pudens."

Chariline bit her lip to stop it from trembling. She tried to smile and failed. Tried to look brave and failed at that, too.

"Chariline!" Theo reached a hand that did not quite touch her shoulder. "We are not finished."

"What if this is God saying no? What if I was never meant to come?" She took a step back, followed by another. "I always knew God did not want me to find my father."

Theo filled the gap between them with a long stride. This time, he reached out with both hands, wrapping them around her shoulders. He drew her forward, until they stood nose to nose. Until they only needed whispers to be heard. Her heart skipped. Theo lowered his head a fraction. She could feel the warmth of his breath on her cheek.

"Yeshua is not against you, Chariline," he said. "Do not give up. Not until God makes his will clear."

She squeezed her eyes shut. *Did* God want to withhold her father from her? Or did the fear of that eventuality make her jump to conclusions about every hurdle she faced?

Either way, it did not matter. She would not hold anything back from Iesous. Not anymore. She looked at Theo. "A wise man once told me that the Lord will be with me, always. With or without Vitruvia. With or without my father. He is with me. I will not give up, Theo. But I will not strive against the Lord either. I will wait, until he shows me the way."

The gray eyes turned molten, warm with open approval.

She felt a chain loosen, a weight lift. She felt a cage snap open and smiled.

As if drawn by an irresistible force, Theo's head bent a fraction more until their heads almost touched. Before they did, he gulped a breath and stepped away.

---

After the evening meal, Chariline showed her drawings for the workshop to Priscilla. "These will not be difficult to construct," she said. "They will double your storage capacity and help keep the workshop organized throughout the day, even when large orders require a lot of leather."

Priscilla studied the designs with interest. "How did you think of this? I have never seen a storage place built under the table like this. Practical, but attractive. I must show your plans to Aquila. In the winter, when we are not quite so busy, he will have time to build them. Thank you for thinking of us, my dear." She looked at the thick scroll of drawings. "You have more?"

"Some are mine, and some belonged to my mother."

Priscilla insisted on seeing every design. Though not acquainted with architectural concepts, she was both perceptive and interested, a combination that made her company a true pleasure. Chariline uncovered a lavish domus designed by her mother.

"This is one of my favorites of hers," she said. Her mother had managed to give the domus, a house designed for urban neighborhoods, the homey welcome of a country estate.

Priscilla said nothing. For a long moment, she studied the domus with an odd intensity. "I have seen this," she said.

"This domus?" Chariline raised a brow. "It's an original design by my mother, not a copy of an existing house. It has never been built."

"Nonetheless, I have seen it. I simply cannot recall where." She traced a finger over the distinctive design of the capitals. "I have seen those capitals. That colonnade. Even the color of that facade."

She rose to her feet. "Let's ask Aquila."

Curious, Chariline followed in Priscilla's footsteps. Likely, Priscilla had seen a villa that looked similar to her mother's plan. Still, she would enjoy seeing a building that resembled what her mother had wished to build.

They found Aquila in the workshop, clearing up the day's clutter. "My love, have you seen this domus?" Priscilla asked, spreading the drawing on the table in front of him.

"What's this? An architectural drawing?"

Chariline nodded. "My mother's work."

Aquila drew the lamp closer and bent over the image. "This looks oddly familiar."

"That is what I said," his wife cried. "Where have we seen it?"

"Let me think." Aquila traced the outline of the portico. "I have it!" He sat up.

"What?" Chariline and Priscilla said at the same time.

"It's the domus we pass when we go to Senator Pudens's house. The one on the corner of their road in the Esquiline hills."

"I knew I had seen it before! The very same house, isn't it, beloved?"

Aquila nodded. "I am no engineer. But as best as I can tell, this is the same house."

"But how is that possible? My mother designed this house twenty-five years ago, and she died not long after. Who could have built it?"

"Would you like to find out?" Priscilla asked with a grin.

———— ✿ ————

Theo had the morning free. When he heard of the mystery of the domus, he offered to accompany Chariline to the Esquiline hills so that she might see it for herself. Priscilla volunteered to show them the way. Without being asked, Taharqa grabbed his cloak and became their rear guard. It was no empty gesture. After two serious attempts on Chariline's life, he did not need Theo to tell him that they had to protect her every time she left the house.

Theo's eyes darted around, vigilant of every shadow as they walked past the arches of Aqua Claudia, the aqueduct completed by Emperor Claudius not many years hence. The urban city of Rome with its high-rise apartments, the tottering *insulae* that rose five and six stories into the skies, and extraordinary public buildings gave way to the hills of the suburbs where the affluent lived.

On a corner plot, perched on high ground, an elegant yellow domus with marble paneling sat behind low travertine walls. As if by mutual consent, they all came to a standstill and stared. There was no denying that this was the same building as that drawn by Chariline's mother.

A small sound escaped Chariline. Without thinking, Theo reached for her hand, and she held on to him as to a lifeline.

"Well? What are we waiting for?" Priscilla asked. "Someone announce our presence."

Theo approached the double gates and stared at the knocker, two dolphins of bronze fashioned into a circle. He had seen that very design in one corner of Gemina's drawing. It felt strange to touch its cold, solid mass. To hear the sharp rap of metal against wood, when its image lay curled in Chariline's arms like a scepter from the past.

The four of them were shown into the atrium by a soft-spoken slave and asked to wait. The small pool in the middle of the room, the curtained openings to small chambers on either side, even the location of the columns were an exact replica of Gemina's drawings, Theo realized.

A tall man of middle years approached from the passageway, beyond which lay the peristyle, the formal courtyard which was the heart of the more private part of the house. His toga fell in perfect folds over his shoulder. "May I help you?" he asked.

In answer, Chariline stepped forward. Without a word, she gave him her mother's drawings.

The man cast a curious look at her before unfurling the scroll. His forehead crinkled as he studied the images before him and read the notations. The color drained from his lean face.

"Where did you find this?"

"It belonged to my mother. That is her handwriting. Her drawing. Her design."

"Who was your mother?" he rasped.

"Her name was Gemina. Daughter of Quintus Blandinus Geminus."

Their host stared at Chariline for a long, wordless moment. "You better come inside."

His invitation surprised Theo. The inner portions of a domus contained the more intimate chambers of the home, reserved for close friends and family. Strangers were usually entertained in the atrium, where they were standing. Seeing as they did not even know their host's name, they could not expect him to welcome them into the private sanctum of his house.

He led them to the airy dining room, a rectangular chamber connected to the garden by a folding door. Wall paintings of the countryside gave the chamber a cheerful aspect. The intricate tiles on the floor, patterned after the ocean, made it look bigger than it was.

"Refreshments for our guests," their host said to the soft-spoken slave who had opened the door to them, before inviting them to sit on the comfortable couches that had been placed against three walls.

"Forgive my rudeness," Theo said. "I am Theodotus of Corinth. May I inquire your name? You see, we only came here because we recognized the house from Gemina's drawings. But we remain in ignorance regarding your identity."

Their host laughed. "This day grows increasingly curious." He extended a hand of greeting to Theo. "I am Aulus Galerius Sergius." His grip was strong and warm. Turning, he faced Chariline. "And you are?"

"I am Chariline. Chariline Gemina."

Galerius shook his head with wonder. "Chariline Gemina, it is a pleasure to meet you. I knew your mother."

Chariline, who had only just sat down, sprang to her feet. "You did?"

"Indeed. Your mother was my wife's dearest friend."

"Your *wife*?" Her throat worked as if she could not quite swallow. "You are married to . . . Vitruvia?"

"How did you know?" Galerius said. "Though she is gone, I'm afraid."

The air leaked out of Theo's chest.

"I am so sorry," Chariline whispered.

"What? No. No, no! I did not mean she is gone to the afterlife. I meant she is not at home. She has gone to visit her father for the day. Which is why she is not here in person to greet you."

Chariline's hand trembled against her lips. Everything in Theo wanted to leap to her side so he could hold her. Comfort her. His jaw ached as he ground his teeth, forcing himself to hold back. Forcing himself to watch her struggle and do nothing about it. It was not his place. The thought wormed into his gut like a drop of acid, burning all the way.

"I never knew of Vitruvia until I found my mother's letters," Chariline said, her voice wavering. "I found them hidden in a secret pouch in these drawings."

Galerius shook his head. "And we never knew about *you*. We never discovered that Gemina had given birth to a child before dying, or we would have sought you out long before this."

# CHAPTER 22

—— ⟡ ——

*There is a friend who sticks closer than a brother.*

PROVERBS 18:24

Like drops of mercury, Chariline's thoughts scattered, rolling away from her grasp. They had come in search of her mother's domus and found Vitruvia! Chariline's mind splintered in a dozen directions. She found it hard to keep up with the unfolding drama, her own life peeling one layer at a time before her.

Ensconced in the graceful building her mother had created out of dreams, surrounded by the shapes, proportions, and colors she had devised, Chariline sat stupefied for long moments. A three-dimensional world had replaced the flat lines of her mother's drawings, bringing them to life. She reached out and touched the door leading to the garden. It felt as though she was touching a bit of the mother she had never known.

Galerius poured ruby-red wine into a glass goblet and, after adding a generous splash of water, offered it to her. "Have a drink, child. It will steady you."

Chariline accepted the cup and took a small sip. By the time Galerius had served everyone else, she had gained control over her runaway thoughts.

"I can't wait to tell Vitruvia about you," Galerius said with a grin. "I may have to revive her from a dead faint. She will be astonished when I tell her that Gemina has a daughter."

"I was equally astonished to know my mother had a secret friend! A friend who was the granddaughter of the great architect Vitruvius. How did this domus come to be built? I thought I had the original plans."

Galerius rose. "Wait here." When he returned, he had a large roll of papyrus under his arm.

Upon unrolling the bundle, Chariline discovered three separate scrolls containing the same drawings that she possessed, but in greater detail. In the corner, with a flourish, sprawled a jaunty note: *Long life to you, dearest Vitruvia. And may you pass to the end of your years.*

"She sent these to my wife as a twenty-fifth birthday present."

"She must have used the one I have as a rough draft."

Galerius nodded. "We saved these plans for years. Vitruvia always said that she wanted to build that domus in honor of Gemina's memory. We both loved the design. A few years ago, we managed to buy this plot and were finally able to make Vitruvia's dream a reality."

"I am certain my mother would have been pleased by what you have accomplished."

Galerius came to his feet. "Would you like to see the rest of the house?"

He led them through the domus, starting with his tablinum,

a comfortable and airy chamber with unusually high ceilings, dominated by Galerius's massive desk. His tablinum was connected to the garden by a folding door. They strode through, finding a partially covered walkway with narrow marble columns and paneling, which gave the outdoor space a sheltered feeling. The sound of trickling water made them feel that the urban city of Rome lay a thousand miles away.

As was customary, the kitchen had been tucked in the back of the garden. What was unexpected was the clever half wall, covered in a vine with aromatic blooms, which completely hid the kitchen's entrance from view. In similar fashion, her mother had created nooks for the household servants and slaves that remained hidden behind discreet doors and panels. A small, private bath and latrine had been built into the opposite corner of the garden. Upstairs, elegant chambers and practical storage rooms lined a long corridor.

Every room had been thoughtfully designed, exhibiting Vitruvius's three main attributes: utility, beauty, and strength. This was a house that would last through the ages. A domus to leave to your children and your children's children for generations to come.

"Your mother was a gifted architect," Galerius said when Chariline admired his home. "Everything here has her touch."

After he had led them back to the dining room, Chariline asked, "When was the last time you heard from my mother?"

Galerius thought. "Gemina wrote one last letter to my wife from Caesarea, telling us of your parents' misfortune. At that time, she still hoped she might be able to sway the Cushite queen. Hoped to be reunited with your father. She must not have known about you, yet, as she made no mention of her pregnancy."

Chariline clasped her hands. "My parents were never reunited. She died without seeing my father again."

"So we gathered. When we did not hear from her after that, we grew concerned. I hired a man to find news of her." He adjusted the folds of his toga. "By then, she was gone. Such a tragic loss. Vitruvia was inconsolable for months."

Chariline leaned forward, eyes wide. "Did Vitruvia know my father?"

"They never met."

"But did she know his name?"

Galerius's brows lowered. "His name?" He waited for a beat. "Child, do you not know who your father is?"

"Until a few weeks ago, I thought my father was dead."

"Then, who raised you?"

"My aunt."

"Ah yes. Blandina, wasn't it? We only met her once. She was married by the time we met your mother and lived in Caesarea. A sweet lady. Your mother was very fond of her. Did she tell you your father had died?"

"No. My grandparents told both of us that story. Grandfather was furious about my mother's decision to elope. I suppose this was his way of evening the score with the man who had, in his words, ruined my mother." She copied her grandfather's haughty voice and Galerius laughed.

"You are not close to Quintus Blandinus, I take it?"

Chariline smoothed the trailing skirts of her tunic over her legs. "For years, my grandparents wanted no part of me. It was not until my tenth birthday that they finally sent for me."

"You must have been eager to meet them, by then."

"Curious more than eager. I had a Cushite friend who

knew my grandfather." She told them about Natemahar. "He is closer to me than my grandfather ever could be. We have adopted each other, you might say.

"When my grandfather sent for me, I asked Natemahar, who was visiting Caesarea at the time, what my grandfather was like."

Chariline still remembered the conversation. Natemahar had considered silently before answering. "I don't know him well. But he is very strict."

"Strict like he has a lot of rules?" she had asked.

"Like that. And more."

"More, how?"

"You know how sometimes you say something that makes me roar with laughter and I pull your braid and call you pert?"

"Aha."

"Your grandfather would likely be offended and send you to bed without supper."

"That doesn't sound nice."

"Well, he may be different with you than he is at the palace."

He wasn't, as it happened. Chariline had gone to bed without dinner many times in her childhood.

Shaking the memory, Chariline said, "When we finally met, my grandparents told me that my father had died and forbade me from ever speaking of him."

Hearing the story of how she had accidentally discovered her grandfather's secret, Galerius whistled. "Gemina always said your grandfather could not bear to be contradicted. Withholding your father from you all these years and lying about it sounds downright cruel to me."

Carefully, Chariline placed her cup on the table. "Did my mother ever tell you my father's name?"

"Not to me. But she may have revealed it to Vitruvia in one of her letters."

Chariline tried to hide her disappointment. God had given her a gift in finding this house. Finding—miraculously, it seemed—Galerius and Vitruvia. If that was the limit of his plan, she would be content.

"You must return tomorrow," Galerius said. "All of you. Come for supper. Vitruvia will be back by then and bursting to meet you."

———⟡———

Theo hired a covered carriage, and Chariline sat cushioned by Taharqa on one side and Theo on the other, her own personal human shield all the way to the Esquiline hills. Chariline suspected that the carriage was not so much for comfort as a way to offer her an extra layer of protection at night, when the shadows could become a weapon in the hands of a trained warrior. No sooner had she disembarked from the undulating carriage than her hostess sprang upon her enthusiastically.

Wide hipped and flat chested, just as her letter had claimed, Vitruvia was an elegant woman of middle years sporting an expensive blonde wig and a brilliant smile. Her hazel eyes were already awash in tears before Chariline stepped foot across the threshold. Wrapping her arms around Chariline, Vitruvia cradled her with the abandon of a long-absent mother. Their tears turned into laughter when Vitruvia's animated embrace knocked her wig sideways.

She reached a hand to straighten the highly decorated

curls. "By Jove's eyeballs! And I did so want to make a good first impression."

"I can't imagine you making a better one, dear Vitruvia," Chariline said.

The weather in Rome had grown warm, and Vitruvia had set up a table and couches in the garden for supper. Unlike Priscilla's courtyard with its wild profusion of potted herbs and flowers, Vitruvia's garden was large and formal, with a shallow rectangular pool that sported a fountain in the shape of a dolphin spewing fresh water.

As Chariline reclined on the couch across from Theo, she caught his eye and waved. If not for Theo, she would not be here. In Rome. In this house. She would not have this gift.

She tried to etch the expanse of her gratitude into her silent gaze. A slow smile curved his lips into a half moon. For a moment, his eyes felt warmer than the breeze, and, distracted, she ignored Galerius and Vitruvia and all the questions that were burning on the tip of her tongue.

Vitruvia rose to direct one of the slaves as he served the first course, breaking Chariline's abstraction. Only three of them had been able to attend tonight's meal since Priscilla and Aquila were hosting a worship gathering at their home.

"In honor of Gemina, I have ordered all her favorite dishes tonight," Vitruvia said. "The first course is herb salad, served with pork cured with myrtle. Gemina used to love this recipe."

"I'm not familiar with it." Aunt Blandina preferred simpler food. Chariline tasted a forkful. "Something just melted in my mouth. Might be my tongue."

"I could eat the whole platter by myself," Vitruvia confessed. "Your mother, now, she had an iron control. Like you, she was slender and tall. Lovely girl. Lovely."

"How did you meet her?" Chariline asked shyly.

"I met her in Fanum, where my grandfather's most famous building is located. I had gone sightseeing at Grandfather's basilica, like any traveler to Fanum. And there she was."

"You had never seen the basilica before?" Chariline asked surprised.

Vitruvia wiped the corners of her mouth with a delicate linen napkin. "Not until then. My father was not a big fan of architecture. Before my grandfather became a celebrated architect, he was a military man and served as an officer of artillery. My father took after that part of Vitruvius. Joined the army and served for many happy years. But he had no interest in architecture or engineering. Never had any desire to visit Fanum.

"I, on the other hand, sprang from my mother's womb with a plumb line in my hand. I never met my grandfather. He was dead long before I was born. But, somehow, I inherited his passion for buildings."

Chariline grinned. "I can understand that."

Vitruvia assessed her. "My father did not. He could never comprehend why I wanted to learn geometry and design. I had to sneak my grandfather's books into bed and read them in secret. It wasn't until I married my dear Galerius, and he was transferred to Fanum, that I was able to visit my grandfather's crowning glory, the basilica.

"Imagine my surprise when I found a narrow-boned wisp of a thing, all golden haired and round eyed, walking alone on the roofed colonnade. And measuring the circumference of the columns when she thought no one was looking."

Chariline laughed. She could almost picture her mother as Vitruvia described her. "What did you do?"

"Asked her if I could borrow her leather strip to conduct my own measurements, of course. Together, we examined the triangular trusses, the capitals, and the floor tiles. We discussed the roof, the foundations, and my grandfather's decision to orient the basilica north to south.

"We snuck into the screened colonnade in the upper story, which is not open for public use, as it is reserved for business. I'll never forget how a toga-wearing man with puce skin barked at us to leave. Your mother drew herself up like an empress. 'It is our business to be here, sir. As students of architecture, I can think of no better place for us to be.' Then, with great dignity, she offered one end of her leather strip to the man and asked him to help her measure the height of the columns."

Chariline snorted. "What did he do?"

"He did as she asked. Most of us did." Vitruvia dabbed her eyes with her napkin. "Your mother was several years younger than I. But it mattered little. That afternoon, we began a lifelong friendship. Understanding and devotion like that are rare, child. I hope you will find someone who fills your heart as Gemina filled mine. No one else has ever replaced her friendship."

Chariline thought of Mariamne and Hermione. Of their loving acceptance. Their loyalty. Their constancy. "I have known friendship like that," she said.

"Then Fortune has smiled upon you."

"God has blessed me. I may not have had a mother or father. But I have had the companionship of the best of friends."

Chariline wondered if the strong bond holding Vitruvia and her mother together had been forged in one short afternoon. "Is that the only time you saw my mother? That day at the basilica?"

"Thankfully, no. At the time, Gemina's father was stationed in Fanum. For five months, we were inseparable. We traipsed through the streets of Fanum, studied the stone Arch of Augustus, and discussed the ingenious tactical walls designed by my grandfather. We dreamed of building our own basilica one day and spent hours designing a city full of buildings. We giggled at jokes only we understood, read my grandfather's books, tried our hands at gardening."

Vitruvia leaned to caress her husband's cheek. "Galerius accompanied us when his work allowed. Sometimes, when he could sneak away, he even took us to picnic on the coast of the Adriatic Sea."

Galerius smiled. "It was an enchanted time."

"When your grandfather discovered that Gemina and I were studying architecture, he forbade us from meeting again. He considered me a bad influence, I think. After that, we had to conceal our meetings and could not be together as often."

"That explains why my mother felt the need to hide your letters."

Vitruvia nodded. "Then your grandfather was sent to Cush and Galerius received a transfer back to Rome. The last time I saw Gemina, she was riding in a carriage on the Via Flamina, headed for Puteoli, where a ship bound for Cush awaited her. We had made arrangements to remain in contact. A friend of Galerius carried letters between us. But we never saw each other again after that."

She reached a beringed hand and caressed Chariline's face. "You have her smile. Her laugh, you know? And the same eyes, though the color is different." She clapped her hands together and brought the tips of her fingers to her lips. "And she called you Chariline!"

Chariline arched an eyebrow. "Why did she give me a *Greek* name? Not a Latin one to honor my grandfather, or a Cushite appellation in memory of my father. But Greek?"

"Don't you know?"

"I asked Aunt Blandina a few times. But she always burst into tears and did not answer."

"Ah. I can understand that. Your aunt had a babe once, you see."

"My aunt?" Chariline gasped, shocked.

"Indeed. Very early in her marriage. A little girl. Her only child. She came too early and did not survive. Your aunt named her Chariline, in honor of her husband's mother. Chariline Blandina. Your mother always said that if she had a little girl, she would name her Chariline. As a consolation to her sister. And here you are."

Chariline bowed her head. How many secrets had her family buried? How much pain lay in the ground of her ancestry? Poor Aunt Blandina. Had she thought of her lost babe every time she called out the name of her niece? Had the honor and comfort her mother had intended by the name become, instead, a constant bleeding thorn under Blandina's skin?

"Speaking of names." Chariline leaned forward, her body straining. "Did my mother ever reveal my father's name to you, Vitruvia?"

Vitruvia's hand made a fluttering gesture. "Galerius told me of your predicament, child. It left me speechless."

"That does not happen often, I can tell you." Galerius smiled at his wife. "My wife can always think of something to say."

"I stayed up half the night trying to remember." Vitruvia shook her head. "I am sorry, Chariline. Your mother wrote me his name in a letter. Only once. It was a distinctive name. Cushite, I suppose." She threw her hands into the air. "And now, I cannot recall it.

"I have dragged half the household from storage room to storage room since dawn, looking for Gemina's letters. When we moved a few years ago, I lost track of them. I know they are here, somewhere. I would never dispose of her letters. But we can't seem to locate them."

Chariline exhaled. Another wall. Another dead end. "Do you remember anything about him? How did they meet? How did they fall in love?" She hoped some seemingly unimportant detail might yet lead her to him.

Conversations stopped as two slaves cleared the first course and served the main meal. Raw oysters served on half shells, sitting over a bed of snow from the mountains; roasted lamb chops with peppercorns; and for the egg dish, an asparagus patina. Chariline watched her companions extract their oysters using the pointed handles of their spoons. She put a forkful of something in her mouth and tasted nothing.

Vitruvia swallowed an oyster and sighed contentedly. "Where were we? Ah yes. How your parents fell in love. It was quite an epic romance. Gemina had been betrothed shortly before she met your father. Your grandfather had insisted on the match, and Gemina had obeyed. Apparently, the young man's father had promised to aid your grandfather's career.

"I was worried for Gemina. I did not see how she could be happy in such an arrangement. The young man in question— I can't remember his real name, of course, but I always thought of him as Varro—"

Chariline laughed. *Varro* meant "blockhead."

"This Varro sounded overbearing, demanding that Gemina give up reading and drawing. Everything she loved and enjoyed." She shrugged. "Young men can be such boors."

Theo cleared his throat.

Vitruvia waved at him. "Not you, child. You are too kind to ever fall into that category." She straightened her slipping wig. "All those pretty muscles and well-formed features don't hurt any either."

Theo turned pink. Chariline had never seen him so visibly embarrassed. She found it a distinctly enjoyable sight.

"Your grandfather had already managed to make an unhappy match for your aunt Blandina," Vitruvia said between bites of lamb. "Sending her off to Caesarea with a man twice her age. He had no idea what his daughters needed. I feared he had created another mess for Gemina. And then, the queen intervened," Vitruvia said.

"The queen?" Chariline turned, instantly alert.

"She is the one the Cushites call Candace, isn't she? The Candace was responsible for your parents' meeting."

"She was?"

"Accidentally. But yes. She had arranged a large formal event to which Quintus Blandinus and his family had also been invited. Your father was the son of the Candace's close friend and was present that night. They were grooming him for some official position. What was it? Let me see. Something to do with numbers or money, I think."

"A treasurer?" Chariline squeaked.

"Yes! That's right. He was being groomed to serve as a treasurer."

Sesen! Sesen was her father!

# CHAPTER 23

—◦⟁◦—

*I will give you a new heart.*

EZEKIEL 36:26

Unaware of the import of what she had just revealed, Vitruvia went on. "It was Gemina's first experience of the Cushite court. As you can imagine, she felt tense and unsure in such unfamiliar surroundings. Your mother was not one for pomp and circumstance. A slave startled her when he showed up silently at her side, and Gemina upended a platter of food on her tunic.

"Dear Varro thoughtfully barked out some rude comment about her clumsiness, loud enough for the whole room to hear. That's when your father came to Gemina's rescue. He assured her that she had done them all a favor since the platter contained some awful food, like pickled crocodile brains and tails. He was making it up, of course, but by the time he was finished, Gemina was laughing so hard the queen asked to meet her. She called Gemina charming."

"The Kandake?" Chariline could not believe the Kandake even knew the word.

"Yes. Apparently, she was quite an intimidating woman, though still young at the time."

"She is still an intimidating woman."

Vitruvia straightened. "You've met her?"

"Not officially." Chariline placed her morsel of lamb back on the plate, uneaten. "Ran into her a couple of times. Not an experience you forget."

"Well, somehow, Gemina managed to be quite a hit with the queen that evening."

"Too bad the Kandake could not remember that when she sent my mother packing for Caesarea."

"Oh, that was your grandfather. The queen merely handed Gemina to Quintus Blandinus and left him to it."

Chariline fought to keep the disgust out of her voice. "No wonder my mother decided to elope."

"Yes. Your grandfather could be callous. But I expect you know that."

Chariline gave a dry smile. "That's the night they fell in love, then?"

"It started then. A few days after the banquet, Gemina ran into him at the cemetery. She sent me a few drawings of those pyramids. Not as grand as the ones in Egypt. But still wonderful. She had gone there to sketch one for me, and your father appeared."

"What was he doing there?" Theo asked.

"Visiting his uncle's memorial." Vitruvia shrugged. "Some

things are meant to be. The two of them began a secret friendship. At first, that was all. All they thought they could have. Gemina was drawn to your father's gentleness, so different from Quintus Blandinus. In the end, they could not pretend to mere friendship any longer.

"They knew that marriage meant they would have to give up everything. Home. Family. Security. They made that sacrifice willingly. They planned to come to Rome. Galerius and I intended to help them."

"But the Kandake captured them before they could escape," Chariline guessed.

Vitruvia nodded. "They came close to getting away. At the very last, they discovered that the Candace had laid a trap for them. Gemina was separated from your father that day and never saw him again."

With a sigh, Vitruvia pushed her plate away. "It is hard to believe such sweet love could end in tragedy. It never occurred to me, when I waved good-bye to Gemina all those years ago at Fanum, that I would never see her again. That she would be lost to us so soon." Vitruvia's tears flowed again.

She reached a hand and caressed Chariline's hair. "But here *you* are. Her daughter. She has left a part of herself in you."

Could hearts crack? Break, shatter, and still beat? Vitruvia's words, meant as a kindness, tore into Chariline, a sharp finger of accusation rupturing their way into old places.

Chariline unraveled.

She felt a fraud, a welcome guest into this home when she was, in fact, the cause of Vitruvia's tears.

"*I* am the reason she is dead!" she wailed. "She died giving birth to *me*." Guilt licked her with its acrid tongue, and she cringed at the pain she had caused this dear woman by coming into the world.

Vitruvia sat up straight. "By Jove's silky beard! You blame yourself?"

Chariline's throat constricted, cutting off her words. Which was a good thing, since she had none to offer.

"Don't you dare, child! I knew your mother like I know myself, and I can tell you this: She longed for a child. She always wished for a daughter. A little girl of her own. She had chosen your name before she ever met your father. And I will tell you one thing more: she would willingly have laid her life down for you."

"I was so big, you see." Chariline choked.

"So? You might as well blame Gemina for having narrow hips. For leaving you motherless. For abandoning you to her dull family."

"I could never do that!" Chariline gasped.

"But you can blame a helpless babe."

Chariline twined her fingers together until they ached. "It was not an even exchange. Me for her. She should have been the one who lived." Not until the words leapt out of her mouth did Chariline realize how deeply rooted they were. How absolutely true they felt to her soul. For twenty-four years, she had carried this burden.

The wrong person had survived that day. The wrong person had been taken.

Gemina, beautiful Gemina. Beloved Gemina. The one whose death had crippled and scarred so many people. The one whose talents still made the world more luminous. Gemina should have lived.

"Chariline," Theo said. Only her name. Nothing more. But in the tone of his voice, the expression of his face, the melting warmth of his eyes, something like understanding passed into her, sank into her bones, settled.

He knelt on one knee before her. "I know," he said. He looked into the sky, lit now with a full moon and a ghostly parade of slow-moving clouds, swallowed, and turned his attention back to her. "I know this thing you carry."

He offered no advice. No correction. Merely the simple grace of understanding. He held her hand tight in his own and smiled a broken smile.

Chariline realized, with perfect clarity, what he meant. That he knew, in his own soul, the same guilt. The same regret. And although he did not explain himself, his words, his gaze, his warmth were enough.

She had reached the bottom of her poisoned well tonight. Pulled from its stinking ground the putrid source of years of contrition. Watched the mirror of her soul and heard the words of accusation that had haunted her silently for twenty-four years.

*The wrong person survived that day. The wrong person was taken.*

It was enough to drown her, that realization. Until she saw Theo. Theo who had no doubt drunk from the same well. Reached the same putrid bottom. He had offered her the comfort of understanding. Soothed her with his knowledge of her pain.

Then he had given her something more. Something beyond the pain they both knew too well. He had smiled at her, and in that broken smile, she had received his acceptance.

—⁊⁊—

Sesen was her father!

As the shattering emotional dust of the day settled, this resounding conclusion returned to tantalize and torment Chariline. That day at the palace in Cush, she had truly found her father. Spoken to him. Now the reality of his plot against the queen came crashing upon her with a fresh intensity. She had to find a way to stop him! However evil the Kandake, she could not let her father become a murderer.

A soft knock sent Chariline to her feet. She opened her door a crack and found Theo standing beyond.

"Did I wake you?"

She shook her head. After returning from Vitruvia's home an hour earlier, she had plopped on her bed, unutterably weary but unable to sleep.

"Will you come to the courtyard with me?"

Chariline nodded, curious. She padded after him, following the wavering light of his lamp as he descended the steps. He had left his writing box on the bench and, pulling it toward him, made room for her to sit.

After she had settled down, he drew out a thin scroll of papyrus. She recognized it as the one he wrote in sometimes. The one he guarded with jealous secrecy.

He swallowed. "You want to know what I have been writing?" Without explanation, he handed her the papyrus.

Her brows rose.

Wetting her lips, Chariline unfurled the sheet. For a moment, she stared without comprehension. Then it finally dawned on her.

Theo, the man who had won the hearts of the people of Corinth with his wild chariot racing, the merchant who had attained enviable success, the ship owner adored by his sailors, the adventurer who had helped save the life of Paul—that Theo had also written this.

A poem.

On the stained, worn sheet of papyrus, where his fingers had left numerous ink smudges, he had composed a poem entitled "Angel Scars."

"You are a poet!"

He winced. "Not a good one." Stretching a hand, he furled the scroll closed. "Before you read it . . ."

"Yes?"

"It's a poem about scars. The scars we bear. In our souls. In our bodies."

He pulled his fingers through his hair, drawing the dark, silky strands away from his forehead, displaying the silver streak he usually hid. "This is my scar."

"The silver in your hair?" she asked, confused.

He gripped the edge of the stone bench, his fingers turning pale. "I was a foundling, you see. An abandoned babe."

She gasped, shocked. For all the hours she had spent trying to guess at his past, trying to unearth his secret, she had never thought of this possibility. "Oh, Theo!"

"My adoptive father, Galenos, found me on the steps of the *bema* on the day of his daughter's birth. He had gone to offer libations to the gods for the safe delivery of his child. On the way, he found me, forsaken."

"Who could ever abandon *you*?" she asked, her eyes big and shocked.

It seemed impossible. Knowing him. Knowing his goodness, his kindness, his loyalty. Who could not have wanted Theo? Was the world mad?

Then a fresh possibility occurred to her. "Were you sickly?" Families sometimes exposed ill or deformed children to the elements. Undesirable babies were left in the hands of the gods to save or to kill.

He dropped his head. "There was nothing wrong with me except for this clump of silver hair."

"But . . ." Chariline angled closer toward him. "You think they abandoned you because of that?" She pointed to his forehead. It made no sense. A tuft of pale hair could hardly count as a malformation.

Theo breathed. Again and again and again. "I always suspected this was the deformity that caused my parents to reject me. And I discovered that I was right. But that is a story for another day."

He touched the silver streak. "This is my scar. The reminder that I was unwanted. The mark of my neglect. The proof that something was very wrong with me."

He licked dry lips. "Most of us have them. Scars from unhealed wounds. Some visible, like a poorly healed cut. Some invisible, always aching.

"The problem with scars is that they tell their own twisted story. They make you see yourself through their distorted mirror."

He pulled his fingers through his hair. "This mark that marred me at my birth, for example. It made me see not only a man who *was* abandoned, but one who *should* be abandoned. A man who deserved to be unwanted."

"But Theo!" Chariline stared at him wide-eyed. She had never known a man more worthy. Worthy to be claimed. Worthy to belong. Worthy to be held onto. Whoever walked away from Theo had to be a brainless fool!

He flicked her an enigmatic glance. "I had a worse problem. This scar made me see a God who would leave me in my time of trouble. A God who would always allow terrible things to happen to me. If God allowed a baby to be thrown out like garbage, what worse nightmares could he have in store for me? It took a long time for Yeshua to teach me differently. To help me see God rightly. To trust him with my future. To trust him with my scar."

Theo looked at his hands, his smile painful. "I tell you this because tonight, you touched your own scar. Touched the lies it tells."

Her throat turned into a desert creek.

*The wrong person had survived that day. The wrong person had been taken.*

This was her lie? Did he think her conclusion as faulty as she thought his?

Theo leaned toward her. "Now your battle begins in earnest. You have to allow Yeshua to tell you the truth. Stop listening to your scars. You are not God's mistake, Chariline. You are his glory."

Chariline's eyes filled with tears. As hard as she tried to repress them, repress the heat in her cheeks and the tremble in her lips, she could not.

"My words will not heal you," Theo said. "Neither will my poem. But they are . . . an invitation. The creaking sound of a door opening. A door to hope. To truth."

Chariline clutched the papyrus to her chest. "You want me to read your poem?"

"I want you to *have* my poem. It's a present." He looked away. "A present from a man not yet fully healed. I know God will not abandon me." His throat worked. "I'm not so certain about people." He shrugged. "I'm still learning, you see. I only wanted you to know that I understand. That I have fought this battle."

She watched him rise, her eyes glued to his retreating back, his steps sure as he melted into the darkness.

He had ripped off a great scab in order to bring comfort to her bleeding wound. Had revealed a secret he would rather have kept hidden. Theo, a foundling! She shook her head. And yet as much as he had exposed of his history, she realized, he had kept more hidden.

What had he said? *I know God will not abandon me. I'm not so certain about people.*

She understood now why he kept her at arm's length. Why he refused to share his past. Shame hides. Shame separates.

It dawned on her, with a shiver of fear, that Theo might never trust her with his past. That he might never fully open his heart to her.

Sitting in the dark, Theo's poem clutched in one fist, Chariline accepted that more than her father, more than her mother, more than all the joys that architecture and design could give her, she had come, over the past weeks, to want what she might never have.

Theo's heart.

The whole of his heart, without conditions, without partitions, without walls.

Because somewhere on the calm waves of the Mediterranean, as he had tended her broken body, Theo had come to fill her own heart with more love than she had ever known.

She took a strangled breath. Then, drawing close the lamp that he had left for her, she unfurled his scroll and peered into his soul.

## Angel Scars

*I met an angel, fierce and bold,*
*battle-scarred and mangled from the wars of old.*
*His face had once been lovely, pure, fiery light,*
*but an ancient wound had marked it, like a livid blight.*

*I asked him to tell the story of that terrible scar.*
*Recount the tragic glory of every gash and mar.*

*His eyes told me a tale of many brutal stings,*
*but his joy was boundless, and I could not fathom its wings.*

*"I faced a demon, once, faithless, and sly,*
*on one prayerless morn, when the battle went awry.*
*He brought me down and maimed me, his talons ice and frost.*
*For one final blow he held me, and I knew myself lost.*

*"Then the Master reached out, extending his hand,*
*grasping the demon's sword like a burning brand,*
*thus, he dispatched the foul one to its native land.*
*Now, here you see me, scarred, and yet I stand."*

*I was confounded,*
*my mind astounded.*
*"Why do you not tremble as you remember that day?*
*Why do you not mourn—lament your loss?" I say.*

*"You mortals are blinded, bound by the Fall,*
*chained as you are, to corruption's call.*
*We Burning Ones know, on good days or ill,*
*whether war rages on, or all is still.*
*Above every din and the force of every pain,*
*we seek the Master's touch and count all else vain."*

*This I can't grasp.*
*I can only gasp:*

*"You have salvation; indeed, you have life.*
*But has God saved you from even worse strife?*
*Recalling that day, won't you weep and fear?*
*Is this scar not a sign you'll lose all you hold dear?"*

*"How strange," he said, "is the memory of your heart.*
*You retain all darkness—but with grace, you part.*
*The threats of yesteryear cast shadows on the morrow*
*until fear becomes your tomb, and joy is consumed by sorrow.*

*"You cannot see the Hand that saved you before*
*has yet more love and grace, more strength in store.*
*Your scars don't point only to the enemy's power.*
*Much more are they reminders that God is your strong tower.*

*He did love you then, and treasures you still;*
*one day your soul will know this; it will drink its fill.*

*"With every hideous pain, you fear much more;*
*but we angels know suffering as a holy door.*

*"The road that leads to valleys will in the end impart,*
*God's hope and his glory: the start of a new heart."*

# CHAPTER 24

—⁌⁍—

*Deliver me from those who work evil,*
*and save me from bloodthirsty men.*

PSALM 59:2

Chariline read through the poem twice. The third reading made her weep so hard, she had to stuff her face into her hands lest she awaken the household. She thought of her scars. The ones she bore from her mother's death. The ones she carried from her father's absence. The ones that lingered from Aunt Blandina's distance. The ones that were left from her grandparents' constant rebuff.

Scars more terrible than the ones that flared out of Sesen's blind eye.

She thought of Theo's angel, who saw his scar not as a reminder of all the harm done to him or as a signpost of more suffering still to come, a finger of indictment against a God who had allowed the battle. Who had failed to protect him.

Instead the angel saw his scar as a reminder of God's protection. As an invitation to a new heart.

Theo had given her this poem, this glance into his soul, this revelation of his past, because he wanted her to become more like his angel. He wanted her to know that God had not made a mistake when he gave her life.

Rolling up the papyrus carefully, she pulled the ribbon holding her hair and used it to tie up the scroll. Back in her room, she placed the poem with her mother's drawings and, tenderly, laid it all safely in her box.

———&#8450;&#8450;———

Theo was eating breakfast in the courtyard when Chariline tiptoed down the stairs. Wordlessly, she approached him. He was nonplussed when she removed the warm bread from his hand and placed it on his plate and drew him to his feet. Without warning, she enveloped him in a tight embrace, arms wrapped around his waist, her head against his heart. She squeezed him so hard, he gasped.

Her touch felt pure, like a sister's. Like a mother's.

But when she stepped away, he saw with satisfaction that there was nothing sisterly in her shy gaze or the heat of her skin.

"Thank you," she whispered.

He had worried, through a sleepless night, that the revelation of his origins might turn her from him. That today he might see pity in her eyes. The kind of pity that makes its object feel lessened somehow. He had wondered if telling her that he was an abandoned child might cause her to want to abandon him herself.

Instead, he found a strange admiration in her regard. As if knowing his past had given her a new appreciation for him.

"For what?" he said, finding his tongue. "The poem?"

"That. And your trust."

His muscles clenched. He had trusted her with little. Given her the tiniest taste of the feast of his burdens. He was not ready to reveal anything more than that. Practically all of Corinth knew that much. But he'd rarely had to say the words. Explain that part of his history, given that it was common knowledge. And he had stayed up sleepless just because he had said those words.

*I am a foundling.*

How could he ever say the rest? To her?

He did not think himself capable of it.

Scratching the back of his neck, he cleared his throat. "Any news from Vitruvia?" Their hostess had promised to send a message as soon as she discovered Gemina's letters.

"Not yet." Chariline went still. "I forgot to say, in all the excitement, that I am quite certain Sesen is my father."

"Vitruvia said that your father was training to be a treasurer at the court. I caught that, too, and wondered."

She exhaled. "Even if Vitruvia does not find my mother's letters, I think I have my answer."

"What will you do next?" It hit him then, with the force of a kick from a cart horse, that they would have to part company, soon. Chariline would want to return to Cush. Perhaps to move there permanently. To live with Sesen. Theo sat down slowly.

She twined her arms behind her back. "I hope to stay in Rome another week or two. Spend more time with Vitruvia and Galerius. Last night, before we left, she invited me to remain with them as their guest. But after that, I must find my way to Cush."

"I see." Theo felt something unravel in his heart. She was leaving already! He nodded, his head moving up and down like a great melon, unable to think of a single word that might dissuade her from leaving. That might persuade her to stay.

There was a loud knock on the door, and Ferox began to bark in the workshop where he sat tethered next to Aquila. From the street, a man stepped inside the dark passageway.

"Greetings!" His deep voice held an accent, which sounded familiar to Theo. He peered into the shadows of the passageway but could only make out the vague outline of a tall form. Instinctively he stepped in front of Chariline.

"I look for Chariline Gemina, granddaughter of Quintus Blandinus." He stretched the word *looook* so that it required an extra syllable. Theo's mouth ran dry. He recognized that accent. Heard it every day, spoken by his friend and captain, Taharqa. It was Cushite.

Cushite!

The assassin had walked brazenly into the house to finish what he had started.

He tried to shove Chariline all the way behind him. To his horror, she evaded his searching fingers and ran toward the dark passageway.

"Yeshua!" he breathed, horror briefly immobilizing him, before springing after her.

She did not slow her steps until she came to a stop in front of the stranger. Theo reached her side a fraction later, his frame tense and ready for a fight.

To his shock, she launched herself at the man. Theo's heart stopped.

It took him a moment to understand the single word she had cried. "Natemahar!"

Long arms stretched wide and wrapped around her, holding her gently, cradling her.

Theo staggered with relief. *Natemahar?* What on earth was the eunuch doing in Rome?

---

"Thank the Lord you are safe and well." Natemahar exhaled a long breath.

Chariline enfolded him in another embrace. She could not wipe the grin off her face. "How in the world did you find me?"

"It's a long tale. Can we sit?"

"Of course!" Chariline drew him into the courtyard. Only then, under the blazing light of the morning sun, did she notice the dark circles under his eyes, the pinched look about the lips, the sunken cheeks. Her steps faltered.

"Come and rest," she said, unable to hide the quaver in her voice. "You have exhausted yourself." Natemahar looked more than tired. He seemed unwell.

She led him to the stone bench near the fountain. "I will fetch you breakfast."

He nodded and smiled at her, his eyes alight with affection. And something wilder. Relief. Her heart squeezed with guilt. She had caused him great anxiety by leaving without a word of explanation. She promised herself to make up for the hours and days of apprehension she had caused him.

Trying to swallow past the fist of worry that had lodged itself in her throat, she heaped a plate with hot wheat porridge.

Fetching a cup, she filled it with *posca,* watered vinegar with spice, and after adding a dollop of honey, set them on the bench before Natemahar.

He pressed folded hands to his belly. "I feared I may never see you again, Chariline."

She threw herself at him, holding him tight, kissing his ashen face. "Forgive me for worrying you, Natemahar! I came to Rome to find Vitruvia. I have sent several letters to Mariamne and Hermione. They knew I arrived in Rome safely. I did not send you a letter because it did not occur to me that you might find out I was gone. I planned to return to Caesarea before you heard of my absence."

Natemahar ran a hand over his head. "The queen told me she had heard a rumor someone had hired an assassin to kill you. She gave me permission to go to Caesarea to ensure your safety."

Chariline nearly fell off the bench. "The *queen?* She knows who I am?"

"She knows you are Quintus Blandinus's granddaughter. And she knows we are close."

"No!"

"So it seems."

"When did you discover this?"

"When she called me into her throne room and informed me, right before revealing your life was in danger. Until then, I thought I had managed to keep you well out of her way.

"Of course, I rushed to Caesarea as fast as I could after her warning. When I arrived, Philip told me you had disappeared in the middle of the night. That somehow you had found passage on a ship and were on your way to Rome.

"His daughters had received your first letter by then and

told me you intended to stay at the home of Priscilla and Aquila, leather workers in the Aventine. Thinking of you traveling alone, I imagined all manner of nightmarish horrors, knowing a murderer was on your trail."

"Oh, Natemahar!"

He shook his head. "I followed you to Rome on the fastest vessel I could find in Caesarea's harbor. Only arrived this morning. Dropped off my belongings at an inn not an hour past and rushed over to find you. To warn you."

Theo, who had been observing their conversation quietly, stepped forward. "Forgive me for interrupting."

Chariline raised her hand in introduction. "Allow me to present Theodotus of Corinth," she said. "Everyone calls him Theo. He is . . . my friend. I owe him my life."

"A life that still seems to be in danger," Theo said. "Natemahar, did the queen know who had hired an assassin to kill Chariline?"

"She did not. But her sources of information are usually impeccable." He placed his cup on the floor, carefully. "Has something happened?"

Chariline cleared her throat. "I've had a little adventure."

She told him of the assault at Puteoli, followed by the incident of the stone pot. "He is clearly not trying to shoot me with an arrow or run me through with a sword. I think he wants to make it look like an accident. But he has been unsuccessful every time."

"Praise God!" Natemahar bowed his head, as though the weight proved too much. "The Lord's hand has preserved you."

Chariline nodded vigorously. "That he has. But Natemahar! Who in Cush would want to kill *me*?"

He shook his head. "I confess, I am mystified."

Theo crossed his arms. "Chariline believes it is the queen. Because she is coming too close to finding her father."

Natemahar's brows furrowed. "That cannot be. She is the one who sent me to help you."

"This matter grows more baffling by the hour." Chariline threw her hands in the air. "I forgot to tell you the most important news. I have found Vitruvia."

The spoon Natemahar had just picked up clattered on his plate. "You've spoken to her?"

"I have! Her husband, too. You will have to meet them, Natemahar. They loved my mother. And you won't believe this. But they have built one of her designs."

"Built it?"

"Yes. They live in a domus designed by my mother. I showed you the drawing, in fact. The one with the triple arches. You remember?"

"I think so. And . . . your father?"

"Vitruvia does not remember his name." Chariline considered telling him about Sesen. But taking one look at Natemahar's ashen visage changed her mind.

"You need to rest, Natemahar," she said. "I will ask Priscilla's permission to take you to my room. I am certain she will not mind."

Natemahar reached for her hand. "First, we need to speak, Chariline. I have something important to tell you."

"Of course we do. Right after you have had a little sleep. I don't mean to be rude, Natemahar. But you look terrible."

"I can rest after we have spoken. I have a room at an inn

not far from here." He stood and wavered on unsteady legs. Theo leapt to support him before he collapsed.

Chariline stiffened with alarm. "To bed with you, old man. Right away." She kissed the top of his head and, ignoring his frustrated hiss, ran to the workshop to speak to Priscilla. In a few short moments, she had the chief treasurer of Cush lying in her narrow bed, where she left him with a promise to return for a long conversation after he had had a few hours of sleep.

Her feet had barely touched the landing when there was another knock on the door.

Theo strode toward the entrance, muttering under his breath, "If it's another Cushite, I will greet him first."

A moment later, Theo returned to the courtyard, followed by Vitruvia's soft-spoken servant. He bowed to Chariline. "My lady sends me with her compliments. She bids you return to her house immediately. She has found the letters you were seeking."

# CHAPTER 25

*The topaz of Cush cannot compare with it.*

JOB 28:19, NIV

Theo dropped Chariline off at Vitruvia and Galerius's home before heading on to the palace. The official there had asked him to be present when the full shipment was delivered from the warehouse later that morning. Theo promised to return by lunchtime to collect her in another covered carriage.

Chariline was shown into Galerius's tablinum, where her host and hostess sat before the expansive marble table with a small stack of scrolls piled in front of them. Vitruvia had not bothered with the blonde wig today. Her own hair, dark brown and shot through with silver, had been arranged in a matronly pile on top of her head, leaving wisps that fell into her eyes.

She rose to welcome Chariline, pushing silky strands of hair out of her eyes with an impatient hand. Galerius took one look at his wife and made an excuse to leave the women alone.

Grateful for this private time with Vitruvia, Chariline

stared at the treasure trove of letters Vitruvia had saved for twenty-five years. Dangling from each was a small leather tag marked with the date Vitruvia had received the letter.

"I had hidden them amongst the books I inherited from my grandfather," Vitruvia explained. "That is why I could not find them. My grandfather left enough books to pave the streets of Rome with."

"You have so many letters!" Chariline said in surprise. She only possessed four of Vitruvia's messages to her mother. Her grandfather must have found some of the letters her mother had not hid as effectively. He would have destroyed those, no doubt.

"I have saved every one of Gemina's letters through the years." Vitruvia sorted through the pile on the table. "I am sorry, Chariline, but I have not found the letter that mentions your father's name, yet. I confess, every time I unfurl one, I get caught up in it and can't put it away. It is taking me far too long."

Chariline smiled. "I am certain I know the name it will reveal, in any case. Take the time you need with them."

Vitruvia pulled out a short scroll and held it up with excitement. "This is the country villa she designed for me the year we met." Chariline and Vitruvia pored over the sketch, younger and less sophisticated than the domus, yet already bearing the hallmarks of significant talent.

"She was only nineteen when she drew this," Vitruvia explained. "I had sent her the first two books in my grandfather's collection, and she designed this villa for me in thanks."

Chariline smiled shyly. "I own seven of your grandfather's books. I have been studying them for years."

Vitruvia straightened so fast, a couple of the scrolls dropped to the floor. "You have been studying architecture?"

Chariline nodded.

"Do you have any designs?"

"A few." She reached for the cloth bag she had brought. "I forgot to give you this when we came for supper. A small gift." She handed the scroll to Vitruvia.

Vitruvia drew the scroll out of its fabric sheath and laid it out before her. Her eyes widened. She splayed the papyrus over the table, using a heavy seal to anchor it on one side and a marble bust of Claudius on the other. For long moments, she studied the design, questioning Chariline's choice of materials and calculations on load.

"By Jove," she murmured. "By Jove!" Her head snapped up and she stared at Chariline openmouthed. "My grandfather could not have designed anything better."

Chariline laughed and waved a dismissive hand.

"Chariline, I do not exaggerate. This shows promise. More. It shows brilliance. My dear!" Vitruvia shook her head. "Do you have more?"

"Not on me."

"I want to see everything. Every sketch. Every line. Every architectural design."

Chariline smiled all the way to her toes. "You shall have them."

"Your mother would have been proud of you. Proud that you have worked at your talent, trained in it. If I had the funds to buy a place in the country, I would build that villa today." She tapped her finger on the papyrus for emphasis. "Lacking that, I will do everything in my power to find someone who can." She grinned. "We won't tell them you are a woman. Not right away. After they have dug the foundations, perhaps."

Chariline raised a skeptical brow. "No one will want plans that come without the architect himself. They will expect me to oversee the project in person. And I cannot hide my gender, Vitruvia. It goes where I go."

Her hostess laughed. "Your mother and I had the same trouble."

"Have you ever been hired to build one of your designs?"

Vitruvia nodded. "A few. Not as many as I would have liked. My name helped to open doors. I am the only scion of Vitruvius's line still engaged in architecture. My age also helps. And Galerius, of course, is a great support. People think a married woman is somehow more capable. As though Galerius would oversee me and keep me from making engineering mistakes. The poor dear can hardly read a map, let alone design a house." She shrugged. "But it matters little. It is enough that he is by my side."

Chariline sighed. "I am a woman. I am young. I am unmarried. And I do not bear the name of Vitruvius. It does not sound very promising."

"You can't give up before you start!" Vitruvia shoved a clump of wispy hair out of her eyes. "Besides. You may not be a Vitruvius. But you have one at your back."

She took a step away from the table, and her slipper caught one of the scrolls that had landed on the floor earlier. She bent to retrieve it and gave a strangled squeal as she placed it back on the table.

"I think this is the one!" She pointed to an ink stain on the scroll. "I remember that stain. Your mother had written this in haste and left this smudge. So unlike her. She was usually impeccable. Which is why it caught my attention."

She unrolled the papyrus. "Let me see." She hummed in a singsong voice as she perused the letter. *"My heart overflows with happiness. When I am near him, I feel like I have finally arrived home. We belong to each other, Vitruvia. He is witty . . . intelligent, handsome . . ."* Vitruvia skipped over a few lines. *"Unusual kindness . . . encouraging. . .* Aha! Here we are."

Chariline leaned forward, her eyes sparkling.

"His name is . . . Natemahar!"

Chariline jerked back as if slapped.

*"What?"* Her voice emerged high, sharp, unrecognizable to her own ears. "What did you say?"

Vitruvia looked up and froze at the expression on Chariline's face. "Is something wrong?"

Chariline tried to lick dry lips. "I could not have heard right. What did you say his name was?"

Vitruvia returned her attention to Gemina's letter and began to read. *"His name is Natemahar. The queen is grooming him to become a treasurer. And he is the man I will always love."*

"Natemahar?" Chariline rose on shaky legs. "Natemahar? But that's . . . that's impossible. Natemahar is a eunuch! He can't marry or have children."

Vitruvia's eyebrows rose. "Was he born a eunuch?"

"Well, no."

"How old was he when he became one?"

"Young. He was young."

"How young? Ten? Twelve? Twenty-one?"

"I . . . I never asked." She had always assumed that he

had been a boy when it had happened, as was the common practice in such cases. But she realized now that he had never said so. It was not precisely a subject of conversation between them. Natemahar had alluded to it once, in vague terms, when he had referred to his ill health. It was a sensitive topic, she knew, and she made a point never to bring it up.

She lifted her hand to her mouth. If Natemahar had become a eunuch later than she had assumed, he could be her father.

Shock radiated through her, like a lightning strike, shaking her to the marrow. Her mind cycled through a dozen emotions with incomprehensible speed, barely registering each, confusion, anguish, anger flowing through her in an escalating whirlwind that left her gasping for breath.

For seventeen years he had lied to her. Called himself friend. Allowed her to believe that her father was dead.

He had even promised to help Chariline find the man. *Find* him!

What a farce.

With sudden clarity, she remembered Natemahar's face when she had first showed her mother's drawings to him. Remembered the way he had traced the drawings with such tenderness. Chariline had thought him moved by how closely they resembled her own style. Now she knew better. He was remembering his *wife*! The wife he had not once spoken of in all these years.

He was a sham. A liar. A betrayer.

His betrayal went far deeper than her grandfather's deception. At least Grandfather had never pretended to love her.

"Chariline, who is Natemahar?" Vitruvia asked.

"A snake," Chariline hissed. "A lying, deceiving, false pretender."

"I take it you don't like him very much."

"Oh, I love him. And I am going to kill him."

———∾∾———

Theo stretched his legs as far as the cramped confines of the carriage allowed. "You need to allow him to explain, Chariline. From everything you have told me about him, Natemahar has always cared for you."

Chariline turned on him. "Obviously, it was all a lie."

"Perhaps," Theo said calmly. "Or perhaps he truly loves you." He shifted closer to her until she felt pegged by his gaze. "The man I saw, gray with worry, exhausted in his attempt to find and protect you, was not *pretending* to love you. Natemahar might have a reason for thinking you were better off not knowing he was your father."

Chariline crossed her arms over her chest. Her back felt so stiff, it ached. "Don't try to defend him, Theo."

"Why would I defend him? I don't know the man. I am trying to protect *you*."

"It's a little late for that," she snapped.

"I don't deny you are hurt. But you could add to that hurt if you simply kick the man out of your life in anger. You need to give him the opportunity to explain. Natemahar must have believed he had good cause to lie to you."

Chariline sat very still, feeling like a volcano before it exploded. A part of her wanted nothing more than to march into the chamber where Natemahar was sleeping and start throwing bitter accusations. Or furniture. Whichever came more handy.

Another part of her didn't want to disturb his sleep. He had looked so fragile. She loathed to upset him.

Chariline vented a bitter laugh. How could she still care? Apparently, seventeen years of affection could not simply be wiped out in one hour. Even now, knowing what he had done, she felt like she needed to shield that lying snake who had fathered her.

When they arrived at the house, Chariline jumped down from the carriage and strode inside, intending to march upstairs in search of Natemahar. She skidded to a halt in the courtyard.

The object of her internal torment was sitting on the bench, clutching the note she had written him before leaving for Vitruvia's house. She had penned the short missive with a light heart, reassuring him she would return quickly. Return with her father's name.

Natemahar shot to his feet and stared at her face. The dark eyes looked tortured, bloodshot, and unblinking. "I tried to tell you before you left."

Chariline hardened her heart against the plea in his voice. "Have you always known?" she snapped. "Since my birth?"

"No! No, Chariline. I was never allowed to receive any letters from Gemina after we were forced to part. No one told me about your existence. It wasn't until that day I met you in Philip's house, when you were seven, that I realized who you were."

Chariline went over the memory of that first meeting. Regurgitated every phrase, every nuance of Natemahar's reaction. Replayed his shock when he heard her mother's name, the stumbling step he took when he discovered who her grandfather was.

She had never suspected the astonishment on his face that day. She had assumed it to be the natural surprise of finding a relative of Quintus Blandinus in Philip's house.

Now she knew better.

"Let us calculate the mathematics of this relationship, shall we? Leave aside emotion and stick to the brutal testimony of numbers. You discovered I was your daughter when I was seven. And now, I am twenty-four." She pretended to count on her fingers. "Seventeen years. You had seventeen years of opportunities. Six thousand two hundred and five days, not counting leap years, when you could have told me the truth. Written it in a letter. Sent a short note:

*"Chariline, I am your father.*

"In a few short moments, you could have set to right the record of years."

Her throat ached as she pushed down a rising wail. "You could not bring yourself to acknowledge me, is that it? To recognize me before others?" Her voice wavered. "Were you so ashamed of me that you could not even tell me I was your daughter?"

Natemahar took a staggering step toward her. "No, Chariline! You misunderstand." He shook his head, looking dazed, as though unable to think of words.

"Chariline, for twenty-five years, I have served as a treasurer. I have had charge of gold and silver, of jewels and coins and ivory. Of the famous topaz mines of Cush. Of forges full of iron and rivers of textiles. For twenty-five years, my job has been to oversee the most precious treasures of Cush." His eyes softened. Filled. "But it wasn't until I laid eyes on you in Philip's courtyard that I realized what treasure really was. The most enchanting little girl I had ever seen. And by some miracle, you were mine! My own jewel.

"You have been my treasure for seventeen years, Chariline. The first name in my prayers, the last name in my intercessions. Other than Iesous, there is nothing in this world more precious to me."

Chariline spun around. "Then why? Why have you lied to me all this time?"

# CHAPTER 26

—— ⌘ ——

*It is not an enemy who taunts me—*
*I could bear that.*
*It is not my foes who so arrogantly insult me—*
*I could have hidden from them.*
*Instead, it is you—my equal,*
*my companion and close friend.*

PSALM 55:12-13, NLT

Natemahar dropped his gaze. "Chariline, you cannot understand how deeply your grandfather loathes me. Your mother was engaged to be married when we met. Not to just any man. But to the son of a Roman quaestor, with ties in Egypt. He had promised a promotion to your grandfather after their children married. Our elopement did not merely embarrass Quintus Blandinus. It prevented his opportunity for advancement.

"He blames me for that. For the years of being stuck in Cush. And he blames me for your mother's death. If I had not gotten her pregnant, she would still be alive.

"If your grandfather had discovered that I even knew about you, he would have hidden you in a hole I could never find. He is a Roman citizen. I am not. I have no rights or standing in regard to you, not if Blandinus decides to set himself against me. And he certainly would. He would never give you up to me.

"I was afraid to tell you. You were a child. A slip of the tongue to your aunt Blandina and we both know she would have been too afraid to hide it from her father. He would have ripped you from me."

Chariline thought of the way her grandfather had blocked any means of her discovering Natemahar's identity, had wiped his very existence out of her life, and had to concede the point.

"You could have taken me. Away from Caesarea. From Cush. Away from him. We could have had each other somewhere, hidden in some corner of the empire."

"That was my plan with your mother. And it did not work out well. It would be even worse with you. Think about it, Chariline. Your grandfather would pursue us to the ends of the earth. Not because he loves you. But because he hates me. What kind of life would that be for a little girl? Never settled, running from city to city. I could not get a proper job. We would live in poverty. In fear. Always looking over our shoulders. How could I do that to you?"

She arched a brow. "So instead you left me with a woman who could hardly bear to touch my hand. Hardly say my name without wincing. You left me, Natemahar! Left me to a lonely life. You abandoned me. How is that better? I could have had my father!" She choked. "I could have had hugs and kisses and everything a little girl longs for. You could have cherished me."

Tears streaked down Natemahar's cheeks. "I did cherish you, Chariline. With every bit of my heart."

"Three or four weeks out of the year? A pile of letters and

notes? You think that made me feel cherished? You think that was a better life?"

Natemahar took a wavering step toward her. "There was not a day I did not long for you, child. I ached from your absence for every hour of those seventeen years."

She took a step back. "Not enough to reveal the truth, apparently. You could have told me later, Natemahar. When I was older. When you knew you could trust me. Confide in me to keep our secret."

"I was wary of the Kandake. As long as your grandfather had an influential position in Cush, she would have disapproved of any connection between us. Your grandfather might be a minor official, but as the only permanent Roman authority in Cush, he has the ear of powerful people. He could interfere with Rome's policy toward our nation. Our semi-independence hangs by a thread as it is. The queen would not allow the nation to suffer because of my personal feelings."

A vein pulsed in Natemahar's forehead. "That was her objection to my marrying Gemina, and it would have been her objection to us living openly as father and daughter. She would never allow it. Not while Quintus Blandinus could foment trouble for Cush."

Chariline smiled, a small, bitter smile she could not hide. "I always knew to avoid her. You had taught me that much."

Natemahar nodded. "Chariline, you . . ." Without warning, he staggered. His knees folded and he dropped to the ground.

"Natemahar!" she cried and rushed to him. For a moment

she forgot his betrayal. Forgot his abandonment. Dropping
to her knees, she put an arm around his shoulder. Theo, who
had retreated to the kitchen to allow them privacy, ran to
Natemahar and carefully hauled him to his feet.

"I will call for a physician," he said.

"No need." Natemahar wiped his brow with a thin square
of cotton. "I sometimes suffer from these spells. What I need
is a few hours of rest. I would like to return to my inn. I will
be more comfortable there."

"Of course," Theo said. "Taharqa and I will take you."

Chariline stared at him, appalled. She had never seen him
this ill. "I am sorry," she said, clutching her arms. She should
have given him a chance to recover from his travels before
pouncing on him.

His eyes shimmered, drowning in moisture. "Child, I am
the one who is sorry. The guilt is entirely mine, as is the contrition. You have nothing to apologize for."

"Come," Theo said. "Sit by the fountain. Chariline, bring
Natemahar a cup of sweet wine while I arrange for a litter."

Chariline obeyed Theo's bidding, her heart in two great
knots. One a gnarl of worry. The other a tangle of betrayal
and hurt and anger. They sat side by side while she held the
cup to Natemahar's lips and wiped his brow with water from
the little pool.

There was a strange intimacy to the moment. Had they
lived as father and daughter, they would have had other such
experiences. In sickness, in weakness, in celebration, in the
daily familiarity of life together.

She wiped Natemahar's perspiring neck. Wiped the trickle

of wine from the corner of his lip. And it came to her in a blinding flash of painful realization: her fingers were touching her father.

———— ⌘ ————

Theo insisted on sending for a physician when they arrived at Natemahar's private chamber. Taharqa added some encouragement in Meroitic that Theo could not understand, and with a sigh, the treasurer gave in.

"Would you like to pray?" Theo asked after Taharqa left to fetch the physician.

"That would be a blessing," Natemahar said in his soft voice. "But I have inconvenienced you enough. You must have better things to attend than wasting your time on a stranger."

"Nothing that won't keep." Theo knelt on one knee by Natemahar's bed. "You are not exactly a stranger to me, Natemahar. Your fame precedes you. Even in the church at Corinth, I had heard of you. It took me a while to realize the friend Chariline spoke of so often was none other than the chief treasurer of Ethiopia, as the Greeks call your nation, and the man who came to faith on the road from Jerusalem to Gaza."

Natemahar gave a pale smile. "I was reading a scroll of the prophet Isaiah in my chariot and Philip ran alongside to ask if I understood what I was reading. I invited him to join me in my chariot and teach me the meaning of the Scripture. I thought he would refuse."

Theo frowned. "Why?"

Natemahar looked away. "Because of what I am. In Jerusalem, I was not even allowed into the Temple, though

I was a God fearer and had placed my faith in the Lord. The Pharisees looked down on me. The teachers of the Law avoided me. But Philip climbed into my chariot and settled next to me as if we were old friends."

"How did you become a God fearer?" Theo asked, curious as to how a man of Cush would have learned of the Hebrew God. Even Taharqa still worshiped the Egyptian deities, though over the years, he had gained a healthy respect for the Lord.

"I owe that to the Kandake, I suppose."

"Your queen is a follower of the Lord?"

A corner of Natemahar's lip tipped up. "Not quite. But when she intercepted Gemina and me on our flight from Cush, she decided I needed the kind of punishment that would leave an indelible mark in my memory. She sent me off to her torture chamber."

Theo's heart sank. "I am sorry, Natemahar."

"So was she, as it turned out. Her man did not have the skills the Kandake supposed. She had only intended to teach me a lesson. The queen wanted to ensure that I would never pursue Gemina again. She expected me to recover fully after being properly terrified. Except that her man went too far.

"Later, my physician told me that the queen had been furious when she discovered the extent of the damage to my body. At the time, I was too sick to know anything but pain. I remember wishing myself dead through the long hours of endless torment.

"To try and save my life, the Kandake sent for the best physician she could find, a Hebrew named Coniah. Coniah dragged my broken bones from the doors of death. But even his expertise could not restore me fully. When I rose from my bed of infirmity, I was as you see me."

A eunuch, he meant. He could not even say the word, Theo realized.

"It took me several months to regain my health. Coniah would speak to me of the Lord as I convalesced. He was well versed in the Scriptures. By the time I recovered, I had walked away from the gods of Cush. Eventually, the Kandake gave me permission to go to Jerusalem and worship my God.

"But I found myself—" he gave Theo a sidelong glance—"not quite welcomed. I purchased a copy of the scroll of Isaiah, hoping to learn in the isolation of my own heart. It was this scroll I was reading when Philip found me and began to teach me about the Messiah."

"Is it true you asked to be baptized before you had arrived at Gaza?"

"Indeed. Why waste time? I have been trained to recognize treasure when I see it. Over two decades have passed since that day, and I still remember it as if it were this morning. The most glorious hour of my life."

For a moment, the hollow, haunted look on Natemahar's face was replaced by a glow not of this earth. Theo stared in mute wonder. Natemahar's faith seemed like a living fire, a burning power that warmed the room.

"I always admired your story of faith, Natemahar," he said. "The way you received the Lord, welcomed him so quickly. I never thought one day to meet you."

The treasurer dropped his gaze. "I am sorry to be a disappointment to you, young man."

Theo placed a hand on the treasurer's shoulder. "On the

contrary. I see a man who wanted to protect his daughter to the best of his ability." Theo tried to make his voice level. "Believe me when I tell you, I wish I had a father like you."

—— ᏣᏜ ——

It took Theo four hours to return from Natemahar's inn. By then, Chariline was pacing the confines of Priscilla's courtyard, wearing a groove in the old mosaics. "What took so long?" she gasped when Theo and Taharqa finally walked through the gates.

"I called for a physician." Theo rubbed his neck. "He will attend Natemahar until he regains his strength. As it is a recurring condition, the physician does not seem overly concerned."

Chariline expelled the breath she had not realized she was holding. She clutched her hair and dropped her chin to her chest. "I thought I had killed him."

"No. No. He is not strong, as you know. But he will recover."

Chariline sat abruptly on the damp floor next to a pot of rosemary. "Theo, I don't know what to do. All I wanted was to find my father. And now that I have, I feel that my heart will break."

Theo lowered himself to the other side of the pot. Absently, he plucked a sprig, crushing the needlelike leaves between his palms, until the camphoraceous scent of them filled the air.

"Remember what I told you?" he said. "Weeks ago, on the ship, I reminded you that the Lord is with you. *Always.* This is the season you need to remember that promise. Your *always* season. You are not alone as you walk through this wilderness."

"Natemahar abandoned me, Theo."

"But Yeshua will not." Theo's gaze slid away from her. "You need to go and see Natemahar."

Anxiety crawled across her chest, a centipede with a hundred legs poking at her. "And say what? That everything is well between us? It is not! That I forgive him? I do not!"

"He does not want you to lie. That will not heal either of you."

"The last time I tried to tell the truth, he collapsed!"

"Yes, I know. But he had been traveling for weeks. He was overtired and anxious. For years, he has hidden this secret, held it from you, borne the weight of it, and finally, it has come to light. That is enough to make anyone collapse. Now you need to finish what you began."

"What? Finish screaming at him?"

"If you need to. Just as importantly, finish listening to him."

"There is nothing he can ever say that will excuse what he has done."

"Perhaps not. But it might explain a few things. Things you need to know. I saw the way you ran to him when he crumpled. Saw the look of terror in your eyes. Saw the way you cared for him. In the midst of your anger and rage, you still offered him tenderness. I know you have lost all trust in Natemahar. But love can bridge your way back to him."

His voice dropped low until she had to strain to hear him. "There is many a son and daughter who has never been loved by a father the way Natemahar loves you."

Chariline wrapped her arms around her middle, trying to hold herself together, trying to keep her bones from shattering with misery.

Theo pried her hand away from her side and held it. She stared at his fingers, long and tapered and strong, swallowing up her own in their clasp. Warmth climbed from his palms, creeping into her wrist, her arm, her neck until her face grew as hot as one of Lollia's cooking pots.

"Listen," Theo said, and Chariline ripped her gaze away from his hands, training her eyes on him. "You have already lost twenty-four years. Twenty-four years of ordinary moments. Of belonging and being known. Don't waste another twenty-four years on anger."

# CHAPTER 27

— ᘓᘝᗒ —

*Instead of your shame*
*you will receive a double portion,*
*and instead of disgrace*
*you will rejoice in your inheritance.*
*And so you will inherit a double portion in your land,*
*and everlasting joy will be yours.*

ISAIAH 61:7, NIV

The next afternoon, Chariline accompanied Theo to Natemahar's inn. She found him sitting at a narrow desk, writing official documents in a pool of sunlight. He dropped his treasurer's seal when she followed Theo into the chamber.

"Chariline." Natemahar rose slowly. "I . . . I did not expect you would ever want to see me again."

"Half of me doesn't," she said honestly. "The other half won."

"I am grateful for that half. Though, I understand the other."

"How are you?" she asked.

"Better, thank you." He indicated a stool to her and the bed to Theo, and they all sat on the edges of their respective seats. An awkward silence filled the room.

Natemahar cleared his throat. "May I order some food for you? Spiced wine, perhaps? The inn provides decent fare."

"Thank you, no. I helped Lollia cook today and for some reason, now I feel quite full."

"You *cooked*?" Natemahar's brows rose. He was well aware that her only acquaintance with a kitchen came from helping to haul food to the table.

"I helped."

"Chariline was the official taster, like the prophet Nehemiah for the king of Persia," Theo provided. "She sampled everything before it went into the pot."

"Very amusing," Chariline said, oddly irritated by Theo's jest. "In fact, I peeled, chopped, washed, fetched, stirred. And, yes, perhaps I tasted a little." She shrugged. "Aunt Blandina and Grandmother do not like me anywhere near the kitchen. But Lollia and Priscilla have been teaching me a few things."

At the mention of Aunt Blandina, another awkward silence filled the room.

"Child, you cannot know how sorry I am," Natemahar burst out. "How deeply sorry I am for the pain I have caused you. I never realized your life was so difficult with Blandina. She always seemed kind to me. Insipid. Petrified of her father. But kind. I had no idea she was cold and distant."

"I never told you. Not everything. What would have been the point? You could have done nothing about it. Or, so I thought." Chariline inhaled. "Aunt Blandina is kind, in her own way. Then again, I took her sister from her. My birth was responsible for her death. I cannot blame her for the grudge she holds against me."

Natemahar's jaw protruded. "I am in no position to judge," he said through grinding teeth.

"No."

Unable to remain seated, she scrambled to her feet. "Natemahar, you could at least have told me the truth when I discovered my father was alive! Why put me through that ridiculous farce? Why read Vitruvia's letters and say nothing? Touch my mother's drawings and not admit who she was? Why let me chase after Sesen?"

Natemahar wiped a hand over his mouth. She saw that the fingers were trembling and had to contend with a fresh wave of writhing anxiety.

"What could I have told you, child?" Natemahar said. "That after all your years of longing, after what seemed like a miraculous discovery, *this* is what you have for a father?" He pressed a hand to his chest. "This broken half man? This fragile shell that is inferior to every normal man?"

She forgot to fill her lungs with air. *"What?"*

"Do you know, in Jerusalem, they would not even allow me to step into the Temple? Eunuchs have no place in the assembly of the Lord. That is what you wanted for a father?"

"What do I care what they do at the Temple?" she cried.

He took a gulping breath. "In the court of the Kandake, I have influence. She has given me a high position. But position means little elsewhere. I will always be less than other men." He shrugged. "They respect me to my face and laugh behind my back.

"I could not bear it. I could not bear the look of disappointment in your eyes. At least, as long as you were chasing after a phantom, you could dream of better things. Now, what do you have? When you introduce me as your father, you will hear sniggers and whispers. You will be the object of scorn. This is my legacy."

Chariline took a half step toward him. "Natemahar, it never mattered to me that you held such a high office. And I cared just as little about you being a eunuch. When have I ever looked down on you?"

Natemahar's gaze slid from her. "As long as we were only friends, it did not matter so much. But to have me as a father?" He shook his head. "I will only bring you shame."

Chariline drew herself up to her full height. "You think a few disdainful comments could sway me from loving you? You think I would be ashamed of you because of what the Kandake's knife did to your body? Do you know me so little, Natemahar?

"Well, I know *you* through and through. I know you are good, kind, wise, caring, godly. Most of the time, you are even honest. No derisive whisper is going to change what I know. If nothing else, all the years of having Quintus Blandinus Geminus as my grandfather have taught me not to care about the opinions of unworthy men and women. You give me too little credit."

For the merest fraction, Natemahar's visage changed, became stamped with a wild hunger, as though for the first time in twenty-five years he was tasting hope. As though her words were an ax that had broken the root of something dark and dreadful. Then, in a blink, the hunger evaporated, and his face returned to its normal, smooth mask.

Only then did Chariline grasp what Natemahar had

hidden from her for seventeen years. Not merely his identity as her father. Something deeper and more powerful lay hidden in the soil of his heart.

Under every decision for silence, for secrecy, lay something far subtler, like the snake in Paradise, slithering on its belly and making sibilant accusations.

Natemahar judged himself unworthy. He considered himself a half thing, an eyesore, an object of scorn.

And he expected her to do the same, not because Natemahar gave *her* too little credit. But because he gave his condition too much.

She thought of Theo's angel who looked in the mirror and saw reflected in his scars a strong tower of protection, pointing to God's love. Natemahar only saw a pointing finger of accusation. Like the angel, some of Natemahar's scars could not be hidden. His broken body forever marked him. When he stepped into a room, everyone knew what had been done to him. And because of this constant reminder, he had never been able to overcome his wound.

With sudden insight, Chariline knew what she had to do. Knew why God had brought her on this long journey of discovery and disappointment.

Chariline did not need a father nearly as much as Natemahar needed a daughter.

The storm of her anger, the mounting tower of her rage, collapsed.

They simply could not bear the weight of Chariline's compassion and love.

She lifted a hand to Natemahar's cheek and cradled it gently.

She turned his face slowly toward her, until his eyes grew level with hers, captured by the inexorable intensity in her gaze.

"Father," she whispered.

The word sounded strange on her lips. "My father," she said and kissed his cheek. "I love you." Kneeling down before him, she kissed the backs of his hands. "I am proud to have you as my father."

Natemahar made an odd sound deep in his throat. A buried wail let loose after years of being shoved down, shoved so far down that his whole being shook as it wriggled out of him. His shoulders shuddered. It was as if his body were an earthquake and his heart the epicenter.

He dropped on his knees, eyes level with Chariline. Several times, his mouth opened as he tried to speak. But no sound emerged. Not even a whisper. He could only produce tears, it seemed, as moisture leaked out of him, spreading across the expanse of his cheeks.

"Father," Chariline said and clasped him to her in an embrace that held the love and ache of years.

She heard, finally, the words he was gasping, as they came broken and half strangled out of his lips.

"My daughter."

Then some floodgate opened that he could no longer shut, and he gasped again and again, "My daughter, daughter, daughter." A litany that changed to, "My girl," "My child," and back again, not stopping until his throat had turned so dry, it could not produce another sound. And still his lips moved, forming a single word.

*Daughter.*

Over his head, Chariline caught a glimpse of Theo, sitting paralyzed on Natemahar's bed, his beautiful face frozen in an odd expression of wonder, eyes wide and unseeing, as if he had witnessed something not of this earth.

——— භ———

In the covered litter that Theo had hired, Chariline slumped against the cushions, dazed. Her life had changed in the course of a few hours.

If not for Theo's insistence, she would not even have gone to the inn. She would not have discovered the wound that had shaped her father's past.

Like a shimmering comet arcing across the night sky, realization dawned. She straightened so abruptly, she hit her head on the roof of the litter. "You knew!" she said to Theo. "You knew he felt that way! That was why you pressed me to go and see him."

Theo smiled. "I suspected." He straightened the edge of his tunic. "Yesterday, while we waited for the physician to come, he told me his story of faith. I noticed that he could not even say the word *eunuch*. It made me realize that apart from his concerns about your grandfather and the queen, Natemahar had a deeper reason for not wanting you to know he was your father."

"You could have warned me."

"It was not my secret to share. This was a conversation only the two of you could have had."

"Didn't you worry that I might make matters worse? Respond with the disappointment he feared?"

"You?" Theo laughed. "Not for a moment. I knew you would never scorn him. You love him too much."

"I do love him." She twitched the curtain and stared blindly into the bright street. It had been an unforgettable hour. But she felt wrung out.

"All these litters and carriages must be costing you a fortune," she said.

Theo shrugged. "I am growing quite accustomed to the luxury."

"You hate being confined inside these things with the curtains drawn! Admit it. I have seen you stick your head out of the window, gulping down the air as if you are about to suffocate."

Theo scratched his chest. "It's very disconcerting."

"What is?"

"Your powers of observation."

"You know what else is disconcerting? The endless coin you are spending on my behalf. I have to find a way to repay you. And we need to catch this mercenary."

"Forget the coin. As to catching this annoying Cushite who hurls pots at women and dogs, you will find a willing accomplice in me. Have you any ideas how we can manage such a feat?"

"Yes."

Theo turned half a revolution and studied her with interest. "Do enlarge."

"What does he want? Me. So, that is what we give him."

Making a disgusted noise in his throat, Theo turned away. "We are not using you as bait."

"Why not? With you and Taharqa there, it would be as safe as Nero's palace."

"Dozens of people have died in that palace." Theo plucked a fluff of lint from his tunic. "Too many things could go wrong, Chariline. We will not play with your life."

She crossed her arms. "And I will not have you spend a fortune on carriages."

"We will ask your father's opinion, shall we?"

Chariline's mouth popped open. "What?"

"He deserves to weigh in on this conversation."

In all the weeks and days and hours she had dreamed of finding her father, Chariline realized, with shock, she had never considered this eventuality. A father would have a say in her life. Have opinions. Have authority. For years, Aunt Blandina had been such a tolerant and placid guardian that Chariline had grown accustomed to having her own way in most things. Those days might be coming to a quick end, it seemed.

———— ◦◦◦ ————

Desperation drove him to recklessness.

His coin pouch had grown alarmingly light, and he could not send for more, not when he had no results to offer. The hours slipped by and the aggravating woman gave him no more opportunities. How he itched to throttle that pretty neck.

Time, he decided, for drastic measures.

When he saw the litter approach the house, he slunk close. Forget accidents. He would just use his long knife like a proper soldier. This cloak-and-dagger business suited women and courtiers. It fell beneath his dignity. He would cut her throat and take her purse and call it a robbery. One of a hundred in Rome. Close enough to the accident he had been paid to arrange.

The vexing young man who had been shadowing her steps alighted from the litter. He had come close enough once to hear the woman call him Theo. The warrior approached, keeping his back glued to the wall, waiting for her to dismount before making his move. He would kill two for the price of one this day.

He saw Theo reach a hand into the litter and prepared to surge forward. But before drawing her out, Theo turned to look carefully, surveying the pavement and the road. His gaze froze when it landed on the warrior.

The warrior growled. He had lost the element of surprise. Theo yelled something and the litter took off, taking the woman out of his reach.

He howled in frustration and drew his knife. With satisfaction, he noted that Theo was unarmed. This should prove quick and easy. With him out of the way, the girl would fall into his hands like a ripe date. Not a bad day, after all.

He grinned and lunged.

The warrior did not see Theo move, but somehow, the young man evaded the thrust, so that the long blade of the knife traveled too far, in a straight line that carried the warrior's arm beyond Theo's back. He managed to pull back just before Theo could grab his arm.

The warrior thrust again, this time aiming for the heart.

Again, Theo sidestepped with an easy dexterity that was almost insulting.

The warrior felt rage rise up, clogging his vision, and forced it down with all his might. He needed calm in this battle. His victory depended on it.

Taking a deep breath, he readjusted his balance. He had underestimated his young opponent. Not a mistake he would make again.

Narrowing his eyes, he feigned dead center, but came in low, intending to cut Theo at the thigh, where a great vein, slashed at the proper angle, would cause him to bleed to death within moments.

Feather light, Theo leapt into the air. Grabbing one of the poles that held the awning above the door, he pulled himself up, evading the knife's sharp edge. Instead of jumping down again, he swung, drawing his hips backward while keeping his legs tucked behind to gain momentum. Before the warrior could move, he found a booted foot in his gut.

Breath hissed out of him, and for a short moment his vision darkened.

Regaining his equilibrium, he swapped the knife to his left hand. Lightning fast, he pulled out the dainty dagger strapped to his side. Taking aim, he pitched the blade at Theo. It was a perfect throw, and the dagger flew fast and true.

The warrior's jaw came unhinged.

For a moment, he could not make sense of what he had just witnessed. He squeezed his eyes shut and opened them again. Was it even possible? The speed! The earth-defying movement as Theo let go of the pole, soaring upward instead of down like a normal human being, arms tucked close to his chest, twirling away from the path of the knife and landing with perfect economy of motion, one knee on the ground, balancing his weight with the tips of his fingers.

The dagger lay buried harmlessly in the leather of the awning.

The warrior's mouth ran dry as the young man looked up, eyes burning feverishly.

He was a warrior of Cush, and no odd, prancing boy would get in his way. Besides, he still possessed the only weapon here.

He shifted his long knife back to his right hand and surged forward. Before he had reached close enough to attempt the choke hold he intended, Theo leapt up, twirled as he flew into the air, and somehow, by the time he was facing the warrior, he held the dagger the warrior had thrown at him.

The warrior went cold. This fight was losing its appeal. And the girl had disappeared from sight. What was the point of facing off with Prancing Boy and gaining nothing?

It tasted bitter, the decision to run. He never ran. Except when absolutely necessary. It did not sit well with him, he thought as he pumped his legs in the opposite direction, to turn his back on a fight.

He ran faster when he heard the young man keeping up behind him. The sun had started to set, lengthening the shadows. Better even than the darkening sky was the fact that carts were allowed to enter the streets of the city once more. The warrior caught sight of a huge one, loaded with terra-cotta statuary, and threw himself in its path. He barely avoided getting crushed. The girl had used the same ploy on him, once, with annoying success. And it worked again, this time to his advantage. He was able to put enough distance between himself and Theo so that the crowds near Circus Maximus swallowed him, making it impossible for his opponent to track him.

He returned his knife to the strap at his side, slowing to a walk. His favorite dagger lost, gods curse the man! He had filched it off a Roman and prized its light weight and perfect balance. Now Prancing Boy had it.

His belly gurgled and he stopped to buy pork sausages and salted peas from a street vendor. Crouching at the base of a public fountain, he tried to plan his next step. The back of his neck still itched and burned from the bee stings, and as he rubbed at the spot absently, he admitted that he was not eager to face that odd leaping boy again. Not even to get his dagger back.

Chewing on the spicy sausage, he realized he would have to distract Theo. Pull him away from her, somehow. He shoved another lump of sausage in his mouth and began a pleasant daydream.

# CHAPTER 28

*And let us consider how to stir up one another*
*to love and good works, not neglecting to meet together.*

HEBREWS 10:24-25

Chariline called a hasty instruction to the men carrying her
litter, ordering them to stop a short distance from Priscilla and
Aquila's house. She wanted, desperately, to run back and help
Theo but knew she would only distract him by her presence.

Dismounting from the litter, she watched the ensuing
drama with amazement. The skirmish lasted no more than
a few moments, but to her, it felt like endless hours. The
first thrust of the Cushite's knife against an unarmed Theo
made her cry out. She expected Theo to emerge bloody and
wounded from that encounter. But he did not.

She watched Theo's body as it leapt in the air, twirled,
and landed with impossible grace. Gasped as he parried the
warrior's vicious blade again and again. She had never seen
anyone move like that. He looked like the famous frescos of

ancient Mycenaean bull leapers, maneuvering with a tempo that defied human speed.

Dumbfounded, she saw him pursue the warrior into the crowds. She had hoped that after vanquishing the man, he would give up the fight. Her shoulders dropped with relief when she saw him return unharmed. Chariline bade the drivers to carry the litter back to the house, where Theo stood at the door, dagger in hand, his face a grim mask as he searched the streets looking, no doubt, for her.

Beyond words, beyond decorum, she leapt out of the vehicle before the men could lower it properly to the ground and launched herself into Theo's arms.

"Watch the dagger," he warned.

"I thought you were going to die!" She wrapped her arms around his back.

His face started to lose its grim cast. Slowly, he smiled. "Did you?" He shifted slightly to allow her body to fit more snugly against him.

She realized how absurdly vine-like her arms twined around him and took a step back. Heat flooded her face. "Thank God you are not hurt."

"I can't believe I let him get away."

"You weren't even armed."

"I am now," he said, flipping the dagger hand over fist. He cast a look toward Aquila and Priscilla's awning and winced. "I'll have to replace that."

"It could have been your throat!" Her voice emerged high and thin.

Theo tucked the dagger into his belt. "No, sweetheart. He didn't stand a chance."

Chariline's lips parted. Had Theo just called her *sweetheart*?

The litter driver stepped forward. "Nice fight, that. You should consider going to the arena."

Theo withdrew a few coins from his pouch and paid the man. "I appreciate how fast you moved."

The driver shrugged. "She don't weigh much." He counted the coins and tipped his head in acknowledgment. "You ever want a litter again, my brother and I will take you anywhere."

When the litter drivers had moved on, Chariline said, "That thing you did."

He arched a dark brow. "Thing?"

"You know. The leaping and twirling. What *was* that?"

Theo's smile, lopsided and pleased, did something strange to her heart. "Just a bit of fun."

"Fun?"

"A man from Crete used to visit the gymnasium where I trained as a boy. He could flip forward and backward and leap from a great height without being hurt. He encouraged us to learn the sport. Most of the boys didn't bother after the first collection of painful bruises. But Galenos's daughter, Ariadne, used to practice with me. Eventually, we became quite proficient. It has been a long time since I have really trained. I suppose after so many hours of practice, the movements sink into your bones and your body remembers."

"You practiced that with a girl?"

His smile seemed veiled, as if it hid a well of secrets. "She wasn't just any girl. The year I won the chariot race at the Isthmian Games, she won the short footrace."

"She competed against other women?"

"A few women. Mostly men, some of whom were professional athletes."

"Impressive."

"Aha."

"I suppose she is also beautiful."

Theo's lids dropped. "She has her charms. She is married to my brother, Justus. Her leaping and flipping days are long gone; she is the mother of a fat little boy now, who they named after me, of course." He seemed pleased by the fact. But Chariline had not missed the blaze of pain in the gray irises before he covered them.

She wondered, with the sudden flash of insight experienced by a thousand women before her, if he had once called Ariadne *sweetheart.*

———— ∾ ————

In the morning, her father sent a note, asking if he may join the family for dinner. Natemahar had assured them they would not need to cook a thing. If Priscilla and Aquila were agreeable, he intended to ask the inn to prepare the meal and hire two servers for the evening.

To Chariline's delight, her hosts accepted Natemahar's proposal. They all knew this was her father's way of thanking Priscilla and Aquila for their hospitality, not only in welcoming him, but also in opening their home to his daughter.

She might never grow tired of those words. *His daughter.*

Her father was coming to dinner.

Her *father* was coming to dinner.

Not her friend. Not Natemahar. Her *father.*

They had decided to serve the meal in the courtyard, and

Chariline set the table with the household's red-glazed pottery, placing Priscilla's cherished silver saltcellar in the center. Next to each plate, she arranged a simple square napkin next to a bronze spoon. She scattered rose and violet petals on the tiles, creating a jaunty pattern around the stools and benches that Theo had pulled up to the table.

This was a far cry from Vitruvia's elegant dinner setting with its roomy couches and silver platters. But, in a way, Chariline preferred the intimacy and ease of Priscilla's house.

She realized she was counting the moments until her father's arrival. Although the pain of Natemahar's duplicity still stung, Theo had been right. Understanding the source of his actions had helped to stop the erupting flood of bitterness that had blinded her.

She still felt the hurt of the past seventeen years. The ache of so much loss. How could she not? They were years she could never have back. But regret and grief did not have the power to swallow up forgiveness the way anger could.

Upon discovering Natemahar's betrayal, all she had felt at first was rage. That rage had eaten up all the joy of finding the father who, undoubtedly, loved her. Now, she found the joy and cradled it close.

What would life be like after this, she wondered? Would her father ask her to move to Cush? Would the Kandake allow an open relationship between them now that her grandfather was moving away from Meroë?

It occurred to her, for the first time, that finding her father meant she would have to leave Rome sooner than she had expected. Chariline froze midstep, a cup forgotten in her clutching fingers, hovering over the table. Whether she returned to Caesarea or Cush, she had no reason to linger here anymore.

No reason to remain with Theo.

She sank onto the stool next to her and stared at the pink and violet petals at her feet. She was not ready to bid Theo good-bye. The very thought felt like a stab from Theo's newly acquired dagger.

She tried to cling to the memory of Theo calling her sweetheart. Theo fitting her body snugly against his, as if he did not wish to let her go. Perhaps he did not want her to leave either.

Then reality took over, flowing over her like a bucket of icy water from the northern springs. A grin and an endearment in the afterglow of danger meant nothing. Theo had never hinted at feeling anything for her save friendship and, perhaps, an onerous sort of responsibility.

He had revealed bits of his past, mostly to comfort her. But he had never revealed his heart to her. Not the way a man would to the woman he loved.

Chariline had sensed strong feelings from him when he mentioned Ariadne the day before. Perhaps he loved this Ariadne. And if so, merely because she had married his brother—which, as far as Chariline was concerned, simply made her a fool when she had had the chance to have Theo—did not mean that Theo had stopped loving her.

That he had a heart to offer Chariline.

Chariline's fingers shook so badly she had to place the cup carefully on the table before she dropped it.

Without the distraction of finding Vitruvia and her father to cloud her mind, she had to face some painful realities. Mercy and grace help her, she could no longer deny her love for Theo. And if Theo loved the extraordinary Ariadne, he would have no reason to pursue Chariline when she left Rome.

———— ୭୧୦ ————

Her father arrived in the early evening, food and servants in tow. Although the Romans liked to eat supper early, lingering over their meal as long as possible, he knew his hosts were working people and needed the afternoon to tend to their leather business. Thoughtfully, he timed his arrival to coincide with the closing of the leather shop.

The servers he had hired, two quiet men with clean hands and carefully combed hair, brought in three large baskets filled with iron pans, pots, and wine amphorae. They had even brought their own serving platters and spoons.

Before long, everyone sat down to a tasty meal of mushrooms and eggs, followed by roasted pheasant, an extravagant treat more suited to the palaces and villas of the aristocracy than the wobbly table of a shopkeeper. Chariline grinned at Natemahar with approval, proud of his generosity.

For once, the women were able to stay at the table without having to run to the kitchen every few minutes. Even Lollia, who had joined them at her father's insistence, did not have to lift a finger except to bring the food to her lips.

Mouthwatering desserts followed the elaborately decorated pheasant. Rich fig cake was served alongside a delicate cheese-and-honey pudding that quivered on their plates like a shy maiden. The servers vanished into the kitchen after bringing each course to the table, leaving the party to converse privately.

While they ate their delectable sweet treats, Priscilla coaxed

Natemahar to recount his now-famous first encounter with Philip. Everyone around the table began to swap stories of faith. Chariline felt as if heaven itself had pierced the world of men and women and wrapped it in a blanket of joy. It was easy to believe, in those God-touched moments, that everything good was possible with Iesous. Every doubt that had plagued her was consumed by the faith that flowed like a river around her.

"And how did you two meet?" Natemahar asked Priscilla.

"We met at the synagogue where I worshiped as a God fearer," she said.

He nodded. "I, too, began my journey of faith as a God fearer. Was it love at first sight?"

She laughed. "What do you say, Aquila?"

Aquila bit his lip. "I was not that clever, I fear. In fact, I admit, I was downright dense."

"I hope you hit him as hard as you hit me," Theo said to Priscilla.

"Well, I did not, as a matter of fact. I save my best blows for you, my dear."

Theo rolled his eyes.

Chariline shook her head. "I'm surprised you were even able to come anywhere near Theo. If you had seen him fight as I did, you would know what a miracle it is that your hand connected with his cheek."

"Clearly, he could not defend himself against me." Priscilla placed a hand on her hip, looking very pleased. "Next time you need someone to protect you, Chariline, you better call on me. Theo obviously can't keep up."

"I had no idea I would have to defend myself against my

own friend," Theo said. "Besides, you look so delicate, I did not realize you could render me unconscious."

Priscilla laughed. "As I recall, you walked perfectly well on your own two feet."

"Sleepwalked, more like. I have no memory of it. Likely, you damaged my brain." He turned to Natemahar. "That was a lovely meal. Thank you."

"Indeed," Priscilla said. "And I did not have to prepare it, which made it twice as delicious. I do enjoy cooking. Even so, it is wonderful to have a night off once in a while."

"Priscilla is an exceptional cook, Father," Chariline said.

Natemahar forgot to put his spoon in his mouth. His hand hovered in front of him, the small mound of cheese pudding quivering in its spoon.

It occurred to her that this was the first time she had called him *Father* in so public a fashion.

He cleared his throat and placed the spoon back on his plate. She tried to read his expression, wondering if she had crossed a line. Wondering if he would ask her, just as publicly, to cease such intimacy. A vein started to pound in her temple.

He dropped his gaze to his hands. When he looked up, his eyes shimmered. "I could grow used to that," he said.

Chariline exhaled. She beamed at him. "I can only imagine the Kandake's face if I say it in front of her."

"Speaking of the Kandake." Theo leaned in. "I have been thinking about this assassin. You told us, when you first came, that the queen would not want Chariline's relationship with you to be made public because she wished to avoid offending Quintus Blandinus."

"Yes?"

"You said yourself, Natemahar, that the queen would not allow your personal feelings to harm Cush in any way. She already ripped you and Gemina apart in spite of the fact that you were married. And she had no problem sending you to a torture chamber. Given how ruthless she is, do you not wonder if perhaps she has hired this assassin herself? Hired him to get rid of Chariline altogether?"

Theo dropped his napkin to the table. "If your queen has discovered that you two are, in fact, in regular communication, maybe she feels threatened. In order to protect Cush's assets from Quintus Blandinus and his desire for revenge, all she has to do is get your daughter out of the way."

Natemahar shook his head. "I don't think that is possible. For one thing, as I mentioned before, she herself warned me about the assassin."

"I realize. But perhaps her intention was to confuse you. She didn't give you enough information to truly help us catch this man. By giving you this insignificant snippet, she won your trust without losing anything. This way, you are not likely to suspect her in the future. Or turn against her."

"I understand your reasoning," Natemahar said. "But it is unlikely. Before telling me about the assassin, the Kandake revealed that she has known about my connection to Chariline almost from the beginning."

"Could she have been lying?"

"She had a trail of information going back years. She knew I used to meet Chariline in Caesarea. Knew about my visits to Philip's house. Knew about the spice shop where I would secretly meet Chariline over the years. She had dates, Theo! Her evidence is irrefutable."

Chariline gasped. "Philip's house? The spice shop?"

Natemahar grimaced. "I thought I had covered my tracks so well. But her system of spies is better even than Rome's." He drew his cloak closer about him, as though chilled. "The Kandake has known about us all this time, child, and I did not realize it."

"She knew who I was? All these years, she knew I was your daughter?"

"I am afraid so."

"But I thought she would destroy us if she knew."

"I did, too. Apparently, because we were discreet, she left us to our own devices." He gave a lopsided smile. "I suppose the queen cares for me in her own way. She has known me since boyhood. My mother was her dearest friend, in the days when she still indulged in luxuries like friendship. I think, after all that transpired, she felt she owed me that little bit of happiness. As long as I kept my connection to you secret and limited, she chose not to interfere."

Chariline dropped her head into her hands. "I feel dizzy. The same queen who tortured you wanted to give you a taste of happiness?"

# CHAPTER 29

—◦⟲◦—

*Without counsel plans fail,*
*but with many advisers they succeed.*

PROVERBS 15:22

Her father ran a hand over his hair. "She is a complicated woman. If not for her, one emperor or another would have swallowed us whole by now. Any freedom we have, any modicum of independence Cush experiences, is thanks to her. She has had to be ruthless to survive a power like Rome. I am not saying she would not resort to swiping my daughter out of the way like a bothersome bug. But she has no reason for it.

"Quintus Blandinus is leaving Cush. He will be gone in a matter of weeks, and his influence with him. No one else will care who I married, or who my daughter is."

Chariline scratched her head. "Perhaps, when she saw me approach Sesen, she felt threatened."

"By what? Sesen may not admit it, but he is not that important."

"She noticed me trying to pass a letter to him, I think.

Perhaps she thought I was . . ." An icy hand chilled her spine. She would have made the connection long before this if circumstances had not interfered. One mounting drama after another had derailed her thinking. She had been so certain that Sesen was her father. That possibility had addled her thinking.

"Perhaps she thought I was part of the conspiracy," she croaked.

"Conspiracy?" Theo frowned.

Her father went still. "Chariline, what are you speaking about?"

She had never mentioned Sesen's plans to Natemahar. Even Theo did not know about them. Though tempted to tell him, she had decided to keep this damaging evidence against the man who might be her father to herself. But the time for discretion had passed. She trusted these people with her life. And now, she would have to trust them with the queen's and Sesen's lives as well. "Sesen is planning to kill the Kandake," she said.

Natemahar blinked. "What did you say?"

"The day I snuck into the queen's palace. You caught me leaving an alcove, do you remember?"

"Well," Theo drawled. "I am glad to hear my ship is not the only place you are able to sneak into. Even kings and queens can't seem to keep you out."

She ignored him. "I was hiding in that little closet to try and speak to Sesen when he finished his business next door."

"I remember," her father said, his face very still.

"While hiding in that alcove, I overheard Sesen speaking to his cohort. Never heard the man's name. But I would recognize his face. They were plotting to kill the Kandake and make it look like an accident."

She paused in thought. "Sesen intends to sink her boat. Initially, his scheme was to have taken place during a trip in the spring. But Sesen said the queen had postponed the journey until summer. He told his accomplice they needed to wait until July to put their plan into action." Chariline rubbed her forehead. "I remember the accomplice was livid about the delay. I think he feared that the queen might ruin him before then. I could not hear every word."

Natemahar's features froze in shock. "She is traveling to Alexandria, on the ides of July. She plans to take the royal barge. The Kandake does not swim. Chariline," her father gasped. "Why did you not tell me of this plot months ago, when you first heard of it? Her life is in danger!"

Chariline squirmed on the stool. "To save the queen's life, I would have to harm Sesen. His plan was four months away. I thought, in time, I would think of a solution to save them both."

Her father rose to his feet. "It's not four months away now! We only have weeks before she boards that barge. We have to warn her."

"I think she already knows," Chariline said. "I expect that's why she has sent an assassin after me. Because when she saw me speaking secretly to Sesen, she must have assumed I was part of the plot."

"She does not know about any plot, Chariline. She still intends to travel to Alexandria. As her chief treasurer, I should know. Everything remains in place for that royal visit to Egypt. More importantly, Sesen has not been arrested. He roams about the palace as pompous as ever. The Kandake would have detained him the moment she had the first whiff of a plot."

Theo cleared his throat. "Perhaps the queen is waiting to catch every person involved in the plan. Leaving this Sesen free might lead her to others in the conspiracy."

Her father considered Theo's words. "She would have told me."

"Not if she believed your daughter was part of it."

Natemahar dropped back into his seat. He contemplated Theo's words in silence, then shook his head. "It is simply not her way. If you betray her, she strikes quickly. No. She does not know about it. I am sure of it."

"I do not mean to harp on this," Theo said, his tone apologetic, "but it seems an important detail. If the queen did not send an expensive Cushite assassin to kill Chariline, who did?"

Natemahar took a sip from his goblet. "I have wracked my brain for an answer. I confess, I have none."

"In spite of your confidence in her, I still believe everything points to your queen. I am sorry, Natemahar."

Chariline had no idea what to think. She bent to pick up a purple petal that had stuck to her toe. She rubbed at the faint blue mark on her foot left behind by the leather of her sandals. They had been a cheap purchase and bled color every time they grew damp. But she had seen them at the market in Meroë and loved their unusual design and colorful beads.

She sat up so quickly she almost slipped off the back of the stool. "My sandals," she gasped.

"Those are your bare feet," Theo pointed out. "Perhaps you should stop drinking whatever is in your chalice."

She shook her head. "This is serious. On the day I over-heard Sesen's conversation, I was wearing my Cushite sandals. They are very distinctive. Blue leather with red and white beads. You've seen me wear them, Theo."

Theo looked around the table like he needed help. "They are . . . very pretty?"

"Never mind that. I wore them to the palace because they are my only Cushite shoes. I did not want to stand out."

Her father straightened. "None of the servants wear colorful shoes at the palace. They are expected to wear plain leather, no beads."

She nodded. "I noticed that when I arrived at the palace. I worried someone might question me about them, about all my garments, in fact. But no one did.

"After I hid in the alcove, I heard Sesen leaving. I tried to sneak a look at him from behind the curtains. But Sesen turned around. I am certain I managed to pull my head in before he could see me."

"But your feet were visible," Theo guessed.

"And Sesen would have recognized your distinctive san-dals!" Natemahar's eyes widened.

Chariline pursed her lips in thought. "You must take into account that the corridor was dark. It would have been hard to catch such detail. Unless he had the eyes of a hawk. Or, er . . . eye, rather, since he only has the one."

"Were the curtains drawn in the room where he had his meeting?" Natemahar asked.

Chariline nodded slowly. "Yes. The windows were covered by a heavy material. Lamps were the only source of light."

"His eye would have been adjusted to the dark. He saw

your sandals and recognized them. He knew, then, that you had overheard him plotting to kill the queen. Not the kind of loose end a man wants to leave behind."

Theo rapped his fingertips on the tabletop. "I have never met these people, so my conclusions do not have the advantage of personal knowledge. Looking at the bare facts, the queen still seems the logical choice. We know with certainty that she saw Chariline with this Sesen."

He turned to her. "She knows you are Natemahar's daughter. In her eyes, that must give you motive to want her dead. To want revenge for what she did to your parents. It would be easy for her to believe that you are part of this conspiracy.

"Whether Sesen saw your sandals in the dark and recognized them is mere conjecture, and a stretch at that, when you consider that he is blind in one eye. He would have motive to want you dead if he knew you overheard him, I give you that. But it's a slim possibility."

Chariline tugged on her ear. "But if Sesen is behind the attempts on my life, that means the Kandake is not aware of the plot. Her life is in danger."

"And we need to warn her," her father said.

"On the other hand, if the Kandake already knows about Sesen's scheme and believes I am conspiring with him . . ."

"Then we need to keep you as far away from her as possible," Theo said.

Natemahar studied Chariline. "If the queen believes you guilty, she will hound you as long as she lives. You may think me imprudent, but I believe you need to face her. Tell her the truth. Convince her that you were not part of this plot, if that is what she thinks."

"The truth? Father, the truth is that I did not warn her as soon as I discovered Sesen's plan."

"If you were a Cushite, that would be a grievous charge against you. But you are a Roman. By coming forward now, in time to alleviate serious danger to her person, you are proving your allegiance."

Theo frowned. "Forgive me, Natemahar. But that is a dangerous gamble. You are speaking of a monarch who tortured you for daring to marry the wrong woman."

Her father dropped his head. "One way or another, Chariline must face mortal danger. I wish it weren't so. But I do not have the power to change that fact. In my opinion, this is the safest course."

Rising purposefully, he faced Chariline. "My dear girl, I have no right to ask this of you. But would you be willing to come to Meroë with me? Tell the queen what you heard? I believe she is ignorant of Sesen's plot. Her life is in danger. I can warn her myself, of course. Save her life, at least of this particular scheme. But you are the only person who can reveal the identity of Sesen's accomplice. The only one able to pull this scheme up by its roots and put an end to any future attempts by these men."

"And if the queen believes Chariline is involved in the plot?" Theo's face had turned an odd shade of gray.

Natemahar splayed his hands like a shield before his chest. "I do not think that is the case. But even so, I believe the Kandake will be able to recognize the truth when she hears it."

Theo's hands fisted on the table. "You are willing to take a chance with your daughter's life, Natemahar?"

Her father drew a trembling hand down his face. "If the

queen has truly dispatched that assassin, she will not give up. Should this warrior fail, she will only send another. And another, until she succeeds. What I suggest might be a gamble. But it is the only way to restore to my daughter a life of security and peace."

He turned to face Chariline. She sensed, in the rigid lines of his shoulders, the fear he could not wholly overcome. "I am so sorry, my dear girl. The choice rests with you. For seventeen years, I stole the decision from you. Made the choice for us both. I will not make that mistake again.

"You have heard my opinion. Theo's concerns also have merit. You need to choose, my dear. Come to Meroë with me, or try to find safety outside its borders. Either way exposes you to danger. Danger I wish I could take away, and cannot. Whatever your decision, Daughter, I will stand by you."

Chariline struggled to swallow. Should she go to Cush? Face that dragon of a woman and admit to sneaking into her palace uninvited? Admit to knowing about the plans set in motion for her demise? Condemn a man to certain death by her testimony? Risk her own life if the Kandake believed her part of the assassination plot?

And if she had not already thought of enough excuses to avoid setting foot on the dust of Cush, she had another more private reason. A bitter taste filled Chariline's mouth.

Going to Cush immediately meant leaving Theo behind.

# CHAPTER 30

—— ᘓᕤᘖ ——

*If any of you lacks wisdom, let him ask God,*
*who gives generously to all without reproach,*
*and it will be given him.*

JAMES 1:5

Chariline tried to sift through the logic of the arguments before her. Her father knew the court of Cush, knew the Kandake. But Theo's concerns were built on rock-solid evidence. How could her father place any confidence in what that woman might choose to do?

Two prudent men whose judgment she trusted, each one offering opposing views.

Either choice came with the burden of a responsibility she did not wish to carry. Whether she acted or did not act, other people's lives would be impacted. Not to mention the fact that both options could lead to her untimely demise. Chariline chewed on her lips, feeling dizzy. How was she to make such a decision? Unexpectedly, Hermione's sweet voice echoed in her mind: *What we need is to ask Iesous. Ask him to show you the way.*

She turned urgently to face Priscilla and Aquila. "I cannot make this decision alone. We need to pray! Would you intercede for me?"

Priscilla beamed. "I have been waiting for someone to ask."

As they prayed, Priscilla and Aquila turned their focus upon the Lord. They thanked him, praised him, sang snatches of song to him, and recited ancient Scriptures that made them more mindful of God than of their difficulties. Bit by bit, Chariline felt the heavy weight on her soul lifting. Felt the grip of fear dissolving.

The cacophonous noise in her head silenced. Within that welcome quiet, she finally heard the call. The call for surrender.

She knew what *she* wanted. Knew the answer she preferred. Now, she needed to willingly accept what Iesous asked of her.

Again and again, God was bringing her to this point. To insurmountable blocks that forced her to accept God's will over her own. Clearly, her soul needed to learn this lesson more than once. Needed to travel down this path over and over until she found it the natural choice rather than a bloody battle.

She nodded to herself. *Show me the way, Lord,* she prayed silently. *Show me your will. I want to go where you go.*

When she looked up into her father's ebony eyes, she knew what to do. Knew the hard path God had set before her. The sacrifice he required of her. To obey Iesous and honor her father, she had to walk away from Theo and any possibility of a future with him.

"I will go to Cush with you," she whispered.

Natemahar drew her into his arms and held her, tucking

her head against his shoulder. "Thank you, Daughter. Thank you," he whispered, not truly understanding what her agreement had cost.

The time of prayer had changed more than Chariline's heart. She caught a glimpse of Theo's expression, and saw that he seemed unsurprised by her decision. His face was a mask of calm. A small part of her had hoped that he might fight this choice. Fight to keep her with him. Not that she would have given in. She knew what she needed to do. But Theo's objections would have revealed something of his heart. This easy acceptance said as much about his feeling for her as it did about his faith, she thought.

She was not worth a fight.

Natemahar addressed his hosts. "My thanks for the welcome you have shown my daughter and me. For the treasured fellowship of this evening. And I especially thank you for your prayers." He dropped his chin in the courtly manner that came so naturally to him after years in the service of a queen. "I am grateful for your hospitality. But I must attend to this matter as soon as possible."

"Of course," Aquila said, also rising. "It's not often the fate of nations rests on our shoulders."

Natemahar smiled. "More often than you might imagine, Aquila. Every time you and Priscilla host a fellowship of seekers and believers in your home, you are affecting the future of Rome. I have no such heavenly influence. But what I have, I must tend faithfully."

Theo held out a hand. "Natemahar?"

"Yes, my friend?"

"I assume you will be looking for a ship to Alexandria, and from there, a river barge to Cush."

"I will."

"I have a proposal. Allow me to take you and Chariline on my ship. I can take you as far as Alexandria."

Chariline's heart stopped beating. She whirled toward Theo, mouth gaping. "But you never take passengers!"

Theo shrugged. "I like your father."

Chariline stiffened. Was that a warning that he was only making this offer for her father's sake?

Laughing, Theo held up both hands. "You look like you are about to spit. It was only a jest."

Natemahar's brow furrowed. "You do *not* like me?"

"Of course I like you."

"I see." Natemahar looked confused.

Theo blew out a breath. "Under ordinary circumstances, I do not carry passengers. Which is why Chariline had to sneak on board my ship. However, your daughter is being shadowed by a trained killer. Boarding some giant grain ship that carries a hundred passengers seems unwise at this time. You need a safe way to get to Cush. I will take you."

Her father's whole body seemed to deflate with relief. "That is very generous of you, Theo. The transport to Cush was my greatest concern. I would be a fool to refuse your offer. But I insist on paying your expenses."

Theo shrugged. "I will pick up more wheat in Alexandria to bring back to Rome. It will cover most of my costs."

"Given our mission to save the queen's life, I can guarantee that Cush's national treasury will compensate you. It's the least I can do."

Theo grinned. "It helps to be chief treasurer."

"At times." Natemahar blew out a breath. "I am glad that is out of the way. Can we leave for Puteoli in the morning?"

"Say the day after. It will take me a full day to make arrangements with the warehouse."

Chariline barely followed the speedy agreement between the two men. A few moments ago, she had resigned herself never to see Theo again. To leave her heart in his keeping without the opportunity for anything other than a handful of memories.

She was still going to be left with nothing more than memories. But at least she would not have to take her leave of him immediately. She would board the *Parmys* again, laugh with Sophocles, feel the wind in her hair, taste the sea on her lips. And she would talk to Theo, draw for him, tease him, and watch him climb his mast to talk to God. It would be enough.

*Lord,* she prayed. *Please make it enough.*

———⟊———

In the morning, Chariline sent a note to Vitruvia, explaining her hasty departure and expressing her regret for not being able to see her again. Without Theo and Taharqa, she dared not venture from the house.

Less than an hour later, Vitruvia showed up at Priscilla and Aquila's door, her broad, old-fashioned litter stopping all traffic while she dismounted. She took a few moments to straighten her linen stola, heedless of the flow of riders, litters, and pedestrians that parted around her like water around a giant rock.

"Vitruvia!" Chariline ran to her side, her heart lifting at the sight of her mother's friend. "What on earth are you doing here?"

"You did not think I would allow you to leave without bidding me a proper good-bye? Or showing me the rest of your designs?"

Chariline grinned. "You are welcome to all of them, Vitruvia. Come in."

"That is well made," Vitruvia said with a glance over her shoulder as they passed under the dark-green awning that shaded the main door. "I see it's retractable. Galerius and I need one in our garden."

"My friends make them. I shall introduce you before you leave. They just installed that one this morning. The last awning was damaged by a dagger."

"A dagger?"

Chariline cleared her throat. "I have so much to tell you."

"I confess, curiosity has been eating at me. Did you try to kill Natemahar? Was it your dagger that ruined the awning?"

Chariline laughed. "I was able to stay my hand. No, it was not my dagger."

"What a charming place," Vitruvia said when they had settled in the courtyard. "No elegant lines to speak of, crooked walls, and yet I doubt Mount Olympus itself could offer such an agreeable spot." She dropped her stola to her shoulders and sighed. "Now tell me. What did Natemahar say when you told him he was your father?"

Without divulging Natemahar's personal history, Chariline told Vitruvia the story of her connection with him and finished by explaining the reason for his presence in Rome.

"Someone is trying to kill you?" Vitruvia cried.

"Apparently."

"Well, they better not succeed," she sputtered. "I only

just found you." She tapped Chariline on the cheek. "So, this Natemahar is in Rome? As we speak?"

"He is staying at a nearby inn."

"You better send for him right away."

"Send for him?"

"You don't imagine I am going to give up my only opportunity to meet my beloved Gemina's husband, do you?"

Chariline wrote a note, asking Natemahar to join them for lunch. She did not mention Vitruvia, wanting to see the surprise in his eyes when, after all these years, he would finally meet his wife's dearest friend.

Vitruvia bid her litter drivers to carry the note to the inn. "And pick up a basket of food on the way here," she instructed. "A hot loaf of *quadratus* bread. Better make that two. Cheese, sausages, and honey cakes. Excitement always makes me hungry," she explained to Chariline.

As they awaited Natemahar's arrival, Vitruvia pored over Chariline's designs. Scroll after scroll passed under her eagle examination. When she had studied the final scroll, she sat back, closing her eyes for a moment. "I wondered, when I studied the villa you designed for me, if it might be a fluke. If somehow you had managed to create something more beautiful than what might be your habit. I see I need not have worried."

She turned to face Chariline. "Your gift shines through every single design. Each one is a small jewel of proportion united with function. What you lack in experience, you make up for in creativity."

Chariline felt warmed through by Vitruvia's words. Hermione sometimes praised her designs. Natemahar, too, thought them brilliant. Even Theo had encouraged her. But none of them really understood the science of architecture. Not as Vitruvia did. Her words of praise meant something more than all the encouragement Chariline had received in her life. And that had not been a great deal. Vitruvia's acknowledgment made Chariline's work feel legitimate, somehow. Validated.

Vitruvia reached for Chariline's hand. "I have brought you a gift." She bent to retrieve a fat scroll, tied up with leather strings, from a cloth bag. The papyrus looked yellow with age, and across the fold, Chariline could read a partial number.

"This was one of my grandfather's own copies. Book VIII of his famous theses on architecture. It is a short book that focuses on water, how to find it and test its quality, with general remarks on aqueducts, wells, and cisterns. Some of his personal notes are in the margins. You told me you had the first seven. Now you own the eighth."

Chariline cradled the scroll in her hands. Vitruvius's own book! "This is astounding!"

"I always meant to give Gemina a full set as a wedding gift. Now, we can start on completing yours."

Chariline shook her head. "Are you certain you want to part with this?"

"I have 131 others. My grandfather had a mania for making copies of his work. Cost him a fortune."

The sound of Ferox barking caused the women to look up. Natemahar approached them hesitantly. "I hope I am not interrupting."

"Father!" Chariline jumped to her feet. "I have someone special for you to meet."

Natemahar did not wait for introductions. "Vitruvia," he whispered, instantly recognizing the woman he had never met. He did not step forward to greet her, but stood apart, his shoulders a rigid plank.

It came to Chariline then, in an avalanche of realization, that she should have warned him. Given him time to prepare his heart. Because meeting his beloved Gemina's closest friend for the first time was no easy thing for Natemahar.

When Vitruvia had read about him in Gemina's letters all those years ago, Natemahar had been a strong, vibrant man. Before this woman who had known him only as Gemina's cherished husband, Natemahar felt too much the eunuch.

Vitruvia, sensing the awkward hesitation in him, took two long strides, covering the distance between them. She folded Natemahar in her arms and kissed his cheeks Roman style. "By Zeus's beard, you are every bit as handsome as Gemina claimed," she cried. "No wonder she ditched that ninny to marry you."

Natemahar's pinched lips relaxed. Trembled for a short moment, before softening into a grin. "He *was* a ninny."

Chariline watched as Vitruvia pulled her father down on the bench next to her and plied him with warmth and questions until Natemahar forgot to be self-conscious. Before long, they were swapping stories about Gemina. Chariline sat, silent as a butterfly, absorbing every word, tucking every anecdote into a corner of her mind, to examine and relish later.

When Vitruvia's drivers returned, Chariline set a table where they could eat together while they reminisced. An hour flew by. Then another. Wrapped up in Vitruvia's and Natemahar's vivid memories, Chariline sat in rapt attention as the food congealed on her plate.

Finally, Natemahar rose. "Forgive me, dear lady. Although I am in Rome, I still have duties to Cush. I must return to the inn to finish some letters before we set off for Meroë in the morning. I cannot tell you what a delight it has been to meet you, Vitruvia. Gemina is never far from my thoughts. But today, I felt almost as though I touched her hand."

"I feel the same, Natemahar." Vitruvia bent to retrieve another scroll from her bag. "A gift for you, if I may."

Natemahar's eyes grew wide. "For me?"

Chariline recognized the ink smudge at once. Her mother's letter! The one that spoke of her father with such effusive tenderness. She watched him as he unfurled the letter and began to read.

His head fell forward, eyes glued to the page, fingertips gently running over the words. "Gemina," he whispered. A single tear ran down his cheek and he swallowed convulsively. He bent down until his lips touched the name signed with flourish at the bottom of the page. "Gemina."

# CHAPTER 31

—ɔıɔ—

*My heart is in anguish within me;*
*the terrors of death have fallen upon me.*
*Fear and trembling come upon me,*
*and horror overwhelms me.*

PSALM 55:4,5

Theo rested against the prow, leaning into the wind as it cooled his face. He felt like a boiling stew, fear bubbling inside him alongside an effervescent excitement. And something more. Something that made him feel at once alive and terrified.

He turned to gaze at the cabin where his guests were staying. Father and daughter had never shared the same lodgings. He wondered how they felt about this new intimacy. Wondered if it was a welcome circumstance or an awkward one.

"Dinner is ready," Sophocles cried, waving at Theo before knocking on the door of the cabin.

Incredible, Theo thought. The old sailor had retained the habit. As soon as he had clapped eyes on Chariline again, he had stopped cursing and begun knocking on doors.

Theo headed for the cabin to join his guests. There was barely enough room to fit all three. But he wanted this first

330

meal to offer a measure of civilized comfort, a table and seats rather than a plate balanced on a lap.

"Sophocles has outdone himself," Chariline said as he entered. "Chicken, Theo! He has made us chicken. And he has added fresh tarragon! It smells wonderful."

Sophocles, who was lingering by the open door, turned an odd shade of red. Theo stared, unable to believe his eyes. He was actually blushing!

"We only left Puteoli this morning," Sophocles said with an offhand shrug. "My stores are full. Easy to make good food when you have fresh supplies." He tried to sound aloof, but as he turned to leave, Theo saw his smile flash, wide and pleased.

"It seems the way to get a decent, hot meal on this ship is to share a table with Chariline," he said dryly.

She grinned. "Sophocles likes me."

He sat on the stool facing her. "I think you have beguiled my cook."

She rolled her eyes. "I compliment his cooking. I doubt he ever heard any praise from the rest of you."

"Because he's a bad cook!"

Chariline sniffed the chicken on her plate. "This smells delicious to me. And did you see the bread? Not a scorch mark on it. I think Sophocles has been practicing while the ship was docked."

"Shall I bless the meal before it turns cold?" Natemahar asked.

"Please," Theo said.

After Natemahar had finished praying, Theo turned to Chariline. "Did you ever think, when we were sailing to

Puteoli, that one day soon you would be sitting in this cabin with your father at your side?"

She gave Natemahar a shy glance. "Not in my wildest dreams. Back then, I was still half convinced that Sesen was my father."

Theo nodded. "I remember." He frowned. "Why do you think Sesen reacted so strangely to you when you first met at the palace?"

Natemahar rubbed his chin. "I have wondered about that myself. Back in Cush, I was bewildered when Chariline first described his behavior. Now, knowing what he was plotting in that chamber, I suspect anything out of the ordinary would have alarmed him. He was taking his life in his hands, after all, planning such a conspiracy.

"Then, in walked Chariline. Servants are not supposed to go to the second floor, though of course, sometimes, it cannot be avoided. But something in Chariline's manner must have caught his eye."

Chariline toyed with a piece of chicken. "Then, why ask my age? Quiz me about my father's name?"

"As soon as Sesen had a good look at you, he would have realized you were no ordinary Cushite. Your light skin, your amber eyes, your hair—everything about you gave away something of your history. You were different, and that made him suspicious.

"After you acknowledged that you were Blandinus's grand-daughter, he would have grown apprehensive. Why was the Roman official's granddaughter acting as a servant? Had Blandinus sent you to spy on him?"

Chariline pushed her plate away. "He said *it fits*. What did he mean? Fits what?"

Theo was pleased when Natemahar pulled Chariline's plate back in front of her. "Eat."

She waved. "I am full, thank you."

"Eat, or Sophocles will be hurt," Theo said, eyes narrowed.

She had lost weight during her sickness, and her appetite had never seemed to return properly. She was not eating enough, and he had worried, over the past few weeks, that she might make herself sick again. At odd times during meals, he had found himself counting her mouthfuls and wondered if he was losing his mind.

His ploy worked and Chariline swallowed a mouthful. Natemahar waited for her to put another piece of chicken in her mouth before speaking again. That intentional delay made Theo smile. If the two of them banded together against her, she would not stand a chance.

"At the mention of your grandfather's name," Natemahar said, "Sesen would have remembered the old rumors. According to the stories that had circulated around the palace for years, Quintus Blandinus's younger daughter had eloped with a Cushite. And there you were, the embodiment of the old gossip. Undeniably, a child of that union. No one knew for certain the identity of the man Gemina had eloped with. Many names had been suggested at one time or another, my own among them."

Chariline's brows rose. "You never mentioned that, back in Cush."

"That is true. Another prevarication in the long line of

my evasions. But Sesen would have heard that old rumor. The possibility that you were my daughter would have made him truly apprehensive, under the circumstances."

"Because he works under you?"

"That, and because Sesen considers me an enemy. He always thought he should have my job. And now, a woman who might be my daughter had shown up in the very chamber where he was having a clandestine meeting, planning the demise of the queen. You must have raised his hackles, my dear. Of course he wanted to know who you were. Who your father was. He had to know if you were a spy. Ascertain if his plot was in danger."

Theo nodded. "That makes sense."

Chariline flopped against the cushions. "And I jumped to all manner of conclusions."

"Some of which were true," Natemahar pointed out. "Sesen did know something about your birth." He wiped his fingers with his napkin. "The whole time you were conducting your investigation, part of me was petrified that you might uncover the truth, and another part of me was proud of how clever and brave you were."

Chariline grinned. "Were you proud when I assumed Sesen might be my father?"

Natemahar rolled his eyes. "In all truth, I wanted to rip his throat out. I couldn't believe you thought that dolt could be your father. I found the very notion offensive."

She gaped. "You were jealous!"

"Eat your chicken. And yes, I was. It might not have been so horrifying if you had chosen a more admirable man."

"I must say, I am relieved not to be related to a killer. I told myself he had good reason for hating the Kandake. But I could not get past the murder part."

Theo watched the banter between father and daughter with a faint smile. Every day, the awkwardness between them seemed to diminish, until there were moments when it was impossible to remember that they had been separated for twenty-four years by painful betrayals.

His throat turned dry as he remembered the image he could not banish from his mind. The image that had tormented him through sleepless hours. Natemahar, looking wounded and so alone, his voice a broken whisper, saying, *I will always be less than other men . . . I will only bring you shame.*

Theo had known, from the day he had heard Natemahar's confession, that he would have to face his own fears, soon. Natemahar had lost seventeen years, wasted all the time he could have had with his beloved daughter, because he had believed himself to be less than other men.

He never gave Chariline a chance since he felt convinced that she would reject him. A rejection he believed he deserved.

Theo had realized, sitting in that chamber, watching Chariline fall to her knees and kiss the eunuch's hands, all the while calling him *Father, Father, Father,* that the only way for him to have such complete acceptance was to open his heart to an equally perfect rejection.

He could not go on making the same mistake as Natemahar. Lose seventeen years of his life hiding his streaked hair and his secrets, burying his heart in the process.

When dinner came to an end, Theo gulped a breath and

came to his feet. He felt his face pale. His stomach revolted. But he forced himself to go on. "Chariline, would you like to go out for some fresh air before you retire?"

She sprang to her feet. "That would be lovely."

"If it's all right with you, Natemahar?" Theo asked, politely.

Natemahar waved a hand. "Of course. It will give me time to prepare for bed."

The night had set up its dark tent while they had been eating. Most of Theo's men had rolled out their blankets on the deck and were preparing for sleep. Some were already snoring robustly. One was playing a soft note on his flute; a couple were engaged in a quiet game of dice, while Taharqa stood at the helm, his body bearing the weight of the steering oar as he leaned into the long wood.

The wind was blowing gently into the sail, carrying them at a decent speed. Theo guided Chariline toward the prow, which was thankfully unoccupied, and stood leaning into the oak railing. In the quiet, he gathered his thoughts.

"Do you know how the steering oars on a ship work?" he asked, his voice soft so that no one but Chariline could hear him.

She cast him a surprised glance. "No."

"Two paddles at the stern of the ship project out into the sea, acting as rudders. They are buried underwater so that you rarely see them, except for their long handles. They are quite small, but along with the sail, they can set the trajectory of a ship. A steering oar can smash you against deadly rocks or bring you into safe harbor."

Her full lips softened, making his heart beat harder. "Thank you for the lesson in seafaring. But I fear I cannot become a sailor. My heart is quite set on architecture."

He wiped a hand down his face. "I was trying to set up an image."

"I beg your pardon," she said, instantly contrite. "Sometimes I forget you are a poet."

"I was too long-winded and technical." He cleared his throat. "All I meant to say is that there are hidden things in the soul, like a ship's tiller. Things that can set the course of your future. Set you careening into rocks.

"I saw this with Natemahar, that day at the inn. His secret belief that he would bring you shame. That was the rudder of his life for so many years."

She was looking at him earnestly, amber eyes glued to his face, lips parted. For a moment he forgot his speech. He could only think about what it would feel like to crush those lips under his. To plunder their soft secrets.

He took a deep breath and turned away, looked at the moon, at the stars that dotted the sky with bright abandon. Anything to distract himself from her ridiculous pull, until he wrenched his mind back to what he must reveal.

That cooled his blood quickly enough.

His hand fisted and he forced his eyes back on her face. "I realized that day that I am not very different from Natemahar. My body may not have been marred, but my soul has."

Chariline wrapped her hand around his fist. "You can tell me anything, Theo."

He tried to swallow and could not. He tried to nod, but his head refused to cooperate. "Remember I told you I was a foundling? That Galenos found me?" He wet dried lips. "He brought me home and raised me alongside his two children. He always treated me with kindness. But his wife,

Celandine . . ." He shrugged. "She found me an offense. The fact that Galenos carried me home the day she had given birth to a healthy daughter—a foundling child whose parentage would forever remain obscure—seemed to her an insult. To Celandine, I remained, at best, a servant. Galenos, of course, could not adopt me while his wife barely tolerated me.

"I never knew who I was in that house. A slave? A son?"

He untangled his hand from Chariline's hold and leaned his arms over the railing. Staring into the ocean, he said, "Ariadne became the only constant in my life. Her brother, Dionysius, was older. He had a brilliant mind for books and preferred study to the outdoors. Ariadne and I had the same interests. She always saw me as a brother. Her twin. We were the same age, and she had not known life without me.

"But in my heart, I never believed I belonged to that family. Even Galenos did not legally acknowledge me as a son until recent years. He had his reasons." He shrugged. "Still, I remained the outsider. Ariadne might have seen me as a brother, but I did not see her as a sister."

"You fell in love with her," Chariline whispered.

"I did."

He heard her intake of breath. "You still love her?" Her voice shook.

He turned to face her. "Not that way. It has taken me a long time to realize it. Watching her with my brother has made me see that Ariadne was right, all along. We are brother and sister. If not for the confusion of my childhood, I would have recognized it sooner. I certainly would have recovered from the pain of that rejection faster.

"What transpired soon after these events, however, almost

crippled me. I cannot regret it entirely as it drove me into the arms of Yeshua. It forced me into a deeper faith than most, I think."

He ran his hand over his lips and found them snow-cold under his touch. In spite of the warm air, his whole body shivered. "Ariadne found a letter from my mother." He waved a hand. "Too long a story to go into now. Suffice it to say that because of that letter, we discovered who I was. It revealed my identity.

"My mother was a slave in Rome. She and Servius, the younger son of her master, fell in love with each other. Servius chose to marry her. He came from a noble family, and his father, enraged by his decision, disowned him. That is how Servius and my mother ended up in Corinth. Galenos knew them since their properties bordered one another. He told me they were devoted to each other and became happier still when Justus was born."

Theo fisted his hands again. "But their lives were shattered. According to the letter, a few years after Justus was born, my mother was raped."

Chariline gasped.

Theo pushed through even though everything in him wanted to stop. To guard this most awful of secrets. "In her letter, she did not name the man. We will never discover his identity now. He disappeared after the attack, and my mother thought the worst was over. That she would heal from this awful violation in time. Then she realized she was pregnant."

"Oh, Theo!"

She must know where this story was headed, he thought. He waited for her to take that tiny step backward, to move away from him. To put an extra layer of distance between them. She took a step. But it was toward him. Again, she wrapped her hand around his fist, opening it this time and holding his stiff fingers like an anchor.

She had not understood, he told himself. Had not grasped where this tale was headed.

He had to force himself to go on. "My mother prayed the child would belong to Servius. When I was born, she took one look at me and knew."

"The silver streak," she said.

Air huffed out of his lungs in a humorless laugh. "Those powers of observation at work again. Yes. The silver streak." He ran his free hand through his hair. "He had it. The man who violated her. When she saw me, she knew whose babe she had carried."

He blinked as Chariline took another half step toward him. He could smell the cinnamon-rose scent of her, feel the warmth of her hand still wrapped around his. Why did she not move away?

"I was her babe. Flesh of her flesh. She loved me. But I was also a constant reminder of a horror she could not come to grips with. I think that divide became too much for her, and she began to crumble.

"Servius must have been beside himself with worry. I do not blame him for what he did. He only wanted to protect her."

"He is the one who abandoned you?"

Theo nodded. "When she found out what Servius had done, she was not angry. She understood that he wanted to shield her from completely falling apart. But she could not live with the decision. She felt riddled with guilt, knowing her younger son was alone somewhere, with no one to care for him. She assumed I had died. The burden of my abandonment became too much for her. She believed if she had been stronger, more able to cope, then Servius would not have been reduced to giving her child away." Theo did his best to keep his voice steady. "In the end, she took her own life."

Chariline covered her mouth with her hand, eyes wide.

# CHAPTER 32

*Let him kiss me with the kisses of his mouth!*
*For your love is better than wine.*

SONG OF SOLOMON 1:2

He waited for Chariline to loosen her hold on his hand. To curl her lip in disgust. Surely now she would walk away.

She clung to him harder than before.

Did she still not understand? He cleared his throat. "This is who I am, Chariline. The child of *that* father. The consequence of unimagined horror."

"Theo!" Chariline's voice emerged, fierce and indignant. "Theo, the circumstances of your conception do not make you who you are."

"Don't you understand? I was the cause of my mother's despair. Every time she looked at me, she was filled with horror. I am the reason she took her own life. After she died, Servius shattered. Justus said his father never truly recovered. That, too, is my doing."

Chariline let go of his hand. He felt it like the severing

of a mooring line. Like the unraveling of a seam. He had always known this would happen if he told the truth. Known she would walk away, repulsed. Known she would find him repugnant once she discovered the full scope of his history. Still, when she let go, something in him caved.

Her hands lifted. Confused, he stood rooted to the deck. Did she mean to slap him? He made no move to defend himself.

Softly, so softly he wondered if it might be a dream, she cradled his face in her fingers. Held them there and pulled until his head lowered and his eyes locked with hers.

"I could not have loved you more if you were the son of a king, and I can't love you less because of what your father did. You are the Theo I love. The man I admire. I have never known a better man. One more loyal or worthy of honor."

Standing on her tiptoes, she pressed her lips against his and kissed him shyly.

Theo was so shocked he never even tasted her lips. His eyes, open and unblinking, just stared at her like a brainless fool.

She drew back and frowned. Her hands dropped to her sides. Her mouth fell open in dismay, and the fingers that had held him so tenderly fluttered between them.

"I . . . Lord's mercy . . . I am sorry, Theo . . . I . . ."

Before she could take another step away, he grabbed her around the waist and pulled her to him. "Come here," he said. This time he lowered his head to her lips without any prompting from her.

Her first kiss, he guessed. Other than the one he had just botched.

He would wipe that from her memory.

Her lips were soft and yielding. He gulped air into his constricted chest. "Come here," he demanded again, pulling her tighter against him. "Come here and never leave."

Theo had gone through a wild season after he had won the Isthmian Games. For a short time, he had had his share of kisses and embraces. But nothing had prepared him for the sweet touch of this woman. For the taste of her, the feel of her, tall and sinewy, fitting perfectly in his arms. Nothing had ever felt so right. "I love you, Chariline," he whispered against her lips.

"Well," she exhaled. "That took you long enough!"

---

"Natemahar, I need to speak with you. Is it too late?" Theo said as soon as he accompanied Chariline back to the cabin.

Natemahar closed a scroll he had been studying by lamplight. His gaze traveled from Chariline to Theo. His smile seemed touched by an odd sadness. "Too soon, perhaps."

"Pardon?" Theo asked, confused.

Natemahar pushed himself from the bed. "A private jest. By all means, lead on, my friend." He grabbed a light cloak hanging from a hook on the wall.

Wordlessly, Chariline kissed her father on the cheek as he was about to leave. Theo noticed the treasurer closing his eyes for a moment, as if savoring her touch.

Theo led Natemahar back to the prow. The lack of privacy on this ship was becoming more of a problem than usual. He swallowed hard and cleared his throat. "Natemahar, I would like to ask your permission . . ."

"You have it."

"Wait. Don't you want to know what I am asking permission for?"

"You wish to marry my daughter."

Theo blinked. "How did you know?"

"I've seen the way Chariline looks at you. She clearly loves you. I knew if you had half the brains you seem to have, you would return her feelings."

Theo barked out a laugh. "Then you give us your blessing?"

"I cannot deny I wish I had more time with my daughter. But that is merely my own selfish desire. Of course I give you my blessing, Theo. I could not have chosen a better man for her myself. You love the Lord deeply. Through danger and difficulty, you have proven yourself loyal, generous, wise, and capable. And you love my Chariline. What more can a father ask?"

---

Chariline leaned back into the railing and adjusted the parasol her father had loaned her to shade her eyes from the sun. He was speaking to Sophocles in low tones she could not hear. They made a strange pair, her father's impeccable purple garments next to the old sailor's stained, short tunic, dark, tight curls bent toward white flyaway wisps.

"Are my eyes deceiving me," Theo said in her ear, "or have those two become friends?"

Chariline grinned. One day had passed since Theo had confessed his love for her. One day since he had held her and kissed her and told her to never leave.

In all the hours that stretched in between, she had blinked and frowned a hundred times and wondered if she had dreamed it. Then he would show up and draw her hand into his, or stare at her lips and murmur something in her ear, and she would realize that it was true. This precious, beautiful man loved her.

"I have a problem," he said now, standing close, arm touching arm, shoulder grazing shoulder.

"And what is that?"

"I am a homeless man."

"That *is* a problem."

"I would like to ask you something important, Chariline."

Her pulse quickened, its beat thrumming in her ear. She had thought hard about their conversation. It had covered a lot of territory. Changed her life and his. But in all the words they had spoken into each other's hearts, she could not remember mention of marriage or anything resembling a proposal.

"Yes?"

"I was hoping . . ."

"Yes?"

"Very much hoping . . ."

"Go on."

"Well. I was hoping you would consider being my architect. I would like you to build a villa on my orchard outside Corinth."

She narrowed her eyes. "I have just the design in mind for you. Big, jagged holes in the roof, a cracked foundation, and crooked walls."

Theo laid his forearms behind him on the railing and crossed his ankles. "I confess, that does not sound appealing."

"Really?"

"I was hoping for something a little more agreeable. A spacious villa, say, with lots of bright rooms and a large garden, like Vitruvia's."

"Were you?"

Theo sighed. "Of course, the problem with a large villa is that it can grow quite lonely."

She felt her lips twitch. "I can ask Priscilla and Aquila to loan you Ferox, if you wish. He makes a very pleasant sleeping companion, I am told."

"That's an excellent idea. Or, conversely, Natemahar could come and live with me."

Chariline dropped her parasol. "What?"

"I don't like the thought of him all alone in Cush, you see. Perhaps we can convince him to give up his influential position at the palace and retire in Corinth. You could design a smaller house for him down the lane from my villa."

"A house for my father?"

"He has such elegant manners. I think he would make me an excellent neighbor."

"Theo, so help me, if you don't stop teasing me, I am going to hit you with that parasol."

Theo tucked his toes under the parasol, made a flicking motion, and somehow, it spun into the air at just the right angle to land in his hand. "This parasol?"

He laughed at her expression. "Dear, brave, funny, talented, beloved Chariline, will you design me a villa and come and share it with me? Will you marry me and be my wife and move into the home I don't have yet?"

The sun afforded them no privacy; too many eyes watched

them. Kisses were out of the question. Instead, the gray eyes caressed her, lingered on her lips, until she felt dazed.

"Some men do anything for a free design," she croaked.

Theo's smile was slow and burning with too many promises. "Is that a yes?" He wrapped a hand around her wrist and pulled. "Say yes, or I'll kiss you in front of everyone."

"Yes! Yes," she gasped, round-eyed. "I will be your architect. No need for threats." And she started to run, skipping over ropes and tackle and swerving around men and laughing too hard to make much headway. Theo grasped her around the waist and pulled her back against him.

"What did you say?" he said.

"I said I will marry you, Theo. I will marry you, my love."

He whooped and picked her up and twirled her around, shouting, "She said yes!"

The whole ship broke into loud cheers, men thwacking each other's oiled shoulders and trying to pat Theo on the back while Chariline still lay against his chest, clutching for dear life.

———— ⌯ ————

The days became a thrilling haze of impossible happiness, melting one into another. Chariline and Theo's joy was a contagion that spread through those around them so that even the crew became more cheerful, the sound of singing and affable conversation filling the corners of the ship throughout the day.

Chariline woke late one morning to find her father gone and the bed made neatly without a single wrinkle. They had fought over who should sleep in the bed, and it was only by proving that Natemahar did not actually fit on the floor that he had agreed to sleep on the cot. Theo had made the tiny space on the ground far more pleasant by having the foresight to purchase a narrow but thick pallet on their last day at Puteoli. It covered the floor between the bed and the wall and made for a cramped but comfortable bed.

Chariline stretched and poked her head outside the door, looking for her father, not surprised to find him sitting next to Sophocles. The two had forged a touching friendship.

Catching sight of her, Theo waved at her from the top of the mast, his smile warming her down to her marrow. She washed quickly, changed into a clean tunic, and wrenched the door open to find Theo waiting outside, knuckles at the ready for a knock.

"Come in," she invited.

He lifted a thick sheaf of parchments. "I have a surprise."

"If that is a poem, it must rival *The Iliad*," she said, eyeing the thick roll.

"It is not a poem."

She looked curiously over his shoulder as he spread the parchments on the bed. "Maps!"

He nodded. "They are of Corinth and its suburbs. I forgot I had them in my chest down below. When I came upon them this morning, I thought you might like to know where our land is."

*Our land.* He had already sewn her seamlessly into his life. Gone from *me* and *mine* to *us* and *ours.* "Theo! That's wonderful."

He spent a moment showing her the different sites in the cosmopolitan city. "And this is Galenos's house where I grew up." He pointed to a spot on a narrow lane. "Galenos still lives there. When I am in Corinth, this is my home."

Theo pointed to a field. "His house backs into this piece of land. And right next to it is the villa where my brother grew up. Justus and Ariadne reside there now with their son."

"So you knew Justus all your life?"

"When we were children, Justus was Dionysius's playmate more than mine since they are closer in age. But being neighbors, I knew him a little. I always looked up to him, especially once he started racing and winning at the Isthmian Games. Neither of us had any idea, then, that we were brothers."

Chariline stared at the map. "I didn't realize how close to each other you lived." She frowned. "Did Servius not recognize you? He must have seen you in the neighborhood."

"He must have. He knew Galenos."

"When your mother became despondent about losing you, couldn't Servius ask Galenos to give you back?"

"I think she died before he discovered where I was. Even if he had returned to the *bema* hours after he left me there, I would have already been gone. I doubt Servius would have spoken to Galenos until it was too late. He was dealing with a grieving wife, while Galenos had to cope with a household that contained two newborns and an irritated wife."

"Your mother took her own life before Servius realized that you were hale and hearty, living next door."

Theo nodded. "Poor Servius. I cannot imagine the horror of it when he realized I was there all along."

"Why do you think he never said anything? After he realized who you were?"

"I asked Justus the same question. He thinks his father was

so broken after the death of our mother that he could barely think straight for a long time. By then, he probably assumed I had grown attached to Galenos's family. Become a part of it. Why uproot me?

"I also don't suppose he relished the thought of telling me that he had left me at the *bema* like a sack of garbage. Likely, he felt too guilty to face me."

Chariline pulled Theo into a fierce embrace. "If only your mother had held on."

Theo's arms tightened around her. "What the Lord is teaching me is that the sorrows of one generation do not have to be visited upon another. The misfortunes of our parents do not have to shape our lives. Not with Yeshua at our side."

He stepped away and pointed to the map. "Now to more cheerful things. We need to put you to work, love. Come and see the orchard that belongs to us and start dreaming of comfortable villas with cool gardens."

"Did you really mean it when you said you wanted my father to move to Corinth with us?"

"Absolutely. I think he would feel your absence too keenly now that he has finally found you."

"I wonder if he would consider leaving his position at the palace."

"He has had a lifetime of position and influence. None of that compares with having you. He told you himself. You are his greatest treasure. His incomparable jewel."

"And what about you?"

"I am a great treasure too. No doubt of it."

She swatted the air between them. "I mean, do you really not mind if he lives near us?"

"Chariline, I grew up without a family. I would like nothing better than to have a whole clan of my own living right next door to me. Your father is dear to me already. He is most welcome to a piece of my land, and an even bigger piece of my heart."

Chariline pulled Theo's lips to hers and tasted in his touch a bit of the vast heart that stretched to make room for so many. She reveled in the way he lingered against her, his whole body a tight knot of longing.

Finally, they parted, breathless, and turned their attention to the map and began to dream of the home they would build together. They were discussing the location of Theo's tablinum when the door burst open.

Chariline's father stood in the threshold, a dazzling smile lighting up his features. "Come along you two. I need your help."

"What is it?" Theo asked.

Natemahar reached behind him and pulled on something. It turned out to be a shoulder attached to Sophocles. "This old sailor wants to be baptized," Natemahar announced.

# CHAPTER 33

―― ᴄ⅃ᴼ ――

*You said, "I am forever—*
*the eternal queen!"*
*But you did not consider these things*
*or reflect on what might happen.*

ISAIAH 47:7, NIV

The journey to Alexandria, shorter than their voyage to Puteoli, proved, in every way, an idyllic time. The wind and the weather conspired to make sailing smooth and as rapid as the *Parmys* could manage.

Theo found it a trip full of unforgettable moments. Chariline's confession of love for him. His proposal. Her acceptance. Their first kiss. Their second kiss. Their hours of planning for a future he once could not have imagined. Natemahar's warm acceptance and welcome. And Sophocles's baptism in the waters of the Mediterranean.

Yet, in spite of the incandescent joy, a heated anxiety was mounting in him. A fear that was taking on colossal proportions the closer they came to the shores of Egypt. First, they had to deal with transporting Chariline safely from the harbor of Alexandria to Meroë. His ship, made for the sea, could not navigate the Nile. They would need to find new transport. With a killer on their trail, every step of that journey would entail danger.

Bearing her safely to Meroë only meant facing an even greater danger: the dreaded audience with the queen.

Theo's belly churned with nausea every time he thought of it. He knew, after praying, that Chariline's choice was the right one. But right choices could get you killed just as effectively as wrong ones.

This mercurial Kandake petrified him. He could keep Chariline safe from warriors and assassins. But how was he to shield her from the power of a queen?

On the morning they arrived at Alexandria's harbor, Taharqa arranged for a berth for the *Parmys* while Theo left in search of a river barge that would suit their needs. When all was prepared, Theo returned to the ship.

"Are you ready?" he asked.

She nodded. Theo adjusted the sleeve of her tunic. They had purchased the outfit back in Rome in preparation for this day. "Is it too bright, do you think?" he asked, frowning.

Natemahar considered the red hue. "I think it's perfect."

She shrugged. "I would have preferred purple. Like his tunic." She pointed to Natemahar's garment.

Theo rolled his eyes. "Just try not to get yourself killed."

She grinned, reminding him for a moment of a wily fox. Their covered litter was waiting on the dock. Time to move. He pulled her stola all the way over her face, and taking her modestly covered arm carefully, he guided her quickly off the ship and onto the waiting litter, pulling the curtains shut as soon as they entered.

They waited in the litter until their barge was almost ready to depart. Theo stepped down and, after scanning their surroundings, helped her out. They hastened to board the barge together and rushed to the cabin in the rear. Just before stepping inside and closing the door, Theo saw a hooded figure board the barge.

"Behave yourself. And stick to the plan."

"Yes, Master," Sophocles said as he lowered the stola to his shoulders, making the few passengers who were taking refuge in the cabin turn their heads in bewilderment.

Quickly, Sophocles stripped off the red tunic and handed the bundle to Theo. In moments, there was no sign of the woman who had entered the cabin. Just an old man with white hair and whiskers, reclining on a seat by the wall.

Theo rolled the red garments and tucked them under his leather belt. The window in the back of the cabin was a little narrow for comfort, and he scraped his arms and legs pushing through it. He ignored the sting as he jumped into the shallows of the Nile just in time to watch the barge embark on its journey down the river.

By the time he doubled back to the harbor where his ship was berthed, a hired carriage awaited him. He climbed in and pulled the curtains shut behind him. Looking at the three passengers inside, he asked, "Is everything ready?"

At their nods, he signaled the drivers and they began their ride back to the river docks. Chariline had told him the name of the ship she and her aunt often used, and he had paid the captain to reserve the cabin for their exclusive use. They slipped inside as soon as they boarded and closed the door.

The barge rattled and swayed and with a groan began its journey. Theo was taking his first tranquil breath of the day when the cabin door swung open slowly. He sprang to his feet, his fingers twitching over his new dagger.

A skinny, half-naked boy crept inside, dark eyes shining with mischief.

"Arkamani!" Chariline and Natemahar shouted at the same time. The treasurer groaned. But Chariline darted forward to enfold the boy in a hug. The boy said something in Meroitic. Theo looked to Taharqa for the translation.

"He said, 'Careful, honey lady. You will wrinkle my loin-cloth,'" Taharqa explained and continued to translate their conversation for Theo.

"Back to working for your uncle?" Chariline said with a laugh.

He shrugged. "It's nice on the boat, sometimes. Cooler on water in the summer."

"Arkamani, we could use your help."

The boy pushed out his chest. "You tell me. Arkamani is your man."

"We are looking for a man in a dark cloak. He has cuts on his cheeks and forehead like a warrior. If someone like that boards the boat, will you come and let us know?"

"You leave it to me. I will call you quick if he boards."

Theo gave Chariline an approving nod. She clearly knew the boy, and it was a good idea to have a spy outside just in case the assassin managed to find his way to them in spite of all their precautions.

Thankfully, the journey proved uneventful. The warrior must still be stuck on the barge that left a few hours ahead of theirs. Sophocles would have disembarked at the first stop and made his way back to Alexandria, where he would wait for them.

Theo had never traveled so far south on the Nile. Chariline, Natemahar, and Taharqa took turns pointing out the ancient sites to him. The coming audience with the queen cast a long shadow on all the wonders he saw along the mysterious, serpentine river. They navigated the cataracts with the usual hassle and arrived at Meroë, tired and hot.

But they were in time to save the queen's life. If she needed saving.

They had evaded the assassin. Now, all that remained was to face the monarch of Cush.

Theo considered finding lodgings at the harbor. He would prefer to show up before the queen well-rested and washed, without the stench of travel on his clothing. Before he could make the arrangements, a royal guard of six soldiers met them at the dock, their shoulders draped in leopard skin and shielded by iron plating.

"By order of the Kandake, we are to accompany you to the palace," their captain said, expressionless.

It did not sound like a suggestion.

"How could she even know we are here?" Theo hissed as they fell in step with the soldiers, three before them and three bringing up the rear.

"I told you she has exceptional spies." Natemahar ran a hand over his tired face.

"What does it mean? Are we under arrest?"

"Given the cordial way they are treating us, I think they have been sent for our safety."

Theo looked to the hard-faced warriors hemming them in as they marched in perfect unison. "You call this cordial?"

"You don't have a spear shoved against your throat, do you?"

———— ᙁᘓ ————

Chariline pressed into Theo's side and held on to Natemahar's fingers. They had been brought into the queen's throne room through a long, deserted corridor. "The queen's private hallway," Natemahar had explained. To Chariline's surprise, even the throne room stood empty. Apparently, this was to remain a private audience. In spite of Theo and Natemahar's reassuring presence, she felt a chill of dread. She tried to be brave and, failing, lifted her head, hoping to look what she did not feel.

Behind the empty gold throne, a curtain twitched. A tall woman strode in, covered in an ankle-length white gown, decorated with a pleated sash that draped across her right shoulder and breast. At the sight of her, the soldiers stood to attention.

The Kandake.

As the queen took time to settle herself on her throne, Chariline had the opportunity to observe her. She looked ageless, her skin unmarred by lines, though she was at least a dozen years older than Natemahar. Henna stained her long fingernails and short hair a subdued red, and on her head, she wore a metal skullcap, which supported a royal diadem.

Chariline's mouth turned dry as the dark eyes landed on her. She felt like she was sitting between a lion's paws. Too late to run now. *Iesous, help us!*

"You look more like your father than your mother," the queen commented.

Chariline bowed. "Thank you, Kandake. You honor me."

"I did not mean it as a compliment. Your mother was a lot prettier. So, Natemahar, what brings you back to Cush in such haste, and with her in tow?" She pointed her chin at Chariline. "I told you to go save her life. Not to bring her back here tucked under your arm like a prized chicken you couldn't give up."

Natemahar bowed with much more grace than Chariline had managed. "Kandake, my daughter has important information, for your ears only."

The queen curled her lip. "Stop spouting about *your daughter* in my palace, if you please. These walls have ears, lest you have forgotten. And a certain person is still on Cushite soil. Watch your tongue for a few more days."

"Your pardon, Kandake. This young woman has some urgent information concerning your safety."

"*My* safety, is it? I thought it was her skinny neck we were trying to protect." She picked up a delicate fan made of silver scrolls and waved it in front of her face. "Well, girl? What is this important information you have for me?"

Chariline felt Theo grow tense next to her. She pressed his arm before letting go of him and stepping forward. "I am sorry to say, my lady, that your royal neck is in as much danger as my skinny one seems to be." She tried to keep her voice steady.

"Indeed?"

"Your Majesty, I am afraid there is a plot to assassinate you."

The queen's face remained still, void of expression. But her eyes widened a fraction, and her long nails curled against the throne.

"Explain yourself," she growled.

Chariline cleared her throat. "I overheard a conversation between two men at your palace. One of them was your treasurer, Sesen."

A muscle jumped at the corner of the queen's lip. Chariline's mouth turned dry.

She forced herself to go on. "Sesen and his companion spoke of your trip in the spring on the royal barge, which had been canceled. Originally, that was when they meant to kill you. Sesen urged for patience until you traveled on the barge this month. They intend for the barge to drown, and you with it, so that it looks like an accident."

The dark eyes flared. The queen surged to her feet, every regal feature stamped with outrage.

Chariline took a hasty step back, leaning into Theo's reassuring warmth. Natemahar had been correct. The Kandake had not known about the plot.

Which meant she would have had no reason to send an assassin after Chariline.

"That toad is planning to drown me?" the queen shouted, her voice sharp as a razor.

"Yes, my lady. You and your ship."

"I love that ship!" She held her breath for a beat. "Wait. When did you overhear this conversation?"

Chariline winced. "Your Majesty . . . Kandake, that is . . ."

The queen took a step toward her. Behind her, three

soldiers also stepped forward in unison, hands at the ready on their sword pommels. "Spit it out, girl."

"In the spring, when I was in Cush."

"Natemahar!" the queen roared. "Did you know about this?"

"I only found out about Sesen's plot after I caught up with Chariline in Rome, Kandake. Which is why we hastened to Cush as fast as possible. She always meant to save your life, my queen."

"Did she, now?" She faced Chariline. "You did not think this was the kind of news you should have brought to me right away, girl?" The queen pinned Chariline with her dark gaze. "You thought it appropriate to wait for three months before informing me, or even Natemahar, that someone wished to drown me in the Nile?"

"I hoped I might be able to change Sesen's mind before this plot went too far."

"Change his mind? We are not talking about his preference in bread. My life hung in the balance!"

"I always intended to warn you, Kandake. But at the time, I suspected Sesen might be my father. I feared for his life if I came to you with the news."

The queen rolled her eyes. "Little fool," she muttered under her breath.

"I hoped to find a way to save you both."

"Well, you have not."

"No."

"If you were not a Roman," the queen spat, "I would have your head for this delay."

Chariline drew herself to her full height. "If I were not a Roman, I would have known Natemahar was my father," she said, mustering her dignity.

The queen's face grew as impassive as the Great Sphinx of Egypt. She settled back on her throne. "I will decide your fate later. First, let us settle the matter of this conspiracy. You say two men are plotting to kill me. Who is the second?"

"Your pardon, Kandake. I do not know the name of Sesen's accomplice," Chariline said. "But I would recognize him if I were to see him again."

"Describe him to me," the queen barked.

Chariline did her best. The queen slashed the air with her hand. "That could be fifty men in this palace. Tell me something that stood out. Did he wear any distinctive clothing? A thinning hairline? Crooked teeth? Anything that would help me recognize him."

Chariline shook her head. "I only saw him for a few moments." She frowned. "He did wear a lot of jewelry. Chains about his neck, thick armbands decorated with jewels. Even his belt had gold embellishments. And he had a distinctive ring. A crocodile biting on an amethyst."

The Kandake went still. Then smiled. "I seem to recall such a ring. Still, I will need your eyes as witness."

"Kandake, there must be at least one other in this plot whose name we do not know," Natemahar said. "The man in charge of damaging your ship. If Chariline is exposed as the witness . . ."

She waved him down. "For now, we will keep her hidden." She pointed to the embroidered linen curtain that hung behind her throne. "She can watch the proceedings through there. If the man I send for is the one she saw plotting with Sesen, then she will send one of my guards to warn me."

"Thank you, Kandake."

"May Theo come with me?" Chariline asked.

The queen turned. Lights from a hundred lamps caught the gold in her crown, making it shine like a star. "Theo?"

"Theodotus of Corinth, Kandake," Natemahar clarified. "He offered us the use of his ship so that we might arrive in Meroë in time to warn you."

"I am sure I will have to pay a fortune for his service."

"He asked for nothing, though I assured him that we will repay his expenses."

The queen waved a hand. "Yes, yes. Now take the ship owner and the girl to my secret room. You two hide there until I send for you. Natemahar, you are with me." The queen nodded to a member of the guard, who accompanied Chariline and Theo to a small alcove immediately behind the throne.

It was a surprisingly comfortable spot, decorated with a couch and feather-filled cushions. A spot made specifically for spying, Chariline realized.

Not long after, the sound of feet echoed from the throne room. A name was announced formally in the chamber beyond, and the guard motioned for Chariline to approach the edge of the curtain. She stood perfectly still and gazed through the slit into the chamber beyond.

# CHAPTER 34

—❦—

*You reward everyone according to what they have done.*

PSALM 62:12, NIV

Sesen arrived first. Chariline was surprised when the queen greeted him in a friendly voice. "I need your help with a dilemma, Treasurer," she said.

Sesen smiled confidently. "It is my honor to serve."

"A young woman has made an extraordinary claim against you."

Chariline gasped. What was the queen doing?

"Against me, my queen?" Sesen asked.

"She claims that you are plotting to kill me."

Sesen took a hesitant step back. "Kill you, Kandake?"

"I myself saw her trying to pass a letter to you. So, the question becomes, was she part of this plot, and then changed her mind due to some division between you? Or is she an innocent, caught in your trap?"

Chariline felt Theo's body grow rigid with tension. She reached for his hand, her fingers shaking.

"I am the only innocent here," Sesen said, his infuriating confidence seemingly unshaken. "Why would I plot against my dear queen? I pledge you my loyalty. Who is this girl who dares to besmirch me with her accusations?"

The queen shrugged. "She is no one important. The salient point is the charge she brings against you."

"Where is her proof?"

"She has given very specific details about time and place."

Sesen frowned. "All lies! I will not even be in Cush for the rest of July. I am leaving for Egypt in the morning. My plans have been in place for months. How could I make an attempt on your life when I am not even here?"

"I never said the assassination attempt would take place in July."

Sesen paled. Just then, another man was announced. Chariline recognized him immediately. The nasal voice, the scowling face, the bright jewels. The guard waiting in the alcove looked to her for confirmation. She nodded gravely, and the soldier slipped into the throne room to whisper in the queen's ear.

"You two know each other, I believe," the queen said.

Sesen's handsome face glistened with sweat. "We have met, here in this very throne room."

"And was it in this throne room you plotted to drown me?"

"*Drown* you?" The nasal voice grew panicked. "Drown you?" he repeated. "Never, my queen."

"I have a witness who says differently."

"Lies and fabrications," Sesen spat.

A guard slid silently into the hall and approached the queen. He spoke quietly so that only she could hear. "I see," she murmured. Turning her attention to the men before her, she said, "My royal barge, it seems, has sustained grievous damage. Inconveniently, the damage is hidden from the casual observer. But one hour on the river in this season of high floodwaters, and it would certainly sink." She leaned forward. Chariline could not see her expression from where she stood. But she could see Sesen clearly. He staggered.

"The damage to my ship was intentional," the queen said, her voice low. "Someone took an ax to my beautiful barge. Never mind trying to drown me. You tried to destroy my ship!"

"I had nothing to do with this atrocity," Sesen cried, taking a step away from his accomplice.

"You can't blame it on me," his bejeweled accomplice screamed.

"It's the girl." Sesen took a step closer to the throne. "You said yourself you suspected her. This is her doing."

"I said I watched her trying to pass you a letter. If she is guilty, so are you. You can't have it both ways, Treasurer."

Desperation washed over Sesen's face. "I had nothing to do with her. Ask her why she wormed her way inside your palace under false pretenses. Ask her why she snuck in here, pretending to be a servant, when she is the granddaughter of—"

"Silence!" the queen snarled. Immediately, one of the guards shoved the tip of a spear under Sesen's throat, effectively shutting him up. "You are a slithering serpent. But you're not very bright. To think I placed you in charge of the treasures of Cush. Your own defense has tangled you. In your desperation to blame another for your guilt, you have confirmed the girl's story."

Chariline wilted. For the first time since they had left the ship, she managed to gulp down a lungful of air. The queen did not think her involved in the plot, after all.

They could hear the men's denials, their cries for mercy. Chariline began to shiver, forced to listen to the plotters' desperate pleas as they were arrested and dragged from the throne room.

She turned into Theo's arms, burrowing against him. "What do you think she will do to them?"

"That is not for you to carry, love. You saved her life. It is all Yeshua asked of you. Now you must give the fate of these men to him."

She remembered Hermione telling her that she might not have the power to save both Sesen and the queen. Chariline held Theo tighter, knowing he was wrapping her in his prayers just as tightly as in his arms.

———— ☙ ————

When the throne room grew silent, the echoes of the doomed men receding down the corridors of the palace, the queen sent for Chariline again.

Theo and Chariline bowed to the Kandake, who was sitting on the edge of her throne, back ramrod straight, face like stone. Chariline thought, looking at the inscrutable features, that the dark eyes betrayed a storm of anger not yet spent. And something more. Hurt.

The queen gazed back at the young couple. Her face softened. "It's never easy to send a man to his death," she said. "You will carry this all your days, Chariline."

"Yes, Kandake," she whispered.

"Then carry this also: You saved not only my life, but the peace of Cush. For were I to die a violent and untimely death, this nation would plunge into civil war."

"Why did they do it?" Chariline asked through dry lips.

"Thwarted ambition can become a sick thing. I did not give them what they asked for. Position for one, and a lucrative deal for the other. I blocked their desires. For that, they thought I should die." Her expression changed. "You must be happy Sesen is not your father."

"Very happy, Your Majesty."

"I suppose I will have to forgive you for not telling me about the plot as soon as you found it out. I may be somewhat responsible for your delusions about Sesen. Had I allowed Natemahar to reveal his relationship to you, you would not have jumped to such ludicrous conclusions."

Chariline exhaled. "Thank you, Kandake."

"At least now we know who hired an assassin to kill you. I will take care of it. You need not worry on that score."

"You are generous, Kandake," Natemahar said.

"But how will you find him?" Chariline asked.

"I have my ways." The queen smiled at the commotion by the door. "And here comes one of them, if I am not mistaken."

Chariline turned as the door to the throne room opened. A skinny boy, dressed in white linen from shoulder to calf, sauntered in.

"Arkamani!"

The boy grinned and walked confidently to the throne to bow beautifully. "Hello, Auntie."

The queen rapped him softly over the head with her fan. "Kandake to you, brat."

"Yes, my lady," the boy said dutifully, eyes sparkling.

"The queen is your *aunt*?" Chariline squeaked.

"Only by marriage," the queen clarified.

"I thought you were my spy," Chariline said, indignant.

"I was under the impression you worked for me," Natemahar added.

"You were both wrong," the queen said with satisfaction. "The boy has potential. I recruited him before both of you." She turned to address Arkamani. "What news, brat?"

"I know where he is hiding, Auntie."

"Kandake, I said."

"Yes, Auntie."

The queen ignored the boy and turned to Natemahar. "We've located the assassin Sesen hired to kill the girl, it seems."

"May I help, Kandake?" Theo offered.

Chariline stepped forward. "If he goes, so do I."

———— ⟳ ————

He counted his dwindling coins dolefully. He had been reduced to downright poverty thanks to that detestable girl and her prancing boy. Both had disappeared from the barge, gone like smoke on a windy day. He was done with them. If that one-eyed courtier wanted to kill girls, he could do it himself. From now on, he intended to stay away from any job that had anything to do with women.

He would have to find fresh employment. He drank the last of his cheap barley water and slapped the cup down.

Donning his old armor, he strapped on his sword, its weight comfortingly familiar, and slung his leather quiver over his shoulder. He looked respectable again, like a proper warrior ought.

Opening the door onto the street, he sidestepped a pile of warm manure. Looking up, he caught his breath. There she stood, like a wraith, smiling at him. She waved, as if she knew him. Glorious day! Good fortune had returned to him. Brought her right to his door. He would get rid of her and be paid the rest of his wages.

He sprinted toward her, and she stood, unmoving, like a lame rabbit, just waiting for him to skin her. He dragged out his knife and let it dance between his fingers, until its cold haft settled like a familiar lover's hand in his palm.

Three steps from her, a broad chest that hadn't been there a moment before smashed into him. "Watch where you're going," he growled and looked up.

Not again! The prancing boy stood in front of him, grinning his manic grin.

The warrior shoved against the broad chest and turned, intending to run the other way, only to find himself face-to-face with another broad chest. Without warning, a whole row of them stood in front of him, blocking the way. The barley water had slowed his brain a touch. It took him a blink and a belch to recognize the uniforms. Royal guardsmen.

He circled fast, only to come to an abrupt halt as he ran into another wall of muscle. The wall parted a little and a woman walked through, tall and stony faced. His mouth turned into a sandy wilderness when he noticed the way the sun's rays reflected off the shining skullcap on her head.

She pressed the tip of her sword to the delicate place where his neck and throat met. "Kneel to your queen, scum."

He fell to his knees. He should have known his end would come at the hand of a woman. "I can give you a name," he croaked.

"I am sure you can," she said pleasantly.

———— ‿ ————

The queen insisted that Theo and Chariline occupy a couple of small, private chambers attached to her own apartments. She did not want Quintus Blandinus Geminus to get wind of Chariline's presence in Cush. In the evening, she arranged for a simple supper in her personal dining room, with only Natemahar, Chariline, and Theo as guests.

"You can stop staring at me like I am going to eat you, girl," she told Chariline as she seated herself. "I had to be sure you were not part of the plot."

"I don't suppose you could have taken my word for it."

"No. I could not." She unfolded her napkin. "So, what do you plan to do now?" she asked as a young Cushite slave with round curves served a dish of vegetables around the table. "Will you go back to your aunt in Caesarea? Blandina, I believe."

Chariline gaped. "Is there anything you don't know?"

Natemahar cleared his throat. "As a matter of fact, Chariline is betrothed to Theo. They will marry soon and return to Corinth."

"Betrothed?" The queen raised a brow. "I see no ring on your finger. Is that not the Roman custom?"

Theo's cheeks turned a light shade of pink. "I have not

had a chance to purchase one yet. I proposed while we were on board my ship, and given our haste to warn Your Majesty, we could not delay the voyage by stopping at a port along the way."

The queen pushed her plate away. "I suppose you are a Roman citizen."

"Not by birth," Theo explained. "My brother arranged for my citizenship several years ago. A merchant's taxes to Rome are gruesome, otherwise."

"I have some knowledge of that myself," the queen said dryly. She turned to address Chariline. "You may be a Roman on your mother's side. But your father is a Cushite nobleman. As such, Theodotus of Corinth, you need my permission to marry her."

Chariline's eyes widened with alarm. She looked to her father for help. But her father seemed as shocked as she. "Kandake," he began.

She waved him quiet. "I am not addressing you, Treasurer. I am speaking to Theodotus of Corinth. Well?"

"My lady?"

"I am waiting to be asked."

Theo came to his feet, stared down at the seated queen. With a smooth motion, he knelt before her on one knee. "Kandake, will you permit me to marry Chariline Gemina, daughter of your chief treasurer, Natemahar?" His voice emerged sure, unwavering. If he felt any anxiety, he kept it tucked up where no one could see.

"Do you want to marry this man?" the queen asked Chariline.

"Yes, Kandake. Very much."

"What does your grandfather have to say about it?"

"He doesn't know, my lady. But my father has given his blessing."

The queen's lip tipped up. "Quintus Blandinus would explode a vein in vexation." She returned her attention to Theo, still kneeling before her. "You may marry her," she said.

Theo bowed his head, managing to look graceful rather than awkward. "Thank you, Kandake."

"I am sometimes in need of a ship that could run an errand or two for me," she said. "Without being too obviously Cushite."

Theo raised a brow, his face smooth. "I can carry scented soap for you, my lady."

"Soap?"

"Soap."

"I am looking for a shipmaster, not a merchant. Can your pomade make or break a nation?"

"Perhaps not. But it can definitely make one smell nicer."

She threw her head back and laughed. "Well, get up from down there. Your chicken is growing cold." She waved to the slave. "Fetch my box. The alabaster and gold."

Chariline watched the Kandake sort through her chest. Eventually, she extracted a trinket that twinkled gold and closed the lid of her box.

"Theodotus of Corinth," she said formally.

"Yes, Kandake?" Once again, he knelt before her.

"Here is a small reward for your services to the queen of Cush." She dropped something into Theo's palm. A beaming smile lit up his face. It was precisely the kind of bright, breezy smile that could make a matron's heart beat a trifle too fast,

Chariline thought. She craned her neck to catch a glimpse of Theo's prize, but he closed his fingers around whatever he was holding.

Theo bowed. "My thanks, Kandake."

"Well?" the queen said. "What are you waiting for?"

"I was thinking of keeping it. It's not every day a man receives jewelry from a monarch, after all."

The Kandake made an odd noise in her throat that sounded alarmingly like a growl.

Theo laughed. Laughed! He flicked the flashing jewel up in the air, caught it with ease, and gave the queen an impish grin.

The dark eyes narrowed. Then to Chariline's shock, the stern lips twitched. "Get on with it, boy."

"Yes, lady." Theo turned to take Chariline's left hand in his. "The queen has helped me with a delicate problem, my love." He extended Chariline's hand and slipped something onto her third finger. She looked down and saw a ring made of polished yellow gold, marked with delicate swirls and etchings on both sides, with a sparkling oval ruby set in the center.

Chariline gasped. "It's enchanting!"

The queen smiled. "I regret I don't possess a traditional Roman wedding ring with a carving of hands clasping. But perhaps you can have a jeweler carve that into the ruby later."

Chariline shook her head. "I would not change a thing. It's perfect."

"I suppose you are going to want an iron band as well," the queen said, curling her lips, referring to the tradition of Roman women wearing a simple iron band for daily use and only donning their bejeweled betrothal ring on special occasions.

"It would be a pity to lose this marvelous jewel, since it is irreplaceable."

"Besides," Theo added, "I intend to have the other ring made from iron mined and forged in Cush, so that Chariline can always have a piece of her second home close to her heart."

"This one is going to go far," the queen said to Natemahar. "He always has just the right words at the ready." She waved the slave forward again, who placed a pouch in her hand. "Merchant!"

Again Theo abandoned his dinner to kneel at the queen's feet. "Yes, Kandake?"

"I gave you your reward for helping to save my life. But I still owe you a payment. Never let it be said the queen of Cush does not honor her debts."

"I was honored to serve, lady."

As Theo resumed his seat, Chariline cleared her throat.

"What now, girl?"

"I have a favor to ask of you."

"Of course you do." The queen sighed. "You saved my life. For that, you deserve a great reward. What is it? You want a ruby bracelet for your ring? Fertile land near the Nile? A pair of matching horses?"

"I thank you, Kandake. But I want none of those things."

"Well?"

"I want my father."

The Kandake's face grew very still.

"I have not had a father for twenty-four years while you have had your treasurer. He has lost everything in your service and never ceased to labor for you faithfully. If he is willing to retire from his position, then Theo and I would like to take him with us to Corinth. He can have his own house on our land. Eat with us every day. Pray with us. Play with our children, should God choose to bless my womb."

The Kandake's hand fisted around her silver table knife. "You ask for much."

Chariline wanted to say that the queen had *taken* much. Instead, she tamed her tongue. "You said I deserved a great reward, and I have asked for one. Having seen the kind of men you have to contend with every day, I know it will be hard to lose someone like my father. A man you can trust. But we both know he is not strong in body. He needs rest, now, and peace. A queen can impart many blessings. But she cannot give the love of a family."

The knife dropped to the table. The Kandake turned to Natemahar. "Is this what you want?"

"I had never thought it might even be a possibility, my queen. It is the first I have heard of it."

"But is it what you want?"

Her father gazed at Chariline. His eyes shimmered. "More than anything," he rasped with a desperation that twisted Chariline's heart.

The queen grew silent. When at last she lifted her head, her whole body seemed to have shrunk a little. "Then you shall have it," she said.

# EPILOGUE

—— ⊂⅋⊃ ——

*Let not the eunuch say,*
*"Behold, I am a dry tree."*

ISAIAH 56:3

They held the wedding in Corinth. Philip and his daughters accompanied Aunt Blandina so she would not have to travel alone. Priscilla and Aquila managed to leave their business for a short while, excited to visit old friends from the church they had hosted in their home while they had lived in Corinth five years earlier. Vitruvia and Galerius also arrived, bearing a cartload of gifts.

Several weeks before the wedding, Theo paid a brief visit to Chariline's grandfather in his new farm on the outskirts of Pompeii.

"I must ask his permission to marry you," Theo explained to Chariline.

She assured him that he need not have this conversation for a third time. But Theo insisted.

"Quintus Blandinus did not receive this courtesy from

your parents when they married. Let us not break his pride again." And so, Theo set off for Pompeii and asked, once again, for Chariline's hand in marriage.

"You must really want me," she teased.

He shrugged. "After a queen with her own private torture chamber, your grandfather does not seem very scary."

Grandfather gave his permission, of course. Who could resist Theo? Even though he had not been born a Roman, he made up for it by being an affluent merchant and a citizen. Besides, he did not argue when Grandfather offered him an insultingly small dowry.

Theo invited Quintus Blandinus and his wife to the wedding but gave so frightful a description of the sea journey to Corinth that both her grandparents decided not to make the trip. A relief, since no one had bothered to tell Blandinus that Chariline had found her father, and he had moved to Corinth.

Because Natemahar's house would be smaller, they decided to build it first. Having lived frugally for much of his life, he was able to hire extra workers so that his house was ready by the time of the wedding in October. Chariline had designed the building to his specifications, with a walled garden and an airy tablinum. It was the first of her designs to be built, and Chariline spent every day on site, supervising the work with an eagle eye.

A few hours before the wedding, Theo found Natemahar and Sophocles decorating the atrium of the new house with the last of the scented jasmine and roses. Natemahar had invited the old sailor to retire from sea life and come to live with him as a steward.

To Theo's surprise, Sophocles had accepted. "I'm too old for the sea," he told Theo. "Can't keep falling overboard. A nice bath is better suited to my advanced age."

Theo found his freedwoman, Delia, directing the two men's effort at decoration. Having once served as a hairdresser to the rich, Delia had impeccable taste and a somewhat regrettable turn of phrase. Her faith in God had tamed her tongue a bit. But when excited, she could still expound amazingly colorful language. "No, don't stick that rose there," she scolded Sophocles. "It looks like a pimple on Venus's cleavage."

Sophocles grinned. "Sounds good to me."

Spotting Theo, Natemahar abandoned his sprigs of jasmine with obvious relief, greeting him with an affectionate embrace.

Sophocles frowned. "What are you doing here, Master, so early on your wedding day? If you are running away, you've come to the wrong house. We will deliver you to the altar bound and gagged if we have to."

"I'm not running away," Theo assured him. He looked at Natemahar. "Could we speak in private?"

"Of course, son." They retreated to Natemahar's tablinum. The sun poured through a window, landing on the black-and-white tiles, making the marble come alive.

"This is for you," Theo said, handing Natemahar the elaborately decorated parchment he had commissioned for his soon-to-be father-in-law.

Natemahar's eyes widened with surprise. He unfurled the parchment, exclaiming with delight at the intricate geometric design that bordered the rectangle. In the center, a few verses from the prophet Isaiah filled the scroll.

*Let not the eunuch say,*
  *"Behold, I am a dry tree."*
*For thus says the* LORD:
*"To the eunuchs who keep my Sabbaths,*
  *who choose the things that please me*
  *and hold fast my covenant,*
*I will give in my house and within my walls*
  *a monument and a name*
  *better than sons and daughters;*
*I will give them an everlasting name*
  *that shall not be cut off."*

Natemahar's lips trembled. "You are not supposed to make me weep today. It's my daughter's wedding day."

Theo clasped his forearm. "I wanted you to know how grateful I am to have your daughter as my wife. And how proud I am to have you as a father."

———— ∽ ————

They stood under the wooden arbor, now decorated with pink and white blooms, while Aquila prayed for them. Priscilla acted as matron of honor, and taking Chariline's hand, she placed it in Theo's.

The air smelled of jasmine and roses. The sky had turned a deep blue, a perfect dome over their heads as Chariline pronounced the words that bound her to her bridegroom: "Where you go, Theodotus, I, Chariline, will go." Her chest expanded until she thought it would explode with joy.

Bending his head, Theo kissed her, his lips warm, his arms secure. Chariline felt her soul knit to his, knit by bonds of love and faith, knit by Iesous's mighty grace, which had brought them together.

The kiss lasted a beat too long as they clung to each other, hungry for more, forgetting everyone else.

The guests cheered loudly, and finally Theo stepped away, grinning.

Theo's handsome brother, Justus, was the first to congratulate them, his eyes damp with joy. "I am so happy to welcome you to our family," he told Chariline.

Ariadne pulled Chariline into her arms, kissing her cheeks twice. "I always wanted a sister. Now I have one." Theo drew Ariadne to his side and gave her a brotherly hug, his manner easy. Whatever love he had once borne this woman had long since been curbed, transformed into something tame and calm.

Little Theo, a dimpled toddler with wide brown eyes, held up his hands. "Me! Me!" he demanded, and Theo swung him up into his arms, where he rested, looking triumphantly down at the world.

Chariline knew just how he felt. She had begun this journey in search of her father. Many were the hours when she had believed she would only come away clutching disappointment. Instead, she had found so much more than the answers to the riddles of her life. She had found Theo. A home. A family. And something more.

In the passing of months, as she had tasted of Theo's tender love, of Natemahar's endless affection, she had finally learned the lesson of Theo's angel. She had learned to look in the mirror and not see a mistake, but to find instead God's jewel staring back at her through the scars of her life.

# THIEF OF CORINTH

❧⟫❧⟪❧

THE FIRST TIME I climbed through a window and crept about secretly through a house, the moon sat high in the sky and I was running away from home. *Home* is perhaps an exaggeration. Unlike my brother Dionysius, I never thought of my grandfather's villa in Athens as home. For eight miserable years that upright bastion of Greek tradition had been my prison, a trap I could not escape, a madhouse where too much philosophy and ancient principles had rotted its residents' brains. But it was never my home.

Home was my father's villa in Corinth.

I was determined, on that moon-bright evening, to convey myself there no matter what impediments I faced. A girl of sixteen, clambering from a second story window in the belly of night without enough sense to entertain a single fear. Before me lay Corinth and my father and freedom. As always, waiting for me faithfully in uncomplaining silence, was Theodotus, my foster brother. Regardless of how harebrained and dangerous my schemes might be, Theo never left my side.

He stood in the courtyard, keeping watch, as I made my way down the slippery balustrade outside my room, my feet dangling for a moment into the nothingness of shadows and air. I slithered one finger at a time to the side, until my feet found the branches of the laurel tree, and ignoring the scratches on my skin, I let go and took a leap into the aromatic leaves. I had often climbed the smooth limbs, unusually tall for a laurel. But that had been in the light of day and from the bottom up. Now I jumped into the tree from the top, hoping it would catch me, or that I could cling to some part of it before I fell to the ground and crushed my bones against Grandfather's ancient marble tiles.

My fingers seemed fashioned for this perilous capering, and by an instinct of their own, they found a sturdy branch and clung, breaking the momentum of my fall. I felt my way down and made short work of the tree. My mother would have been horrified. The thought made me smile.

"You could have broken your neck," Theo whispered, his jaw clenched. He was my age but seemed a decade older. I boiled like water, easily riled into anger. He remained immovable like stone, my steady rock through the capricious shifts of fortune.

The tight knots in my shoulders relaxed at the sight of him, and I grinned. "I didn't." Reaching for the bundle he had packed for me, I grabbed it. "The gate?"

He shook his head. "Agis seemed determined to stay sober tonight." We both looked over to the figure of the slave, huddled on his pallet across the front door, his loud snores competing with the sound of the cicadas.

"I am afraid there's more climbing in your future if you really intend to go to Corinth," Theo said, his voice hushed. He took a step closer so that I could see the vague outline of his long face. "Nothing will be the same, you know, if you do this thing, Ariadne. Whether you fail or succeed. It's not too late to change your mind."

In answer, I turned and made my way to the high wall that surrounded the house like an uncompromising sentinel. Grandfather had made it impossible for me to remain. I should have escaped this place long ago.

I studied the daunting height of the wall and realized I would need a boost to climb it. By the fountain in the middle of the courtyard, the slaves had left a massive stone mortar that stood as high as my waist. It would do for a stepping-stone. The mortar proved heavier than we expected. Since dragging it would have made too great a clamor, we had to lift it completely off the ground. The muscles in my arms shook with the effort of carrying my burden. Halfway to our destination, I lost my hold on the slippery stone. With a loud clatter, it fell on the marble pavement.

Agis stirred, then sat up. Theo and I dropped to the ground, hiding in the shadow of the mortar. "Who goes there?" Agis mumbled.

He rose from his pallet and looked about, then took a few steps in our direction. His foot came within a hand's breadth of my shoulder. One more step and he would discover me. Blood hammered in my ears. My lungs grew paralyzed, forgetting how to pulse air out of my chest.

This was my only chance to break away. If Agis raised the alarm and I were apprehended, my grandfather would see to it that I remained locked up in the women's quarters under guard until I capitulated to his demands. He held the perfect weapon against me. Should I refuse to marry that madman, Draco, my grandfather would hurt Theo. I knew this was no empty threat. Grandfather had a brilliant mind, sharp as steel's edge, and a heart to match. It would not trouble his conscience in the least to torment an innocent in order to get his own way. He would beat Theo and blame every lash on me for refusing to obey his command.

The fates sent me an unlikely liberator. Herodotus the cat came to my rescue. Though feral, it hung about Grandfather's property because Theo and I had secretly adopted it and fed the poor beast when we could. My mother had forbidden this act of mercy, but since the cat had an appetite for mice and other vermin, the slaves turned a blind eye to our disobedience.

Just when Agis was about to take another step leading to my discovery, Herodotus ran across his foot.

"Agh," he cried and jumped back. "Stupid animal! Next time you wake me, I will gut you and feed you to the crows." Grumbling, the slave went back to bed. Theo and I remained immobile and silent until we heard his snores split the peaceful night again.

This time, we carried our burden with even more attentive care and managed to place it next to the wall without mishap.

I threw my bundle over the wall and stepped cautiously into the center of the mortar, then balanced my feet on the opposite edges of the bowl. We held our breath as the stone groaned and wobbled. Agis, to my relief, continued to snore.

The brick lining the top of the wall scraped my palm as I held tight and pulled. I made my way up, arms burning, back straining, my toes finding holds in the rough, aged brick. One last scramble and I was sitting on the edge.

Theo climbed into the mortar next, his leather-shod feet silent on the stone. I leaned down and offered my hand to him. Without hesitation, he grasped my wrist and allowed me to help him climb until he, too, straddled the wall. We sat grinning as we faced each other, basking in the small victory before looking down into the street.

"Too far to jump," he observed.

On the street, next to the main entrance of the house, sat a squat pillar bearing a dainty statue of Athena, Grandfather's nod to his precious city and its divine patron. At the base of the marble figurine the slaves had left a small lamp, which burned through the night. I crawled on the narrow, uneven border of bricks twelve feet above ground until I sat directly above the pillar.

As I dangled down the outer wall, I took care not to knock Athena over, partly because I knew the noise would rouse Agis, and partly because I was scared of the goddess's wrath. Dionysius no longer believed in the gods, not as true beings who meddled in the fate of mortals. He said they were mere symbols, useful for teaching us how to live worthy lives. I wasn't so sure. In any case, I preferred not to take any chances. Should there really be an Athena, I would rather not draw her displeasure down on me right before starting the greatest adventure of my life. She was, after all, the patron of heroic endeavor.

"Excuse me, goddess. I intend no disrespect," I whispered as I placed my feet carefully on either side of her, balancing my weight before jumping cleanly on the street.

Being considerably taller, Theo managed the pillar better. His foot caught on the goddess's head at the last moment, though, and smashed it into the wall. I dove fast enough to save her from an ignoble tumble onto the ground. But her crash into the plaster-covered bricks had extracted a price. Poor Athena had lost an arm.

"Now you've done it," I said.

Theo retrieved the severed arm from the dust and placed it next to the statue on the pillar. "Forgive me, goddess," he said and gave an awkward pat to the marble. "You're still pretty." I caught his eye and we started to laugh, half mad with the relief of our escape, and half terrified that the goddess would materialize in person and punish us for our disrespect.

"What are you doing?" a voice asked from the darkness, sharp like the crack of a whip.

I jumped, almost knocking Athena over again. "Who is there?" I said, trembling like a cornered fawn.

The speaker stepped forward until the diminutive lamp at Athena's feet revealed his face.

My back melted against the wall as I made out Dionysius's familiar face. "You scared the heart out of me," I accused.

"What are you doing?" he asked again, his gaze taking in our bundles and my unusual garments—his own cloak wrapped loosely about my figure, hiding my gender.

I swallowed hard, struck mute. I was running away from

my mother and grandfather. But in escaping, I was leaving behind a beloved brother. Dionysius was Grandfather's pet, the son he had never had. I think the old man truly loved him. He certainly treated him with a tenderness he had never once demonstrated toward Theo or me. Grandfather would not stand for Dionysius leaving. He would follow us like a hound into the bowels of Hades to get him back.

My escape could only work if my brother remained behind.

I told myself Dionysius loved Athens. He fit perfectly into the mold of the old city with its rigorous intellectual pursuits and appreciation for philosophy. Athens suited Dionysius much better than the wildness of Corinth. I was like a scribe who added one and one and tallied three. I lied to myself, twisting the truth into something I could bear.

Dionysius had a more brilliant mind even than my grandfather, a mind that prospered in the academic atmosphere of Athens. But he had inherited our father's soft heart. The abrupt separation from Father had wounded him. To lose Theo and me as well would cut him in ways I could not bear to think about. Not all the glories of Athens or Grandfather's affection could make up for such a void.

I had not told him of my plan to run away, convincing myself that Dionysius might cave and betray us to the old man. In truth, I was too much of a coward to bear the look on his face once I confessed I meant to leave him behind. The look he was giving me now.

Theo stepped forward. "She has to leave, Dionysius. You know that. Or the old wolf will force her to marry Draco."

My brother shifted from one foot to the other. "He is angry. He will cool."

I ground my teeth. Where Grandfather was concerned, Dionysius was blind. He could not see the evil that coiled through the old man. "He threatened to have Theo flogged if I refuse to marry the weasel. One stripe for every hour I refuse."

"*What?*" Theo and Dionysius said together. I had not even told Theo, worried that he might think I was running away for his sake more than my own, and refuse to help me.

"He has no scruples when it comes to Theo. Or me."

"Mother—"

"Will take his side as she always does. When has she ever defended me?"

I rubbed the side of my face, where the imprint of her hand had left a faint bruise, and winced as I remembered her iron-hard expression as she hit me.

Two days ago, Draco and his father, Evandos, had come to visit Grandfather. After drinking buckets of strong wine, the men had crawled to bed. The wind had pelted the city hard that evening, screaming through the trees, making the house groan in protest. The rains came then, sudden and violent.

I had risen from my pallet and slid softly into the courtyard. I loved storms, the unfettered deluge that washed the world clean. Within moments, I stood soaked through and grinning with exultation, enjoying the rare moment of freedom.

An odd sound caught my attention. At first I dismissed it as the noise of the wind. It came again, making me go still. The hair on my arms rose when it came a third time, a tortured wail, broken and sharp. No storm made that sound. My heart pounded as I followed that unearthly wail to a narrow shed on the other side of the courtyard. I slammed the door open.

He had brought a lamp with him, and it burned in the confines of the shed, casting its yellowish light into every corner. My eyes were drawn to the whimpering form on the dirt floor, lying spread-eagle. In the lamplight, blood glimmered, slick like oil, staining her thighs, her face, her stomach.

"Alcmena?" I gasped, barely recognizing the slave girl.

"Mistress!" She coughed. "Help me. Help me, I beg!"

I turned to the man standing over the slave, his face devoid of expression. "You did this?"

He smiled as if I had paid him a compliment. "A foretaste for you, beautiful Ariadne. I look forward to teaching you many lessons when you are my wife."

"Your *wife*? Get out of here, you madman!"

"Your grandfather promised me your hand in marriage. We drank on it earlier this evening." He stepped toward me. His gait was long and the space narrow. In a moment, Draco towered over me. He twined his fingers into my loose hair and pulled me toward him. The smell of the blood covering his knuckles made me gag. Without thinking, I fisted my hand and shoved it into his face. To my satisfaction, he staggered and screeched like a delicate woman. "My nose!"

"I beg your pardon, Draco. I was aiming for your mouth."

He rushed at me, hands clenched. I screamed as I stepped to the side, missing his bulk with ease. I had good lungs, and my voice carried with eerie clarity above the howling gale.

He faltered. "Shut your mouth."

I screamed louder.

The muscles in his neck corded as he hesitated for a moment. Then he lunged again, and I braced myself for a shattering assault. It never came.

Dionysius and Theo burst through the door, causing Draco to skid to a stop. My brothers seemed frozen with shock as they surveyed the state of Alcmena. Relief washed through me at the sight of them, and I sank to my knees next to the slave.

"What have you done?" my brother rasped, staring at the broken girl who could not even sit up in spite of my arm behind her back. "You brutal maggot. You've almost killed her."

Theo placed a warm hand on my shoulder. "Are you all right?"

I nodded, crossing my arms and trying to hide how badly my fingers shook.

Grandfather sauntered in, my mother in tow. "What is all this yelling? Can't a man sleep in peace?" He wiped his bristly jaw.

"Draco hurt Alcmena," I said.

My mother had the grace to gasp when she saw the slave girl, though she said nothing.

"He asked my permission to take the girl, and I gave it." Grandfather tightened his mouth when Alcmena doubled over and retched painfully. "You must have drunk too much, boy. Go back to your father."

Draco bowed his head and left without offering an explanation.

"He is crazed," I said. "He claims he will marry me. That you made an agreement with him earlier this evening."

"What of it?" Grandfather said, his voice hardening.

I expelled a wheezing breath. "You can't be serious! Look at what he did to the girl."

"The boy is a little hotheaded. Too much wine. Things

got out of hand. Nothing to do with you. I have made the arrangement with my friend Evandos. It is done."

"Grandfather!" Dionysius cleared his throat. "I think we should ask Draco to leave the house."

"We shall do no such thing. If an honored guest wants to abuse your furniture, you must allow him," Grandfather said. "She is my slave, and the damage is to my property. I say it is of no consequence."

"She's hardly a woman. Younger than I am," I cried. "What do you think Draco will do to me if he gets his hands on me? You should be ashamed of yourself for even entertaining the notion of my marriage to such a man."

Calmly, my mother raised her arm and slapped me with the flat of her hand, putting the strength of her shoulder into that strike. I tottered backward and would have fallen if Theo had not caught me.

"Don't be rude to your grandfather. Now go to bed."

*Furniture.* That's what the poor girl amounted to in the old man's estimation. And I was not far above her in his classification of the world. In the morning, Grandfather insisted that my betrothal to Draco would stand. He expected me to honor his precious word by marrying Evandos's brutal son. My mother watched this tirade, eyes flat, as her father bullied me. She expected me to obey without demur as any good Athenian girl would.

With effort, I pushed away the memories and returned my attention to my brother. "Mother informed me yesterday afternoon that she had started to work on my wedding garments."

Dionysius blinked. In the flickering light of the lamp his

eyes began to shimmer as they welled with tears. I knew, then, that he would not hinder us. Knew he would cover our departure for as long as he could, regardless of the pain it caused him.

I encircled my arms around him. Grief shivered out of us as we tried to make the moment last, make it count for endless days when we wouldn't have each other to hold. I stepped away, mindful of time slipping, mindful that we were far from safe. Theo and Dionysius bid a hurried farewell, locking forearms and slamming chests in manly embraces that could not hide their trembling lips.

Grabbing my bundle, I threw one last agonized glance over my shoulder at my brother. He stood alone, blanketed by shadows save for a luminous halo of lamplight that brought his face into high relief. I swallowed something that tasted bitter and salty and entirely too large for my throat, and stumbled forward.

Theo and I started to run downhill through the winding streets of Athens, our initial excitement dampened by the grief of leaving Dionysius behind. Before the sun began to rise over the hilltops, Theo came to an abrupt halt. "You should cut your hair now, Ariadne, while it's still dark."

We had decided that a young girl traveling with a boy, even a boy as large as Theo, would attract too much attention. Instead, we had concluded that we would travel as two boys. Dressed in Dionysius's bulkiest tunic and cloak, with my chest bound tightly beneath its loose folds, I looked enough a boy to pass casual inspection. Except that my hair remained long and uncut, a fat braid hanging to my hip.

I pulled out a knife from my bundle and handed it to Theo. "You do it," I said, trying to sound indifferent. I was vain about my hair, which was thick and soft, like a river of chestnuts.

Theo took a step back. "Do it yourself. Your father would skin me alive."

I threw him a disgruntled look but had to concede his point. Theodotus was courting untold trouble for agreeing to accompany me on this desperate escapade. Grandfather's outrageous threats aside, my mother would have him whipped for encouraging me, if she could get her hands on him. My father, I hoped, knew me better. If ever Theo and I were embroiled in trouble together, he would realize who had led that charge.

I held out my braid with my left hand and started hacking at it with the knife, wincing with pain as the strokes pulled on my scalp, until the long rope of my hair sat in my palm like a dead pet. With a grunt, I threw my feminine treasure into a ditch and we resumed our journey toward the Dipylon Gate, Athens' double gate on the west. I remembered to make my steps wide and swaggering, imitating Theo's athletic gait.

There were two ways of getting to Piraeus, the seaport for the city of Athens. One was through an ancient, walled corridor, which led from the Pnyx hill straight into the seaport, and the other, by means of an open road, which led southwest. We chose the open road, reasoning that if our absence were discovered earlier than expected and Grandfather sent men to find us, we would be able to hide better in the surrounding fields than the confines of a walled avenue.

To our relief, no one followed us. Save for a few inebriated men weaving through the winding streets, Athens seemed deserted, and we made our way into Piraeus unmolested.

The Aegean Sea greeted us with deceptive decorum, its aquamarine beauty muted in the predawn light. The air tasted of salt and fish. My mouth turned dry. The outlandish plan that I had hatched in the wake of the furious exchange with my grandfather never accounted for all of the obstacles we were bound to encounter in Piraeus. How could we find an honest captain who would not try to cheat us or, worse, conscript us into forced labor? We had no sealed letter from a recognized official to lend us legitimacy and were too young to travel abroad on our own.

I looked about, trying to find my bearings in the large seaport. There were three different harbors built into the port, two of them strictly for military use, and the third for commercial business. That is where we headed. The sprawling harbor was dense with ship sheds, where vessels could take shelter from bad weather. We found the port stirring with activity in spite of the early hour. Ships were getting ready to sail, bustling with sun-browned sailors stocking their ships and getting their cargo ready for transport.

"Let me do the talking," I said.

"How would that be different from any other day?"

I asked a sleepy man in respectable clothing which ships were sailing to Corinth that day. He named three and pointed them out in the harbor.

"What do you think, Theo?" We studied the ships in silence for some time. One was a narrow Roman trireme, sleek and fast, transporting soldiers. The second, a massive Greek merchant ship, bulged with amphorae of imported wine and vast earthenware vessels of grain. Hired mercenaries as well as passengers crawled all over its deck. Our eyes lingered on the third ship, which stood out in the harbor for her dark-colored wood and an elegant design that contrasted with her huge, odd-shaped sails. Her sailors had skin the color of a moonless night and laughed good-naturedly as they worked.

"That one." Theo pointed his chin at the odd ship. "They are small enough to be happy for a bit of extra income. No soldiers or passengers to ask awkward questions, either."

I nodded and surreptitiously wiped my damp palms on my clothing. We approached the captain. "We want to buy passage on your ship, Captain," I said, my voice an octave lower than its normal pitch.

"Do you, now?" He looked me up and down, his hand playing with the hilt of the dagger that hung from his waist. "What brings two fine fellows into the sea so early in the day?" His accent lilted like music.

"We are looking to make our fortune," Theo said.

The captain laughed. The sound came from deep in his belly and flowed out like a drumbeat. He loosened his hold on the dagger's hilt. "Fortunes cost money. How much do you have?"

For my sixteenth birthday, my father had sent me a gold ring domed with a red carnelian, along with a modest purse of silver. If he had sent them in the usual way, my mother would have apprehended both ring and silver before I ever caught sight of them. But he had dispatched his gifts by means of a friend who had delivered them to my brother in person.

I wore the ring hung on a strip of leather under my tunic. The purse would pay for our passage.

I haggled until the captain and I settled on the price of our passage, which left us with a few pieces of silver for food and emergencies should we run into trouble before finding my father in Corinth.

"How long does the passage take?" I asked.

"Five hours if the wind blows right."

"Is it blowing right today?"

The captain lifted his face and sniffed the air. "Right enough." He told us to sit in the bow of the ship while the crew readied for departure, out of the way of the sails. We sat quietly, hoping the sailors would forget our existence. Hoping the captain wouldn't change his mind.

We discovered that the Kushites called their ship *Whirring Wings*. They told us that the ships in their land were all called by that name.

We found out why when we set sail an hour later. As those tall sails, so awkward-looking at rest, unfurled fully, they looked like wings, stretching out from our hull. For a moment, I wondered if we would take off into the air like an osprey. Once we left the shelter of the harbor and found our way into the Saronic Gulf, the other part of the ship's name began to make sense. Something about the fabric of the sails caused them to flutter and shiver in the wind, sounding like a thousand birds in flight. The noise was deafening, making our attempts at conversation futile.

The vibrations wormed their way into your ears, into your head, into your heart, and it became impossible to hear anything but their noise. I found the experience strangely familiar. In a way, this was how life had felt at Grandfather's house for the past eight years. The whirring wings of everyone's demands, the noise of their expectations swallowing my voice, drowning out life and desire and dreams, so that only they could be heard. Once in Corinth, there would be blessed silence and I would live again.

We had sailed for two hours when dark clouds whipped across the sun with sudden ferociousness. A fierce squall shook the hull of our ship. Lulled into sleepy stupor by the calm of our passage, I snapped awake as a huge wave rolled over us, followed by another. Wind gusts snapped at the sails viciously, and before the sailors could pull them down, the largest tore in half.

Another wave broke over us, raising the ship as high as a two-story building, and flinging it back down into the restless sea with such force that Theo, who was sitting near the stern, flew bodily into the air, and to my horror, was thrown overboard.

I lunged after him, and at the last moment was able to grab at his ankle. By then, half of my own body had sailed overboard and I dangled into the stormy sea, salty water spurting into my eyes and nose. Both my hands held on to Theo's ankle with a strength I did not know I possessed. To let go of him meant losing him to the storm. But with my hands thus occupied, I had no way of securing myself. The force of Theo's weight pulled on me, and I slipped over the edge.

There is a thin line between courage and stupidity, and I crossed it with a frequency that pointed to a lack of wit rather than a surfeit of bravery. I did not know how to swim, not even in calm waters. I certainly would not survive a dunking in this tempest. I tried to anchor my feet into the edge of the ship's railing and found it a losing battle. One deep breath, and my head sank into the waves.

# A NOTE FROM THE AUTHOR

You might be scratching your head, wondering why I have described Natemahar as a Cushite rather than an Ethiopian. After all, he is based on the eunuch in the book of Acts, who is described as an Ethiopian court official working for Candace, queen of the Ethiopians (Acts 8:26-27). It turns out that *Candace* is not a proper name. Rather, it is the Greek word for *Kandake*, which is what the Cushites called their queen.

Are you baffled yet? I was, when I started my research. Was the eunuch a Cushite or an Ethiopian? Or was he an Ethiopian working for a Cushite queen?

Most scholars now agree that he was a Cushite (or Kushite, if you want to use the scholarly spelling). Greeks and Romans referred to the lands south of Elephantine as *Ethiopia* and called the natives of those lands *Ethiopian*. Technically, the word means "burnt face." In biblical times, *Ethiopia* seems to have been a catch-all term for a large geographical area whose people had dark skin, not the nation we now know by that name. And since the book of Acts was written in Koine Greek, its author, Luke, uses the common Greek term for Kush, which is—you guessed it—*Ethiopia*.

It seems likely, then, that our eunuch hails from the Kingdom of Cush, located in modern-day Sudan. He would have called himself a Cushite, not an Ethiopian. Respecting his heritage, that is what I chose to call him as well.

The language of the people of Cush, Meroitic, which has been preserved in various documents, has never been deciphered, leaving us with a regrettable dearth of knowledge regarding this significant civilization. We know they flourished on the shores of the middle Nile for over a thousand years, leaving behind over 250 extraordinary pyramids, temple ruins, and rumors of enormous silver and gold mines. Their kings served as pharaohs in Egypt for a season. In time, their queens rose to power alongside their kings. We know the names of many of these monarchs, but except in the case of a handful, the exact period of their rule remains a mystery. Hence, I never named my Kandake, though some sources seem to believe her name might have been Nawidemak.

When I first began to outline this novel, I wanted to have one of the daughters of Philip the Evangelist as my main character. A short email from a fan upended my plans. A young lady wrote to tell me that she loved my books. But, as an African American, she wondered if I ever planned to have a character who looked like her. Because, she explained, it was important for her to see heroines who reflected her.

I realized that as a writer of biblical fiction, I had a responsibility to this young woman and others like her. But where was I going to find a heroine that fit the bill in the New Testament? The only character I could think of was the eunuch. How was a eunuch supposed to have a child? Well. Now I had a book, didn't I? I ripped up my outline and never looked back. I did keep the name Chariline, which according to some church records was the name of one of Philip's daughters. And I kept two of his daughters for Chariline's friends.

According to some early church documents, the eunuch was called Bachos, or Simeon Bachos. People of that time period often had two or three names: the one they were given at birth and another Greek or Latin name in deference to the international world that was the Roman Empire. And the Ethiopian eunuch might have also had a third, Jewish name, since he was a God fearer before being baptized into Christ. I felt that Natemahar, born in Cush, would have a Cushite name, and that is what I gave him. Whether in his lifetime or afterward he came to be known as Simeon Bachos is a puzzle beyond my scope as a novelist.

Marcus Vitruvius was a real person, and what I've written about him is mostly accurate. Except for the fact that he had a granddaughter called Vitruvia who followed in his architectural footsteps. That didn't happen. But wouldn't it have been fun if it had?

Both Chariline and Theo are fictional characters. To read more of Theo's story, check out *Thief of Corinth* and *Daughter of Rome*.

To read more of Natemahar's real story, please refer to Acts 8:26-39. I am a novelist, which is to say, I make up stuff. My words cannot begin to replace the glory and power of the Scriptures. If you have never read this story, or the book of Acts, or if it's been a while, do yourself a favor and read it. You may encounter the vastness of God's grace and mercy just where you need it most.

# ACKNOWLEDGMENTS

This book was written under challenging circumstances. We had some health concerns in the family already when the pandemic hit. My brain turned to mush. I found it hard to write. I would spend a dazed hour with Jesus and another in the garden and manage to eke out a couple of pages of words. My dear editors, Stephanie Broene and Kathy Olson, were grace personified, giving me two extensions without complaint. I can't thank them enough for their kindness and support. God, in his grace, made up for all those delays. This book required the fewest edits I have ever needed with any story, so it ended up being released on time. A special thanks to Kathy Olson, who accepted the extra edits I threw her way, absorbed the expanded work, and never protested. People like that, both kind and talented, don't come around often.

My brilliant husband is the one who introduced me to Vitruvius. He bought me a couple of books on ancient Roman architecture and came up with the idea of having Chariline meet Vitruvius's granddaughter. As if that wasn't enough, he helped me with the research for the Fanum basilica, cooked for me a few times, baked unbelievable cookies, and gave me a lot of hugs. He even managed to create the maps that you find in the front of this book. Yes, I am blessed. Grateful to have this man in my life.

407

A very special thanks is due to Dr. Barry J. Beitzel, author of the award-winning book *The New Moody Atlas of the Bible*, who wrote me long emails in answer to my pesky questions about sea voyages in ancient Rome. The travel scenes in this book are so much better thanks to Dr. Beitzel's guidance. Any mistakes you find are mine.

I am grateful to my capable agent, Wendy Lawton, for her help and encouragement; the gifted fiction team at Tyndale; and the wonderful sales team who manage to place these books in the hands of readers.

Most of all, thanks to my readers, who return for more stories and share these adventures with me. I have the most amazing fans! Please keep those prayers, letters, and emails coming. Even when I don't have time to answer, I read every word and thank God for you.

# DISCUSSION QUESTIONS

1. Even before she knows of their true relationship, Chariline rejoices in her lifelong friendship with Natemahar and the way it helps to make up for her lack of a conventional family. How has God used friends in your life, either in place of or in addition to the people you are related to?

2. When Chariline is tempted to focus on the bad news of not knowing her father's identity rather than on the good news of knowing that he's alive, her friend Hermione reminds her, "Sometimes, in the frustration of what we don't have, we forget to rejoice in what we do." Why is it often easier to focus on the negative? What are some practical ways we might remind ourselves to rejoice in what we do have?

3. Chariline is certain that God wants her to find out who her father is, but Hermione urges her to ask for the Lord's guidance. She points out that often "God starts to tell us something, and before the sentence is out of his mouth, we finish it off the way we prefer. We assume. We presume. And we jump to false conclusions." Can you think of examples of this, either from the Bible or from your own experience?

4. Natemahar chooses to keep his relationship to Chariline a secret. Do you feel he has a legitimate reason to conceal his true identity from his daughter? Is Chariline justified in her anger with him when she finds out? In what ways can secrets be harmful in our relationships, and when is it appropriate to have them?

5. Chariline promises Theo not to go off on her own in her search for her father, but then breaks that promise. What are the consequences of her impatience, both for her and for those who care about her? When has impatience gotten you in trouble?

6. Priscilla challenges Chariline about her intense desire to find her father: "It's not the nature of your longing that is at issue. It is the fact that God does not reign over it. Finding your father has become the jewel you refuse to part with. Not even if God asks it. In that part of your heart, at least, your flesh still rules. The problem is that when you are flesh-driven, you cannot be Spirit-led." Has there been anything in your life that you've had a hard time being willing to part with?

7. Once she starts to seek God's will about finding her father, Chariline begins to wonder if every hurdle is a message from God telling her she's on the wrong track. How can we tell whether or not a particular circumstance is actually a message from God?

8. Both Chariline and Theo struggle with challenges related to tragic circumstances surrounding their birth. Near the end of the book, Theo says, "What the Lord

is teaching me is that the sorrows of one generation do not have to be visited upon another. The misfortunes of our parents do not have to shape our lives." Are there generational hurts that still need to be healed for you or your loved ones? How can your relationship with Jesus help overcome them?

9. For a long time, because of what happened to him as an infant, Theo struggled with his sense that God was not a loving Father, but rather "a God who would leave me in my time of trouble. A God who would always allow terrible things to happen to me." Have you, or someone you know, struggled with something similar? What are some ways to address this?

10. Eventually Theo comes to see his scar not as a reminder of something bad that happened to him, but as a reminder that even in his darkest moment, God was with him, protecting and guiding him. Do you have any "scars" like this—reminders of times in your life when God was present and active, even though you weren't able to see him at the time?

# ABOUT THE AUTHOR

Tessa Afshar is an award-winning author of historical and biblical fiction. Her novel *Daughter of Rome* was a *Publishers Weekly* and ECPA bestseller. *Thief of Corinth* was an Inspy Award finalist, and *Land of Silence* won an Inspy Award and was voted by *Library Journal* as one of the top five Christian fiction titles of 2016. *Harvest of Gold* won the prestigious Christy Award in the historical romance category, and *Harvest of Rubies* was a finalist for the ECPA Christian Book Award in the fiction category. Tessa also recently released her first Bible study and DVD called *The Way Home: God's Invitation to New Beginnings*, based on the book of Ruth.

Tessa was born to a nominally Muslim family in the Middle East and lived there for the first fourteen years of her life. She then moved to England, where she survived boarding school for girls, before moving to the United States permanently. Her conversion to Christianity in her twenties changed the course of her life forever. Tessa holds a master of divinity from Yale University, where she served as cochair of the Evangelical Fellowship at the Divinity School. She worked in women's and prayer ministries for nearly twenty years before becoming a full-time writer. Tessa speaks regularly at national women's events. She is a devoted wife, mediocre tomato grower, and chocolate connoisseur. Visit her website at tessaafshar.com.